THE JERUSALEM JOURNEYS

The Forgotten Wise Man

A NOVEL

John H. Timmerman

INTERVARSITY PRESS
DOWNERS GROVE, ILLINOIS 60515

©1993 by John H. Timmerman

InterVarsity Press® is the book-publishing division of InterVarsity Christian Fellowship®, a student movement active on campus at hundreds of universities, colleges and schools of nursing in the United States of America, and a member movement of the International Fellowship of Evangelical Students. For information about local and regional activities, write Public Relations Dept., InterVarsity Christian Fellowship, 6400 Schroeder Rd., P.O. Box 7895, Madison, WI 53707-7895.

Cover illustration: John Walker

ISBN 0-8308-1676-3

Printed in the United States of America ∞

Library of Congress Cataloging-in-Publication Data

Timmerman, John H.
    The forgotten wise man/John H. Timmerman.
        p.   cm.—(The Jerusalem journeys)
    ISBN 0-8308-1676-3
    1. Bible. N.T.—History of Biblical events—Fiction. 2. Jesus
Christ—Fiction. 3. Jerusalem—Fiction. 4. Magi—Fiction.
I. Title. II. Series: Timmerman, John H. Jerusalem journeys.
PS3570.I46F6   1993
813'.54—dc20   93-19199
                                                         CIP

16	15	14	13	12	11	10	9	8	7	6	5	4	3	2	1
05	04	03	02	01	00	99	98	97	96	95	94	93			

For Pat and Ecko,
Gary and Nancy,
Don and Nancy—
in appreciation for many nights
at round tables

Prologue

"The moment has come." We were sitting at the Table of the Brother-hood when all fell silent, stunned by the realization that it was now time to leave. It was the moment the Magi had been expecting (and had been trained to expect!) for hundreds of years. A small, knowing smile crept across Balthazzar's handsome face as he said it.

But that was like Balthazzar. And everyone there believed him. That was always the way.

I have often wondered how some people, Balthazzar for one, command such thorough and instant obedience. Was it because Balthazzar always seemed physically in authority, set apart by those eyes like dark coals that flashed without warning, as if charged by some inner fire? Or was it the chiseled muscles that laced his torso like hewn rock? He was, quite simply, the rock of our strength, and perhaps for that reason the others of us burned with envy for him, yet were also proud to be of the Brotherhood with him. Or was it, perhaps, because of his mind, quick as a spring stream, always shifting and sliding into the right course with a fullness and vigor that were far beyond me at least? Balthazzar was born a leader. Born a Magus.

But not I.

I didn't follow until too late. And because of that I saw more than any of them. This I don't understand. They saw the beginning; I, the ending. They saw the glory; I, the horror. Maybe I am cursed above all others. Or maybe blessed above all others.

BOOK ONE
KINGDOM OF SAND

CHAPTER ONE

I t didn't happen as quickly as that, of course.

For several weeks our anticipation was high. We seemed to live during the nights, studying the stars carefully, trying to decipher their cold, remote secrets. We also lived more in the past during that time than in the present, as we tried to link old prophecies with the signs in the heavens. We were obsessed with this.

It took no special instruments to see the two stars moving into conjunction. It was Gaspar, a true wizard of the heavens, who first detected them. That had been months earlier. In his slow, methodical way, Gaspar plotted their courses. He would not speak until he had irrefutable proof. Then, and only then, did he lay the charts before us during that afternoon session, while the sun stood hot above the dry and wind-blasted palace at Babylon. Silence followed, like the stillness before storm. Then Balthazzar declared, for all of us, "The moment has come."

* * *

In those days there were just four of us Magi left. Dying men in a dying breed. The world was changing under our very feet, and we, above all mortals, knew this. It is not easy to know yourself the last of a kind.

Few are aware of their daily dying, refusing to think of it until death has its long nails caught deep in the body, until it takes only one hard, abrupt squeeze to shut life down.

It is different for the Magi.

The Magi are trained from birth to be aware of dying. The first lesson for a Magus, upon reaching adolescence when the serious training starts, is to ask this question each morning: "Shall I die today?" Does that sound foolish? It is the world's great absurdity, for every nerve in the body wills to live. But the will itself must choose to live. I cannot control the day. I can control how I will meet that day.

Unlike mere mortals, who sense death only when it squeezes the heart, the Magi are trained to detect its first cold fingernail slipping into the body. To affirm life is to fight death at its earliest skirmishes. That is why we clung to this sign like life itself.

Understand that once the Magi were the rulers of the world as we knew it. For almost a millennium we held sway over kings and peoples by our special gifts—knowledge of the stars, understanding of histories, interpretations of dreams and prophecies. Never were we more powerful than when we took those small tribes, the Israelites, into captivity. For they held, we believed, the secret to life itself.

That is why, as Gaspar and his assistants pondered their charts and studied the night skies, others of us undertook a study of the old texts. The sign of life lay in the heavens. This we knew. The promise of life itself lay in the old texts.

Such study was not for me. I understood nothing of the texts, little of the stars. For all the study and training to which I had been so arduously subjected, I often wondered whether there was any truth at all in it. I pretended knowledge and often wondered whether the others were pretenders also. But they seemed so certain in what they knew and what they longed for that, in time, I too was infected by their madness. Not truly believing, but a believer by indoctrination. It is a difference of the heart.

The Magi were royalty by status, by their very separation from the common people according to their gifts. This had been so throughout their history. While they held no political power, their knowledge often guided the most powerful of kings.

And since being a Magus had always been determined by the gifts of a person, by character, and not by marriage or politics, none of the Magi had ever married. To be a Magus, one had to be chosen. Just how this choosing was done, I'm not sure. Many were offered; few were chosen.

There had been no new Magi in my time. I had seen parents bring a bewildered child to the palace for entrance to the Magi. Some brought purses of money with them; some, merely a scrawny goat or a weary camel as an offering. All had been denied. The Magi believed that if marriages were permitted, there would be the temptation of inherited status and the danger that one with inferior gifts or a contrary spirit would inhabit the Brotherhood. The risks were high enough without that.

I know now that it is all false, and this is one reason why I still, to this day, struggle against belief. For what I was told was all a lie, especially what I was told, or not told, of myself.

For example, I was told only a few facts about my mother, who was called Selaina. She was obtained at great expense by the late Necomar. She did not live long in this inhospitable land. But I remember her. While I remember nothing of Necomar, save the treatises he left—he was the Earth Master of the Magi, the position I inherited—I shall never forget my mother. She stood apart from everyone, tall and beautiful. Eyes like ebony pools. Ah, I remember her eyes. Her skin was as dark as night, a velvet skin. She had no need for the jewels the Magi draped her in; for she wore royalty in her flesh.

My mother died only a few days after my confirmation as a Magus. I was twelve. I don't know how old my mother was then. She seemed but little older than I. She was my only friend in Babylon.

The sheets were damp from her fever when last I saw her. Her body shivered uncontrollably. Her dark skin turned the color of cold ashes; her eyes were squeezed shut against the pain that riddled her body. When she opened those eyes at the sound of my weeping, I looked into the halls of death itself. I knew that I was losing her.

At that time, Balthazzar cared for me like the father I had never known. My leader became my comforter, and for one brief moment our hearts were knit in a shared sorrow. I did not understand then. I knew only that he met my need.

At twelve it was I, in the absence of a father, who followed my mother's corpse to the funeral bier in the forecourt of the palace and struck the fire that consumed her.

At twelve, I, Elhrain, became the fourth Magus at the Table of the Brotherhood. Left without parents, I had a home and family only with the Magi—Gaspar, Balthazzar and Melchior, these remnants of a dying race.

And at twelve I already knew I didn't belong. But I was bereft of a way home, as the Magi were bereft of a lineage. Not only had I no means of leaving, nor any knowledge of a place to go, but I also had the unsettled feeling that the Magi would be loath to let me leave. At times, I believed that I could not leave even had I wanted to.

* * *

Now, at age twenty-one, the youngest by far of any of them, I found myself fighting the excitement of discovery, the disclosure and fulfillment of six hundred years' prophecy, for, it seemed to me, it would prove our final undoing.

That morning I met with Melchior at his request. He still considered me the upstart, the unbeliever, but he wanted my alliance at the Table of the Brotherhood that afternoon. As a Magus, after all, I would carry a vote, and in this matter every vote was important, even if the outcome were a foregone conclusion. The Magi had a rage for unity. We met in his room, and from the start his voice was urgent, hurried.

"The Book of the Exile, quickly," Melchior muttered to his assistant. Melchior stood before the large desk in his room, the walls about us lined with shelves upon which the parchments lay rolled in silken canisters. These shelves reached from floor to ceiling across the north and east walls.

"Careful, there," Melchior admonished the assistant. He walked to the window and looked out over the forecourt. His mind was six hundred years back in time. I knew the look in his brooding, narrow eyes.

"It can happen, Elhrain," he said. He turned to me. "Do you know how we were at the pinnacle of our authority then?"

I must have winced. Although a full Magus now, I still felt I was being tutored, and I resented it. "Yes," I said. "Well I know."

"Don't take offense, Elhrain." His eyes were opaque. "Everything we have waited for is about to come to pass."

"If you are right."

"I *am* right. There are the signs. Here, fool!" he shouted at the assistant. "You're in the wrong row. That's it. The Book of the Exile, top row, fourteenth cabinet. Handle it like your life, boy."

He turned back to the window slit. "Six hundred years ago, Elhrain. We were lords of the earth. We held sway in the mightiest kingdom this earth has ever known."

"The Romans are no small people," I reminded him.

"Pah! They are dogs of war. We ruled by the gods themselves." His voice softened. "Still, the time is desperate," he admitted. "In fact, this couldn't have happened at a more desperate hour."

"Maybe our desperation makes it seem a reality."

He shrugged. "Is not that the risk we always take? Have faith, my son. If these things are not true, then we are fools and finished. If they are true, then we will once again rule the world. As is our duty."

"But the Holy One is the One to rule. According to the prophecies, anyway. Doesn't that mess up everything?"

"Elhrain, sometimes I think you never fully understand." He caught my expression of annoyance. "Oh, don't be aggrieved," he said.

I wasn't. I was angry.

"We experience our rule *through* kings, not by playing king. It is a far better thing to have knowledge and authority than power. The problem during these last years is that there has been no real *king*, no divinely appointed ruler to rally us. Here is the matter of import, for Belteshazzar himself—"

I interrupted. "You mean the *great* Belteshazzar."

He chuckled as if enjoying a private joke. I sensed bitterness behind it. "One of us had to bear his name. Of course I mean Belteshazzar of the exile. Oh, here, assistant, you have the right one."

Melchior spread the parchment on the desk. It was not my task to know this language. I was never sure what my task was. Gaspar: Master of the Stars. Balthazzar: Master of Dreams and Signs. Melchior: Master of Histories and Oracles. Elhrain: Master of . . . The line is blank. They call me Master of Earth, the title Necomar held. Harmless occupation.

Melchior read rapidly, moving from right to left.

"Here. Here's the promise of the great Belteshazzar himself. See, he has a vision. That in itself is the mark. Belteshazzar was a master of dreams, as he was of all things. He was the Magus of all Magi, the three in one: Stars, Signs and Language."

I nodded. I had heard the litany of praise so often it made me sick. Some befuddled old man from a foreign land. Ah, but the Magi were desperate. Desperate enough to turn *back* to look ahead. They were desperate for survival itself, to engage this mad errand. Perhaps my purpose, I thought, is to pen their epitaph.

Melchior's finger moved up the page. "Notice, Elhrain. Here's the mark of truth upon it. Belteshazzar writes that in his vision—this is truer than any experience now—one appears before him who looks like, here's his words, 'The Ancient of Days.' "

"The Almighty God," I filled in. I knew the passage, if not the words, as well as any. I had been a quick study, mind you, to be confirmed a Magus at twelve rather than the traditional twenty-one. Or perhaps this was just another sign of their desperation?

" 'Wearing white raiment,' " Melchior went on unperturbed. " 'Seated on a throne of fire.' That is to say, his abode is above the stars themselves. He is the one who made the stars, and, therefore, all the stars carry meaning. Look. He speaks in flames. 'A stream of fire issued and came forth before him.' That is the significance of Gaspar's sign. The stars tell the truth, and here is the message in it. The great Belteshazzar foretold all things."

I nodded politely. The poor assistant stood ready to fetch or carry manuscripts, but Melchior was lost six hundred years in the past that he read as the present. I would have preferred an alliance with the Romans.

"And here, Elhrain, is what the great Belteshazzar sees. 'One like a son of man.' Interesting, no? The Divine One becomes the Human One. But most important, 'To him . . . this Son of Man . . . was given dominion and glory and kingdom.' Our eternal future. 'His domain is an everlasting dominion.' "

He looked at me, positively gloating in triumph. "People have discarded us, Elhrain. Written us off as of no account. But we'll show them, won't we? The eternal kingdom! Think of it. The Divine One becomes the Son of Man. And to think it's happening in my lifetime. Oh, they'll see." He glanced out the window. "We must hurry now. It's nearly time to meet. To decide."

With that I left him, certain that I would never go with these madmen.

* * *

In the forecourt of the Palace of the Magi the afternoon sun shone with a hard, crystalline light, flooding the blue-tiled mosaics, firing their gold-leafed edges. One had to look twice to see the signs of decay, but they were there.

Like everything here, the forecourt was old, nearing ruin. It must have been magnificent once, all shining and new. Now it was merely decadent, diseased by age and inattention. Plants around the pool wilted in the sun. Little the Magi cared, consumed as they were with their mad quest for a world ruler.

I tarried by the pool on my way to the meeting. Between the pool and the central gate stood the funeral bier. The sun lit its smoke-charred bricks, seeming to fire a flame into their black hearts. For a moment I again felt the brazier in my hand, held it to the wood and watched the flame engulf my mother. It had been my task, supposedly my honor, to strike the flame that would carry her spirit heavenward. She had been wound in white linen, and when the flames touched her burial clothes they seemed to explode and fall away from her. For one moment I saw her corpse high above the flame, then the flesh charred, and the flame engulfed her.

I remembered these old men chanting at my back. Their words were meaningless then, and were meaningless now. I loathed them.

My reflection was broken as Gaspar and Balthazzar entered the forecourt, each trailed by assistants, on their way to the Table of the Brotherhood. Balthazzar led, of course, his powerful shoulders thrust back, black hair shining in the sunlight. Gaspar hurried next to him, his hands gesturing rapidly.

I wanted to avoid the meeting altogether. I even wondered if there was some way I could decently miss it.

Then, two things surprised me. Through the gate, alone, but walking as if he owned the place, strode Kruspian, the local military leader. Something about him made me nervous. There, for the first time really, I understood that the Magi were really serious about this prophecy. And if they meant to go, they needed someone to organize. They needed Kruspian—the military man, the consummate politician. To me, it was a sign of just how thoroughly the Magi's authority had declined. They were going begging now. Begging with the serpent, Kruspian, the military conniver. So, authority and power tended to meet, after all. I nearly laughed at the irony of it all, but the second surprise checked me.

It was the way Balthazzar paused and turned toward me. He hesitated silently, the hot sun glittering off the heavy golden necklace he wore, then he walked to me. His eyes held uncertainty. Or was it mistrust, now that his moment had arrived?

"You're not forgetting the meeting, surely?" he asked.

I held his dark eyes with my own; obsidian, hard eyes against his deep brown. I did not reply. His gaze turned to the funeral bier as if remembering.

"We have much to discuss, Elhrain," he said.

"With him?" I nodded toward Kruspian.

"It may be necessary."

Or foolish, I wanted to say. Instead, I followed them into the high court. Even then, I cursed my foolishness. I should have turned and left. Lord me no lords!

CHAPTER
TWO

They nodded and babbled around the table like a coop of hens. Ancient Gaspar's small head bobbed at the end of a skinny neck, layers of loose skin trembling as if some palsy afflicted him. He shifted his charts of the stars and planets, trying to explain what we had already observed. It was his task, after all, and Gaspar was harmless. He was Master of Stars, and some thought he lived among them.

Melchior, Master of Histories and Divine Oracles, moved coolly about the Table of the Brotherhood. He examined certain parchments while Gaspar babbled. Melchior's massive intelligence was like a visible aura. While he kept the parchments, attended by a half dozen assistants, he had little need to read them. When he did, it was to refresh himself on a minor point. Melchior held hundreds of years of history tucked in the folds of his mind like a library.

After all these years, I was still something in awe of Melchior, and he alone of the Magi I thoroughly respected. Physically, he was not distinguished: medium height; thinning black hair, a bit unruly; his skin too pallid, perhaps, from his many hours in the library. It was almost as if some god, having deposited that enormous intelligence inside his narrow skull, decided that he would need physical plainness just to survive.

I felt closest to him, even though his mind was leagues beyond my own in learning, beyond everyone's. Melchior never stopped amazing me with the way he could pull whole pages of history, minute in its detail, from that monster of a mind and recite it in uncanny clarity, as if he were *there*, at the precise moment the events unfolded.

Melchior saw himself, I believe, as my mentor. At least, he took time to explain things to my plainer mind.

I said I respected Melchior. What, then, did I feel for Balthazzar? Awe? To be sure. Balthazzar compelled me, as he did all others. Fear? Somewhat. Who didn't fear this compelling commander, this general of metaphysics and men?

He was nearest to me in age. At nearly forty he looked closer to my age, except stronger, more powerful. He exuded strength. He always spoke with the most urgent tones. There was no denying Balthazzar. The forceful glint of his brooding eyes, the ripple of his powerful muscles shifting under his robe, the weight of his mind and will—these were the weapons behind his authority. Next to him the two old men—Gaspar and Melchior, both in their sixties—seemed pale twigs of humanity.

And I, Elhrain: Master of Earth. Not *the* earth, mind you. But *earth*. Of course, all our sciences overlapped. My training in constellations and literature was thorough. I could read the heavens as well as the past. But from the start, my mastery was given to the earth.

I could speculate on why this was so. It has to do with my foreignness, for one thing. I vaguely remembered the desert waste of my native land, and was adept at understanding this desert waste. I also loved the earth, sensed its fragile beauty even in this land of broken promise. The Magi recognized this gift in me.

Whatever my gifts, I stood out like rock in the living stream of the Magi's heritage. They were olive-skinned men. I was black as the night sky, desert-born and desert-bred. Their pasts reached back through centuries of noble lineages. My own, beyond the little I knew of my mother, was a mystery.

The one blessing of my mastery was that I could be absent for days from the confining decadence of Babylon. With one or two assistants and a handful of guards, I made foray after foray into the surrounding countryside, sometimes for a week or more. The Magi came to expect it. I think they secretly willed it. I was not at home in my home here. I knew it; they knew it. I was bought at a price. I was determined to make it expensive.

Often during these lonely expeditions, seated at night before a scanty fire that tossed a handful of light into the vast blackness of the desert, the camels grunting behind the tents, I felt an eerie and desolate longing for someplace other than this to call home.

*   *   *

"For an old buzzard, you're too impulsive," Melchior shouted.

Gaspar fumed and spat. "Impulsive! How much time do you think *you* have?"

"Bah! One foot in the grave and with the other you want to set out . . . when? Tomorrow? A thousand miles, old man!" He looked to Balthazzar for support.

Balthazzar gazed silently at the vaulted ceiling, as if studying one particularly interesting tile.

Melchior raised his hand and pointed a long, thin finger to the window. "Out there lie a thousand miles between here and this . . . toad of a city. Jerusalem. You can hardly get out of bed. Don't be in such a hurry."

"The heavens proclaim it!" Gaspar shrieked. "The stars are right. We must seize the moment." The folds of skin at his neck flapped like a wounded turkey.

Oh, wisdom. This is what it amounted to. I nearly laughed aloud.

Balthazzar raised his hands to silence the two angry men. "Planning," he said. "Of course Melchior is right. We can't rush off into the desert like a bunch of pack rats sniffing out some morsels."

"Melchior is a coward," Gaspar seethed. "He wants his luxury. Know what he wants?"

"I want some order!" Melchior said.

"No. You want the little girls in their silken pajamas, you old goat. Snuggle your skinny haunches up to them! You're afraid of the desert."

"Of course I am, you old fool."

Again Balthazzar interceded. "And well you should be. That is why I brought Lord Kruspian along."

Kruspian nodded officiously as attention turned to him. He had been almost forgotten. Two golden bracelets clinked softly at his wrist.

"We need a plan," Balthazzar continued. "One with the full weight of military logistics. We need papers. Letters. Supplies. Foreign currencies."

That silenced them.

"Especially money. Kruspian estimates forty camels."

21

Gaspar sucked in his breath. "Forty?" he asked.

"At minimum," Balthazzar said. "Listen, this journey will take up to a year, over some of the most brutal terrain in the world. Melchior is right. We can't afford to go hastily. The price would be our lives."

"Wrong," said Melchior. "The price will be the lordship of the Messiah. The price will be the authority of the Magi themselves. This is *our* moment, but a moment enduring not less than forever. It is our chance to write a history for all time."

"Well," said Balthazzar, "something like that. For the moment we would do well to think of the task at hand. While Gaspar has been plotting his stars and while Melchior has been propounding his histories, I have asked Kruspian for his hand in a plan."

Suddenly, he turned to me. "But first, you must understand the reality of the journey. Elhrain, what can you tell us about the land?"

I shrugged. "Nothing that you don't already know. The land is wretchedly hard for travel, vast stretches wholly unpopulated. You should aim to leave in the winter season in order to cross the high desert before summer. In the summer the heat would fry you all like a bunch of cracked eggs."

I paused for a moment. I hadn't intended the comment, but once spoken I let it sink in.

"The greatest challenge is to transport enough water. Kruspian says forty camels? I wish it were a hundred, all of them bearing water. Thirst is your greatest enemy, and you will travel for days, weeks, in land so dry the rocks crack from the heat. Without enough water the human body starts to feed on itself. It withers as it reaches inward—"

"Spare us the biology lesson," Gaspar snapped. "Stick to the land."

"Very well. You will be in desert until you hit the coastal mountains. Then you might even find snow in the high passes. But getting across the desert will be your biggest battle. You cannot count on the land to guide you. Along the way, there is the threat of sandstorms. The sand flies with grains so fine it literally enters the pores of the skin, rubbing it raw from within.

"You cannot rely on fresh meat. Oh, it's there. But you'll never find it. Rabbits burrow five feet under the ground. Jackals move by night in packs. All you will see are lizards and scorpions. They will comfort you at night by crawling into your bedrolls."

"Thank you, Elhrain. That's quite enough." Balthazzar turned to the others. "You see the formidability of the task, gentlemen? Planning is the key to survival."

"How many assistants may we take?" muttered Gaspar.

Kruspian answered. He was in command now. "No more than three. In addition, you need drovers and guides. They will be my men, serving also as guards. In all, thirty-five men on forty camels."

"Assuming all of us go," I said.

Balthazzar, then Melchior, turned in amazement. Melchior spoke. "What do you mean? Of course we will all go. Don't you realize that this is the ruler of the world? What this means to us?"

"It sounds like madness to me," I said. In a moment I had decided. I turned to go out.

Balthazzar blocked me, raising one arm to hold me back. His muscled arm seemed as thick as a log thrust in my way. But his voice was gentle, almost pleading. "Wait until we have finished," he said. Then added, "Please."

I waited. Kruspian outlined his plans. At the very earliest we could depart in four months. This would place us in the winter season. He needed letters of safe passage. That in itself could take several months. He needed to plan the safest and fastest route. And the supplies! A horrendous expense. And then, an estimated ten months for the journey itself.

"Ten months!" Gaspar exploded. "I might as well lie down and die now!"

Kruspian stared him down.

"So we arrive, at a minimum, fourteen months from now?" Gaspar said. "How will we even know this king, then?"

"The king will be an infant," Melchior interjected. "Hardly ruling yet. If the prophecies are right, as of course they are, seeing as you, Gaspar, construe them, then we are to usher in his reign."

"We must leave sooner," Gaspar said. He banged a skinny fist upon the table and winced at the pain.

"If your gods are sending a ruler," Kruspian said coldly, "surely they can control those circumstances. Are your gods so rash that in six hundred years of planning, they couldn't foresee fourteen months' travel?"

"And what do you care about the gods?" Melchior asked.

Kruspian shrugged. "You hire my services, not my beliefs. I can get you safely where you're going."

Suddenly I saw through Kruspian. He wanted the glory of rule. The realization shook me. How far was Balthazzar in league with the man? Was that Balthazzar's aim, too? It was impossible to tell. Balthazzar stood impassively. As if feeling the weight of my gaze, he turned and looked at me, looked long into my eyes while old Gaspar fumed. He turned slowly back to the others.

"It is expedient," he said abruptly. "Simply expedient. By ourselves we are incapable of mounting such a journey. Incapable of the logistics. Incapable of control. Incapable of withstanding the desert outlaws."

"Bah," Gaspar said. "The Lord is on our side. Why worry about outlaws?"

"The Lord?" I asked.

"Read the prophecies, pup," he snarled. He dismissed me with a look of complete scorn. "We will find the Lord of the great Belteshazzar," he snarled.

"True," said Melchior. "It's all there in the texts."

Balthazzar raised a hand. "Even so, it would be foolish to mount such a journey unprepared."

"What will it cost us?" Gaspar said after a moment's reflection.

There was an uncomfortable pause. Then Balthazzar said simply, "Everything we have. Right down to the palace itself." He let that sink into the astonished faces. Kruspian let the faintest smile ease his lips. This was the moment of truth for him, and he knew it.

"But," Balthazzar said, "if this is, indeed, the right moment, as we believe, then we will also have everything we have ever wanted. True?"

After a moment the two old men nodded. No one consulted me.

"Except," Kruspian said quickly, "the gifts you will hand-carry to the king."

"Very well," Balthazzar said after a moment's silence, "we are agreed?"

He turned to Kruspian. "You may proceed. My personal attendant, Bara, will see to your needs." It was a dismissal. "And before you leave, Elhrain," he turned to me, "a word with you, please."

We walked outside to the reflecting pool. Balthazzar held my elbow, steering me slightly. I felt the slightest pressure against the bone, as if he were reminding me that he could break my arm like a mere twig if he so chose. I permitted him his indulgence.

Even the reflecting pool was shallow and scummy. It once held floating flowers that seemed like clouds suspended above its polished marble tiles. When I was young, small darting fish charged from shadow to shadow. I pretended they were gold and silver birds flying underwater. Today, the pool was nearly empty under the pitiless eye of the sun, and algae crept from every corner.

Balthazzar released the pressure on my elbow. For all that, his face was not angry when he turned to me. Rather, I saw some odd, superior humor alive in his eyes.

"You don't like the prospect," he said.

"It's crazy. Insane."

"Indeed?" His left eyebrow raised. I often wondered how he did that. How he could lift one eyebrow in a gesture mixed of dispassion and scorn.

"It is the futility of old men afraid to die," I said with some heat.

"I see." He clasped his hands behind his back and looked out past the wall of my scorn. In the distance, desert heat shimmered above sand dunes. "If so, then why are you afraid to go?"

"I'm not."

"Yes, you are. I see myself in you, Elhrain. I too am afraid to die."

I looked at him sharply. I could never tell when he was telling the truth or merely toying with me. At times I wanted to embrace him, and weep on his shoulder like a son. At other times I hated him with every ounce of energy I had.

"You're joking."

"Oh? No, I don't think so, Elhrain." His eyes held mine steadily.

"Then why not stay here? They would listen to you, not to me."

"Maybe that's why."

"I don't understand."

"I'm not sure I do." He smiled then. His white, even teeth gleamed behind his black beard. Then, in one instant he was deadly serious. "All I know is that here we are dying slowly. Isn't it better to try the impossible rather than the interminable? Besides, maybe they're right." He waved in the direction of the palace, the Table of Brotherhood.

"Surely you don't trust Kruspian."

He looked at me steadily. "No. I don't," he said. "That's why I want you along."

"Why?"

"Because I don't trust you also?" It was a question. I didn't answer. "Because . . . because *I* need you, Elhrain."

I couldn't resist. Who could resist Balthazzar? Yet, even as I nodded, I wondered if he knew this and if it wasn't just some clever trick of his.

CHAPTER
THREE

Within weeks it was clear why we needed Kruspian. The enormity of the task was overwhelming. Empty rooms in the palace became storehouses for supplies. Huge bags of grain and long-necked water jugs lined the walls. Kruspian's guards and drovers moved into the unused rooms at the back of the palace. The smoke of their cooking fires seemed to permeate every inch of the building. Noise and stink and supplies—our palace became a warehouse.

The guards paraded and performed each morning in the courtyard. Under the command of an iron-jawed, fierce-eyed Egyptian, they slammed their boots against the mosaics as if grinding them to shreds.

For that entire first month we did not even meet as a brotherhood. Each went about individual studies and studied nothing. The faces of the Magi were tight and pinched like meat left too long in the desert.

Each thought of the desert, of those insufferable months that lay ahead. The fear of the unknown. Each, quietly, one by one, sought me out for my knowledge of the land. To each I repeated my litany. The seasons would be little different from here in Persia.

"But we have no seasons," Gaspar said.

"Theoretically we do," I said. "Hot and dry. Cold and wet."

"Bah. Maybe one year out of ten it follows a pattern. I have lived out rainy seasons when not a drop of rain fell."

"True," I agreed. "And I have seen with my own eyes ice on the desert sands where a month before the rocks cracked in the heat."

"Well, that I don't believe. Even if it happened," muttered Gaspar.

"The desert is the deceiver, Gaspar," I said.

"Yes," he murmured, stroking his chin with those long, narrow fingers that looked like a bundle of thin twigs. His bloodshot eyes peered intently into mine, as if probing for some revelation. "Will we make it, Elhrain? I mean," his eyes darted like two little fish, "is it possible?"

I shrugged. "Who knows," I said. "Maybe if we get some help from this God we seek. We just might."

"Ah, you still don't believe."

"I'm comfortable where I am," I observed.

To avoid their questions, I began spending most of my time in my quarters. The living quarters of the rectangular palace spun like webs off a vaulted, central corridor. From this corridor, doors opened to the main living room of each Magus. Behind the spacious living room, several smaller rooms, serving as bedrooms or study areas, backed up to the outer wall of the palace. There were three or four such smaller rooms to each cluster, designed for friends or close attendants of the Magus.

The layout was designed for comfort, privacy and, most of all, for security. The back bedrooms held slit windows to the outer court. If the palace ever came under attack, which had not happened in hundreds of years, defenders fought from the outer ring of bedrooms and from the long corridor while the Magi sought the safety of the living rooms. Such was the plan. In actuality, the palace now had only a handful of guards supplied by the prince. It was easy duty for them.

Of twenty clusters, only four of them were now in personal use. The vacancy was dreary, sometimes even morbid in the quiet heat of long nights. My own chambers were approximately midway down the hall.

One night I was in the living space there, sitting at a table playing a game of bah-lah with my assistant, Haggai. The game was an inheritance from my mother and one of the few things in the kingdom I truly valued. I kept each ivory game piece, intricately carved into human and animal shapes, in an individual velvet pouch and kept the whole, including the game board, in a tightly fitted box. It was a demanding game, requiring intense concentration, and Haggai was the only one I had been able to teach it to.

That was curious because, although he now ranked as my chief assistant by virtue of our long association, Haggai had received no formal training in the arts of strategy and warfare—the two skills for any competition, and especially for the mental warfare of bah-lah. He was more comrade than assistant.

His younger sister, Doval, now a beautiful young woman of about fourteen, was also more friend than servant to me. Although technically she had no rights whatsoever in this kingdom, she was a part of whatever odd household I kept. In fact, she seemed more like my daughter than anything else.

While Haggai and I battled wits over the bah-lah game board, Doval sprawled in her thin sleeping gown on some pillows, playing with her cat. It was the way I enjoyed my rooms in the evening. A knock on the door shattered my concentration. Without waiting for an answer, Balthazzar entered. I disliked being disturbed at night in my chambers, and a curse surfaced to my lips. Balthazzar detected it immediately. A grimace crossed his face and a hand rose to his forehead.

"Forgive me, Elhrain, I'm getting so busy that I forgot my manners."

He always had the same effect on me: half irritation, half awe. "That's okay," I muttered. He *was* busy I knew, trying to oversee every step of this mad venture, not quite content to let Kruspian have his way entirely. "What can I do for you?"

"For me," Kruspian said. He had slipped in behind Balthazzar. He wandered to Doval, standing insolently over her, hands on his hips.

Self-consciously, Doval drew up her knees, hugging them to cover herself from his gaze. She averted her eyes nervously. The cat arched lazily and wandered to the windowsill.

"As you may know," Kruspian continued, eyes raking the girl, "I have campaigned often in the desert. What I want . . . would like you to do for me . . . for all of us, is to. . . ." He slipped a toe of one boot behind Doval's calf, stretching her legs out.

"Don't touch her," I commanded.

He looked at me with surprise. "A slave girl? Is she something special to you?"

I stood up from the table. Not a small or a weak man, I think the only man I have ever feared physically was Balthazzar. That was not because of the layers of muscle corded about him. It was . . . because he was what he was. Kruspian, however, I simply scorned, and at that moment he knew it fully.

He stepped back and chuckled disarmingly. "Well, well," he mused. He looked again at Doval. "And such a pretty little whore too. Well, if you don't know what she's good for, send her my way."

"Get out," I ordered.

Balthazzar intervened. "We will. Make your request, Kruspian."

Kruspian had quite forgotten his request. "Oh, yes. Maps. Maps of the north desert. Do you have any?"

I looked at Balthazzar.

"If you please," he said.

"I will locate them in the morning," I said. "Haggai will deliver them before noon. But I caution you. My expertise is *not* in maps, nor in directions."

"I thought you were the Earth Master," Kruspian sneered.

Even Balthazzar took offense at his ignorance. "Elhrain *is* Earth Master," he said emphatically. "Maps only chart surfaces; his knowledge is of conditions, the earth itself."

Kruspian arched an eyebrow as if to say, how ludicrous. "Whatever," he said. "Let me see them tomorrow."

Balthazzar sighed wearily. "Pardon us, Brother," he said. "The days are long."

Only after they left did I muse upon the fact that it was entirely odd for Kruspian, who claimed such expertise and experience, to want maps at all. "Why don't you pack up the game, Haggai," I said. "I want to think a while."

"Will you need anything?"

"No, you may go."

Doval stood with him to leave. She had her own room in my quarters, adjoining Haggai's room in small alcoves off from my own.

"Doval," I said as I studied her lithe form under the sheer pajamas. "You're not a little girl anymore."

She smiled.

"What I mean is . . . some men will look at you in certain ways . . . They will want to use you."

She looked puzzled. "What do you think I should do?" she said.

"Be careful," I said.

No, I didn't want her to change. I needed that inviolable trust, that winsome innocence. I needed a daughter.

When they left the room I picked up the pillow she had been lying on and hurled it across the room. It did no good.

I personally delivered the maps to Kruspian the next day. He said nothing.

* * *

The days slipped by. The courtyard bawled with activity. Balthazzar brooded over the scene with dark intensity. Melchior and Gaspar kept babbling away.

Beyond the courtyard gates I could see the camel herd grazing where they were penned by the river. Noisy, stinking camels.

Beneath an azure sky, flawlessly deep, unblemished by hint of cloud, the land sprawled like a festering brown sore toward the horizon. Where the river etched its narrow path between rocky banks, clumps of greenery held firm. The river's girdle of trees was intact. In low-lying areas, some green fields ripened to tawny gold. But the effects of the prolonged drought were undeniable.

The screeching of the camels seemed to echo the land.

I walked out to them once with Haggai. "I hate riding those things," I muttered as we stood watching them.

Haggai laughed nervously. He didn't hate the prospect. He was terrified of it.

The camel is an odd creature, all weird angles and flaps of clammy skin and sinew. A grotesque, elongated head ends in a set of lips as big as baskets and a nose like a flap of raw meat. A necklace of scruffy fur girdles its neck above the forelegs, and a hump of flesh on its back is ridged by a mane of fuzz like a bald man's bristle. The body collects toward a set of preposterously high and oddly connected rear legs, knees protruding in the stupidest places. Its rear haunches stretch out in the air like flags with a little mop of tail that flaps like a dusty rag. Wretched.

They were all dirty brown, the color of sand, save for two that were brindled with black, sooty fur, and a mean-spirited female with nearly white hair. They belched and spit at anyone who walked nearby. Their drovers were no better. They were weaselly, little, dark-skinned men who kicked at the camels' thick rumps and cursed them unimaginatively.

The drovers were force-feeding the camels huge amounts of grain and water. Each camel wore a feed bag strapped over its blubbery lips. With every breath, almost, the beasts inhaled grain. Their bellies were swollen obscenely.

It all reminded me a bit of beasts being fattened for slaughter. In the old days, before the great decline, we used to receive offerings bred like that. Yearling cows with distended bellies and marbled haunches donated for the wise men's delights. How things changed. Now we fattened the beasts to flee the land, an offering to despair and desperation.

Turning away in disgust, I walked with Haggai through the old city, on streets I seldom saw. I was restless, discontent in the noisy confines of the palace. Children in rags huddled in the doorways of brick hovels. Their little bellies were swollen with famishment. While our camels were bloated with grain.

Haggai pressed close to me as we wandered along the streets, hands snatching at our clothing, hands outstretched, begging alms. Once these people had reached out to shower gifts upon us. Was there no king left in this land who cared about the people? That tyrant-prince in the palace at the opposite end of town from ours—(a grand design of two opposing but communal palaces: power and authority conjoined in tense harmony!)—waged half a dozen petty wars at a time with neighboring kingdoms.

Well, it was one way to solve the problem of starvation. Put a sword in the starving man's hands and send him off to die in battle. How weary I was of it all. Perhaps that was the reason I began to think I would go. To seek a solution. Or a way out.

Haggai started plucking nervously at my sleeve. Evening shadows lengthened in the narrow streets. I let him steer me back to the safety of the palace, although I saw no threat in these people. Maybe the threat was there. Maybe some of these old men could lift their skinny limbs off the desiccated earth and try to attack me for the shining baubles I wore around my throat.

The wind shifted, and we caught the acrid scent of camels as we returned to the palace. There they lay, heavy-bellied, satisfied. Behind us the whining pleas of the beggars.

What madness was this?

I dismissed Haggai at the palace gate. I wanted to be alone to think. Impossible to do these days with the noise and hurry around the place.

I sat by the empty pool, looking toward the funeral bier.

I sat that way for a long time, enveloped in noise and smells like a package. And like opening a package, my mind seemed to unravel. Curiously, it was there in the courtyard where I decided, for the first time really, that I would go along with this quest; worse, that I wanted to go.

The truth is I no longer knew the truth, nor the right way to find it. The truth is, I wanted to begin all over, from the place where I now stood. And what a place! It was only a framework of glass, so fragile it was ready to break at the slightest provocation. The only reason it had held for so long was because so many hands of the Magi strove to hold it up. So we erected a thin shield of glass we called the truth, and everyone believed.

Here is my discovery. That glass was actually a mirror. It reflected our own failure and that of the god we had made in our image.

Adept at probing the stars, we thought we could reach beyond them and seize the *design* of the stars. Since we seized it, grasped it with our minds, it was *our* design. We *were* gods. Thus the glass of truth became a cloudy mirror.

I speak of *we* here: let me confess. The sin was mine also.

Here is the rest of the paradox, however. The design we invented behind the stars is only darkness. Either that, or it is a mystery beyond the hope of human comprehension.

I can no longer aspire to some god without, some god above, beyond the stars. If there is a God, if there is *some* design behind the stars, lurking there like a hunter in the darkness, then he, she, it, must come *down* to me.

I am too weak to find God. Whoever, whatever, it is—this God—he must be powerful enough to become weak. To become ungodded. That is the final paradox.

I don't know if my thinking settled anything for me. It simply revealed that there was no point in staying, and that I had to engage the absurd risk of seeking. Whatever the case, I felt better than I had in days. When I got up from the courtyard and turned toward my rooms, I had decided I would go. I wanted to go. I went quickly to find Haggai.

Not immediately seeing him on the grounds, I headed for my rooms. Halfway down the corridor, I heard a sudden smash of a vase and a startled scream.

CHAPTER FOUR

As I ran down the hall toward the sound, Melchior flung open the door of his room. Clad in a worn silken robe that looked like an old sack flung about his skinny body, he stood wide-eyed and frightened. A young female attendant cowered behind him, peering around the edge of his robe.

"I heard a scream," I shouted at him.

His eyes were dazed with sleep. "In your room, I think," he said.

I raced down the hallway with Melchior's naked feet slapping clumsily at the tiles behind me. My doorway was wide open. Across the living room I could see Doval's doorway standing open. The canopy of her bed had capsized. Doval lay on the floor in a heap. I stormed into the room in time to see a young man in dark clothing escaping through the narrow slit window.

I lunged for him, grabbing a handful of his hair. He had squeezed almost all of his body through the slit, a space far too narrow for me to get through to pursue him.

I wrenched at his hair, trying to tug him back. His head twisted, and I saw the darting young eyes, full of pain, staring from a dirty face. Not a man at all; he was a mere boy, no older than Haggai. But he was as tough and wiry as an animal. He tried to swing at me but his body was compressed in the window frame. He writhed desperately. I felt my grip on his greasy hair slipping.

In the corridor behind me I heard the pounding boots of the palace guards. "Outside," I shouted. "Get him outside!"

The boy twisted and grabbed at my elbow. Pulling my forearm to him, he sank his teeth into the flesh. The pain shot down to the bone. My grip loosened, and he was gone, squirting through the window frame, a dark shape scuttling across the courtyard and clambering over the wall as the guards pounded laboriously behind him. They didn't stand a chance.

For a moment all was chaos. Poor Melchior clucked about the room helplessly, all his learning worthless at the moment. Doval sat on a pillow, leaning against the wall and rubbing at a bruise along her neck. Haggai had come in and held her, letting her cry out her fear. I sent Melchior and the guards on their way, pulling the shutter closed over the window slit and relighting the wall sconces. The light flickered fitfully over the disheveled room.

Doval's gown was torn to fragments hanging from her shoulders. She clutched the loose ends to her thin body. I wrapped a blanket over her as I bent to her, and lifted her to the bed. The bruise on her neck was turning a livid purple. I feared the worst: rape in my own rooms. She shook her head numbly in response to my question. My sigh of relief was audible.

She was no coward, this Doval. It didn't take her long to relax and to let anger replace fear. Yet, she shivered whenever she glanced at the shuttered window.

"It's locked," I said. I got a woolen robe out of her dresser and draped it around her. She leaned against me.

"Hold me a minute," she whispered. I sat next to her on the pillows, one arm around her small shoulders, while Haggai sat across from us, his eyes flickering angrily.

"Tell me about it," I said, keeping my voice dispassionate. She didn't need my outrage right now. Even so, with my arm around her shoulder I was mindful, as I was increasingly of late, of her small, muscular body swelling toward womanhood. How I treasured this child-woman. She astonished me with her seeming unawareness of her own lithe, graceful body. Her eyes darted to the window and quickly averted.

"He must have come in through the window," Doval said. "I was getting ready for bed. All of a sudden he was there."

"Go on," I said.

"At first he just stared at me," she said. "He seemed . . . to be trying to tell me something. But mostly he seemed scared. Really scared. Maybe I should have waited."

"Waited? Why? What did you do?"

Doval laughed, a nervous release of fear that gave way to trembling. How thin and fragile she seemed. She had her brother Haggai's deep almond eyes. They flushed restlessly in the light of the oil lamps. I squeezed her shoulders. She glanced at me, and the light of the lamps caught a glittering fleck of gold in her right iris.

"I told him to get out. I went over and grabbed his arm. He got scared and tried to get away. He shouted at me, then tried to get out the window." Doval panted angrily, as if reliving it. Her thin hands gestured like floating birds. "I should have let him go, but I was angry. I mean, this is *my* room! I grabbed at him and shouted for the guards, then he panicked. That's when he grabbed my throat, pushing me away. To get loose from me. Somehow my robe ripped. I think he got tangled in it." She stood silently for a minute, her shoulders heaving against me. "It was an old robe anyway," she said, and I wondered at her comment.

I searched her eyes, trying to tell how far to push this. "Why do you think he wanted to get in here?" I asked. "Then run away?"

"Probably had second thoughts," Haggai said. "Doesn't say much for the guards, does it?"

Doval was reflecting. "I'm all right, anyway."

"Why don't you sleep in my room," I offered. Then thought otherwise. She was not, after all, my daughter. "Or with Haggai?"

"No. I'm not a coward."

"Yes. That's a problem. Anyway, I'll have a guard posted outside. But I don't think he will be back. He seemed more terrified than anything else."

"That's just it," she exploded. "He didn't want to be here." She paused. "I think I remember what he said."

"Oh?"

" 'Don't go.' He said, 'Don't go. Tell him, don't go.' "

* * *

I lay in bed for a long time that night without sleeping. That in itself is not unusual. In fact, I often arose during those long hours of the night, when the palace was even more quiet and solitary than usual, when the whole earth was wrapped in darkness. Sometimes I would light a lamp and work. At other times the restlessness would drive me outside. Somnolent guards nodded at my passing. If I strayed beyond the palace gate, a guard would fall in several paces behind me, the jingling of his weapons the only sound in the whole vast universe as I walked to the great dunes or down by the palm-lined river.

I used to wonder what stories the guards told their comrades in the morning, then decided it wasn't worth my while worrying about it. Let them gossip as they wished. I had learned to live with my night demons.

This night I lay awake because of a vast, unexplained loneliness. It was not just the events of the evening, although that may have been part of it, for my thoughts turned often and restlessly to Doval and Haggai.

Even here, in this matter, I was the odd one, the misfit. While the other Magi kept several attendants, even in these lean times, I had few. Of those, Haggai and Doval, brother and sister, were the only ones I had regular contact with and permitted to live in my quarters.

Tonight I began to realize just how precious they had become to me. It had begun with their need for me; now I needed them no less. This is what made it so difficult, for I had to tell them just what the intruder had told them. "Don't go. This quest is not for you. Because I love you, because I need you, I cannot subject you to this madness."

But whatever on earth would I do without them, I who needed *them?*

I sat on the edge of my bed, head in hands. It was on such a night as this, steamy and desolate and restless, that I had found them. This would have been only a few years after my confirmation. Hard to remember now. Six or seven years ago? After my mother's death, surely, for I had no one then.

I had gone walking into that vast emptiness of night, the guard trailing wearily behind me. I had made my way to the palms by the river, leaning back against the grooved bark of a tree and watching the moon bend silver lines across the river. A fish leapt free of the water and glided across the surface of the moon before snaring an insect and disappearing. Somewhere in the dunes a jackal hooted at the stars. I heard the guard sigh behind me.

The bushes along the river's edge rustled. "A small animal," I thought.

A figure broke free of the brush, crawling down to the river. It bent and lapped the water. Behind it, another figure followed, walking upright, and I knew that they were small children. They drank of the water, then splashed it over their faces. One of them giggled quietly.

They did not hear me coming behind them. I bent down and with one hand seized the larger one by the neck. Not brutally. Just to hold him. His body was wiry, hard and whiplike, under my grip. I held him by his shoulders and lifted him while he kicked out and swung his fists. Not a word did he say. The smaller one attacked my legs, kicking resolutely against my shins. It began to annoy me.

I called the guard and handed him the larger one. The guard wrapped the boy in a massive arm and held him tight. Only then did the child speak. "Let me go," he hissed.

I held the smaller child and recognized her in the silver moonlight as a young girl. For a moment she batted away at my shoulders, her breath gasping. I began walking back to the palace. By the time we reached the gate, she was asleep on my shoulder, one tiny arm flung about my neck.

Like the ooze of water seeping slowly from a hole dug in a dry stream bed, their past trickled out a drop at a time. It had been buried deeply, under protective layers of denial. I am not a patient man. I am accustomed to giving orders and expecting instant obedience, yet I realized immediately that this slow ooze of pain could not be rushed. If it were, like water bursting a dam, it could destroy them. For weeks I listened, coached them at opportune moments, let them fall silent when they wished, swallowed my impatience, and thereby perceived bits and pieces that I could finally puzzle together—a flat, superficial portrait of two little lives. During the whole of that time I studied them like caged specimens, rather than any really human life. Daily, I was astonished at their animal vitality. And very nearly animals they were. They would not eat until I left the room, then they devoured their food, licking the platters. They couldn't get enough, eating every meal with a sort of desperation as if it would be their last. They were wary, cunning creatures, always on the lookout for escape. I posted a guard outside their door.

After her first subconscious gesture of affection, falling asleep on my shoulder, the girl, whom I then judged to be about seven or eight, kept a studied distance. Often she retreated behind her brother when I approached, darting glances at me past a crook in his arm. As for the boy, he was adamantine as a small block of granite. A kind of fiery energy surged constantly behind his masklike features.

Their primitive, raw emotions approached too close to the surface for my comfort, and I was tempted to abandon them. But I kept coming back, making conversation that was met by silence or only the barest minimum of words. It became a perverse kind of game for me. In such a way I learned that they were orphans, left to the desert after their parents had died, and that they had learned to survive by hovering around the edges of villages and rivers, scrounging or stealing the food they needed to survive. How long they had endured this way and just where they had been, I had no way of knowing. A year possibly. They refused details.

They had learned to distrust everyone and everything merely to survive. Their trust had been violated and was not easily won again. Simply being there, day after day, being *present* for them, was the first step toward trust. The hours spun thread-fine cords between us, each one so fragile, but growing in tensile strength as they wove around and through each other. They learned to trust—if not me entirely then my being present.

But trust is easily confused, I have learned, with dependence. So my greater challenge was to unravel the strands of dependence, one by one, and give them back. For soon the trust of Haggai and Doval became a slavish dependence. Their eyes grew wide with fear whenever I left the room. They clung to me; huddled their small bodies to mine. As much as I craved that warm comfort of flesh, I wanted them mindful of themselves. I could be savior to no one.

I set them on a course to be saviors to themselves. I forced them apart, not only from me but from each other. How they protested! But they found interests and then skills.

Curiously, it was Doval who proved adept at the skills of the athlete. She loved the river even as the small child she was then. She loved simply being there, frolicking in its shallows or simply watching the smooth glide, the timeless flow suspended over a gravelly bottom. Then she began fishing. Not with a net, for that would place her too far in the flow, but with a simple hook and line. Often she brought her treasure of fat river carp to me.

Her body too took on the firmness and slim, muscular strength of an athlete. She loved tumbling, running, even the rudimentary sword play that she enacted with a blunt stick in the forecourt of the palace. A warrior-child, this Doval.

Haggai grew inward. Had I not known better, I would not have guessed him for Doval's brother. Nearly any hour of the day I could find him in the library, poring over the parchments, fascinated by maps. Somehow, perhaps by manipulating Melchior, who delighted in anyone who took an interest in his work, Haggai secured inks and painstakingly copied the maps. They were so perfectly drawn I couldn't tell the copy from the original. He didn't stop there. Copying was the apprenticeship only. He began drawing buildings, starting with an intricate and precise plan of our palace, and from there began designing his own buildings in odd shapes that I could not recognize. I began to worry about the course of his mind.

With that worry I knew that trust was complete. They had been set free enough—had been permitted to be free enough—to be worried about. When I gave up control, I could only worry from a distance. That is the difficulty of allowing someone to grow up to be free.

I couldn't help wondering if I had ever had that freedom. Or perhaps I was given too much freedom. Who, I wondered, worried about me?

I don't really know what created the breakthrough. I had taken them out walking for exercise one morning. This was about a year after I found them. We hiked along the river, and I held their hands, although I no longer feared, nor much cared, that they would bolt off. Perhaps they sensed this. Since it was not yet hot, we walked up into the dunes.

North of the palace there is a high bluff. From its crest one can see the winding of the river to the east and a vast quilt of dunes rolling to the west. Here the wind saws continuously, but on cloudless days one feels like he's afloat in space. The world is hugely empty, the landscape polished clean under a brilliant blue sky. On impulse, I led them up the perilous pathway to the crest of the bluff. I had to lift them, urge them, over the dangerous places where the sheer edge dropped to the desert floor. I even began to enjoy their fears, their complete dependence upon me. They hung close to my ankles as we climbed. I laughed and encouraged them, pushing them on.

When at last we reached the peak, they huddled on the rock gasping, peering far into the distance. They sat with their hands clinging to the rock, as if they might slide off. We were well-rested and ready to climb down when a small band of ragged wanderers entered the gap below, heading toward the city. Three of them, all well-armed. Probably outlaws. Two rode donkeys. The third walked, striking the ground angrily with a wooden staff. Suddenly both children crouched against me.

"They're the ones," the boy hissed suddenly.

I was startled. He had hardly spoken to me before, and that only in response to my most direct questions.

"Who?"

He pointed below. "They killed them."

"Those men? Killed whom?"

"Mother and father."

"And sister," said the girl. "They got sister too."

"Who is sister?" I asked.

"Our sister. Older sister. They did bad things to her."

"We don't know they got sister," said the boy.

"Yes we do," insisted the girl. "I saw them get her."

"Do you mean those men are the same ones?" I said in astonishment. "They killed your father and mother?"

"And sister," said the girl adamantly.

"How do you know?" I asked. The three men had turned out of sight, crossing behind the flank of the dune along the village road.

The boy looked at me, as if debating with himself. "I know," he said resolutely. He held me with fierce brown eyes.

"You mean, they looked like the men who could have killed them."

He shook his head. "The same," he said.

"He was wearing father's clothes," said the girl. "I saw."

The boy nodded. "They are our donkeys."

They stared at me with the solid determination of the rock we stood upon. It unnerved me. What right did they have to burden me with this? Yet, they asked for nothing. It was a kind of test, I realized. Do you really measure up, wise man?

Quickly I seized their hands. We hurried down the mountain as best we could, far too quickly over the dangerous trail. We arrived at the palace, and I notified the chief guard, instructing him to send a message to the prince. He was, after all, the civil authority.

The prince took it seriously. His guards captured the three that evening. Without hesitation, the children identified some of the goods the men carried, small pieces of jewelry, a knife inscribed on the hilt. It sufficed. The three men were beheaded in the town square the following morning. Their heads were impaled upon stakes at the village gate, as was the custom of the place, and were to hang there for thirty days. Their empty eye sockets stared out at the desert from polished white skulls, picked clean by the carrion birds. Eye for an eye. It was a minor triumph for the prince. Relationships between us were never better.

From that day forth the children and I were inseparable; I had listened to them, and acted. I gave their basic care over to the peasant-cook, an old crone named Lachiska who had lost nearly all her teeth. She was grateful for the service that ensured her place in the palace a few more years, and insofar as I could tell, did her duty by the children. From that day, they were a part of my household, and I was surprised now by how very deeply those bonds, which had begun so simply, had grown.

Now I wanted to tell them to stay here. They *could not* join this . . . this crazy dream which, I was convinced, would end in nightmare. Yet I had no one, Lachiska having grown aged and senile during the intervening years, to leave them with. The logical choice would be to give them to the royal palace. Some lackey there would welcome the well-bred attendants of a Magus. He would also work them to death, perhaps even sell them at a high price into slavery.

During the long hours of that night, this dismal fact sank in. I had no choice but to take them. At least we could die together.

CHAPTER
FIVE

A t the start of a journey the blood surges in expectation, energy
soars, the excitement seems overwhelming. As we set out from
the palace and, with the first dune, left the royal city of Babylon behind,
the whole thing felt like a wonderful adventure rather than a quest. Laughter, sometimes nervous, was on every lip, and voices were unduly loud.

Even the overburdened camels accepted their riders and loads willingly
enough. After long rest, the beasts were fat and frisky. They stretched out
in a long single file under a bright desert sky and cool air, their ungainly
haunches galumphing along like drunken soldiers.

Behind the leather saddle of each camel assigned to the Magi was secured a box, about a foot in length and half that in width and depth. They
were crafted of wood and secured by metal hasps that girdled the box and
locked with three separate mechanisms on top. By a series of intricate
loops, these were affixed directly to the saddle, where they would remain
in the security of the Magi themselves.

There was not much secrecy about what they contained. These were our
passage to the throne room of the king we sought: our gifts. They were
all we had, and we wondered aloud whether they would suffice.

In Melchior's cask, the heaviest, lay a velvet bag filled with gold coins.
The denominations and site of coinage were insignificant, gold being the
universal payment. There were coins whose minting was unknown even

to us. Some had been in the possession of the Magi for hundreds of years, from kingdoms that we didn't even know and that probably no longer existed.

In the cask of Balthazzar nestled six small bottles of the unguent frankincense. He had carried the potent incense back from a great southern kingdom on one of his voyages years earlier. How he had come by it, he never told us. The thick, resinous liquid was, perhaps, more valuable than gold. It was treasured by monarchs in our world who lusted after its sweet perfume. Just a drop or two in an incense burner perfumed a king's palace for days. It had been a great while since I had smelled it in our own, the most recent during the visit of a head of state several years earlier.

The myrrh carried in Gaspar's cask was similarly an incense brought back by Balthazzar. Although less powerful than frankincense, myrrh was used to induce such reveries and visions that one could by them read the lessons of the stars. It aided dreams and prophecies. Our store had been much depleted, since this was the task of the Magi. Only two small bottles rested on the velvet cloths. We had questioned this gift but concluded that such a king as we sought—one who was himself the fulfillment of prophecy—would have an appreciation for it.

And in my cask?

This was my own arranging. I was given the keys to the treasure room, deep under the Palace of the Magi, a small room reached by an underground passage and through doors opened by the manipulation of certain levers and devices. Yet, as I stood in that underground room lit by a feeble candle, I was dismayed at the poverty of our riches. Everything lay in a thick coat of dust.

On shelves lay rows of heavy, ornate silver plates and goblets, handed down, I had been told, from the exiles six hundred years earlier. Far too heavy for this voyage. Some ancient manuscripts were on another shelf. They were worthless; we ourselves didn't understand them, or they would have been on Melchior's shelves.

From another shelf, I raided a jewel box of several brilliant stones, discarding some of the bulky, heavier pieces as too awkward. Carefully I wrapped a polished sapphire as large as a small egg in velvet cloth. I selected a small figurine carved from some green stone I wasn't familiar with. The figure looked like a woman huddled over an infant. I thought it appropriate. Lastly, I selected a small ring. Too small for my fingers.

It bore a winking diamond that flashed brilliantly even in the candlelight. A small serpent lay intricately engraved on the band, so that the jewel formed a sparkling eye. It caught my attention. I wrapped it and slipped it also into the cask.

Some small boxes and bags lay tumbled in straw on the lower shelves. They had been untouched for years, looking like gray piles of dust. I didn't bother to search them. Certain I would never return, I locked the door, leaving all the rest to whoever might locate this chamber in some future year.

Haggai and Doval packed their things, along with some clothing they thought I would need. I let them make their own choices. Both had acquired desert cloaks for travel, and finally took little else. My heart jerked once when I saw Haggai study his pack, then thoughtfully remove the bah-lah game from it and set it aside. He knew that the time for childhood was over.

On impulse, I took the game back to the treasure room and thrust it on a shelf. The memories, at least, were precious.

*　*　*

It was the cool season when we left, the winter rains having dissipated and the skies now clear and crisp, newly made each morning by the power of the sun, spun out of molten blue. The advantage of the season, besides the moderate temperature, lay in the rain-compacted sands and the quiet breeze that fanned us gently as we traversed the dunes.

It all seemed so glorious, so blessed and happy. One might have thought it all worthwhile.

In moments, we crested the first dune and Babylon lay behind. That was the reality. Behind us lay home. Ahead of us lay endless days at the mercy of the desert. Surely a man could walk faster than these barrel-fat camels. But not so far. They were the ships of the desert seas, their scarecrow legs like oars punching the surface of the sand, their great horny feet splashing dust in their wake. Each of us knew that in time these ponderous beasts would grow unruly, ornery, weary. But for this time we managed to enjoy it.

If truth be told, there was much to enjoy in the desert, especially after the rainy season, before the sun began its furious summer reign. Haggai and Doval delighted in the lessons I taught them, and even I began to believe this might last.

Each day's travel was painfully short, no matter how hard we pressed the beasts. We were, after all, Magi. This meant that we had to stop long before sundown to erect the tents before darkness. Since the drovers, some of them simply young men plucked from city streets or borrowed from parents on run-down farms, did this clumsily, we often assisted. The drovers then had to herd and feed the beasts. The guards, who had next to nothing to do but guffaw with rude laughter all day, would then have a fire started and be eating already. Our attendants, meanwhile, prepared our dinner, which we took with Kruspian before Balthazzar's tent.

Our tents were arranged in a circle about the small fire. Around them were arrayed the smaller lean-tos of the guards. The drovers slept in the open a short distance away with the stink of their camels.

We saw little of the drovers and guards. They kept their distance; we kept ours. The idea was that we would be protected from association with them. Occasionally we saw travelers, but these were rare even though we were on the main caravan route from Babylon to Al Achor, where we would reprovision for the long leg of the journey to the west. A few of these travelers paused to watch us pass by. It was obvious to them that royalty of some sort was near, and, like all people, they had a fascination with royalty.

After days of travel, the monotony hardened into a grinding routine. Our conversations around the fire grew increasingly terse. Kruspian seemed to take a peculiar delight in needling old Gaspar. One night Kruspian slapped him familiarly on the back while Gaspar was taking a long drink of water from a flagon. "Good water, Gaspar?" he roared.

"Good," spat Gaspar as he choked on it. "It's water, fool. Please don't clap my back like that."

"Ah, Gaspar," said Kruspian expansively. "Aren't you glad I'm along? Fresh water. Everything in order. Your every wish is my command."

"Can't see what difference it makes," Gaspar muttered.

"Oh, you will, Gaspar. Believe me, you will. You'll thank me yet, my friend."

Gaspar stalked off. "Patronizing idiot," I heard him mumbling as he crawled into his tent.

Gaspar was a tough old bird. I think he would have been content voyaging by himself. Probably all night, looking up at the stars. Trouble was, he'd wind up walking in circles, or end up some place he hadn't expected and wonder where he was.

In the mornings, of course, all the tents had to be broken down and repacked, a laborious process at best. The camels had to be outfitted, packed and mounted. Generally it was midmorning before the first steps were taken, and the days ahead looked even longer.

To break the monotony, when we struck camp in the evening, I often took Haggai and Doval a short distance into the desert. At first Kruspian protested.

"Your safety is my responsibility," he insisted.

"Look," I said. "It's still daylight. I don't see any outlaws around, do you?"

He sneered at me. "*You* wouldn't see them if there were," he insisted. "They could rise up behind a dune in a moment."

"I'll take my chances."

"Besides," he added, "hyenas and jackals always trail a caravan."

This much I knew to be true. They had picked up our trail a day out of Babylon. As soon as we struck camp in the morning they descended like locusts on the site, scouring for scraps. They would only grow more voracious the further we went into the desert. Given the opportunity, they would descend like a cloud of jaws and ripping claws upon a lagging camel or a wanderer.

"We won't go far," I said, to reassure Kruspian. In the end, he permitted us, as long as a guard followed at a distance. Having time to ourselves was worth the risk of jackals.

The desert at this time of year burst with an incredible fullness of life. I spotted a gecko hole, and we lay on our bellies in the warm sand for a long time waiting for the tiny lizard to poke its grayish head above the sand. When it came, two little eyes like polished marbles studied us. Doval began to giggle. The gecko darted up, gave a flash of pink back, flipped in the air, and dove back into its hole.

Another time we tracked the spindling trail of a viper, its thrusting lunges having left a series of stitched tracks in the sand. When we located its nest by a red boulder, we studied it from a distance. It took some time to separate the thick, dangerous body from the rock against which it lay. Nearly all its body was curled under sand, the immobile head protruding like a fat, scaly twig.

I taught them to be on the lookout, always, for scorpions. Beetles and spiders darted everywhere, and I permitted Haggai to take along the dried shell of a scarab beetle that he kept like an amulet, tied to a piece of string about his neck.

After days of travel like this, midway to Al Achor and the real start of the journey, we camped by an oasis. Seeing our sizable caravan coming, people moved aside to permit us room by the water's edge.

The place was a miracle of plant life that battled the desert's dryness beyond the pool of water. Here and there primroses folded their delicate petals for the night. In another week or two they would dry up as the hot season approached, entering their long wait again for the winter rains. Stunted trees edged up to the water, and their long fronds whimpered in the evening breeze. I wished we could have stayed there longer, so I could show Haggai and Doval the dens of animals that I knew would be hidden in the surrounding dunes. Instead, we studied their tracks in the damp sand down by the water.

The drovers replenished the waterskins. Al Achor, as a desert town, would have limited supplies, well-guarded and expensive even after a good rainy season. The village hoarded its water in underground cisterns and supported itself as a replenishing depot.

As we prepared to embark at dawn the following morning, Doval asked me if she could bathe in the oasis. I agreed under the conditions that I walk with her and that we go to a sheltered area, removed from the camp.

We passed a number of the drovers and young guards splashing water on themselves in the shallows about the camp. It would be a late departure. No one was in a hurry to leave.

We reached the shelter of the palm trees, and I settled back on the sandy bank while Doval dipped under the fronds, stripped quickly and slipped into the water. She swam outward a short way, her smiling face beaming at me above the water. Playfully she slapped water in my direction.

After a few minutes I called her to come out. She protested briefly, made a face at me, then paddled back to the fronds. As she did so, I became aware of a figure crouched behind the trees, well-hidden in the brush. How long he had been there watching, I couldn't say. I shouted as Doval rose from the water.

The figure in the bushes leapt to his feet, started to run and stumbled headlong over the root of a palm tree. I dove at him, but his body was so thin and wiry he would have slipped out of my grasp if Doval hadn't grabbed his ankle and tripped him. I had my weight on him then, but it was like trying to subdue some panicked animal. He was all sinewy leanness, squirming in the wet sand. I got one arm around his neck and twisted mercilessly. For a moment he tried to bite and kick while I squeezed down on his windpipe. Then suddenly he fell limp. Still, I kept my hold on his neck while I twisted one arm behind him and lifted him to his feet.

I heard Doval suck in her breath, giving a thin, strangulated cry.

"What is it?" I said. The thin body I held squirmed like a fish.

"He's the same! The same one in my room."

I pulled on his hair, twisting his head around to get a look at his face. I couldn't tell. It had been too dark. He had the same dirty face, the too-long black hair and the desperate cunning eyes of thousands of slum-life boys.

"Are you sure?"

"Yes."

"Doval," I said as calmly as I could. "Put your robe on."

She shivered with sudden embarrassment, throwing her robe on and cinching the belt.

I kept my grip on the boy's hair and spoke in his ear, "Now," I hissed, "tell me your name and what you're doing."

He bit his lip and squeezed his eyes shut, as if he wanted to close out the world about him, pretend it wasn't there. He was terrified of me. I saw this, but I wanted answers. I drove him to the ground, put my knee in his back and held his head above the water.

"Tell me!" I feared my own voice, its cutting anger and what my own arms were doing. I couldn't stop myself. I plunged his head under the surface and felt it jerk spasmodically for air. Strangely, it made me all the angrier. I felt all my rage at this insane journey, this rupture of reason, surge in me and pulse through my arms to the skinny form I held. I jerked his head up.

"Tell me!" I shouted in his ear.

The water streaming from his hair, his clenched lips and closed eyes made me furious.

"Don't . . ." he began to say, but I didn't let him finish his protest. I plunged him under again.

I felt Doval pulling on my shoulders, heard her voice whimpering behind me.

It dragged me back to reality. I loosened my grip. The boy lay gasping for air. Suddenly, I was sickened at my own anger. Disgusted. He was just . . . a boy. I let him up, choking and gasping, and my stomach churned.

"He . . . means to kill you. All of you." He gasped the words in heaves of breath.

"Who?" I demanded.

The boy shook his head, squeezed his eyes again as if warding off some pain. I pulled him to his feet, keeping his arm twisted behind him. The thin fabric of his worn shirt tore with the movement, and I saw the latticework of whiplashes across his shoulders. I stepped back appalled.

"What is this?" I asked. Even then the words sounded foolish to me. I knew little of suffering, protected in my shining palace. The boy merely shook his head. He would say no more.

"Very well. Let's see what you have to say to Balthazzar." The boy trembled under my hand. Again, I jerked his arm up behind him and marched him toward the campsite. I would have answers! But even as I went, I loathed what I was doing. Let Balthazzar handle it. Or Kruspian. Or whoever was in charge of this mess.

I am grateful for one thing. As we neared the campsite, Doval plucked at my sleeve. "Don't hurt him," she pleaded and ran ahead into the tent. I hope she didn't see what followed.

Kruspian and Balthazzar stood before a tent, each holding a cup of water while Kruspian pointed into the distance. They were probably planning the day's travel. A light mail shirt flickered brightly over Kruspian's hairy chest. He wore a silk cape to shade his body; leather boots, laced to the knee, protected his feet. As always, he was armed. At one side of his waist he wore a short scimitar, at the other, a dagger.

As I approached, he turned and stared at me insolently. For a moment, I felt like a fool with nothing to say. When I spoke it was to Balthazzar.

"This boy," I said, "was spying on us while Doval was bathing."

Balthazzar merely frowned.

"He is the same one who broke into her room and attacked her before we left."

Kruspian reached out a hand and spun the boy around. He landed a backhanded blow that rocked the boy's head back, his jaw snapping.

Blood flew from his lips.

The boy's eyes widened. He turned toward Balthazzar. "Don't trust him!" he screamed. "I wanted to warn—"

His words ended in a gasp and a long sigh, as if air had been expelled from a bloated waterskin. He crumpled forward as Kruspian's fist drove into his chest. From the boy's back several inches of the scimitar protruded. He hung that way for a moment, then Kruspian jerked the blade back, and the boy collapsed.

For a moment I stood speechless, motionless, unable to believe what I saw. It seemed part of a play—an act, unreal. Kruspian leaned over and deliberately wiped the grooved blade of the scimitar on the boy's ragged pants.

"What are you doing!" I finally exploded. There was a wild throbbing in my temples, a terrible insanity.

Kruspian looked at me calmly. His face was completely impassive. "I'm cleaning my blade," he said, as if mocking me. "Nothing is more effective than running it through the sand. However, it dulls the blade."

"Are you mad!" I screeched. Some guards who had drawn close, like flies surrounding the smell of blood, chuckled. I noticed, even then, that they arranged themselves near Kruspian. Not us.

I whirled on Balthazzar. His eyes seemed rooted on the boy. The blood had stopped flowing already, as if he had always been lifeless, frozen forever in a small, crumpled heap on the sand. Flies sang over the wound like mad celebrants.

Kruspian turned toward the guards. "Strip him and throw him out of the camp," he said irritably. "We're already late. Get those drovers busy on these tents!"

I grabbed Kruspian by the shoulder, whirling him around. His face flushed red, and he reached automatically for his weapon.

"Get your hands off me," he hissed through his teeth.

"You killed him. For what? For spying on a girl!"

"No. I disciplined all of them," Kruspian said evenly. "If you don't like it, why didn't you handle it yourself?"

He had himself under control, the cold, rigid captain of the guard. Two of his men reached for the body. I shoved them away. Kruspian's hand fell on a muscle at my neck, paralyzing me with pain. The strength in his hands astonished me. I struck out, meeting only air. The guards hooted with laughter. I slashed a forearm upward, jarring Kruspian's grip.

"You black mongrel." He spat the words at me and dropped into a fighting stance. "Come on, then."

Suddenly Balthazzar stood between us, massive and threatening. His eyes shot fire. He said nothing. He did nothing. Yet the guards saw the corded muscles of his arms and fell back slightly. His anger seemed to make his shoulders and neck swell even larger than usual so that the heavy golden necklace about his neck seemed at the point of bursting.

Kruspian stepped back from him.

"We will take care of the corpse," Balthazzar said. "See to the tents."

Kruspian sputtered. "I can't tolerate insubordination if we are to succeed. Nor," he added, "an attack on one of our own."

Balthazzar stared him down. The weight of those eyes was ponderous, undeniable. Kruspian suddenly turned away shouting orders with undisguised fury, kicking angrily at any guard or drover who didn't move quickly enough to suit him.

Balthazzar motioned to me. We picked up the body and carried it out of the campsite. We scooped out a hollow at the far end of the oasis, other travelers watching fearfully. None dared intervene. We piled some rocks over the shallow grave. It was ineffective; the hyenas would have it open within the hour.

I wanted to talk, to defend myself, to find answers. Balthazzar sensed this. He paused and laid a hand on my arm. "We are late," he said. "We must leave now."

"You can just leave it like this?"

"Maybe in Al Achor I can pursue it."

"He's a madman."

"True. He's also all we have to get us through. The journey, Elhrain, has hardly begun."

"Yes," I muttered. "And what a start."

As the caravan departed, I heard at my back the howl of a hyena, and I shivered.

CHAPTER
SIX

E ven before we reached Al Achor I pressed Balthazzar to separate
from Kruspian. Melchior and Gaspar seemed to take no interest
one way or the other. Already the journey was taking its toll on them.
I didn't see how they could possibly survive the whole voyage. Each night
they staggered off their camels, ate briefly, and, as soon as their tents were
up, fell soundly asleep. They seemed to live in their visions, in their huge
hope.

Hope can be a vital, if dangerous, prod. Unfortunately, I did not have
it. With each step hope seemed, to me, the soul-kin to madness.

Balthazzar's responses to my pleas were noncommittal. "We'll see," he
would say. Or, "We're into the game now. We can't change."

It was a means of denial, and it took its toll on Balthazzar. On all of
us.

I could not drive from my memory the explosion of blood from the
boy's body. It kept rehearsing itself in my mind, in intricate detail, as if
preparing for a reality that had already occurred. Worst, perhaps, was the
wan withdrawal of Doval. She would not speak to me, would not listen
to my rationalizations. Even I knew they were worthless. She spoke only
to Haggai. I understood. They were once again waifs of the desert, fleeing
their past.

Whatever hope I had for change was dashed when we arrived at Al

Achor. Foolishly, I expected another Babylon. I expected at the least some civilized structure. I was wrong.

We had planned to reach Al Achor in slightly over two weeks. Already a month had passed. And the weather had shifted decidedly. The cool days and nights of the late rainy season had fled. For the last few days we had not seen a single cloud in the sky. The sun grew daily more harsh, a searing flame that hung in the sky and scalded the dry earth.

Nonetheless, we spent four days at Al Achor, letting the camels replenish themselves. You could almost see their flesh expand as they lounged around the oases. The guards, ever vigilant against pillaging townspeople, stood shifts throughout the day and night.

The village men, on the other hand, stood as vigilant against the guards. They were stunted men, as if shriveled by desert life. They squatted under thin capes that they wore hooded over their heads, ever watching. We began to feel like a people under siege. For the first time I began to understand the necessity of the guards.

One of them approached us at the evening meal on the third day. He was the man Kruspian had made arrangements with for the replenishing. While he was some sort of village leader, he bore all the authority of a scurvy dog. His clothing was a motley assortment of rags. He seemed inordinately fond of jewelry, sporting a fistful of rings, a gaudy bead necklace from some far northern country, and a gold ring in one ear. A thin, livid scar ran from the ear across his cheek to his upper lip where it disappeared in some ragged bristles of a beard.

He walked up to the campfire and stood at the edge of the circle awaiting an invitation. Kruspian ignored him. I found this curious, for he stared at Kruspian as if he knew him better than their one brief meeting would suggest. At last Balthazzar stood and extended the courtesy of a greeting.

"I am Racbah," the man announced as he glided to the edge of the fire and squatted. His body was thin and sinewy, seeming to curve in upon itself like a snake. The firelight glinted on his greasy hair, upon his sharply defined features including a nose that hooked like an eagle's claw.

"What can I do for you?" Balthazzar asked.

"Pardon," Racbah said expansively. He drew a heavy flagon out from under his desert cloak and passed it to Balthazzar. "It may have been some time since you have tasted good wine." He held the flagon out. "For you," he said when Balthazzar hesitated.

Balthazzar held the man with his eyes, then took the flagon and raised it, shooting a stream into his mouth. When he tipped his head back, his heavy golden necklace flashed in the firelight, and I heard Racbah gasp audibly. Balthazzar set the flagon down for whomever wanted to sample it.

"Very good," he said. "Thank you."

"Pardon me, sir," Racbah whined. He wiggled where he sat like a fawning puppy. "I couldn't help noticing your necklace." He paused.

"Yes?" Balthazzar pierced him with his eyes.

"It's not from these parts. Is it?" Racbah's voice buzzed like a honeyed whine.

"No," Balthazzar said shortly. He stood up and walked into his tent.

Racbah had little interest in speaking to me. In earlier travels into the desert regions around Babylon, I had noticed that the villagers of these small towns were a reclusive and protective people. While many of this region are burned by the desert sun to the hue of dark brown, few such people have seen a man like me, bearing black skin. People in the larger cities, like Babylon, that carry on foreign trade, seem not to notice any peculiarities whatsoever, being more content to judge a man by what's in his purse. But in the more reclusive villages—and Al Achor was as reclusive as they come—the villagers reacted with silence and suspicion to my skin color.

It irritated me. I got up and left Racbah in the presence of Kruspian and some loitering guards. My guess was that, having to deal with the surly Kruspian, Racbah would return to his village in minutes.

There were other interests on my mind.

*　*　*

I waited until the camp was asleep. Kneeling along the billowy sides of Balthazzar's tent, I listened for sounds of his breathing or moving about. Nothing. Only the faint glow of a shielded oil lamp. I had hoped to find him awake. About to sneak back into the darkness, I sensed a shadow against the light within the tent. A slight shift, really, in the intense darkness all about, as if someone had moved from the lamp. Crawling belly down in the sand, I crept to the door flap. A guard passed nearby, and I flattened myself.

After a moment, I lifted a corner of the flap an inch or two. Balthazzar was seated on the ground before the oil lamp, its light so low I could hardly distinguish the features of the man.

"You may come in," he said softly.

I didn't move. How could he know I was there?

He chuckled softly. "Come, Elhrain. Tell me your sorrows. I have been waiting for you."

I darted in quickly.

"Sit down." He patted the ground. He lifted the flagon of wine that Racbah had left and handed it to me as I sat.

"Surprisingly good wine," he said. "I wonder who they stole it from?"

"You think the same then?" I asked after I jetted some wine from the flagon into my mouth. It was good indeed.

"What? That they're thieves and outlaws? Of course. We didn't expect our voyage to occur without incident, did we?"

"I don't trust them. None of them."

"Nor do I," he said. At times Balthazzar had a way of lowering his eyes upon a person, the gaze so intense and predatory that he wanted to scream for a way out. But he also had a way of looking at someone that made the person feel as if he were the only other one in the world. That he was special, a soul-mate. I had to avoid those eyes to say what I wanted to say.

"Why do we do it, then?" I asked.

"Oh, Elhrain. Do you lose sight of the goal so quickly? Take it as confirmation, Elhrain. The more difficult the quest, the more important the goal."

"I wish I could believe that easily."

"No. Don't make that mistake. It makes it all the harder to believe. The time for easy belief is long behind us. The demons of denial rise up against us. Therefore, we go on. *Because* of that, we go on."

"I concern myself with people, not demons."

"Kruspian?"

"Yes. He's a killer, Balthazzar. A bold-faced killer. You saw him. He ran his sword through that lad and never flinched. It meant nothing to him. And you did nothing."

"What *could* I do, Elhrain? Kill Kruspian?"

For a moment I was going to say, yes. Kill him. But I realized, too, that if we pursued this quest we were in all practical effect Kruspian's prisoners. At the very least, we were at his mercy. The knowledge hit me, in my weariness, like a physical blow, and I recognized that Balthazzar had understood this all along.

I stood up. "Goodnight," I said.

"Sleep well, Elhrain. We will talk again?"

It was more an order than a question. I did not answer. I stepped outside and darted into the shadows.

As I slipped back toward my tent, some muttered words from the darkness arrested me, and I froze. There, a few yards away, I made out the familiar shape of Kruspian. And the man with him who had raised his voice for a moment, gesticulating, arguing a point? I would have sworn it was the thin, reptilian shape of Racbah. In a moment he was gone, and Kruspian stood by himself in the night.

I turned back toward my tent, slinking through the shadows. It was a moonless night, the darkness such that it seemed to suffuse palpably into the body. All I wanted to do now was sleep, to pass into the sweet oblivion. My mind whirled, as it had for days.

I must have been half asleep already. I darted around the corner of a tent, Melchior's I believe, and tripped over the guy wire to the peg, landing heavily against some supplies stacked alongside the tent. I pulled myself to my feet, looking wildly for an avenue of escape. Then I remembered myself. I *am* a Magus. This is *my* journey. What have I been reduced to, slinking about in the darkness like a scared rabbit? I cursed and kicked at a loaded container.

Kruspian stood before me suddenly, as if he had been transformed out of thin air. He seemed to reach out a hand to help. Then I saw a glint of shiny metal in it.

"Put that away," I ordered peremptorily.

He hesitated, but sheathed the dagger. He did not move, effectively blocking my way.

"Wandering around?" he asked. "Looking for something?"

I had a lie on my lips: stepping outside to relieve myself before sleeping. Then I thought, who am I to have to lie to this . . . this soldier? I refuse to be his minion. Should I confront him about Racbah? No.

"What are you doing here, anyway, Elhrain?" he asked impatiently.

My anger rose like a flame in my throat. He dared question me? He seemed to sense the tension across the darkness between us.

"You don't belong. You know that, don't you?" His voice was a hiss.

I willed myself to relax. I would not be goaded. I sensed where his questions led. Get inside his mind, I told myself. Like knowing the land—know the enemy. Even as I spoke that word in my mind I felt the shiver of fear. Enemy. I countered him. "A misfit, you mean?"

"A misfit. Unfit. You don't fit, that's for sure. You're as out of place as a snowstorm in the desert."

"Snow is white, Kruspian. Hardly an apt analogy. You can do better than that."

"Right. You belong in a closed room, black man. Where it is dark. These are not your people."

"Don't anger me, military man."

"You anger *me*, black man. I can't abide your stinking color. If you think I will defer to you because you pretend to be one of them, you're dead . . ." he paused upon the word, "wrong," he finished. "You're as dead as a desert night."

"Perhaps, Kruspian, in that night I'll yet prove to be your nightmare." I couldn't resist goading him, even though I knew it was the wrong approach, a stupid approach.

"Watch it, stranger," he hissed. "Don't you dare threaten me. I won't fail in this, and you won't get in my way."

"Your way? What is it you think you'll get, Kruspian? Just where is your way?"

"I'll get whatever I want. And everything I want."

My anger was ready to explode. He recognized the point he had pushed me to—and relished it. Before I was able to reply he turned and disappeared into the darkness. I was about to pursue, thinking, too late, of all the things I might have said to him. I heard the jingling of armor, a subdued chuckle. His guards had been there in the darkness all the time. Shaking with fury, I returned to my tent.

I threw myself down upon the sleeping pillows, but I did not sleep. I lay on my back, tense as a bow string, hands behind my head, and stared into the darkness.

I loathed them, but his words, as if guided by some diabolical sorcery, had touched my deepest fears. I did not belong. Stranger in a strange land. I did not want to think of this. Nor could I stop thinking of it.

I found my mind, against my will, ferreting out my own past, probing at the sore points of memory. I wanted, more than anything, to know myself and felt like crying out into the darkness, "Who am I?"

* * *

I had been a mere child, three or four perhaps, when I left my native land with my mother. I remembered little of the time before leaving. I remembered a palace, to be sure. And a freedom I had there. People took care of me. I must have been . . . what? I don't know.

I could not remember a father. There was an older man. His skin, like that of my mother and me, was jet black. He wore golden jewelry like another skin. Perhaps he was royalty. He seemed to care for me. I was sure of that, but I was too young then to know anything else with certainty.

Perhaps my earliest clear memory was the leaving. My mother was weeping. We set out on a ship and were at sea many days. I remember having no room to play. Just staring out at the endless expanse of water. And being sick. Mother kept me near her, and she seldom left her tiny cabin.

The ship was a trading vessel. I knew this, even at that age, because the deck was crowded with barrels and crates, and when I climbed among them the sailors—harsh, rough men—chased me away. Other than that, no one spoke to us. We were alone. Many days.

When we at last docked in this hot and sullen land, men and camels met us. They took us north, to the palace at Babylon. I was given a small room of my own at the back of the palace, far from the Magi's rooms. I didn't even know where my mother slept. Almost immediately I was pressed into studies, and I saw her only on holidays and at official functions. She looked very much like a queen to me then, very beautiful, but then she always had.

At those official functions I saw the way others deferred to her, the way they revered her. She sat darkly shining, with her jet-black hair wrapped up carefully in gold-trimmed braid, dressed in flowing white robes. When she stood near me and placed her hand on my shoulders, I nearly burst with pride.

That is all I remember.

And it was not enough.

When Necomar died, I spent more time with Melchior and Gaspar.

Seldom was I with Balthazzar. Yet, he always seemed to be there watching me. Waiting.

Then, for many days, I did not see my mother.

My twelfth birthday and the confirmation arrived. She appeared briefly at the ceremony, seated in her white robe, and her face was as empty and pallid as a desert cloud. I could hardly follow the proceedings, so intent was I upon her suffering. She left before the ceremony concluded, guided out by two attendants who seemed to support her rather than follow her. I remember Balthazzar starting from his place at the head of the table, then, as if by an act of will alone, forcing himself back down.

It was Balthazzar who awakened me the night she died.

He entered my room, now the room of a Magus off the central corridor, in the darkness of full night, shaking me awake. In my sleep, I resisted. He sat on the edge of the bed. At last I awakened fully, and saw him sitting above me. Saw those *eyes*, rather. Those piercing, hawklike eyes. And they were suffused with tears.

"Get dressed," he said softly.

"What?"

"Get dressed. I'll wait for you."

He stood with his back to me while I dressed, following some strange decorum. I fumbled with my clothes. He led me down the long central corridor in the darkness. I was surprised when we arrived at a door which I recognized as leading to his own rooms.

Without a word he led me in. The room was lit with oil lamps that drove back the darkness. The furnishings were opulent. He strode across the room as if completely unaware of its beauty and led me to a door off the primary chamber. He opened it quietly and pushed me through.

My mother lay upon a large bed so full of pillows that she seemed afloat on them. For a moment, I remember, I had the feeling of being at sea. My feet were unsteady.

She was dying. I knew that the moment I laid eyes on her. Her rich, dark skin had flushed to a dirty gray. Her breathing was like the heaves of storm. I flung myself upon her and she had barely the strength to lift an arm about me. I held her thus for what seemed a long time, then felt Balthazzar's hand on my shoulder. I released her.

Balthazzar pulled me to him and placed one thick arm tenderly about my shoulders as we sat on the floor by the bedside. I fell asleep that way, in his arms.

When I awakened in the morning I lay in his bed. I hurried out to the adjoining bedroom. The bed was empty. Even the pillows had disappeared.

Three days later I again saw my mother. She lay on the funeral pyre, and the flames licked at the linen cerement cloths.

* * *

Piece by slow piece, I relived those days during the night. I still had not fallen asleep when I sensed a small form sitting inside my tent by the doorway. I was not even aware of her entering.

"Doval?" I said.

I heard her whimper. "I'm afraid," she said.

"Come here," I whispered hoarsely.

She crept to my bed, and I enfolded her in my arms. At last we slept.

CHAPTER
SEVEN

Our convoy left Al Achor without fanfare. We were making pitifully slow progress, and because of that now faced the cruelest season with the very worst the desert had to fling at us. Al Achor was the last known outpost. In all likelihood we would not see anything resembling civilization until we had crossed both the desert and the western mountain passes. As we forged out of town that morning, I kept asking myself, why go on?

The answer never changed: because there is no place else to go and nothing to return to. I cared only for the safety of Doval, who smiled shyly at me this morning as if sharing some secret, of Haggai, who seemed wrapped in an intense, dark blanket of worry, and of myself. That was all that mattered. I, and those dear to me, would survive.

Kruspian tongue-lashed his men savagely. The camels themselves seemed to sense what lay ahead and were loath to leave the oases. At last the overburdened beasts staggered to their feet and we set out.

Past the sullen, cold-faced stares of the villagers. I did not see Racbah, although even the thought of him sent chill tracks down my spine. I turned and forced a smile at Doval. She bravely responded.

Immediately beyond the village, with its annealing touch of the interlaced oases, the desert rose to meet us. Over one dune and we lay in its defiant grip. You dare invade me! it seemed to announce. None of us was adequately prepared, mentally or physically, for the full effect of its heat. One could never prepare for it. A rage of fire fell from the sun above and rose from the earth below, clamping our small band in a hot fist. We had clever canopies, stretching across poles from the camel saddles, erected over our heads. They blocked the sun, but seemed only to intensify the heat.

On the seventh day west of Al Achor, we confronted the first of the desert sandstorms. The camels sensed it before the men. While the sky was still clear, they huddled restlessly on the trail, stumbling, burying their noses in each other's flanks. The drovers whipped them fiercely, puzzled by their sudden indolence. The camels herded more tightly together, squeezing us into a ball of brown hide.

Then, far in the west, we spotted the tan pall lying like a heat wave above the desert. It seemed like a living thing, arching its brown back higher and higher. We could make out the twisting shapes of blown sand as a cloud rose like a wall from the earth itself, soaring thousands of feet into the air. The sun disappeared. The sky turned brown. The drovers shouted, whipping the camels into a circle while we stumbled hurriedly off their backs.

Then it was upon us—sand so fine and winds so fierce that the scythe-like particles flayed the skin. We huddled with backs turned to the storm, trying to breathe through layers of cloth. The dust worked into nostrils and throats so that the very lungs felt abraded. The dust curled under eyelids, no matter how tightly squeezed. Every blink felt like an abrasive rubbing across the eyeball.

The storm raged for most of the afternoon, then lifted suddenly past us. The winds died, and it was gone. The brown wall, eerie with its coiling spumes, moved eastward. It looked like some demented fiend leaving us; its heart was as dark as a demon.

We made camp where we were that night. Everybody was subdued. The only sounds were the hacking of dry lungs. Six inches of powdery dust muffled the sound of our movements.

In the morning we discovered that during the night seven of the camel drovers had snuck out of camp and retreated toward Al Achor. They had taken advantage of the powdery dust to take with them the two mules, laden with water and supplies. Kruspian ranted and raved. He had the two guards for that area whipped until their backs were sheathed with blood.

Little good that did. We were seven hands short, which meant that all of us had to pitch in with the chores of loading up that morning.

The camels balked. Ornery, spiteful beasts in the best of times, the sandstorm exacerbated their meanness. They refused to get up, spitting and snapping angrily at the drovers who switched their backsides. Finally one of the drovers dug out some hot embers from the fire and carried them in a cup toward the lead camel, a particularly ugly and mean-spirited brute. The drovers chuckled among themselves in anticipation. The flame-carrier sneaked up behind the camel on hands and knees, scooped a little hollow under the camel's back haunches, and poured the coals in. He darted quickly away.

The camel tried to ignore it. Little puffs of smoke started up. As the coals seared its hide, the camel lifted its head as if sniffing the air. Then, with an angry bellow, it lurched upright, chasing itself in clumsy circles until the singed hide cooled.

The other camels clambered to their feet and fell in line.

The disappearance of the drovers seemed to make our band just a bit less formidable as we set out, not that we worried about outlaws. We had all heard the stories of the pillaging and terrorizing desert bands, those people who knew the desert intimately, living for months in its barren wastes and raiding stray caravans. Still, we were a large group, heavily armed. We felt vulnerable not to outlaws, but to the desert itself.

Kruspian doubled the guard for the following week, presumably for protection, in reality to prevent any others from leaving. By then Al Achor lay so far behind us that one would be better off risking the unknown ahead. To leave now would be a guarantee of death, a suicide.

Even so, turning back sometimes appeared the better course. Our spirits dropped daily. Each morning we flagellated bodies into action by an act of will. And by Kruspian's imprecations. He seemed to grow daily more anxious. Each morning and each evening he walked out into the desert a way, trying to locate some high point from which to take bearings. He pored over the maps I had supplied. One evening I suggested that we veer to the north, toward the mountains, the better to locate water. He shook his head angrily. "We'll stay on this course," he snapped. I didn't bother arguing.

Each night we staggered off the camels in a stupor of exhaustion. Royalty seemed to drop away from us as we bent our backs to common tasks.

The remaining drovers and guards seemed strangely elevated by comparison.

Perhaps it was that stripping away of customary routines that led Balthazzar to draw me into the conversation that, in many respects, was to change the course of my life. Had it not been for that breakdown of his normal reserve, I have no doubt my bones would now lie bleached under a desert sun. After the evening meal one night, he beckoned to me. We walked a short distance from the campsite. We had found a few dry twigs and branches around an arid oasis that afternoon, and he carried a bundle of faggots for a fire, along with a small waterskin.

We exchanged small talk while he worked sparks from the faggots and started a fire. It sputtered fretfully, casting a scant light into the vast, surrounding darkness. I wondered why he wanted to be apart. When we sat down his words did not seem to come easily. And the words, from the start, seemed strange to me.

"Elhrain, have you ever thought of who your father is?" he asked abruptly.

"Who he was, you mean?" But why did he ask this? And why *now?*

"Yes. That's what I mean." He looked around, as if to assure himself no one was listening in. I had never seen him this uneasy. We were not far from the camp, only forty or fifty paces over the rise of a dune. Occasionally we heard a raised voice from the camp; otherwise we were wrapped in the eerie quiet of the desert night.

"My mother wouldn't tell me," I replied. "She told me of my land. She told me a bit about the people of the land." I shrugged my shoulders. "I was young then, as you well know."

"Yes, a tall and beautiful people. Your mother's, I mean. Beautiful. Skin as smooth as polished stone. Not the gritty fissures of this . . ." he swept his hand as if encompassing the world, "this desert. Tall and beautiful like your mother, Elhrain."

"Why are you telling me this? To tell me I don't belong here? I don't need the reminding."

"Oh, you belong, Elhrain. Yes, you belong."

"If I'm a Magus, it is only by training. Not by birth."

"Elhrain, no one is a Magus by birth. You know that."

"I know the legend. It is why the Magi never marry. So that they won't make the mistake of kings—thinking their offspring are royal."

"It depends on how you look at it. The Magi *are* royal, but by gifts given, not by lineage. Not all royal offspring are so gifted. That's the mistake we seek to avoid, Elhrain. Ours is a sacred, a timeless, calling. Not a time-bound function dependent upon lineage and the whims of common people. Surely you see the difference."

I let out a hollow laugh. "It all seems so ludicrous to me."

"Maybe so." He sighed wearily. In the firelight I saw something in his face I had never seen before. The flames played in his dark eyes and in them I saw regret. Perhaps even Balthazzar no longer believed.

Those eyes turned on me and held my own for a long time. It seemed so difficult for him to talk, to live outside his customary role. "Maybe it would have been better the other way," he said. "Then we would not be, as we appear to be, at the end of our line."

"Do you think we are?"

He did not answer my question. He cradled the cup of water in his powerful hands and sipped thoughtfully. He set it down on the sand and folded his hands.

"If we are," he said, "it may be time for the truth."

"I thought that was always our aim." I couldn't keep the jeering mockery out of my voice. He pretended to ignore it.

"About you, Elhrain. For you are the lie to our virtue, to our selection."

"I'm not a Magus? That hardly surprises me. This has never made a great deal of sense to me."

"This what? Looking for the truth?"

"Not looking to the land. We lose ourselves in stars and histories and prophecies when the people need direction. Need food and clothing. Need security in their homes and families. I would rather take these gifts," I waved vaguely toward the camp, "these jewels and incense and gold and feed the people with them."

"There you have it. Perhaps they will do just that. It's possible, of course, that the truth we seek will also be an answer to the people's need. But that is the point. You see the need."

"So I'm not a Magus."

"Oh, but you are. You are also, Elhrain, a king."

"Hah!"

"I said it was time for the truth. Your mother was the daughter of one of the most powerful kings on earth. His kingdom is far from here. Your people are a mighty people. Your mother is firstborn of the mightiest in the kingdom. The king is revered as the son of the gods."

"How do you know this?"

"I'm not sure it is time for that story. You will have to trust me, Elhrain. You are the king's grandson, and you were in line to a throne after your mother."

"Does the king live?"

"I don't know."

"So, if you tell the truth, and I have no way of knowing that, I am a king, not a Magus. I am still the pretender at what I do. What I am. It is too late for me now to play king. That much is obvious. King of the hyenas, perhaps." I glanced angrily toward the desert.

My comment was spurred by the eerie howling in the distance. The ugly creatures had darted around the fringes of our caravan for days, fighting for the scraps we left in our passage. Even the sandstorm had not thrown them off track. Sometimes I could see their high, knobby flanks dart over a dune. Often their disconsolate howls pierced the night with a chilling ululation.

"But there lies the paradox," Balthazzar said softly. "You are also Magus; your gifts are tested and proven. King, or prince I might say, and Magus at once. The fruit of a king's daughter and a Magus."

The words hit me like blows. I dared not look in his eyes. Who! How! I gathered some desert sand in my hand and squeezed it, and it felt like my heart.

"How do you know this?" I hissed.

"I told you, Elhrain, that it was too late not to tell the truth."

Balthazzar's voice became gritty, as if the words caught in his throat and he had to force them out. Those cordlike hands folded tightly above his knees. In the firelight little muscles flickered at his wrists.

"I was a young man when I left Babylon. Younger than you. If I am truly a Magus, my gift must be that of the Seeker. Never content . . . no. That's not even the right word. I was content while seeking. Ah, Elhrain. There are lands and seas to the south and west of us that beggar the imagination. Great seas. Lands draped with greenery. Great trees so tall and thick they form a palace of shade."

He seemed lost in those lands for a moment, seeing them in his memory. "It is from trees, by the way, that the incense is derived."

"Frankincense?" I asked.

"And the myrrh." He waved a hand. "That is beside the point. Don't let me wander now," he said, as if forcing himself to the point at hand.

"The things I have seen! I was gone five years, by leave of the Magi. You see, to be Master of Prophecies *is* to be the Seeker. Do you understand that?"

I nodded. I'm not sure if he even saw me. He was seeing the past unscrolled in his mind.

"Ah, this land. Fair land. Farther west yet than the land we now go to."

"You've been to this place before! This place we're going?" I couldn't keep the surprise from my voice.

Balthazzar laughed softly. His teeth flashed in the firelight. For a moment I felt like a little boy, before the father I never knew. Listening to stories at his knee. Balthazzar seemed to sense this. He leaned forward to reach out a hand and squeeze my shoulder gently. He let his hand linger a moment before removing it.

"No," he continued. "If I had taken that route, I'd still be traveling. Heavens above, my feet would be worn!" He laughed again. "Either worn or dead," he mused. "There's something I haven't told you about that, Elhrain. The people whose land we seek are also our bitter enemies."

"Oh, great. You haven't told the others?"

"They can guess. We, that is our kingdom, held these people in bondage, Elhrain, for four hundred years. We held their princes in exile, and used their common people for slave labor. They are a people with long memories."

"And now we come with a handful of trinkets for their king."

"Well, our king, if the prophecies be true."

"Slim chance of that."

"Be that as it may. That would have been one way I could have gone. My way was by sea. My interest, gold. We had long sent ships on the southern seas, plying the coast of this distant land. We traded for spices, for ivory and animal skins, and occasionally slaves. It was a long voyage, but not particularly dangerous."

"Who were these people, then?"

"They called themselves the people of Kush. Their land, Nubia. Many leagues inland from the coast. A great river flows there. One that makes our river look like a mere stream, a trickle."

"Don't speak of water now."

Balthazzar stared at the cup and sipped sparingly. "Yes. Well, it will get worse.

"These people, these Kushites or Nubians," he continued, "were a proud and ancient race. Along the river they built towns. They erected temples and palaces that make ours seem like hovels. They bury their kings in mausoleums of white marble. It makes our custom of the funeral pyre seem primitive. Their knowledge of the earth, and of the heavens also, is vast.

"From the coast we traveled many days by caravan to their sacred city, Jebel Barkal. Oh, we were received royally, I and my retainers. We traveled in rich style in those days. But they were a proud and secret people and were loath to let us leave. That's why I stayed five years.

"The courtyard of the temple, Elhrain, framed by white pillars, was larger than our palace. There was gold everywhere. The people wore rings and necklaces of purest gold like baubles."

"Why did you leave? Or, how did you escape?" His story had me now. I could visualize the buildings he described.

Again, that disarming smile. Then he stiffened slightly. Some camels grunted and stirred in the distance.

He relaxed, listening to the night. "Odd," he remarked. "The hyenas are gone."

I listened also. The distant howling, the closer scuffle of feet over harsh sands, had fallen quiet. The night was eerily silent. "Maybe they have found some prey elsewhere," I ventured. "First time in days. Maybe we're getting near an oasis."

He frowned. "We still have weeks. And the hardest part to travel at that. Oh, well. Where was I?"

"How you left."

"I had to earn my freedom." Again Balthazzar paused for a long time. His chiseled features stood before me like a statue propped between firelight and the inky vastness of the night sky. The emptiness of the desert night was as profound as eternity, and he sat there like a bronzed obelisk, a demarcation. Here is life; beyond lies . . . what? I wanted to reach out and touch him to see if he was still real.

He shivered slightly. A noise, a jingling of armor, seemed to awaken him. Probably one of the guards checking the camels. Balthazzar rubbed his hands and tugged at the cloak he had flung about his shoulders. The night had grown cold. The fire had died to a few winking embers.

"Outside Jebel Barkal lies a sacred mountain," he began again. "A most sacred place to these people. Odd that all these religions pick mountains as the place where the gods come to earth. If I were a god, I would come to a river." He chuckled. "Of course, if I were a god, I wouldn't thirst."

"If you were a god," I pointed out, "you wouldn't be sitting here."

He laughed in genuine pleasure. "This mountain," he said, "rears hundreds of feet above the plains of Jebel Barkal. Its top splits into two peaks, the one a flat bluff, the other an arching spire. The spire was the sacred place. It narrows and bulges like, some say, a serpent prepared to strike. The spire was a madness to try to climb, beyond human capacity. Therefore it was a place of the gods.

"Something's out there," he said suddenly, peering into the night.

At first I thought it was part of his story. Then I felt an uneasy shiver. "Just one of the guards," I said. "I heard his armor a moment ago."

"Oh. Where was I?"

"The spire. Of the mountain?"

"Yes. The mountain had been climbed just once. By a priest, who did it to earn immortality. He etched the sacred name of the god in solid rock at the summit of the spire. Just getting there was an impossible feat; to labor there, unthinkable. He took with him no food and only one flask of water, to carry him to his mission's end. He carried ropes on his back to hoist his tools, and also pieces of gold film. His aim was to etch the letters, then hammer sheets of gold over them so the god's name would be visible for miles around."

I couldn't help it: I snorted loudly.

"What is it?" he asked.

"All these quests," I said. I couldn't help motioning back to the camp. "To honor some god. People suffering, tormenting themselves to honor a god. When will there be a god who suffers to honor people? Give me that god for a change."

"An interesting point," he observed.

"I'm sorry," I said. "Please. Back to the story. I won't interrupt again."

"The people couldn't see how he managed to climb it, for he set out one night during a full moon. The next morning he was there. They knew he labored there, for each morning he would fling down a rock to let the watchers know he was at work. Then one day, no rock fell. Days went by, and the watchers knew he had failed."

Once again, he paused. He seemed to be listening to the night, his back slightly stiff, leaning toward the darkness. I heard nothing.

"So?" I said, urging him on.

"So I volunteered to finish the task," he said. "In exchange for my freedom.

"That was when the king called me to his throne room. Whatever I wanted, up to half of his kingdom, was mine for the deed."

"Would he have done that?"

"Probably not. It was just a way of saying I could name my price." He chuckled. "It seemed a safe bargain. Except that I succeeded."

"You climbed the mountain?"

"Indeed. For I had tricks up my sleeve. Actually, I had studied the precipice at great length. Others, you see, simply looked at it and saw that it was impossible. They saw all the mass, the height. I studied it as a thing in itself, and saw that with a little imagination and a lot of luck, it was possible. I climbed the bluff, which was a fairly easy task, as long as you didn't look down. By fastening ropes to an outcropping rock, I was able to swing across to the spire.

"I found the ledge where the priest had worked. His body had long ago been picked clean by birds. So much for sanctity. He had succeeded in chiseling out his inscription. It took me only a few days to hammer the gold plates in place. When the morning sun struck them, the whole mountain seemed to glisten. There was one problem, though."

"What was that?"

"I hadn't thought of how to get down."

I laughed aloud. "Obviously you found a way," I said.

He grinned. "I was never so scared in my life. I had hauled up the ropes the priest had used. He had left little bundles of rope, wrapped in oiled skins, on the top of the bluff. I had no idea if they would hold my weight. Each time I came to a sheer drop-off, I cut and secured a section of rope, closed my eyes, and flew. Each time I landed within feet of the next ledge. I severed the rope and continued to the next drop-off. As far as I know, the ropes still hang there. So I made it. I've been scared of heights ever since."

71

"And soon we enter the mountains?"

"By paths, Elhrain! And we'll go around more than up! This I swear."
Balthazzar chuckled softly again, that deep melodic sound that seemed to
rumble in his massive chest. He stroked his beard thoughtfully.

"What is it?" I asked.

"Actually," he said, "there was an easier way down. At least I think
so. Before coming down as I did, you see, I studied the mountain pretty
carefully. Things look different when you look down, from on top, rather
than looking up, Elhrain."

"Hmmm. Sort of like a Magus?" I observed.

"How so?"

"Looking down upon the people. Ever wonder what it's like being a
gutter-sleeper? Always having to look up?"

"Oh, yes. I have wondered."

I snorted. "Tell me about the mountain," I said.

"On the back side, which fell not to the plain where the people lived,
but to a tangle of hills running into the jungle. See," he motioned with
his hands, though I could not follow them in the darkness, "the spire
seemed to be a freakish outcropping from a ridge that ran back into the
mountains of the jungle. Anyway, the rock on that back side seemed
ledged and worn, unlike the sheer drops on the other sides. From the
ground no one could see that, of course. I would have wagered I could
have climbed down without using a rope. But remember, the biggest
mystery of the mountain was not how to get up. The people thought it
would be even more of a miracle to get down. Especially since the priest
had not made it."

"Why didn't you?"

"What?"

"Climb down the back side?"

He chuckled again, that dull rumbling sound in his chest like horses'
hooves. "Can't you guess? I had touched the home of the gods, Elhrain.
The people expected a miracle, not a slow climb like a mere mortal. When
I swung through the air on the ropes, my heart pounding like thunder,
the people screamed and hid their faces. Then they shouted praise each
time I landed safely. Elhrain, they were ready to make *me* a god!"

"So, you do have a god-lust."

His smile vanished. "Don't make that mistake. The people needed a hero. Then, at that time and place, they needed a deliverer. Besides, I was just young and foolish enough to think I could be one. I would have used the ropes if there had been a stairway carpeted with velvet."

"I bet you would." Still, it was hard for me to imagine Balthazzar as a young man, before the weight of authority and position settled upon him. A young man boiling with daring, free to take risks, needing adventure like a nutrient. "And did you get half the kingdom?"

"Oh, something much better."

I laughed. "And what might that be? A return to the decayed Palace of the Magi in the Persian desert?"

He didn't laugh with me. Slowly he lifted a hand to the gold necklace about his neck. I saw it glitter in the firelight like a live thing. He snaked a finger through it and lifted it over his head. "I got this," he said.

With a flick of his wrist he threw it toward me. I just caught it, a shot of glittering light in the darkness. I looked at him, wondering.

"Put it on," he said.

Its weight felt strangely warm and heavy about my neck. The pendant amulet of two twined serpents, carved in bas-relief against a golden shield, felt like a living thing against my breast.

"I got that," he said, "and a king's daughter."

The pause was long enough to walk around in. There was something he couldn't bring himself to say. Something he wanted terribly to say. I began to fear what he would say.

I touched the golden necklace, running my fingers over the heavy amulet, began to lift it off. He reached out a hand to stop me.

"Don't," he said. "It's yours."

I began to protest. The word *why* was on my tongue when suddenly screams filled the night. The camels sputtered and brayed as a dark cloud rolled over them. The cloud separated into shapes, and light glinted on weapons.

CHAPTER
EIGHT

I have thought, sometimes, how it might have ended differently.

We were some distance from the main encampment, Balthazzar and I. Suppose we had just kicked out the embers of our fire and hidden in the vast night? Watched the mayhem before us? What then? Would Balthazzar and I have escaped unscathed? And how would we have lived with the knowledge of our cowardice?

But that is dangerous thinking, and that was not the way it happened. The way it did happen changed the course of our lives, and the course of my heart, forever.

* * *

Balthazzar rose up from the sands like a tower of strength. He—I swear this is true—actually smiled. "I knew it," he said. "Now we see how it goes. Come, Elhrain." There was no panic, only a strange eagerness in his voice.

Then he was running down the side of the dune, *toward* the camp. A cry of outrage, such as I've never heard—some weird battle cry from one of his distant lands, perhaps—broke from his lips, shattering the night, louder than the shrieks of fear, the yelling of the outlaw raiders. He never looked behind to see if I followed. He was, at that moment, not Magus, not prophet or king. He was the warrior.

I did follow. Balthazzar never doubted I would. Heart pounding with fear, I stumbled down the dune in his tracks.

The camp was consumed with the struggle. Already tents were burning. Outlaws scurried about, screaming fiendishly. Long scimitars slashed through the night, reflecting the fire manifold times.

It was impossible to tell how many there were, even who fought whom. The attendants of the Magi, those before the blazing tent of Balthazzar, those surrounding Gaspar and Melchior in a protective circle, fought valiantly. But *whom* they fought was uncertain. Guards in armor stood against them, then outlaws. Then other guards fought against guards. All was a screaming, bizarre confusion.

My feet seemed rooted in the sand. I didn't want to join them! Ahead of me, Balthazzar slammed into the melee barehanded. His arms closed upon an outlaw, lifted him the way one lifts a rag doll, and hurled him bodily into the blazing inferno of his tent. Balthazzar spun around to face the others, and, in the one moment I saw the light flicker on his face, I saw a wide grin. This was a Balthazzar I had never known but always suspected. Then he lunged, his powerful fists exploding into bodies, weird shouts erupting from his lungs. Several of the guards suddenly fell in alongside him, aiding him. They had found the leader they needed. I recognized two of them as the ones whom Kruspian had had whipped at Al Achor.

Kruspian himself I did not see.

I stood there stupidly for a moment, watching. Then a body hurtled backward into me. The man's scimitar seared my hip, and I felt a sudden jarring pain that forced me into action. I whirled as he turned toward me. My motions were rude and awkward, but now the violence had seized me. I knocked his thrust aside with my forearm, grabbing his wrist. I snapped the arm around, and slammed my fist into his face. He toppled backward with a groan.

Then I was swept into the storm of it. Even aged Gaspar tried desperately to wield a sword with clumsy strokes. Someone struck his legs, and he collapsed moaning in a heap.

Above it all rose the defiant rage of Balthazzar, like some mad tower pivoting at the center. He held no weapon. His weapons were his fists and the brute power of those massive shoulders. He fought with the ferocity of some desert beast, leading a phalanx of three guards into the heart of the outlaw band, into other guards who aided them. His arms swung like clubs. I followed him into the fray. Weapons bit at his flesh, leaving his cloak torn and turning wet from wounds that he didn't seem to notice.

Even in the very heart of the insane noise, with roars of rage cascading from my own lips, I heard a solitary scream, a woman's—Doval!

Hands ripped at me, tearing at my cloak. I felt the edge of more than one weapon. I struck out to ward off one blow and felt my hand slice open to the bone. One of Gaspar's attendants rose behind the man and brought a sword down on his skull. Averting my eyes from the sickening sight, I saw his weapon drop to the ground. When I broke free of the pack, I held the slain outlaw's scimitar in my lacerated hand, its hilt slippery with my own blood.

Surprisingly, my own tent had not yet been set afire. Flames surged up all around. A camel slammed through the camp, a tent rope caught about its neck, trailing flaming cloth like an avenging demon. In the light of the fires I clearly saw inside my tent as I stormed through the entrance.

Haggai lay dead across the threshold, his neck severed by a stroke.

Doval knelt before the saddle bag we kept in our tents, her hands fumbling with the locks of the jewel cask. The keys trembled pitifully in her hand.

Kruspian had his fingers knotted in her hair and held his scimitar to her throat. When she turned to me, eyes wide and pleading, the blade drew a thin trickle of blood.

"Get over here," Kruspian rasped. "Open it or the girl dies."

I raised the scimitar. I couldn't help it. My hatred for him was an animal thing pushing the weapon upward.

"Don't!" he shouted. He jerked back on Doval's hair so violently that she cried out.

"Now!" he hissed. "Open it."

I stepped forward. I couldn't stop the scimitar from rising. I wanted his blood. His life. The traitor!

I sensed movement behind me from shadows in the doorway. I turned.

Racbah's scimitar thrust downward. I raised my arm and took the full force of the blow on my forearm, feeling the pain explode up to the shoulder. I swung on him, heard a heavy grunt as my weapon met his rush. His eyes started wide in surprise. His mouth opened as if to speak, yellowed teeth gaping in the dark hole of his beard. Then his body fell heavily upon me.

Before I could turn, I felt the force of a blade burn into my back like a cautery. I stumbled and felt my leg snap as a weight hit at the ankle.

The tent whirled and blackened, and I heard that war cry of pure outrage. I saw Balthazzar surge through the tent door like a whirlwind, his powerful arms now holding a scimitar in each hand. Then I could see nothing as the blackness sucked me down and down.

* * *

A golden fire touched my closed eyelids. It burned through and fired bright white lights that exploded at the back of my skull. I tried to open my eyes to let the fire out. I felt pain then, and the darkness came back.

In the darkness my body was wet, shivering. All night the heat attacked my body from the inside out. Yet, I was very cold in the darkness.

I tried to call out. My lips wouldn't pry apart. They sealed the heat in. If only I could let it out. Someone pried my lips apart. Someone held my jaw open and squirted water between my lips. I could not swallow. The water ran down my cheek.

The heat has lessened. I feel the pain now, but cannot isolate it. Sometimes it felt like my whole body. But then it was in my back, and I remembered. Then it was my arm, and I saw the blade falling.

My leg wouldn't move. It was as heavy as stone, and it hurt to move it. An insect crawled along my leg, and I could not drive the thing away. It bit and stung me.

* * *

The pain was in my lungs, and I couldn't breathe. Someone squirted water into my mouth again. It was cool, but would not go down. I heard voices and angry words. The voices were very loud. I tried to open my eyes and couldn't.

Someone carried me. It felt like my father. I wanted someone to hold me. I wanted my father. I heard voices again, and they went away. I tried to cry out: father. And the word stuck in my throat, burning like coals.

* * *

It felt different. I squeezed one eye open. They were all gone. It was dark. A fire was before me. My body was no longer hot. I felt the pain now in places. I tried to move my arm, and it was bound tightly to my body.

When I opened both eyes it was daylight. There was a tent flap propped above me on poles dug into a sandbank. I was lying under the sand.

A black bird stood outside the flap, beyond the cold embers of a fire. It did not know what to make of me. I tried to shout, and no sound came out. But the bird stepped back awkwardly.

When I awakened again it was night. A snuffling sound awoke me. I looked into the darkness and saw green eyes glowing.

The beast smelled like death.

I worked the arm that I could move free of the sand and the cloak I was wrapped in. I reached out for a piece of wood. When I threw it at the hyena, the beast stepped back and lay down on its belly. Watching.

* * *

In the daylight there were more of them. They lay outside the tent flap waiting, and they angered me.

With my one good arm I worked free of the sand. I saw a flagon half-buried in the sand. I had to worm on my belly to reach it. The water was so cool it hurt my head. A pounding behind my eyes. I sipped again. The water carved a course down my throat.

I could lift my head. Look around. Several flagons of water lay buried in the sand. A small packing crate—food, perhaps.

Someone had ringed tent poles around me. I understood I was in a cage. The animals could not get in. They whined hungrily.

I hauled my body into a sitting position, head against the tent post beside me, and sipped more water. The skin over my chest and belly was drawn tight, like a drum. Rib bones protruded. How long?

I felt something heavy about my neck. I reached up and touched cool metal, and I remembered. Balthazzar's necklace.

I studied my forearm and wounded hand. Someone had stitched the wounds. What a task. The scimitar had laid open the entire forearm from elbow to wrist. Thin pieces of animal hide—camel?—stitched through the skin held my flesh closed.

I shivered when I looked closely. The arm was alive. In between the garish sutures dozens, hundreds, of white maggots crawled.

I tried to wipe them off on the sand, slamming my arm down into the writhing maggots. Then I fell back, exhausted.

When I awakened again, it was evening. The maggots were still there, crawling in my flesh. But the flesh was healing. I let the maggots be. *They will eat out the poisoned flesh.* I tried to chuckle at the discovery, and my stomach ground hollowly.

I tried to sit up and noticed my leg bound rigidly in splints. It did not hurt at all anymore. I could see, though, just above the ankle, where the bone had broken. It was a dark purple bulge under my black skin.

Shoving myself with my good leg, dragging the other, I wormed toward the crate. My breath flagged through dry lips. I reached the crate but had not the strength to pry off the lid. I tried to curse and only a dry hissing sound came.

A small, sheathed dagger lay alongside the crate, nearly covered by blowing sand. I dragged it out, and it seemed to weigh so much I could hardly lift it. I waited until the dizziness passed, then lifted the knife and pried the lid loose.

A rolled piece of parchment, tied shut, lay on top. I dug past it, brushing it aside. Dried meat. Some dried figs. Grain. I took out one fig, placed it in my mouth, and had not the strength to chew.

* * *

When I awakened, my mouth felt clogged, and I turned over, retching dryly into the dry sand. The bloated fig fell out. Carefully I cleaned off the particles of sand, took a sip of water, and chewed the fig.

With it came understanding: I was forsaken in this vast wilderness. Doval! Haggai! For the first time I thought of others. But they were gone.

A hyena snuffed at the tent-pole fence. I seized the dagger and lunged forward, collapsing in the sand. The hyena hooted angrily at me and crept a short distance away.

I peered beyond the fence but could see no signs of the former encampment. Suddenly the details came back to me. The horror of screams. The whirling figures in the firelight. Doval huddled in the tent with Kruspian's fingers at her throat.

And Haggai lying dead across the threshold.

What happened? Balthazzar had entered, like a whirlwind bringing death, a scimitar in each hand. Were they all dead? They must be. They would never desert me.

Shadows lengthened beyond my small space of safety. How long would the hyenas wait there, before their bodies slammed into the stakes?

I crawled to the box of food. I had noticed some tinder and twigs piled alongside. Yes. Inside, I found a flint and stone. I struck them feebly over and over again with my numbed fingers. At last the spark came. I breathed on the tinder—more a ragged gasp. A flame. Like life itself I nurtured the fire.

When at last it blazed freely I was too exhausted to eat. Another fig, a sip of water, and I slept.

* * *

When I awakened during the night, I was hungry.

Quickly I tossed the remaining twigs upon the embers of the fire. Glittering eyes peered back from beyond the tent stakes. How long would they hold back? How long until they overcame their instinctive fear of humans to assuage the ravaging instinct to feed upon flesh?

My own hunger spurred me. I ransacked the box for food, eating now like one famished. Which I was. I shoveled figs in my mouth desperately, as if I would never get enough. Then stopped.

Forsaken! Deserted!

These were all the provisions I had. I replaced the lid.

The eastern sky flushed pink. I sat panting back at the hyenas as the sky lightened. When the sun crept over the wide rim of sand, a sudden red ball rising, the hyenas circled and drew apart. I studied the landscape beyond my cage. I did not recognize the place. I was certain it was not the place of the attack. How did I get here?

My arm itched. Unconsciously I scratched the wound, then started. It was dry. I looked at it closely in the daylight. The maggots had done their work, eating out the putrid ooze of decayed flesh. The skin lay closed in a rough ridge along the stitches of camel hide. I flexed the arm. The muscles responded with fiery protest—but they did respond.

Taking the dagger in my left hand I laboriously cut away the stitches. Small spots of blood welled up in their place. They would heal.

I leaned forward, grasping the bars, and looked out. The sun was a white ball, evil with energy.

How long had I been here?

My stomach groaned for more food. I turned back to the box, seeing there the scrolled parchment where it had fallen. Clumsily I lifted it, cutting the ribbon with the dagger since my fingers still functioned too awkwardly to untie the knot.

The words were minuscule and precise. I recognized Balthazzar's writing and I trembled. As I read the words, my heart turned to ice.

If you read this, our worst fears are realized. You are alive. Believe me, when we laid you here, we were uncertain.

We go on. We must go on, Gaspar, Melchior and I. We, the few attendants and the few faithful guards left to us. For seven days we waited, having removed ourselves slightly from the place of battle, the stench of the dying and already dead.

I suspected Kruspian all along, of course. Still, we needed him, and I could not share my fears with you. He might have proved true. I was not certain until several of the guards, desperate for escape, told me of the plot.

We lost nearly everything. All the drovers mutinied. We have left a half dozen camels and the few supplies we managed to save from the fires.

The pillagers, fortunately, were cowards. When they saw their comrades falling, they fled with what they could carry, setting fire to what they could not. I am grieved to say that in searching the morning after, Doval was neither present nor among the slain. May the gods have mercy upon her.

And upon us.

For seven days we remained, certain each morning that you too would be numbered among the dead. Yet you lived. How, I do not know. Your wounds were grievous. We forced down water and mashed figs when we could. Then you could swallow nothing.

On the seventh day we left. We had to leave the place or die ourselves. We could not go back. Our only hope is to complete our quest, or else all our hopes are vain. We still have the gifts we bear. Rude gifts from a ruined race. Yours was the only one we lost.

We strapped you to a camel for the journey, swearing to take you with us as long as we could. Ah, Elhrain. My son. To leave you is death itself. To take you certain death for you. Can you understand this? Bouncing there on the camel's back, unprotected from the sun, your wounds opening again and bleeding, the desert flies swarming relentlessly over your body, it was death itself. You could not have lasted another hour. Nor could we wait.

We give you now to the mercy of the gods. Perhaps even the god we now seek. Our weakness, the weakness of all the Magi, is hope. I dare not even hope that you will someday read this. When hope is gone, there is only mercy.

Can you ever forgive me?

Hope? I laughed, a dusty rattling in my throat. Forgiveness? Oh, I will survive, Balthazzar. I will survive. For I *will* have vengeance for this desertion. Your throat under my fingers—let that be the only hope that sustains me! Henceforth and forevermore.

CHAPTER NINE

I waited two more days before leaving my cage, this little patch of sand and sticks, among jackals and hyenas. I waited, carefully dividing the food to replenish my body, and wondering how I would endure this sunscorched earth. Though it was impossible to stay, I was afraid to leave.

My meager supply of firewood disappeared. I had started burning the tent stakes. The only thing remaining between me and the carrion beasts was the threat of the flame. Yet the faster I burned the stakes, the more susceptible I became and the more important the fire. Several times I had to poke at their grinning, savage faces with lighted stakes, and once I hurled a flaming brand into their midst. They whimpered like children and milled about uncertainly.

Even as this physical fire died, another seemed to flame to incandescence within me. I stared at the wasteland of sand, imagining the departing tracks of the Magi there. I imagined their figures, hunched upon camels, their backs to me, leaving over and over again. I nursed my outrage in my heart, like a white-hot blaze that coruscated through every artery in my body.

I no longer thought myself one of them. They were my enemies. I wanted them on their knees before me, pleading for their lives, especially Balthazzar; for the decision, finally, would have been his. How could he leave me? The very love I had for him turned into a hunger for his destruction.

This would be *my* quest: to vilify and destroy the very name *Magus*. And to do so by ensuring the end of them.

I fondled my hatred like a lover, caressed it moment by moment while my strength returned. Let it eat up grief and loneliness, let it consume me! I would survive by believing in nothing but myself. Never again would I dare trust others. Thus I vowed.

The fracture above my ankle would be my greatest danger. It was tender yet even to the touch, the bone skewed under the swollen flesh. Gradually I forced weight upon it, nearly howling aloud with the pain at first. I flexed and massaged it hourly.

Then I parted the tent stakes and hobbled out into the sun, carrying the dagger with me. When the hyenas circled close, I crouched and hissed at them, and they drew back, their pinched sides panting with hunger.

I sharpened one of the remaining tent stakes—the heaviest I could find, a straight post fully six feet long—into a spear. The wood was well-tempered, as hard as stone; it took a long time to whittle the blunt tip to a point. I liked the weight of it in my hands. It felt like an extension of my own arm, but stronger.

I baited the hyenas, lying perfectly still, letting them creep close. I waited as breathless and silent as a dead man until I heard their snuffling almost in my ears. Then I whirled and plunged the spear wildly into the closest one, driving it deep as the beast reared back, twisting and turning, while the others ran yelping away. I pulled the spear out with trembling hands. The beast limped a short way off, lay writhing on the ground, and then lay still. It was all far easier than I expected. During the night I heard the others feeding upon their dead brother.

It was time to leave. My body felt stronger now. I could walk on the leg if I splinted it carefully. Yet, even with my new weapon, I dared not forsake the protection of my shelter while the hyenas were nearby.

A way was given me.

Toward late morning of the next day the hyenas milled nervously. Something bothered them. One by one, they sat back, lifted pointed snouts into the air and whined. They shifted anxiously about into a milling pack. It seemed they wanted to crawl into each other for protection.

The sun grew cruelly hot, beating against the tent top and encapsulating me in an oven of heat. The air seemed overfull, thick with storm. But it was well past the rainy season; there was no moisture in this air.

Toward noon the sky seemed to turn a dusky brown. Far in the distance a strange humming sound rose above a thorough and profound silence, as if the very earth held its breath.

The hyenas outside continued to mill about. They moved off a short distance, lay down, then rose, whining tentatively, pushing their pointed snouts into the sides of companions. One large, old beast topped a rise and howled into the darkening sky.

The dust came first. A fine cloudiness infiltrated the air. The humming sound grew louder, as if rough surfaces were scraping upon each other. I slipped out of the tent, climbed awkwardly up the small dune behind me and peered toward the west. The entire horizon was a roiling mass of sand, before which small geysers rose from the desert floor and spun ahead of the storm. Out of the mass the first advance winds struck, hurling fine pieces of sand at me. Then, like an explosion, the storm struck with full force.

My tent had been built into the side of the dune for protection and shade. Against this storm there was no such thing as protection. The wind ripped at the fabric I huddled under. I drew the waterskins and the nearly empty crate of food close to me. A rip opened in the tent fabric. Within minutes the material was in tatters, beating wildly against the tips of the remaining stakes. They slowly bent over, like broken legs unable to bear the weight of the wind.

A gust reached in, caught the embers of the fire and whipped glowing sparks out into a maelstrom of sand. I wrapped myself into a huddled ball, pulling the cloak over my head, while the storm bent its full force. Dust worked through layers of cloth into my eyes and nostrils. I was choking on dust, suffocating. There was no air anymore, only dust and sand in waves.

Out of the storm dry sheets of lightning cracked and lacerated the earth. Above the howling of the wind, thunder rocked and blasted.

Had it not been for the protection of the dune, I am certain the sand would have flayed me alive. I huddled there, burrowing into the sand, clutching my waterskins, letting the sand rise about me like a blanket.

This went on for the better part of the afternoon. It was as if the pit of the underworld opened and sucked me down amid flashes of lightning. It went on and on.

I awoke to darkness, thorough and profound. I shook off the layers of sand and stood up. Stars burned in the sky as if newly torched. The whole landscape had changed. Only the tips of the tent stakes protruded above the mounds of sand, bearing tattered remnants of cloth like surrender signals. In hours the desert had been transformed.

There was no sign of the hyenas. They had either burrowed nearby or had tried to escape the storm's fury. Perhaps they had lost my scent altogether. I determined not to let them find me again, to make a blessing of the storm. I gathered up the waterskins, took the remaining food out of the box and wrapped it in some remnants of fabric from the tent, bundled it all together and slung it in a kind of sack over one shoulder. I had the dagger sheathed at my waist and clutched the hand-fashioned spear in my fist.

With one final look around to see what else I could salvage, I set out.

* * *

For four days I trekked those remote, featureless sands, guiding my course toward Al Achor by the stars. I was sensible enough by this point to travel entirely by night. By midmorning the sun blistered the sky. When I found a protected spot—a litter of boulders offering shade—I stopped. The air sucked the moisture out of the skin, and I could feel my body protesting. For the last two days I had not even urinated.

Already weakened by my wounds, it seemed that I drew energy for each step from some deep well within. And I knew what nurtured that well—vengeance. Without that I would have lain down and died.

My food was gone. I had eaten the last of it, a few dried figs, the morning before. I had one waterskin left, and I fought not to suck it dry. Just a small bulge of water lay in its bottom.

I would die. Alone in this vast wasteland.

This morning the hyenas found me.

They kept their distance yet, as if some primitive instinct reminded them of the bite of dagger or spear. I did not want to be torn by their teeth. I know this made no sense. If I were dead, it would hardly matter what happened to this body. Let them have it. Yet, having lost all faith—no, having willed away all faith—I had only this left: I love myself. That and vengeance. Small comfort.

I collapsed among some red rocks I had found. They were small, offering little shade. The ground was littered with them here. I could not remember having seen this place before. I nestled alongside the largest boulder I could find, drew my knees up, laid the spear across them and fell asleep.

I awakened, startled by a noise. I looked around for the hyenas and did not see them. Something had startled them off. No. I saw a brown shape flick over a dune.

The sun had moved overhead and beat fully upon my exposed body. Perhaps that had awakened me. My lips felt scorched. I rolled over and reached for my waterskin. Go ahead. Empty it and die.

A hiss rippled through the air and stopped my hand midway. My body went rigid. The sun still seemed to be working behind my eyes, and they would not focus. I blinked slowly, trying to bring moisture to them.

I had placed my waterskin alongside the rock, protected by my body. I let my eyes drift down my outstretched arm to my hand and beyond it to the coiled and rearing neck of a viper. Its head was poised motionless, its eyes transfixing my own, hypnotizing me into immobility. The sliver of tongue slipped in and out of its open mouth. The hooked fangs were rigid.

The viper had coiled its body about the waterskin as if claiming it. Inch by minute inch the blunt head moved, measuring the strike.

I dared not withdraw my hand. It grew heavy. It began to fall. The viper arched, stiffening. I closed my eyes.

Over my shoulder a brown blur slapped past my head as swift as a strike of lightning. Like some tongue of an immense serpent, it snapped at the viper's neck with a crack so sharp and loud I thought I had been struck. The brown thing snapped backward, and I was staring at the viper, its head ripped loose from the body. The stalk held there rigidly for a second, gushing blood from its severed neck. Then, in a spasm, the body arched and jerked and coiled on the ground and lay still.

I heard a chuckle behind me and twisted around in the sand, the spear held before me. My glance traveled upward from booted feet to tunic-covered legs. He had a desert cloak thrown over his shoulders, but its draw-string was open in front, exposing the powerful swell of his chest and shoulders. The hood was flung back from a head of curling black hair and a short beard on a painfully sun-scorched face. Casually he coiled the whip and tied it to a thong at his belt. He placed his hands on his hips, stared at me and chuckled again.

"And I thought I was lost!" he said, and laughed aloud. "By the gods above, man, what are you doing out here?"

I recognized the language as Latin. During the last century the Magi had, of necessity, mastered the language. Still, it was rusty on my tongue. While I could decipher a Latin missive with ease, I had not spoken the language more than a dozen times in my life. I tried to speak but had to take a sip of water first.

"Yes. It's precious," he said. "Go sparingly."

I looked past him. Twenty men, standing alongside camels and pack mules, waited silently. I caught the glint of sunlight off weapons. They were Roman soldiers.

"Thank you." I said. I could still feel the sand in my throat.

He reached out a hand, grasped mine and lifted me to my feet.

"Not much left of you," he observed. "No camels. No others?"

In fumbling speech I told him as sparingly as I could of the outlaw attack. I omitted all reference to our quest, saying only that I had been traveling by caravan to the west.

"Well," he said, "and that's where we come from. But we are powerfully lost. These sandstorms. Just when we think we're getting someplace, we discover that everything looks the same. The worst of it is that our navigator died along the way, and no one else, although I hate to admit it, knows how to use his blasted instruments. So we've followed our noses."

"And all sand smells the same," I said.

He laughed appreciatively. "Indeed," he said. "From the look of those wounds, the outlaws took their toll on you."

I rubbed the raised welt of the wound on my forearm self-consciously. "The worst is my leg," I admitted. "It was broken in the fight, and I can't get far on it."

"Well. We can help you with that. With the supplies we've used up, we have more than one mule at your service. You can ride a mule, can't you?"

"Yes. Where are you going?"

"To Babylon, of course. For certain negotiations. Can you lead us?"

For the first time hope brightened in me. I *would* survive. It hardened to a bitter thing. Survive and avenge.

"Indeed, I can," I said.

When we walked back toward the waiting men, I flicked a glance over my shoulder at the snake. The tip of its tail twitched once. I shivered.

* * *

Riding a mule is quite unlike a camel. I felt every bone in the mule's body attacking me like clubs. No rhythm at all. The beast jolted along as if delighting in the torture it rendered. Particularly painful was my back. I had nearly forgotten the stab wound, but this creature seemed to sense every stressed ligament in it.

Still, as the days passed, and as I ate freely from the Romans' supplies, I felt steadily stronger. The travel passed far more quickly than the clumsy, laborious work we had made of it going out. I found myself wondering how Kruspian would have fared with genuine military people like these.

The commander's name was Lycurgus. My rescuer. It was clear that his men fairly worshiped him. He never had to repeat an order or raise his voice to issue it. We made and broke camp with a quickness and ease I wouldn't have believed possible.

We began travel in the early evening, moving during the cool of the night, and made camp in early morning. Several times sandstorms arose during the day but none with the violence of the earlier one. By night the skies were clear, and I plotted our course without hesitation. Nor did Lycurgus, once having given me leave, question my direction.

It was not unpleasant riding with Lycurgus and his men. For days I had had no one to talk with, and it seemed at first that my mouth was fuzzy, my tongue thick. In time, though, I remembered more of the language, and soon it came easily to me.

It was obvious, too, that Lycurgus's relation with his men was more than merely a military command. They seemed more a family of brothers than a military command. They did their tasks quickly, efficiently and without grumbling.

I wondered why this was so, this sense of a family that I had never known. I couldn't say. Lycurgus was obviously a leader, bold and forthright. He exuded power but not in the darkly threatening way that Balthazzar did. Next to Lycurgus, Balthazzar would have seemed a dark storm—beautiful but dangerous—on the verge of explosion. Lycurgus's every motion was graceful, fluid.

Most curiously, for all the loyalty evidenced by his men, Lycurgus seemed not much older than I. A year of two, perhaps. Yet I pictured my wasted, ebony-black shape alongside his, and I seemed far the elder.

As we traveled under the night skies, I pointed out the constellations to him—stars I knew as intimately as a lover—and he listened avidly. Within a few days, I felt that he no longer needed me. I was equally certain he would not leave me.

On the morning of the seventh day of travel, a route that had taken us nearly three weeks on the way out, we approached the village of Al Achor. I would liked to have ridden boldly into the city, and see the villagers flinch before the power of these men.

Lycurgus would not permit it. We circumvented the city and camped along the oasis. Quickly the men stripped camels and mules and let them water. After the men had settled, Lycurgus sought me out.

"We'll lay over here two days," he said, "to rest the animals. How far is it to Babylon?"

I reflected. "At the rate you travel," I said, "you can be there in ten days. Two weeks at most."

"Good. You have guided us well, Elhrain. I'm grateful. Still, we'll have to resupply tomorrow."

"It is a village of outlaws," I offered.

"That's obvious. Not the first we've seen either. The western desert is full of them, preying upon travelers such as your band. But they have what we need, and we'll drive a hard bargain. I think they will be glad when we leave."

"You say there are other villages. Out there?" I waved my hand westward.

He laughed. His laughter rolled from him, seeming to arise from some easily replenished well within. "Of course," he said. "The closer you get to the mountains. They're scattered all over. This is one of the things we wish to talk about with your Babylonian king."

"Then there's a chance," I mused aloud, "a chance they made it."

"Your people?"

"My former people. There is only one I still seek. A young girl."

He laughed again. "It's that way, is it? Yes, one gets attached. My men would dearly love to get into this village. I'll let some go tomorrow."

Quickly, too quickly, I objected. "It's not the way you think. She . . . she's more like my daughter."

"Oh. I see. Who knows, Elhrain. I can't offer much hope. Maybe she lives in some outlaw's tent now. Maybe sold into slavery. Pray to your gods about that."

"I have no gods," I said bitterly.

He paused, looked at me and left without speaking.

*   *   *

No men from the village came out to meet *this* group. The village seemed preternaturally quiet. People ducked into the mud-brick huts if Roman soldiers ventured toward them. Like any village dependent upon travelers, Al Achor had several rude inns where they could pursue such pleasures as they wished. Lycurgus sensed the magnetic attraction of it upon his men. They were military men, weary from long travel, eager for pleasure. Late on the second day, he took with him a small group of men to barter for supplies. When the men returned, they were laughing and restless. They had gained permission to visit the inns in sequenced groups that night.

As the night drew on, I found my curiosity growing. I hardly expected to find Racbah here. For all I knew he lay dead in the desert. Yet I would not be satisfied until I knew for certain. With the last group out that night I tagged along. The men were hardly aware of my presence. I had no interest in their pursuits.

It was a clear night. The loud boisterous voices booming from the inns carried far. The inn-keeper would honor the Romans' money and be glad to see them gone. They headed straight for the largest inn, drawn by the sounds issuing forth.

I entered on their heels. The air was thick and smelly. Homely, tough women delivered huge flagons of wine to the men sprawled on benches. Torches shot smoke into the air. Some man plucked painfully upon a lute and warbled his idea of some melancholy tune. I couldn't make out a word of it. When a young girl, wasted and thin as a rail, stepped from behind a curtain and began to dance, the men roared in appreciation. More than one soldier disappeared into the back room of the inn with his arm around the waist of a brutish desert woman.

I heard a voice in my ear, and looked into the watery eyes of a woman. She seemed drugged, plucking at my sleeve and grinning beguilingly with a mouthful of decayed teeth. She leaned close, and her breath reminded me of the desert hyenas. I shrugged her off and stepped outside, her curses ringing in my ears.

I stopped at another inn down the street. There were no soldiers in this one, and the mood was much subdued. Men squatted on the floor smoking water pipes, and the scent of the drug was overpowering. No one so much as looked at me.

I was about to step back out when a crashing noise startled me. At the back of the inn two men rose, shouting in angry voices. One knocked a table askew, and dishes flew onto the floor with the smashing sound of pottery. One of the two leaped at the other, clawing at his face. He darted out a back door, the other on his heels.

My heart was pounding. My mind cold with rage. Kruspian and Racbah.

I started to run through the room toward the back door. One of the figures sucking on a water pipe stuck out a leg and tripped me. I felt hands upon me. I struck back. Then they were on me, tearing at my hair and digging for a purse. A hand at the golden necklace about my neck twisted it, determined to break it free. I lowered my head against the pummeling of blows and fought back as best I could.

Then came a silence. The hands fell away. I heard a familiar crack-crack. The report of the whiplash exploded in the room. I shoved myself to hands and knees and looked directly at the boots of Lycurgus.

He reached down a hand. "You have a penchant for trouble," he muttered. As he lifted me, he said, "If I didn't need a guide, I'd leave you."

"The outlaws," I gasped. "The ones who robbed us. Who took Doval."

His eyes hardened. "Where?" he hissed.

I pointed at the back door. With his hand upon my shoulder he bulled his way through the crowd, the drugged men falling back.

CHAPTER TEN

Lycurgus fairly ripped through the back door with me on his heels like a desperate hound. We exited upon a maze of alleys, leading off like twisted spokes from a hub, squat little hovels backed up to impossibly narrow spaces. The alley stank of garbage and human waste. In a nearby hut we heard a child crying, the sound of a blow and silence.

I stood panting at Lycurgus's side. He had his hand on the shaft of his whip and, as far as I could tell, had no other weapons. I was not afraid in his presence, nonetheless. He walked the night as if he owned it.

Yet there were so many alternatives. We started down one path, so narrow we could touch the brick walls of the houses on either side.

Suddenly we heard shouts, a cry of pain. It seemed to come from our right. Finding a space between two houses, Lycurgus dashed through. An angry pig in a fenced yard charged at us, receiving a whip-crack before its nose that stopped it short.

Another cry. Straight ahead. We ran out into another alley. I recognized the crumpled body immediately as Kruspian. Footsteps pounded down the dark alley. Lycurgus ran off in the direction of the sounds. I bent to Kruspian, feeling the wrath surge in me. He lay huddled on the ground. I seized his hair and twisted him around, driving a knee into his abdomen.

Kruspian doubled over in pain and coughed wetly. Even in the darkness I could feel the sticky spatter across my wrists.

"Help me," he groaned.

My anger was so violent that I was, at first, outraged that the man was dying, for he surely was. In the cold light of the stars I saw the dark stain spread across his chest. The man was drowning in his own blood. Even more than vengeance, I needed answers. I raised his head in my arm so he could breathe.

"Now tell me, Kruspian—"

Before I could finish he groaned. "Yes. Yes. I did it. Did it with Racbah. Get him. Kill him, Elhrain."

His eyes started open.

"It is you, isn't it?" he gasped in surprise. "Elhrain. You're not dead?"

"You're dying, Kruspian. You left me for dead."

"No! They drove us off. It all failed."

"I want answers."

"The jewels," he gasped. "Racbah has . . . the jewels. I can tell you where they are."

He coughed violently. I twisted away from the spray. For a moment I thought he was gone.

"Listen, Kruspian. Or I'll throttle you where you lay."

"It would be a mercy. Kill me."

"Doval. Where is she?"

"Who?"

"The girl. The one I kept with me."

The most horrifying thing I have ever heard was the strangled gasps of Kruspian's laughter. An eerie croaking sound more animal than human sputtered from his lips.

"Tell me!" I insisted.

"You have missed her by nearly two weeks," he chortled. "She brought a high price."

"A high price!" Without my willing it, my hand slipped to his neck. He felt the pressure.

"Do it," he hissed.

"Sold to whom? Tell me, Kruspian."

"Traders."

"Slave traders?"

"Who knows." His lungs gurgled thickly.

"Which way?"

"They were heading south. Or west. Who knows, Elhrain. I am dying."

"Indeed you are." I set his head down in the pebbly sand underfoot.

Suddenly I was aware of Lycurgus standing behind me. He was panting slightly.

"You didn't find him?" I asked.

"He got away. These alleys are like mazes. He's in the desert by now. It's hopeless."

I nodded.

He tapped the shaft of his whip against his leg. "Does she mean that much to you, Elhrain?"

"She was a daughter to me." I meant to say, "like a daughter." I don't know why it came out that way.

"Shall I finish him?"

I shook my head. "He's gone," I said.

But Kruspian wasn't. Summoning some terrible power, he grasped my sleeve, raised his head slightly, and said, "They're all gone, Elhrain. They'll never make it."

His head slipped back. Once more he spoke.

"Have mercy, Elhrain."

"I have none left, Kruspian. I left it all in the desert."

I stood and walked away. Lycurgus followed me. "We must leave tonight," he said. "We still have a journey to make."

"Any time," I replied. I did not know if I would find a trace of Doval in Babylon, that great and awful city. But I would not stop there. If not there then south. And west.

And for the first time the idea entered my mind. South and west. To Kush. To my people.

"Grandson of the king," Balthazzar called me. Well, I would find out. If that were so, I would hold this world in my hand, in order to crush three kings. And their king.

I couldn't get ready to leave quickly enough.

I rode out with Lycurgus at the head of the column, and we traveled slowly in deference to the soldiers' wine drinking. We would not get far that night, that much was obvious. Lycurgus noticed my hurry.

"Do you want to run with the wind?" he asked after a while. "Or are you driven by the wind?"

I tried to force a smile, tried to relax. "You could make your way without me," I said. "You know the stars as well as I."

"But you taught me. So I cannot leave you."

I pondered that.

"Do you hate them so much?" he asked.

"Is it that obvious?"

"Indeed. You wear it like a garment, Elhrain. But what can you do about it?"

"Hunt them down. Eventually. After I find Doval."

"Yes. And what then?"

"Leave them for dead."

"The way they did you."

"Yes."

"How long do you intend to go on dying, then?"

"What do you mean?"

"You let hatred destroy you. There are better ways."

I was silent.

"If you wish, Elhrain, I can try to use my influence to locate Doval."

"Yes. Do that."

"I can ask around, involve the military in Babylon."

I wondered just how much influence Lycurgus had. "You're no common soldier, are you, Lycurgus?"

It was his turn to be puzzled. "What do you mean?"

"Your men. They don't just obey you. They . . . live for you."

"No. They don't. They live for the ideals I give them."

"Ideals!" I snorted aloud.

"Yes. I would rather have it that way. Justice, Elhrain. Peace. Oh, we have seen enough of war, my men and I. Each one here has been tested in battle. But now we work toward a peace that all can share, hence my mission."

"Babylon is a dying city in a dying kingdom."

"True. Maybe they can be taught to live." He was silent a moment. "Where will you go if there are no answers in Babylon?"

Briefly I related Balthazzar's story about Kush. Even as I told it, some long-buried memories stirred within me.

"Being a king's son is a heavy burden, Elhrain."

"You would know, wouldn't you?" I meant to question. I had long since guessed.

He laughed uneasily. "So you find me out. Yes, the emperor's son. By his concubine, though. So you see, a king's son with no claim. I run royal errands now, having proven myself indispensable in the wars. I wear no rank. Some men selected me to lead them." He sighed wearily. "But I am content. Indeed, what I long for now is a simple command in some remote village. As a centurion, perhaps."

"A centurion is hardly simple, Lycurgus."

He laughed. "It has to be simpler than being a king's son." He pulled up, slowed. His eyes cut across the darkness toward me. "The highest thing, Elhrain, is justice, not vengeance." He paused, reflecting. "In fact," he added, "sometimes one has to suffer for justice to be done."

He looked behind him at the straggling line of men and laughed. "I think we will make camp," he said, and called out the order.

In all my life, I don't know if I enjoyed a week more than that one toward Babylon. These twenty soldiers of Lycurgus had accepted me without question, and Lycurgus himself treated me like a brother. I look back at it now, all these years later, and I wonder how it is that one person appears in a life, however briefly, and somehow leaves an imprint that never disappears. Is it a matter of personality—laughing at the same things, the sense of ease with each other? I had known such pleasure before, but never in quite this way. Is it a matter of intellect—that here is a mind a match for one's own? I had grown up in the company of some of the greatest minds of the time, but never had this sense of common inquiry I shared with Lycurgus. Or is it simply a matter of shared and met need—here is one person at one place in time whose solace was indescribable, whose mere presence placated the demons raging within me? Whatever, I think I have forever after borne some of Lycurgus in me, and perhaps that has shaped the course of my life since.

*   *   *

By the time we reached Babylon, my nearly visceral hatred of the forsaking Magi had much dissipated. It had not disappeared, to be sure. I would keep the vow I had sworn. But it had diminished.

I thought more often of Doval and my heart bled tears for her. I tried to picture her: bewildered in the custody of some foreign people, bereft of the sympathy I enjoyed. I would tear the world apart to redeem her, pay any price, sacrifice any life.

From the moment I set foot in it, I knew Babylon was no longer my home. I returned to the Palace of the Magi and found it already usurped by the political authorities. I was locked out of my own palace.

Here too Lycurgus exercised his authority, which was far more potent than I had guessed. He bore with him letters of negotiation from the emperor himself and represented him well. Before riding into the city the troops stopped. Each man bathed in the river. They shed their filthy travel clothes and broke out of packs their full military gear. It was a stunning sight, silver armor and weapons dazzling under the desert sun. Lycurgus himself seemed transformed.

He was true to his word also. Within hours a military sweep of the city was mounted for Doval. It amounted to nothing, but the effort was thorough. Lycurgus accompanied me to my former palace. The riffraff that had moved in fell back before his presence. The palace was in a state of squalor. He accompanied me down the underground corridor to the treasure room, which had not yet been located and pillaged. I limped slowly down the steps on my still-swollen ankle. Nails of pain drove up the length of bone.

I worked the secret locks on the doors and admitted him to the room. Two of his soldiers stood guard with flaring torches. Lycurgus sucked in his breath as the door opened. The torchlight fell across the shelves of silver dinnerware, the orange tongues of flame reflected like dancing serpents over the dusty surfaces.

"Help yourself," I said.

He shook his head. He made straight to a lower shelf in the tiny room, seizing a small golden statue draped with a velvet cloth.

"Do you know how this got here?" he asked in surprise. He knelt before the statue, examining it closely.

"I'm afraid I've never been much interested. Technically, it was in Balthazzar's keeping. Although we all had access."

"But how did it come *here?*" he insisted.

"I don't know. Remember that the Magi have always been royalty in this kingdom. I assume these things came as a share of booty."

"Yes. Probably."

"Something special about that one?" I asked.

"It's Etruscan," he said. "Early Roman. It's a figure of Diana. If you don't mind . . ."

"I meant what I said. Take whatever you can carry." I had not meant my voice to be curt. "Listen," I said. "I would like it if you would also take gifts for your men. They took me in when they did not have to. They became like brothers to me."

He smiled at that and stood up. He put a hand on my shoulder. "I will," he said. "And, Elhrain. You are a brother to me."

He moved to the silver dishes and goblets. "Interesting," he mused. "Hebrew in origin."

"That I can explain," I offered. "Those would be from the exile. The king that started this madness." For the first time, then, there in that dark, small room while the soldiers stood patiently and impassively with their flaring braziers, I told him the whole story. He did not laugh, even at the wildest prophecies that I now considered lunacy. Indeed, he sucked the words in with an intentness that disturbed me. When I finished his eyes were glittering.

"Then it is time," he breathed.

"No. It isn't," I said. "It is madness."

He smiled at me. "Perhaps I will see for myself when I have finished here. Didn't I say I was looking for a small outpost? I have had too much of war, Elhrain."

We had to call additional men. Lycurgus let me present gifts to them in the name of the Magi. To each of the soldiers I gave a silver goblet from the shelf. A macabre sense of humor, to be sure. I told them that with their interest in wine, they could remember me thus. You would think I had given them the world. I was amazed that none of the political usurpers in the palace interfered. They were nowhere in sight, a testament, again, to the authority Lycurgus wielded.

As for myself, I took only those things that could be readily convertible anywhere I traveled. The coinage was all gone, of course, used to finance the Magi's quest. I approached the last of the jewels, thinking as I did so of the flawless sapphire I had taken as a gift to the messiah. It was now held by Racbah if he was still living. I gave a short laugh at the thought.

My hand paused at the small box holding the bah-lah game. Why leave it for others who would not understand? Memories flooded over me. I left the game lying there. That life had ended.

Poking through the dusty shelves, I found sufficient pieces remaining to ensure my well-being for many years to come. In a bag tucked under some straw in a corner I found several small gold bars.

But under that bag, thrust beneath the straw almost as an afterthought, my fingers stubbed against a small, wooden box. It was intricately carved and peculiarly heavy. I unlatched it. On a velvet tray lay a few jewels. Very well, I would take them along.

I fingered the jewel box mechanically, merely glancing at the baubles within. Suddenly a spring latch snapped, and a panel in the wood popped loose. I must have triggered a secret lever. I studied the box. Yes, there it was. The head of a rearing serpent engraved in the wood. I pushed the panel in, pressed the head with fangs bared, and the panel popped loose again. Clever. Under the panel was a tiny knot. I pulled lightly, and the drawer slid out. It held a dozen heavy golden coins, each embossed with the form of a rearing serpent, arched above its coils, its thick head angled to strike. They reminded me precisely of the twined serpents on the medallion about my neck. I smiled and slipped the coins into a pouch. I wasted no time wondering how they got there, nor how they had been overlooked.

We left only the larger dinner plates and some odds and ends. Lycurgus wrapped the small figurine carefully and carried it out. Out of perversity, I triggered all the locks on the doors. Let the usurpers work for what was left.

Within a week I had bid farewell to Lycurgus and his men and prepared to travel to the coast, hoping to board a ship to the south and west. The passage of my new life was about to begin.

Book Two
Kingdom of Gold

CHAPTER ONE

Putting Babylon behind me without a backward glance, I left on a mule, leading another that carried provisions. It would not be a long journey, and I made no allowances for guards or companions despite the gold I carried. I wanted to be alone. If I were attacked again then that was it. I didn't even carry a knife to defend myself.

As it happened, the journey to the port of Rilad was uneventful. The region was stony, but its gullies and ravines offered more shade than had the desert to the west. When I arrived at the city, I sold the mules at the docks, for some coins and a dagger. That night I slept at a tavern, where I had my first hot meal and a bath in the seventeen days since leaving Babylon. By the next day I had booked passage on the first vessel out.

The sea brought back curious memories that surfaced only in fragments. I saw a young boy who was my earlier self frolicking upon a deck that seemed as huge as a field and its stacked cargo as puzzling as a maze. How the lad had resented it when his mother, her concern and fear huge in her liquid brown eyes, called him from that playground to the cramped cabin below. It seemed I had been in prison ever since, as if I had never had any choices. Oh, to recover that adventure of youth, where all the world is a playground. Too soon, we discover that it is littered with hidden dangers that we stumble over day by day. The wonder is that we retain any memory of the frolic at all.

Now the deck itself, once so huge, seemed cramped. I stalked it like a caged animal, pausing only when those sifted memories filtered to the fore. Then I would sit and watch from the bobbing deck that heaved from wave to wave, watched the resolute march of the sea toward the gray horizon, watched the gray turn to evening and suffuse with violet wings of cloud that framed the sea. Time suspended. My mind was a raging thunderstorm. But at such moments I clung to the reveries and peace like a lonely thing, a heart I had lost.

I fed on my loneliness during that long sea voyage, but in so doing devoured it and began to set it loose. I would take the adventure at hand, and resolved never again to let someone else make choices for me. I put death and despair behind me, further behind with each new-risen sun, each blazing violet sunset. Distance was measured in days, not in miles, for on the sea one is always moving while seeming to stand still. It is the inversion of traveling by land, where motion is measured by the distance crossed over a steadfast, unmoving solidity. The very action of the waves forced me inward, drove me to the still point at the center of my being.

As a paying passenger I was not required to work, but I grew restless on the small, heavily laden vessel. At first the crew thought I interfered. And I suppose I did. The swelling above my ankle had gone down, but it felt awkward, like a club. Pain gnawed continuously at the joint. It would never be whole, but I forced it to bear weight.

Under the hot sun I stripped to a loincloth, like the crew, and labored under sails and ropes. There was always work to be done: cargo to be shifted; decking to be cleaned; oarlocks greased; ropes stowed, coiled, unleashed; sails to be mended. I began to feel alive for the first time in months. I came to the serving window of the galley famished, ate heartily, felt muscles grow sore, ache, then grow in mass and dexterity again. The flaccid muscles in my forearm began to swell. I had never known or really tested my own strength in manual labor. The new curl of muscle and ligament felt good. With some surprise, I began to look down the length of my body, and, looking past the heavy necklace I had inherited from Balthazzar and which, out of perverse allegiance to my vow, I now wore constantly, I seemed to see the lineaments of his body beneath it.

When we spotted the shores of that western land for the first time, I was disappointed. We embarked at a crude trading port and for two days underwent feverish loading and unloading. I was in the midst of it, clumsily hoisting barrels and carrying them up and down the ramps. I decided to sail further down the coast. We had put in at two more ports when the captain called me aside. I had overstayed my fare, he pointed out, and while he appreciated my labor he could not afford to pay me. Moreover, the ship would be heading back to Rilad after this last port of call. The cargo had changed almost entirely. The ship's bays, which had been packed with fabrics and quilts and barrels of figs and dried fruit, now held bundles of ivory horn, animal hides, small caskets of spices and incense.

When we put in at this port some strange hope arose in me, some stirring of my spirit. I had forsaken any belief in divine signs, having buried my life as a Magus back in the wind-blasted desert west of Al Achor. Yet, I could not deny the quickening of my heart. I don't know why. The signs were subtle, but they were there.

It was unlike the other ports at which we had stopped. We customarily put in at the angry sprawl and noise of the docks, choked by cargo and wagons and sweaty, cursing men. Filthy huts tumbled to the water's edge In the doorways of some, women loitered, awaiting the day's trade in human flesh and need.

Instead of spindly docks and ramps of treacherously insecure wood planking, balanced precariously atop some rock foundations, this port, Tamal, had two long stone wharves jutting out into a quiet bay. To the south and west of the village, a forested range of hills jutted up, forming the mouth of the bay and protecting its quiet water from the ocean storms. The village itself was neatly laid out along a dusty street that dwindled across a plain to further hills. It was incredibly, almost intolerably, hot and humid, but toward evening a fresh breeze flickered down from the hills, cooling the bay. Dozens of small fishing boats plied the water, heading back toward land with the evening sun.

Several hopeful vegetable plots had been carved out of the soil along a river that meandered into the bay. Around the nearer houses, rows of bright red flowers like shattered rubies spilled about doorways. I had not seen flowers since leaving Babylon. For some reason, they stirred my spirit immensely, drawing me. Even as we docked, the air seemed to turn rich with the sweet perfume of flowers, although a contrary wind brought the intermittent smell of fish, pungent and sharp, as the fishing vessels docked neatly and knives began to flash over the silver bodies of the catch. And the people I saw, most of them anyway, were dark-skinned. Like me.

I stumbled quickly to my cabin, cursing the pain at my ankle as I tripped down the ladder, grabbed the two knapsacks that held all my belongings, bade farewell to the captain who over the several months voyage had become something like a friend—as much as I was willing to permit anyone to be—and stepped ashore.

At a lodging place I inquired, through an interpreter from the docks, about quarters for a long stay. This place seemed as good as any. Some old men conferred, their bald heads bobbing like wizened monkeys. At last one of them stood, bandy-legged and foolish-looking. He motioned me to follow. He turned his back and stamped down the path, his feet kicking up little spirals of dust in his wake. His thin body, hunched in the shoulders, looked like a crooked stick blown before the wind.

He led me to a small house with the omnipresent garden against the south wall. A woman answered his cough at the open doorway. They jabbered in a high-pitched, rapid language. The woman pointed to the heavy, gold necklace around my neck. The old man shook his head and jabbered some more. Suddenly he wheeled and grabbed my knapsack. I started to seize it back. He held up a hand to stop me and rooted through it. He picked out two small coins from my purse, handed one to the woman, bit the other one hard, grinned and walked off with it in his hand. The woman motioned for me to enter. She pointed to a bed behind a curtain, gesticulating firmly. I nodded; I had a place to stay. I walked to the bed, put my knapsacks between me and the wall, lay down and soon fell asleep.

During the night it began to rain, breaking suddenly in huge, pelting drops, then in cascading torrents. I awakened and stumbled to the doorway, watching the storm sweep across the valley. Lightning scoured the black clouds, tripping through the sky like some clumsy runner looking for the finish line. The heavens careened with flashes. I watched until the storm moved out to sea, then went back to bed with the distant bellowing of thunder still rumbling in my ears. The storm seemed to purge me.

I slept late in the morning, even though the bed seemed all night to be rocking to the rhythm of waves. It was my first stable port in months. When I awakened, I was startled by a ring of soft brown eyes in silent faces watching me intently. I stared back at the children, six of them. Not all hers, I hoped. One of them reached out and touched my forearm lightly, just above the jagged scar tissue. When a muscle twitched involuntarily he jumped back. The others giggled.

The mother entered and shooed them away, their legs tumbling like puppies. She smiled broadly, revealing a mouthful of missing teeth; it was a kind-hearted smile. She babbled recklessly at me, then threw up her arms and returned to the kitchen.

My first task, I decided, was to learn the language. One is forever a stranger until one learns the language. In this my training as a Magus stood me in good stead. Admah was a good teacher, patient and careful. Soon I was speaking the language with ease.

I was to stay in the village nearly two years, at peace in the home of Admah the widow. Only two of the children, I was grateful to learn, were hers. I had plenty of money for the simple lifestyle. The minor baubles I had taken from Babylon translated richly here. I don't know how long I would have stayed in that peaceful village. I had no plans. I simply waited for something to happen to me. When that something occurred, it happened suddenly and irrevocably.

CHAPTER
TWO

M y time in the coastal village of Tamal was a time for healing, a time for plotting.

The need for the former was obvious. I would be forever lamed by the broken ankle. Although the muscles and bones accepted the burden of motion, I was forced to hobble slightly when I walked, the ankle skewing the direction of the foot slightly so that I placed my weight on the inside surfaces. Aboard ship, I had been able to stagger short distances on deck barely noticing the infirmity. On land, where there were distances to cover, the twisted bone felt like a painful weight at the end of my leg. The foot seemed to grow even more twisted to accommodate my awkwardness, but slowly mobility returned. I felt my muscles strengthen almost daily, often taking long walks that pushed me beyond pain to rehabilitation.

The scars on my forearm constricted to a pink, keloid ridge. The muscle had been irretrievably damaged, but some dexterity remained. It was more ugly than awkward. One had two arms, after all. Daily I practiced grasping, throwing, testing the pressure on the enervated muscles that remained. I walked along the shore, tossing rocks at the endless waves. In time, the arm proved capable, if not competent. Similarly, the dagger wound in my back healed. It felt like a handful of hard roots under my probing hand, low on the back. When I passed beyond walking on the lame foot to a kind of staggering, uneven trot, that wound stitched with sharp pain. But that too passed away. I was healing.

The internal pain was less quick to heal. I continued to nurse my hatred and my desire to thwart not just the Magi, but also the power they represented. For, while my initial impulse was vengeance, I had little doubt that they had not survived the desert. Still, I often dreamed I held one of their throats under my hands, and forced them to see my mangled flesh as I squeezed tighter. Often I awakened in the night, bathed with sweat, and with angry curses on my lips.

Around the marketplace at Babylon there had always been those individuals, usually sailors, who had become addicted on their travels to certain drugs. Upon their return, they sprawled in the marketplace, feasting on the narcotics. When the drugs ran out, they entered the horror of longing for more.

I was addicted to wrath. The withdrawal was more time-consuming and no less painful than that of the drug addict. But like the addict, I knew that it could flare anew at any moment; the fire never went entirely out. For the time being, I knew peace, but always that beast inside was plotting. To get vengeance—maybe not on the Magi, but on their type, the strong, the arrogant—I needed power. I began to crave power, even as my life grew outwardly, day by day, more calm.

I traded a few of the small gold bars for some local currency with the money-trader at the docks. His eyes bulged as he worked the scales. He had to return to his shop twice to find a sufficient number of the little rough pieces of brown metal that passed for coinage with these people. I had no idea whether he cheated me. I had more than enough money.

On the way home I purchased furniture and had it delivered to Admah's home. I bought supplies that had to be carted by ox. She stood speechless when they arrived, falling at my feet with her face pressed into the hem of the peasant's cloak I had bought myself. I had to force her upright. I gave her more than she needed, perhaps too much. But she and her two small sons were kind to me, and kindness was a treasure beyond price.

I spent much of my time walking about the countryside exercising. I always wore the heavy gold necklace with its pendent medallion hidden inside my cloak. I had started the practice shortly before docking at our first port. The captain had drawn me aside. He had looked out toward the sea, expertly avoiding looking at me. "None of my business," he said. "But were I you, I would keep that charm well out of sight. Places where we're going a man would slit your throat as readily as spit for the thing." He turned on his heel and left. I listened.

I hid it now to move freely among the people. I wanted nothing between me and them. I walked to the fields where the peasants labored under the tropical sun. Although I had dozens of suggestions at hand to improve their rude methods, I kept silent. Perhaps I would offer them at the next planting season. They were simple people, eager to please. And a pious people, whose lives were infiltrated everywhere by deities and spirits. How simple belief is, really. If it made them happy, fine. I had long ago given up such foolishness.

It was while I was returning from one such walk that I found the village in a hubbub. Houses on the outskirts were deserted. From nearby fields, peasants streamed toward the village square. I followed, my interest quickening.

In the square a number of soldiers had arrayed themselves, most of them having ducked into the shade of shops; others milled by the docks. Their horses, magnificent animals, were being rubbed down and fed in the pens that often held mewing sheep and gangly oxen for trade. A small squad stood guard by a horse-drawn chariot. But it was the gigantic figure standing by the chariot that drew my attention. He was the largest man I had ever seen, with limbs ponderous with fat. He couldn't have been older than his early twenties, but his flesh weighed on him like years.

Oddly, his face was a different color than his body, a light, mottled tan, above a frame as black as ebony. The tan rose from a ring of fat above his shoulders and lightened toward the polished skull. The obesity afflicted his face also; his flesh hung in discolored flaps from his cheeks and chin, pushing in on his broad nose and thick lips so they seemed on the point of collapse. The cheeks were stippled like some diseased fish.

Tempted to glance away, I was yet compelled to continue looking. For while everything else about him suggested indolence and flabbiness, his eyes, black as some infernal caldron, burned with fierce intensity, locking grips with a person, devouring him.

His body was sheathed in a scarlet robe from which a linen undergarment protruded like a dirty skin. Both were wet with sweat, even though the guards had hastily erected a canopy over him. Despite his foreboding presence, he chatted amiably with the village elders, smiling broadly, putting them at ease. He reached behind him into the chariot and passed around a heavy flagon. There were good-hearted smiles all around as the elders drank deeply. The flagon made another pass. The elders smiled and chatted back.

I nudged a villager standing nearby. "Who's this?" I muttered.

He spoke without turning to me, his eyes large with the regality and power of the visitor. "An envoy of the king," he said abruptly. His tone implied, "You fool."

King? I did feel foolish. I, who had played the very games of royal power, had naively assumed that the village was self-sufficient, an island apart from civilization. Of course there would be a king somewhere, a powerful one who enabled this village to appear peaceful and self-sufficient. And I knew immediately what the purpose of the visit was.

I asked anyway. "Why is he here?"

The villager turned, dumbfounded at the naiveté. "Oh, it's you," he said. "Of course you wouldn't know anything of such matters."

"Of course," I replied.

"It is Prince Kurdash," he said knowingly. "He has grown some since last we saw him. Collecting taxes."

"Will they be here long?"

"No longer than necessary. We have no place to put up the guard." He jingled a few coins in his pocket nervously.

"Are the taxes heavy?"

"King Komani has always been most fair."

It was the party line. His voice betrayed him; he was scared.

The village elders were producing scrolls and setting up tables under the shade of an awning.

"In effect," I said, "he'll take all he can get."

He whirled, as if I had spoken blasphemy. Then he smiled. "Watch your tongue, Elhrain. Or you may lose it."

I smiled with some surprise. I couldn't remember having told the villagers my name. Nothing travels faster in a small village than gossip. I wondered what tales they told behind my back.

Already people were lining up as Prince Kurdash walked toward the table. He moved easily for such a large man. Beneath the soft coating of fat, muscles rippled over those extremities that projected out of his robe like logs. He stood behind the table while several of his men joined the village elders on stools behind him.

A young man about the same age as the prince stayed by his side at every step. I nudged the villager once more.

"And who is that next to the prince?" I asked. "He seems an officer of rank for one so young."

The villager peered hard for a moment. "Eldrad," he said. No further embellishment.

He set his shoulders firmly and moved toward the line.

I spotted Admah and her sons standing back in the shade. Tocqui, the younger boy, clung to her skirt. Donqua pranced in and out of the crowd. She was lifting Tocqui to her hip as I approached.

I greeted her. She smiled nervously.

"What's the matter?" I asked.

She stared bashfully at the ground. "It is two years since they came," she said. "My husband was alive last time."

I puzzled over her comment. "So?"

"I don't know if they will believe me."

"The elders are here."

"I know."

Suddenly it dawned on me. She didn't know if she had enough money. I called Donqua over to me. He came readily, always up for something new. I knelt down before him.

"Listen, Donqua. On my bed"—he nodded vigorously—"there is a pouch in my knapsack. I want you to get it."

He shook his head.

"No? Why not?" I tried to look stern.

"Mother told me never to touch your things."

"That is very good of your mother. But this time I say it is okay. Do you understand?"

He looked at his mother. She glanced at me indecisively. "Do it," I said sharply. For a moment, I was Magus again, ordering a menial. Fear slipped across her eyes like a wet veil. I softened my voice. "It's okay. I need it."

She nodded to Donqua, who hurtled off in a flurry of legs and dust. In moments he returned, breathing hard, and handed me the pouch. I tucked it under my belt.

I had never been on this side of the bureaucratic bench. I loathed it.

The line moved with interminable slowness. Bodies, hot and sweaty, jostled against each other. At first there was laughter and gossip. As the afternoon sun bore down like a white hot weight on our shoulders, conversation died out. Admah stood tense and silent next to me, sweat dotting her dark face. Several times I told myself I had no part in this. Walk away. See a new world. Leave them alone. But then I saw her slight frame grow tense, her lips working nervously as if rehearsing lines, and I waited.

I had not known there were so many people in this area. The line moved by social caste—traders and shopkeepers first, craftsmen next, farmers and the disenfranchised last. It was a very long line. Soon the only sound was the mechanical jingling of coins as people perspired nervously, wondering if they had enough with them. As people left the table, their faces were tight and drawn. They hurried away.

Slowly, we neared the table. Then we were next in line. I studied Kurdash's bland impassivity. What a monster of a man he was. The young man next to him, Eldrad, seemed pleasant enough. He bore a long homely face, but his eyes were keen and intelligent. He shifted. Even in the shade, rivulets of sweat tracked his features. Kurdash seemed bathed in it. His body emitted a nearly feral odor.

The man ahead of us was protesting. The village elder studied his scroll. "Zindash," he said, "you own a house in the village, a square of land. Ten drachmas is the tax."

"But that's double what it was last time!"

"Last time there had not been a war," Kurdash spoke. His voice was loud enough for all to hear. He had probably repeated it many times that day. "If you were now under foreign rule, you would have nothing! Pay it and count your blessings."

Zindash paid and left the table muttering.

"Ah, Admah," said the elder as we stepped up. He turned toward Kurdash. "She's recently widowed."

"Who is the man?" Kurdash asked, glaring at me.

"A boarder. A foreigner."

"Indeed! If she is able to take boarders, she pays the full price for a householder. Five drachmas."

"But widows pay half," the man protested.

Kurdash said nothing, his eyes boring into Admah.

"Do you have five drachmas, Admah?" the elder asked.

She shook her head mutely, palmed up a handful of small coins I recognized as ones I had paid her.

"It's not enough," he said.

Angrily I stuffed a hand into my purse, fastened upon a heavy coin, and tossed it on the table. "Is that enough?" I demanded.

The coin spun dizzyingly on edge. Even before it flipped over, I heard the gasp from the elder. He whipped a glance over his shoulder at Kurdash. The elder's hands were trembling as he reached for the coin, which now lay flat, the rearing serpent embossed in the gold shining like a living thing in the sunlight. Before the elder could reach for the coin, a huge black hand, as quick as the flicker of the serpent's tongue, darted through the air and seized the coin.

Kurdash held the coin in his hand. Something registered in his eyes. It may have been fear, perhaps hatred. His whole body leaned forward.

"Where did you get this?" His voice was a rumble, a thunder storming in his chest.

I locked eyes with him. Studied him. He resisted. It *was* fear. I looked at the man Eldrad next to him, whose mouth hung open, staring at the coin.

"In a distant land," I said.

"Who? Who gave it to you? No, you stole it."

I became aware of guards shifting, suddenly ringing us in a loose circle.

"It's possible, Kurdash," said Eldrad. "Indeed, it is possible."

"Answer my question," Kurdash said. His eyes never left mine.

"I cannot," I said. "The coin is mine by legal right. What is it to you?"

A fury washed over the big man. I was surprised, nonetheless, by the evenness of his voice. "I think you will come with us," he said. Immediately the hands of the guards fastened upon me.

"No," Eldrad said. I was surprised at his brashness, for I sensed even then that my life hung in a balance. "He will come as our guest," he said. "This is not a kingdom of renegades." I didn't understand what authority this younger man carried.

Kurdash nodded. The fury dissipated. The guards loosened their grip, but they did not step away.

When the company left for Jebel Barkal the following morning, I was among them. I was allowed freedom to go with them. I believed I would be dead if I resisted.

CHAPTER
THREE

Leaving Tamal, we wound through a tangle of hills, verdant with tropical foliage even in the summer's heat. I flicked one final glance over my shoulder at the shining expanse of the sea, then we dipped over the crest of the hill.

Despite the often circuitous route we took through the hills, we traveled rapidly. The horses were magnificent animals, high-spirited and muscular. I laughed, remembering the desultory camels I had ridden. Yet I was grateful for the experience I had gathered riding them. The soldiers cast expectant glances my way at first, awaiting the tumble. They were disappointed. While I had much to learn about riding, I could ride. And, despite my uncertainty, it was a joy to ride these animals. They rampaged across the valleys, jostling eagerly up hills. At a gallop, the uneven, rocky plains leveled under their flashing hooves like a carpet.

If I was under guard, it could not have been more loose. I looked upon myself as a firmly invited guest. I ranged about freely, even riding a short distance from the others occasionally to survey an area of interest. Of course, I had no doubt the others could have caught me in a moment. I rode the horse, but hardly like one raised in the saddle. Always someone among the others seemed especially intent upon watching me.

Several times Eldrad drew alongside to chat with me. He was delighted with my skill at the language, but listening to his cultivated, formal speech after living with the villagers was like experiencing different languages altogether. He was patient, laughing good-naturedly at mistakes, smiling at my meager word-hoard, occasionally correcting me in a gentle way. I liked him the moment I laid eyes on him and found my liking growing. His long, homely face knew no guile. He wore his feelings openly, mostly his good cheer. His dark skin had been pitted by some illness in the past, and his face twisted crookedly when he laughed. It made him seem oddly vulnerable, but he himself seemed unaware of it. His body was slim but powerful. Muscles rippled like little streams along the forearms and calves that protruded from the light riding cloak. He pitched in with the menial labor when camp was made, yet he rode with the natural authority of a born leader, so different from the sullen and remote Kurdash, who flailed the horses of his chariot like a possessed man. Some strange bond lay between the two. As we rode along one afternoon I asked Eldrad about it.

He had been talking about the temple at Jebel Barkal, describing his royal city with pride and delight. "I wasn't there at the building, of course," he said, chuckling. "Although I sound like it. Really a fascinating thing. How they quarried the marble, dragged it all those miles, then floated it down the river to Jebel Barkal."

"Sounds like you've studied it pretty thoroughly," I observed with the listener's technique of eliciting information without telling anything yourself. I wanted to protect my anonymity, although I was thinking of the Palace of the Magi in comparison.

"Oh, yes. Someone has to preserve the past," he said. "Maybe I was born too late." He cast a glance at Kurdash. I let the comment pass.

"Many of these temples, or palaces for that matter, have secret corridors. Passageways underground?" I let the question dangle. I might need the information if an escape became necessary. I wasn't sure where I stood here.

"Hah!" he exclaimed. "You know your royalty." That questioning glance slid across me. "You're right. They are a vanity of kings, whether to hide themselves or others, I don't know. Rest assured that Komani has no need for that, though. We have long been at peace, probably because Komani mastered the art of compromise with the northern powers. Even this 'war' that Kurdash spoke of was nothing more than a minor clash over territory with some southern tribes. I can't remember the dungeons' ever being used."

"Dungeons?"

"Isn't that what you meant?"

"No. Well, yes. I suppose. I just meant secret passages."

"Well, we do have some secrets, I suppose." Again, I felt his probing glance. "Perhaps we all do," he added.

When I looked at him, he was staring out over the plain, smiling.

"Funny thing," I said. "When I first saw you and Kurdash at the village I thought you were the royal representative, he the bodyguard."

"You think I'm his bodyguard?" he asked.

"Aren't you?"

"No."

"Then . . ."

"Then you'll see, won't you?" He smiled and rode off.

I had the uneasy feeling I was touching upon a sore point. I would be careful to avoid it again until my own status became clear.

* * *

I lost count of the days of travel. It may have been ten, maybe less. Several times Eldrad chatted with me. He seemed to have forgotten entirely our earlier conversation, and I didn't force it.

The last leg of the journey lay through a strange landscape, as if desert and wet land fought each other for the upper hand. Barren landscape, littered with jutting rock and stony soil, attacked small clumps of watered and cultivated land. Where the river wound, a green stitchery followed its banks. So much promise lay here with so little knowledge to develop it. My eye scanned potential farm sites—in the bend of the river, across a fertile valley. Perhaps they flooded in the rainy season. Perhaps the plain grew dry early in the season. But dikes could be built to divert the floods; channels carved to irrigate. My mind itched with possibilities. I pointed these out to Eldrad, while he nodded with surprise.

"It could be done," he murmured.

The hilly terrain fell away to broad plains. We wound past thickets of prickly weeds and black boulders the size of small houses strewn at random on the plain as if whimsical gods had once played a game upon the broad spaces. Small streams were numerous. Hugging the shores, thick strands of brush with lacquered green leaves grew tangled and thick.

The riders seemed to change with the landscape. Occasionally they broke into random song—an odd, off-beat chant, really—as we headed west.

Then the first settlements appeared, little farms carved hopefully out of wilderness. But it was *not* true wilderness. I recognized this with a surge of excitement. The land was a fair and good land, able to support agriculture. The farms mocked that promise: a testament to ignorance.

I was so intent on studying the river and farms that I scarcely noticed the hills rising to the south and west of us. Their distant ridges were tinged with a green that grew increasingly dark and heavy as we rode. In late afternoon, storm clouds rose over them, prowling the ridges like robbers.

The chants of the riders grew more avid, their faces eager with anticipation. We rode fast, near a gallop, the horses blowing clots of lather that caught on our legs like fleece. We surged up a long hill.

And there below us lay Jebel Barkal. The great river, the recipient of the tributary we had been following, lay like gray glass reflecting the storm clouds. Small fishing boats, dots in the distance, hurried toward shore to beat the rain.

The city itself rimmed the shore of the river, a maze of streets winding toward the shining bulk of the palace that soared like a white marble shout of defiance against gray cloud. It was the city of dreams—but dreams with broken wings and crippled feet.

Irresistibly, my eye was pulled beyond the city to a great monolith of stone. It rose like a freak of nature, macabre and disturbing, above the latticework of farm and plain beyond the city. An odd, rocky spine arched from the distant hills, suddenly erupting into an immense pillar. The spire, however, dominated everything. It soared straight up, as if reaching for the clouds that stormed above it. Its top was split like two great, groping fingers clawing the sky. No, not fingers; from this angle it looked precisely like the head of a rearing snake. Twin heads, perhaps, swelled off one thick body.

Was this the mountain Balthazzar described? Could it be? The recollections seared across my mind. I gasped aloud, but no one noticed. Their chants had risen to a deafening chorus.

Jebel Barkal itself lay in a sprawl about gleaming marble buildings that formed the heart of the city. As if on command, a shaft of late sunlight splintered the clouds and illuminated the palace and temple. They glistened in the distance like ivory models. The chant that the soldiers had

118

been babbling all day rose into a cavalcade of shouts. Howls, ear-piercing screams, filled the air as we rode downhill to the city. Hooves thundered.

People streamed from the houses as they saw us coming. They broke into awkward little dances in their excitement. Dust clouds rose about their feet. The people hooted back at the riders, raising a weird ululation, primal and urgent. A cloud curtained the shaft of light. Thunder rumbled. A crash of lightning scorched the clouds, turning loose the rain. Drops splattering off their bodies, the soldiers rode at a heart-pounding gallop down the hillside into the city, the horses' hooves kicking up mud in heavy clots. All the while the crescendo of song broke from them, as if they could outshout the thunder. Soldiers peeled off toward clusters of huts, while a small band headed by Kurdash's chariot found the main street and continued directly toward the palace. Children clapped and frolicked in the rain, kneeling as Kurdash's chariot rumbled by.

I had fallen far behind in the melee, stunned by it. It was as if I had been forgotten.

The milling mass of bodies, mud-splattered and rain-soaked, ignored me in the jubilation of homecoming. Someone gestured me off my horse and led it away to the stables. I began wandering awkwardly down the street. Could I just keep walking, out of the city and away from the people in whose care I didn't know if I was prisoner or friend? Suddenly Eldrad was there, tugging on my sleeve. A woman held his arm tightly, her head bent politely to avoid my gaze.

I followed numbly as Eldrad led us toward the palace grounds, its central gate thrust open to a broad, walled expanse. Kurdash's chariot had rumbled on ahead, and I saw two guards help him plod up the long flight of marble stairs to the palace entrance. The palace glistened with rain. Even under the dark clouds, it shone. We passed through the gate into the courtyard, but turned off to a series of mud-brick houses arranged along the eastern wall.

I knew enough about palaces to know that we were heading toward the homes of either the king's relatives or of the highest-ranking military commanders. I looked at Eldrad with surprise. He was much too young to be a military commander. Was he a prince, then? And what of Kurdash?

Eldrad led me into a well-lit, spacious house. Oil lamps flickered from shelves on the wall, and a fire roared in the hearth. A young boy ran about closing shutters against the downpour, laughing as rain swept in and puddled across the tiled floor. He turned and flung himself into Eldrad's arms.

After a moment, Eldrad remembered me standing awkwardly in the doorway. He seized my arm, drew me in and introduced me to the woman, Alsace, whom I took to be his wife, and to the boy Kanaha. They greeted me politely.

Alsace moved to a kettle of steaming food over the hearth. She gave me a friendly smile as she bent toward the fire. She was truly a beautiful woman. Her skin, filmed with moisture from either the rain or the fire's heat, shone so deeply black it seemed almost purple. Her features were as smooth and flawless as polished statuary. When she flashed that sudden smile, her eyes lit up like stars. A gay, happy woman, this Alsace. Eldrad hugged her from behind, running his hands over the swell of her pregnancy. She shook her head, playfully slapping at him.

Suddenly, in the doorway to one of the side rooms stood a tall woman. From that first moment her eyes seemed to bore into me and seize my very heart. I stopped as if struck.

At first, it was simply at the sheer surprise of her skin color. For in this kingdom of black-skinned people, she was startlingly fair-complected. Her flesh was browned by the sun to the hue of polished oak, but she was beyond doubt a foreigner from the north, a foreigner—as was I. From that first meeting, something—call it a kinship of forsakenness—sang between us. I couldn't imagine what she was doing in this home, unless it was as a slave or servant.

Eldrad chuckled behind me. "And this," he said, "is our sister Taletha."

I bowed slightly. "Elhrain," I said, trying to keep the surprise out of my voice. Sister? She couldn't be.

She nodded in return, her dusky eyes fixed relentlessly upon me.

Everything in the room seemed fixed in place.

"Well," Eldrad said. Then, "Well, well." He chuckled again. "Perhaps we can eat?" He nudged me, "She rarely speaks, Elhrain. But be careful what you say."

Her eyes flashed angrily.

* * *

After dinner, when the storm had rumbled off to the east, Eldrad walked with me about the palace grounds. The air held that charged, fresh atmosphere that follows a storm. We picked our way around puddles that reflected stars.

"Perhaps tomorrow you would like to meet my father," Eldrad said.

"I would be delighted. Does he live here?"

"Oh, yes." He smiled.

"Nearby?"

"Right here." He pointed at the palace.

He saw my surprised look. "Komani," he added. "My father is the king."

When we returned, he showed me to a spacious bedroom. The house seemed to go on endlessly along the palace wall, a long corridor opening off the front room to a series of bedrooms. Someone had spread pillows and blankets on the floor.

I had great difficulty sleeping. Perhaps it was because I had become accustomed to the rude cot in Admah's home or to sleeping in the open with the troop on the way to Jebel Barkal. The pillows kept shifting under my tossing body. Each time I hovered on the edge of sleep, however, I seemed to see the flashing eyes of Taletha and came fully awake.

A rooster was crowing somewhere when I finally dozed off.

CHAPTER
FOUR

Despite my confusion upon first entering Jebel Barkal, I sensed that all the noise and hurry and press of bodies had not been threatening. The people had been joyful. So too, many of the years that followed were to be for me a kind of jubilation.

Those years were not always easy, for living in joy is not for one moment living without challenge or threat. Indeed, I discovered during those years that jubilation, which is the other side of sorrow, can occur even while living *in* sorrow. There's the odd thing. I have wondered since, after having walked not just in sorrow but in the very pit of blackness where the demons of desolation rage, whether one can truly know joy without having known sorrow.

In any event, I had no opportunity to be bored at Jebel Barkal, from the confusion of the tumultuous welcome home to the day I fled in panic. I was tested to the limits of my physical and intellectual endurance, and I proved worthy. No, even more than that, I excelled.

*   *   *

The area I excelled in—knowledge of earth and soil and plant life—was precisely what the kingdom needed. Only by its fabulous wealth of gold had the kingdom staved off a disaster, but it was a disaster waiting to happen. The people had the river for fish; they had a thriving trade in spices and ivory and skins for foreign goods. But of farming ability they had little. The farms nearer the city were no more prosperous than the sparse and crooked little ones I had seen on the outskirts. Everything was slapdash and ineffective. The bottomland around the river, however, was just rich enough to permit this style of farming. My challenge was to change it from haphazard to healthy and thriving.

I continued living for the time, until I found my own quarters, in Eldrad's spacious home. I had nearly complete freedom of movement, hampered only by the miles of desolate terrain surrounding Jebel Barkal and by the king's armies that protected that territory. Still, I often felt, if not watched exactly, then at least studied. So I particularly enjoyed the freedom of wandering across the agricultural fields.

I brought it up with Eldrad one night. We sat in the large front room that caught a breeze through open windows. The scent of jasmine from the garden perfumed the air. The sun lowered past the willows of the palace portico, half of its fire hidden behind the mountain that stood like a guard over the city. In the kitchen Alsace talked with a friend, her hands folded over the bulging mound of her pregnancy as she leaned back on one of the few chairs in the house. We reclined on pillows. I had been there a month, and Eldrad sensed my restlessness.

"What do you think of the land?" he asked.

I tugged my eyes reluctantly from the splendor of the setting sun. "Underused," I replied.

"Underused?" he said with surprise. "But it gives us all we need."

"Listen," I said, sitting up awkwardly on the pillows. "The people farm as if they don't care. They scratch in the earth, plant their seeds, then pretty much sit back and wait. They don't work."

"Should they?"

"Should they!" My voice was louder than I intended. "Look, Eldrad, surely you know the weather goes in cycles. They are storing up nothing. They plant for the present, and because they have enough for now they think all is well. What will they do during the dry years?"

He reflected. "I can't remember any dry years," he said. "There has always been sufficient food. And the river always provides water."

"But *will* it always? Look, man. You live nearly surrounded by desert."

"Wrong. The jungle lies to the west and south. Rain comes from the jungle."

"Rain comes from the sky, Eldrad. It's the desert I fear. And, believe me, the lean years *will* come. I have lived all my life in the desert."

"But wait a minute, Elhrain. You say my people don't work. That's because all their work has been done."

"What! They should be doing more. What do you mean their work is done?"

"Yes. I mean that. They have done their work. The sacrifices began months ago. They were observant."

"Sacrifices? To what, pray tell?"

He ignored my pun. "The gods granted the land," he said. "The people sacrificed for a good crop. They are devout." He spread his hands. "Now it is in the gods' hands."

"You can't be serious."

* * *

I met King Komani shortly after arriving, and even though I had lived nearly all my life among royalty—had been royalty as a Magus—I had been impressed.

As in any palace, steadfastness, glory and protection were the architectural themes. The flight of marble steps was attended foot and head by armed guards. Behind huge wooden doors, strengthened by strips of metal and flung open this morning to catch the fresh air, lay the main corridor, open to the south and intersected by passageways running east and west. Directly across the corridor was the central court, a room elevated by another flight of stairs offering guards a final point of defense if an attack should ever infiltrate the palace. In the court itself, six guards stood on both sides, each dressed in a loose, short loincloth, and bearing a long spear. High on the walls, narrow windows admitted the sun, flooding the chamber with light. The windows were some ten feet above the tiled floor, and a fighting parapet ringed them so archers could climb to the catwalk and shoot through the narrow openings.

The walls, once polished white marble like the outside, were gray with soot from the fire pit in the center of the room. In one corner, laborers were washing the walls with pieces of rough animal hide wrapped around heavy, flat stones. Behind them a band of white marble appeared from their labor, fading back into dusty gray as they progressed about the room. The fire pit was empty on this warm morning. Puddles of water, where the rain blew in through the windows, were being mopped up from the tiles by several women.

The room was a full forty paces in length. At its end, on a raised dais, stood the throne chair of King Komani. It was vacant at this early hour.

Eldrad talked easily with the guards while we awaited the king. I spotted two of them from the group I had traveled with, already taking their turn on duty. They looked pleased to be back home.

One of the guards barked a command. The ranks snapped to rigidity, not an eye blinking, as the king entered the room.

Komani stood in the doorway a moment, and then, seeing Eldrad, hurried toward us. They met in an embrace. As they did so, Kurdash entered the throne room behind them, attended by his two guards. His eyes glared like hot fires. He almost seemed to shake with some invisible anger, then he lumbered past Eldrad and Komani to his seat behind the throne, where he kept stony silence. People slipped through a side door, passing scrolls to him for his signature and whispering urgently in his ear, even as Komani and Eldrad strode to the throne.

Komani was a large man in stature, somewhere between Kurdash's bulk and Eldrad's whiplike body. Under the red robe cast over his shoulders and hanging open over his torso, his body was still leanly muscled, fuzzed slightly with graying hairs. His head also was fringed with gray. He sat down with some care, and immediately an attendant slipped him an enormous pipe, which he sucked at greedily. He sighed luxuriously and exhaled, then looked at me as Eldrad presented me. I bowed more for the kindness toward Eldrad than for the authority of the king. I would never bow unwillingly before a man or a god again.

His eyes sparkled. He sensed the resistance. He offered me the pipe, and I declined. The tobacco smelled as foul as sewer sludge. He closed his eyes, sucked at it again, then set it aside.

"Awful habit," he said. "Smells bad, too."

Behind him Kurdash rumbled with laughter. Someone had brought him a bowl of fruit, and he devoured it in huge, sucking mouthfuls. Some chewed fruit dribbled down his chin. Kurdash wiped it with a thick finger and sucked it clean. He took pains to ignore us.

"Welcome," said Komani. "It's good to have you as a guest."

"You rule a great kingdom," I offered. It was a general courtesy. One would say it to a dumpy sovereign of a diseased colony. I was surprised how easily the old amenities rolled off my tongue.

Komani grunted derisively. "It *was* a great kingdom," he said. "Actually," he paused and, using a silver tongs, relit his pipe from a small canister of coals by the chair. "Actually, we are held on the leash of a greater kingdom. Oh, we were great once." He waved the smoke away as if also waving away the past.

"The kingdom of Kush ruled lands north and south. To the east, of course, is the ocean. To the west . . ." He shrugged and puffed. "Well, we were called the Kingdom of Gold then, hundreds of years ago. The gold came from the interior. But where there's gold, there's war."

He set his pipe down and rose from the chair. He walked down to the fire pit, staring at the gray ash in a bed of sand.

"And so, we found ourselves at war. But we are also a powerful people, strong and beautiful. Powerful at arms." He raised his voice and looked at the guards. A few smiled in agreement. They were, indeed, powerful men.

"But also wise," said Komani. "Why should we shed our precious blood? We also knew the art of compromise. And that's where we are today—compromised."

"The kingdom seems vital, healthy," I said.

"Oh, it is. Compromise is a good thing. We pay them so much every six months; they don't invade us. They even offer their name as protection. Of course, it is in name only. If someone invaded us, I would guess that they're too busy with their own affairs to bother. But a name can be a powerful thing, Elhrain."

"What is the name of these people? Not Persian, surely?"

He chuckled. "No. Those who stopped the Persians, actually—Egyptians. The alliance hasn't been all bad, if largely one-way. We have had Kushites marry into their royal families, serve in high offices. Ah, a name can be powerful. Like yours."

"Mine?"

"To be sure." He looked at me quizzically. "You don't know the meaning?"

"Well, I never thought of it. Still, it always struck me as an unusual Persian name."

At that he laughed outright. "You think you're Persian, lad? *Elhrain* means Lord of the Mountain. How many mountains are there in Persia?"

I changed the subject. Komani made me slightly nervous, as if he knew things about me that I didn't know myself. "Where did the gold come from?" I asked. "Surely not from around here."

"The gold," he snorted. "Always the gold. Sometimes I wish we never had it." He walked back to the chair.

Kurdash, gorged with fruit, had fallen asleep and was snoring loudly.

"In truth," said Komani, "I don't know." He saw my surprise. "You tell him, son," he said to Eldrad. "I want to smoke in peace." He hoisted the clay pipe. In a moment the area was thick with the stench of his smoke.

Eldrad nodded. "This was years ago—centuries. Men came out of the west, following the line of the hills. Jebel Barkal was a tiny kingdom then, really, based closer to the seaport where we met you. Trade was our main industry. The men who came bore flakes of raw gold, some as large as a fingernail, to trade for the cloths and weavings we had through trade. The gold was nothing to them; a piece of silk, a rare treasure. Being a trading kingdom, we knew the advantage."

I nodded. It was not my place to point out that the advantage was pretty one-sided.

"This trade endured some years. Then suddenly it stopped. But not before we had become wealthy. And having wealth, we needed to use it. It was when we began using the gold to build this city of Jebel Barkal, trading gold for the marble of our temple and palace, that others took notice.

"A few nearby invaders tried to overthrow us. We defeated them easily and annexed their lands. Thus the kingdom grew.

"But the finest marble came from Egyptian lands, and that's how we met our compromise."

"But you have gold left?"

"Oh, to be sure. Only not so much that we can avoid collecting taxes."

"Taxation is good for the people," Kurdash rumbled, evidently not sleeping as soundly as we thought. "Never forget that. They have to do something for their government."

Eldrad didn't bother to reply. Nor Komani. I began to sense a tension here.

After a moment, Komani said, "What gold we retain had been specially minted into coinage. It is most carefully controlled. Only through this court, in fact. And so, when you displayed one such coin in Tamal, it naturally aroused some attention." He looked at me seeming to expect an answer. I merely nodded.

Komani chuckled. "You're shrewd, Elhrain."

"How do you mean, Your Majesty?"

"You know all the graces of the court. You also know when to keep your mouth shut."

"Forgive me." I laughed. "I am just a wanderer."

"Then ask him, father!" Kurdash's voice rasped.

"Silence, Kurdash," said Komani.

"No. Ask him about the necklace."

I started. Since my first days in Tamal I had kept the necklace concealed under my garments. It lay now against my chest, under the cloak I habitually wore.

Kurdash raised himself from the chair, his massive body trembling. His face was contorted. For the first time I saw him as a fearful thing.

"Ask him!"

"Whatever its past, the past is done," snapped Komani. "Silence!" he thundered.

Kurdash fought to control himself. Then he sat down and gnawed angrily at a remaining piece of fruit.

Komani nodded at Eldrad and we left.

Eldrad and I walked in silence from the palace. First the guards, then the people on the street bowed and smiled as we passed by. We cut down some back streets toward the river, the strong fish scent a beacon.

"Do you like it?" I observed.

"What? The river?" Eldrad replied.

"The bows, the courtesies of the court."

He laughed. His homely, guileless face broke easily into a grin. I liked him more each time I saw him. "I don't even notice it," he admitted. "One gets used to it."

"And Kurdash?"

He paused and sighed. From where we stood we could see, beyond the dark glitter of the river, the patches of neighboring farms. "Ah, yes. Kurdash. That's another story."

"Is he your elder?"

"Yes, by three years. My mother died during my childbirth. Why do you ask?"

"He covets power."

Eldrad reflected. "True," he admitted. "And he can have it."

He touched my arm, steering me to a cliff bank above the river.

"You asked about agriculture," he said. "And you're right. We have been too long at ease in Jebel Barkal. A people at ease can become weak. If you want it, the job is yours."

I looked at him in puzzlement.

"Minister of Agriculture," he said. "You'll have the full authority of the court. You might need it. A people at ease also doesn't like to change."

"Authority to do what?" I said. While my voice was calm, my head was hammering. Here was a task indeed.

"Whatever you think fit. Make us self-sufficient. Make the land produce. Give us grain to barter."

"And the sacrifices?"

"Ah, yes." he observed. "You don't have to participate if you don't wish. But the people will want to."

"Very well. I'll serve the people, never again a god."

"Perhaps people will see you as one if you succeed, especially if this drought you talk about comes to pass."

"Their worse luck," I muttered. "But I also will need granaries."

"The people store their own food," Eldrad said in surprise.

"Not during a famine."

"Very well. You'll have laborers to build your granaries."

"We'll build them on the plain, close to the temple where they're easy to defend."

"A nice touch. A gift to the gods."

"Tell that to the people. That will do."

Eldrad laughed. "You drive a hard bargain, Mr. Minister."

"Mind if I ask you a question?"

"It seems you have been doing that."

We sat down on the cliff, feet dangling over the edge. On the river a fisherman drew in a net of fish. His small boat bobbed precariously as he hauled it aboard.

I drew the necklace out and fingered it. The sun shot glittering rays from the twined serpents. Eldrad sucked in his breath. I slipped it back in.

"Perhaps it is best so," Eldrad said.

"Hidden?"

He nodded.

"Tell me about it."

"That's your question?"

"Yes. And the bargain. Tell me and I keep it hidden."

"The necklace is one like the House of Kush, kept by the reigning monarch of the land. Except that long ago, many years ago, one kept by the monarch, my father, was lost."

"Lost?"

"Well, given. You see, Kurdash and I had an elder sister. Her name was Sulani. Since she was in line to rule, the medallion of the House of Kush was bestowed on her at her twentieth birthday as a sign of her right to the throne."

He fell silent. I felt my heart hammering. My need to know forced me to intrude upon his pain.

"How long ago? What happened to her?"

"I don't know the details. It was not a matter to be spoken of. Sulani fell in love with an eastern king, one that stayed for a time in Jebel Barkal. They left for his land with promises to return, but never did. All this I have only secondhand. Kurdash was a mere boy, I was born the year Sulani left, and my father was loath to speak of it. So, you see, when you arrived, and the medallion was seen, immediately Kurdash took an interest. Especially since you also used a gold coin minted by the House of Kush."

"I see." I didn't see. My mind reeled.

"Sulani's husband," Eldrad continued thoughtfully, "may have been a god."

"What do you mean by that?" I saw that his face was composed. He actually meant it.

"He was called Conqueror of the Mountain. It is believed, since she did not return, that the gods took her. That he was really a god all along."

It was clear that Eldrad could tell me no more. He had told me enough.

"One question yet," I asked.

He sighed, no longer smiling.

"Taletha. You call her sister, yet she obviously is not of your family."

"Sister, daughter, friend—none of these and all of these. Taletha was sold to my father by a coastal trader a number of years ago. I remember the day. She looked so fearful. So distraught. And she would not speak a word. Komani loathed the traders, later outlawed them. But he took pity on Taletha, you see. There was, *is* something special in her. Instead, she became a part of the family. That is the way of our people, you see. Who knows whom the gods may send to us?"

"Maybe the gods had nothing to do with it."

Eldrad stared at me for a moment. His normally friendly attitude was stirred by anger.

"You know something?" he said. "You have a problem. I don't know what it is. If you want to tell me about it sometime, fine. But you have no right to cast spite on my beliefs. Understand? If they do not agree with yours, I'm not imposing them on you."

"But it's such perversity," I offered. A bit lamely, I thought.

"More perverse than believing in nothing? How do you *know* the gods haven't sent her? Or yourself for that matter?"

"Good point. I'm sorry."

"Don't mistake not caring for not knowing. Sometimes we do one to deny the other."

"Enough!" I said. "I don't want to talk about it. I'm sorry I upset you."

"Okay." Eldrad leaned back on his elbows. "Anyway, since Taletha doesn't speak about it, or speaks so little at all, we have no way of knowing. Still, I'm glad she is with us. I've often wondered what Sulani was like."

"Probably not like Kurdash," I offered.

Eldrad laughed. "Nor like me. She was, so I'm told, very beautiful."

"Oh, then surely not like you."

He laughed good-naturedly. "Listen. I have work to do. You do what you think is best."

"Minister of Agriculture, huh?"

Eldrad stood up. "You've got it," he said.

"I want it," I replied.

CHAPTER FIVE

K anaha shimmied all over, like a fish in a net. His hand darted out, then he would snap it back, anxious to move his ebony bah-lah piece. At first, I thought I would have an easy time with him. He was only seven, after all.

Imagine my delight when I came to the house of Eldrad and Alsace one evening and found Kanaha setting up a bah-lah board on the table. My eyes started. I hadn't seen the game since I played with Haggai in Babylon. I felt my heart tripping.

"I have a game for you, sir," Kanaha said. He still persisted in calling me that despite my protests. "Will you play?" I saw the cunning in his small, dark eyes and nodded.

"Perhaps you should tell me the rules," I said as I squatted by the low table.

"The rules are easy," Kanaha said.

"But every game has them."

He nodded. Quickly he ran through the rules, his hands flashing out moves to demonstrate. It was precisely as I remembered, each move permitted from each square neatly configured.

"I think I can try it," I said. "If you help me along."

"I will," he said decisively.

I planned to let him win a few games. But when he beat me two straight with unexpected moves, I threw aside kindness. His fingers had flown automatically over the board, skipping from hook moves to cross and circle patterns with a geometrical precision far beyond his years. On the third game, he beat me with a trapping counter move I had long forgotten.

"You've played before," Kanaha said.

"Yes. I have."

"You tried to trick me."

"And I couldn't, could I?"

"You should play Taletha," he said. "She's really good."

I looked up in surprise. Here this little scrub had beaten me three games straight. Okay, I was rusty. But Taletha was "really good"?

"Anytime," I said.

In a flash Kanaha stood up, and Taletha glided gracefully into his spot. I had the feeling I was being set up. Something was backfiring badly here.

Within the first few moves, I realized what Kanaha meant. Yes, she was really good, but it was the strategy and daring of her plays that surprised me. Haggai and I had always played a methodical, plodding game, opening with predictable moves in hope of eventually wearing down the opponent and outmaneuvering him. Kanaha had approached the game in much the same way, but with a skill that spoke of long practice. Playing against Taletha was like playing a different game altogether. It went beyond mathematics to imagination. Instead of "I can do this," it was "this might be possible." After each move she lifted her bright eyes to me as if saying, "Do you dare try this?"

In a half-dozen moves she had me helpless, cornered on every side. I studied the board ruthlessly, but she had blocked every retreat. I looked up. She rested her chin on her hands, studying my expression.

Taletha began to giggle. She knew she had me beaten.

I scowled at the bah-lah board, looking for a way out. She had the ivory leopard—my last piece—trapped by three ebonies, and had anticipated every move. Even the L-jump I had maneuvered for as my last gamble.

"This is a serious game," I muttered as she giggled again. She was watching me, not the board. I threw my hands up in capitulation.

Eldrad leaned over her shoulder. "She's got you," he said. "Got you tied up, locked up, put away."

"Nice game," she murmured softly.

In reflex, and surprise, I lifted one eyebrow. She laughed aloud and got up to help Alsace. Then I remembered. It was precisely what Balthazzar had done to me so often. Lift one eyebrow, the other stationary. I had never done that before.

* * *

I met with Eldrad several times during those summer afternoons to go over my plans. The land drowsed under a hot sun; flies brushed against the fabric stretched over the windows. Often, as the afternoon wound down in a discussion of an architectural plan or a system for organizing workers, I simply stayed on for dinner. I felt I was more than friend, almost a member of the family. Alsace and Taletha busied themselves in the kitchen, and toward evening the odor of the spiced foods filtered into the room, calling us to dinner. My place would be set at the table.

Sometimes the table would be shoved back, the benches turned against the wall, and we would sit cross-legged upon pillows eating from a large pot of stew. Fingers would fly, dipping in bread, scooping out a bowl. The children, Kanaha and the new baby girl, seemed everywhere, the baby passed from lap to lap as we ate and Kanaha incessantly trying to intrigue someone in a new game.

We were sitting just so one evening, when Taletha excused herself early. She had things to attend to in the village. I was still disturbed by the fact that she spoke so little. One evening, when I had taken it upon myself to accompany her on a shopping trip, I had tried to question her. Each time she turned the question back to me.

"Do you feel at home here?" I asked.

"Do you?"

"Well, I feel at home with you people. I mean, with my friends. It's hard to believe, I've been here nearly half a year already. It seems like I've been here forever."

She nodded but didn't speak.

"Do you know what I mean?"

"Yes," she said, busying herself with a package she held as we walked back.

"You don't come from this country," I observed.

"Where do you come from?" she asked.

I began to tell her, describing the desert reaches around Babylon. It seemed that I was listening to myself make noises only, although she nodded politely. Then we were back, and I realized she had told me nothing.

That is why I asked Eldrad about it after Taletha left that night. We rested on the floor pillows. The baby had fallen asleep. Kanaha was puttering with some toys in the corner.

"She never talks," Eldrad responded to me easily. "Don't worry about it. For a long time I thought she *couldn't* talk."

"She can speak," Alsace said. "Is able to speak, rather."

"Then why doesn't she?" Eldrad looked at his wife, not entirely amused. "She has been in my father's household for years, and hardly a word has she spoken."

"I don't know why," Alsace countered tartly. "She hasn't told me."

"Bah!" he said. "One talks too much; the other not at all." He winked at Alsace and received a scowl in return.

"All I know," said Alsace, "is that one has to listen in order to hear." Eldrad looked puzzled. "Listen . . . to hear? But I listen!"

"Then you would hear her. Perhaps she isn't ready to talk to you. To the children, though, and to me, indeed yes."

"Hmm." Eldrad nodded. "It could be."

It was a puzzle to me also. But I grew comfortable with the silences between us. It was just that there was, almost always, *only* silence between us. Taletha seemed to withdraw when I approached, as if retreating from some memory. If she had chosen a world of silence, would it be all the more profound than if she had never spoken? If she had *willed* it? The will, the power to choose and hold steadfast to it, was a powerful thing.

It was disquieting. There was so much I wanted to tell her, so much I wanted to hear her tell me.

* * *

The days stretched into weeks, then months. I began to feel at home, as if my past had been put behind me. Yet sometimes the past slipped through. Sometimes it even thundered through the walls I erected against remembering. This happened one evening after I had spent the day with Eldrad surveying the outlying farms.

After we parted, I wandered to the bluff above the river. The sun was warm on my back, and I shed my cloak, letting the sun's heat seep into my dark flesh. Little beads of sweat collected on my shoulders, gathering to trail down my chest.

How good it felt to be among these people. Even as the thought flitted through my mind, I named the feeling. I felt I was at home. Yet, on the heels of that thrill of belonging—among people that looked like me at least—another feeling crept upon me like tiny rats' feet, feeling its way tentatively and unnamed.

By now it seemed that I had lived in Jebel Barkal all my life. I spent hours in the fields, talking with the farmers, trying to understand them before I tried to change their methods. All the while I planned. Soon I would begin acting on my plans. But often I had this longing to be alone.

At such times, I wandered down to the river, sometimes to fish, sometimes to study the glide of water over polished stones. So it was that evening.

Fog lowered over the dusty banks with evening shade. Little tears of mist gathered upon the rocks. I sat by the river fishing, but I fished to be sitting, not to catch fish. Something about the water moves upon the mind. The rocks along the shore held the sun's heat, and I leaned among them, my feet dangled in the water, flickering just under the surface. A river carp slid up to nose my toes. I slapped the water once, and it twisted lazily away to the dark undercurrents. I felt at one with the river, its current sustaining the flow of memory.

It was something within me, like a darkness insinuated into my blood. It welled up from some past vacancy that had always lain there within me. Perhaps this new sense of belonging only made me mindful of how long I had felt otherwise as an outsider. A thick, tentacled weight dragged its feet over my heart.

This time I named it—loneliness.

It had always been there. Oddly, it took companionship and belonging to recognize it. At first I thought it was simply the inevitable other side to the happiness of this new home. Seeing Eldrad and Alsace steal secret glances, hold each other and love each other, informed me of what I knew only by absence. But that wasn't it entirely. They included me whenever possible in their games, their hospitality, their home life. They even gave me chores so I wouldn't feel like a guest or an outsider. Instead of alleviating the loneliness, their kindness sometimes seemed to abet it, reminding me all the more forcibly that they were doing this *for* me, not with me. At least, I perceived it so at times.

Seeing oneself as outsider places one forever on the edges, unable to penetrate either to the core of oneself or the core of the other. But I now understood that *I* had placed myself on the edges. It was my doing, and it prevented their undoing of my loneliness.

I dared admit something else to myself: Taletha had taken a large place in my heart. Something about her troubled me, more profoundly than her inability or unwillingness to converse. Sometimes I caught her watching me, and her eyes flashed with embarrassment. Occasionally, I accompanied her on shopping trips, although I found quickly that she had no need of my voice. She was quick, even shrewd and authoritative with the merchants, conveying more in the shake of her head and flash of her brown eyes than I could in words. I went with her only to be with her.

It was not my aim to gain the love of a woman; at first, only her respect. Perhaps that made all the difference. I find it easy to write that—years later, far removed from that land, a changed person in a different world. It is far too easy, for it is a judgment, and, while altogether true, it bears all the neat simplicity of a judgment.

The reality always works otherwise, of course, for reality is all too often a rude fumbling among confusion. Life itself seems like a game—not one we play, but one that plays us.

Nothing quite so summarized my relationship at this time with Taletha as confusion. Always before, what I had wanted I simply demanded. Then I would discover that I hadn't wanted it anyway. But the people I wanted more than anything in the world—Haggai and Doval—were ripped from me. I did not trust *wanting* again and had forsaken its other face, desire.

I decided I did not desire Taletha. This I told myself, forced myself, who would believe nothing, to believe only in the negative—not desiring.

There was no remarkable beauty in her, I told myself, not the kind that would set a man's head spinning, his feet stumbling awkwardly. But, just so, everything about her was beautiful. Her dark hair, often caught in a knot behind her head and held in a bright red scarf. Her skin the hue of polished wood. Her body so slim, and supple as a young girl's. But mostly her eyes, that flashed with such raw vitality.

A fisherman docked his boat nearby and waved. "You need a boat and a net," he called. "Only children fish from the shore." I waved, and he went away, carrying a basket of fish atop his head, balanced precariously with one hand.

My thoughts turned back, unspiraling like a scroll. I thought of the widow Admah and her two rambunctious sons. How long ago that seemed.

I wondered what would have happened had I stayed with Admah. Could it have gone on indefinitely? Need deepening to friendship deepening to . . . what? Looking back now, I saw ties growing there that I had not even been aware of—familiarity, domesticity, being cared for, and caring for others.

My mind continued working backward. At length it fastened upon her like something tugging at the line and hauled up to light through all the dark undercurrents of memory. It bypassed Melchior, Gaspar, Balthazzar—these with whom I had lived and might even have loved had things turned out otherwise. Without the madness of gods! It fastened on Doval. My heart, hooked and opened and bleeding hard, felt uncontrolled spasms of love and loneliness. I realized suddenly that only she had loved me as deeply as I had loved.

Oh, my daughter!

For one moment I nearly went wild. As if the rocks were walls closing in upon me. But the naming also brought peace. I knew my pain.

I knew also the cause. Had it not been for the Magi—cursed lot!—I might at this moment be with her. Had it not been for the Magi, I would never have known her. The paradox of loneliness and love.

Would *I* have been? *This* kingdom felt like my home. As if it always had been. These black-skinned, proud, beautiful people were my people now.

I rose from my fishing and walked back in the darkness toward the home of Eldrad.

I saw her in the distance, and for a moment in my distracted state I thought it was Doval and began to run to her. But it was Taletha, and when I drew near, I saw panic in her eyes. She seized my arm and pulled me urgently toward the palace grounds.

CHAPTER
SIX

Inside the palace, the guards had been shoved aside by the temple priests. Thick smoke choked the air. It rolled in clouds toward the windows.

A fire roared in the central pit and the blood of goats slathered the tiles in a sticky, slick mess. The priests babbled and waved their arms about, eyes bulging, as they carved the sacrifice and flung it upon the fire. Flames engulfed the chunks of flesh, sending off the clouds of smoke that stank like a garbage pit. The guards choked and wheezed by the windows.

We hurried through the throne room to the back corridor, unchecked by the miserable guards or the frantic priests.

Although I had lived in Jebel Barkal some time now, I had never been to the private rooms behind the throne room. Noting my hesitation, Taletha seized my hand and led me swiftly, with intimate knowledge, through the labyrinth of corridors.

It was quite literally a maze of walls, a room full of cunning twists and turns, dead ends and surprise openings. Taletha unerringly led me through to the stairwell. Lit by torches, it curved upward and crossed a small archway, leading to another upper-level hallway. From the arch I could see the maze below, twisting around the room, and I saw its purpose.

The entire palace had been cunningly planned as a system of final defenses: the great outer stairs, the outer hallway, the throne room with its open space and fighting parapets, and now here the crested archway from which guards could rain arrows upon an enemy stumbling through the maze. I wondered at this clumsy way to live, always having to deal with threats, imagined or real.

Taletha tugged my hand impatiently. She led me into the upper level hallway, past several doors, and stopped at last before one where two guards stood. Their normally impassive features were twisted into lines of worry. They moved as if to stop me, but Taletha brushed by them into the room.

Eldrad sat on a chair by the king's bedside, head in his hands. Komani was propped in a mountain of pillows, as if swallowed in silk. His body seemed a thin gray thing lying there. I could hear the labored groans of his breathing the moment we crossed the threshold.

A priest lay flung flat out upon the floor, his arms spread-eagled. He wore a headdress of brightly colored feathers and a loincloth of leopard-skin. I recognized him as the high priest, Wamala. We had to step over his prostrate form to get to the bed.

Eldrad lifted his head, his eyes red from weeping, and embraced us both.

"Alsace just left," he said. "I asked her to stay with the children for a while."

Taletha nodded. She bent by the bedside and lowered her face to Komani's outstretched hand. Her body trembled with sobs.

"He was walking to the throne," Eldrad explained. "I had to be there because it had to do with a trade treaty. The ambassadors were already there."

I nodded. Among the official duties Eldrad held was the position of Negotiator of Commercial Treaties, determining rates of exchange, pacts and routes with neighboring states.

"And then," he continued, "just as he was walking to the throne, he seemed to stiffen. Then he just caved in. Collapsed. The guards carried him up here right away. He can't move. Or talk."

I stared at Komani. His eyes were shut and his breathing a rasp. His color had drained, leaving an ashen pallor.

"How did they carry him through the maze?"

Eldrad looked at me in surprise. "Taletha took you that way?" he said. Then he smiled. "Of course she did. It's quicker for her. There is a back stair, though, that can be sealed off by rocks during an attack. Komani never takes the maze anymore."

"What can I do?" I asked.

Eldrad shook his head. The worry on his face deepened. I sat quietly in a corner of the room and waited.

* * *

Kurdash did not make an appearance until late in the day, lumbering into the room wheezing like an elephant. He shook off the support of the guards and stared at his father.

"Where have you been?" Eldrad asked. His voice was as sharp as a rapier.

"Busy," rumbled the big man.

"Preparing?"

Kurdash whipped his large head around and glared at his brother. Again I was mindful of the muscle under that bulky carcass. He was a fearful man. And hateful. His eyes blazed with it.

"Someone has to mind the state," he hissed.

Eldrad did not reply.

* * *

I felt like an intruder with Kurdash there. I caught Taletha's eye. She nodded and stood up.

The priest had long ago taken himself back to the temple, muttering about sacrifices. Alsace had come and gone once, promising to return with food for Eldrad, who refused to leave his father's side.

I walked out with Taletha and followed her back down through the maze. Her dark hair hung disheveled about her shoulders, reflecting in tiny red lights the glow of the torches.

Crossing the throne room, I reached for her hand. She jerked it free and whirled on me. "Hey," I said in surprise. "I just . . ." Her face softened and she turned toward home, but she kept her hands folded tightly before her.

* * *

Komani did not die. For a week he lay battling death. Eldrad faithfully spooned mashed fruit between his lips, tilting his chin and forcing Komani to chew and swallow. As long as the liquid mass slid down, Eldrad clung to his hope. Then, after a swallow, Komani's eye, his right eye only, flickered open. His lips trembled ever so slightly, as if trying to smile.

Incredibly, the king gathered strength during the following days. He looked like a pale semblance of his former self, aged almost beyond recognition, but his spirit battled for life. The left side of his face seemed rigidly frozen, the eye sealed shut and the left corner of his mouth inflexible. The paralysis extended a short way down his body to the shoulder and left arm. But he lived—a haggard, deformed, but living king.

Within a month he sat up in bed. He vowed to return to the throne, but in the meanwhile assigned most of his duties to Kurdash, who was seldom seen in the sickroom. Every evening Eldrad, Alsace, Taletha and I met there.

Often I sat in there and studied the remarkable, calm beauty of Taletha's features. I drank her beauty in like a thirsty man. Her cheekbones were high and flaring under skin of flawless brown. Her nose was straight and narrow, so unlike my own! She often pursed her lips, as if aiding her concentration. When she felt me watching, she turned her eyes on me, and they flashed with embarrassment. Other times, she let her gaze linger, returning my own. She would smile, a tentative flash of bright teeth and eyes.

But when I walked home with her, there would be silence, as if something crept up out of the darkness and chilled her soul. Sensing this, I placed my arm about her one evening. She stiffened involuntarily, then forced herself to relax. But as soon as she could, she darted into the house as if escaping me.

I cursed myself: a grown man tormented with the thoughts of a boy and behaving like such. I burned whenever I saw her, so that I could barely stand to look at her and could not bear to be apart from her.

By day I threw myself into my work with an urgency and fury I had never known in any task. It took me a full six months simply to arrange the details for building the granaries.

I exercised my newfound authority by appropriating a broad stretch of land, to the north of the temple, mollifying the high priest, Wamala, by pointing out that the granaries would, perforce, bring traffic to the temple, a renewed interest in religion and a steady flow of drachmas. He became one of my chief supporters then, publishing the need for laborers and materials.

Stone would be carved from a quarry north of Jebel Barkal and floated downriver. We would cut a canal from the river to the site so the stone could be floated as far as possible. I was looking for laborers to cut the canal, to fashion tools and to hew, haul, lift and mortar stone. I needed hundreds of them, all of whom had to be paid.

This had to be negotiated through Kurdash, who held the strings of the treasury. Surprisingly, though he loathed the idea of the granaries, he authorized the funds without comment. I suspected the influence of El-drad. While Kurdash generally approved my requests each time I asked after that, he did so grudgingly and with an attitude of condescension that made me feel like a worm he could crush underfoot any time he pleased. He made certain I understood that his very giving of the funds was an act of power over me.

It was during the time when we constructed the foundations for the granaries that I moved out of Eldrad's household into a small house in the village. Eldrad and Alsace protested. How could I tell them I could not bear being with Taletha? She was inscrutable, and it was not just her unwillingness to speak. Something stormed in her each time we met, and I felt responsible.

I left one morning in a matter of minutes. I could not avoid hurt feelings, and wanted to make the transition quick. I settled on terms for a small mud-brick house, just two rooms, near the gate of the palace. I made arrangements with a housekeeper for meals and cleaning, and that was it. I was on my own.

The months passed as I continued to assemble laborers and foremen. The details of the undertaking were mind-boggling; the individual projects necessary to start the larger ones were time-consuming. It took us nearly a year just to hew the short canal from the river to the plain. But I wanted it done right, not just a ditch cut in the ground—one that would wash out with the first rain—but a dredged and lined canal, built from the plain to the river as straight as an arrow. Its banks were reinforced with heavy slabs of stone to support the equipment needed to move granite and marble blocks. We took it one step at a time.

The temple plain yielded easily to excavation. We hit bedrock about twelve feet down and laid the foundations for four of the ten planned granaries before the rainy season interrupted our work.

The rains were feeble. Wind gusts swept the valley. Lightning cracked and thunder rocked the mountains, but the rain itself was scant. I sensed the drought coming. The coastal villages would not be affected drastically, but all of the huge central valley depended upon crops. I forced the laborers to work even during the rainy season and tried to loosen Kurdash's purse strings. Since I had not seen him for some time, I followed the formality of sending a messenger requesting an appointment.

When I went to see him that morning, I was amazed to enter the throne room and find Komani reclining upon a couch at the head of the steps. The throne had been removed to a side position.

After the days of smoke and ashes, the room itself seemed restored. Scrubbers worked upon the sacrifice-blackened walls. A light haze of mortar dust, raised by some workmen on the upper portico over the main entrance, sifted through the sun-shafts. They were replacing weakened stone, and their hammers rang out like a cry.

King Komani lay sprawled across the wide couch, blankets tossed around him like waves suddenly frozen into scarlet billows. Months of illness had enervated his body. Seeing me coming, he smiled crookedly, the paralyzed muscles forming a rude rictus of a grin. He flicked the wrist on his right hand. Noises slipped through the crooked mouth, and I took it to be a greeting. I bowed at the foot of the bed without hesitation and with genuine appreciation; I surprised myself.

"Enough," he gasped. "Don't bother. Here," the right wrist pointed toward a chair. "Sit."

The words came in urgent, breathy exhalations, the frozen lips only partially shaping the sounds. He called an attendant and had her prop him up on the pillows. It seemed to make his breathing even more ragged.

"Can I do anything, Your Majesty?" I asked.

"Yes, slip a little poison into my wine," he said. I wasn't certain that he was joking. "This old husk has carried my spirit around too long. Now they'll keep me alive here, I suppose, as long as they can."

"They want you to live," I said. "The people love you and grieve for you."

"Yes, yes. Well, the people," he muttered. "Tell me, Elhrain, can Kurdash do it?"

"What, Your Majesty?"

"Rule! Rule this kingdom."

I thought about how to answer him. Did he want the truth? Or comfort? I gave him the truth. "No," I answered.

"Yes, you're right."

He sat reflecting. His eyes closed, and I thought he was asleep. Then they snapped open. "How about you? Could you do it?"

"*Could* I, Your Majesty?"

"That's what I said. I have enough trouble talking without repeating myself."

"I'm not certain what you mean."

"Suppose I declared you king. Could *you* rule?"

"No, Your Majesty."

A wheezing sound that mimicked a chuckle slipped through his lips. I was staggered by the thought. The last thing on earth I wanted was to rule. Surely he jested with me. As if reading my mind, he said, "I'm quite serious, you know."

"Yes, Your Majesty."

"We'll drop it for now. Ah, Kurdash. What am I to do?"

I didn't answer. Evidently the king was baring his heart to me. Why, I couldn't imagine. Yet it affected me strangely that someone so powerful would talk to me like a friend.

"There is Eldrad."

"Yes. He is your friend, isn't he? He has told me of his affection for you." He was silent a moment, as if gathering his strength. His body looked fragile, mere skin and twiglike bones.

"But that would never do," he said. "Kurdash would crush him in an instant, and I could never subject Eldrad to that."

"But you would me?" The question was out of place. Komani chuckled.

"Oh, he would never crush you, Elhrain. You were born a king."

We sat in silence for some moments. He offered no further explanations. At last I stood.

"In fact," I said, "I came to see Kurdash about appropriations."

"Not necessary," Komani said. "It was only a formality anyway to appease Kurdash. Spend what you need. You're doing a fine job."

"Thank you, Your Majesty." He looked exhausted by the struggle to speak coherently. "I'll leave you now."

He raised a hand in dismissal.

Crossing the throne room, I thought of the smoky sacrifices that had

145

befouled the place only months before, leaving a fresh deposit of greasy soot upon the walls where the sunlight slanted through the high, narrow windows. Several of the guards nodded familiarly to me.

That's right, I thought, I am an official now. Minister of Agriculture. Well, I better go minister to something.

Past the throne room lay the intersecting hallways before the palace entrance. At the entrance stood Kurdash.

Was he waiting for me?

No attendants were with him. Despite his huge weight, I never suspected that he really needed them.

"How is he?" Kurdash asked.

"Quite well, thank you."

He frowned. "And what do you want here?"

"The usual. Settling appropriations."

"Yes, I heard. Well, see to it then. Although it's all a waste of time."

"Perhaps so," I said.

He wanted more. He wanted an argument, deference, something other than what he got.

I wondered what it was, what the design of this huge man was. But I had work to do.

There was one other meeting on that morning that, as I reflect on it now, formed a turning point in this twisted maze called life.

As I passed through the palace gate, I stood a moment at the threshold. Taletha appeared at the lower gate, climbing the stairs with her fresh, energetic step. She saw me and slowed her step uncertainly. Her hood was thrust back, the sun falling full upon her dark hair that seemed to blaze with light. She paused and smiled, walking more slowly up the steps to meet me.

I had hardly seen her during these recent months, having moved to my own house and become obsessed by my work on the granaries. I realized, suddenly, how desperately I missed her. For a second, time was suspended. The sun stood still. The hammers of masons on the upper portico seemed to fall silent.

I stepped through the doorway to meet her. She looked up expectantly from a few steps below me. She was glad to see me! I had a greeting on my lips when suddenly her face twisted in panic. A guttural sound wrenched through her frozen lips. She sprang toward me, even as I heard the sickening, sliding sound above me and tried to twist my head upward.

She tackled me around the waist, twisting her body so we tumbled sideways. Her strength was incredible. Pulling me, she rolled me over her down the steps. The noise rose to a rumble, and a hail of stone slammed against the steps where I had stood only seconds before.

We came to rest at the bottom clutching each other, both bruised by the fall. My body ached in a dozen places. I had tried to protect Taletha as we fell, but she had taken my full weight upon her.

I looked up. The board that the masonry stone had been piled upon tipped into space, caught a draft of wind, and tumbled harmlessly out over the steps. By the parapet I saw the face of a workman for a second. Then he disappeared.

Guards were flailing through the mound of debris, running toward us. I pulled Taletha upright. She rubbed her bruised shoulders with trembling hands and stared at the parapet.

"You saved my life," I said.

She fell against me, trembling and sobbing, as the guards stood about, uncertain what to do. I shouted at one of them.

"Some accident up there," I said. "Get that clumsy oaf."

Taletha grasped my face in both her hands. She shook her head violently.

"No?" I said. "No what?"

Suddenly I felt her fear, pulsing through the trembling fingertips that held my face.

"No accident?"

She nodded fiercely.

I stared into her wide eyes. "You mean . . . someone pushed it?"

She nodded. "I saw him," she whispered.

As I guided her back to Eldrad's house, a couple of guards approached us. The masons who had been working on the portico had simply disappeared. The palace mason claimed no knowledge of their work at all, assuming they had been hired by some underling.

I waved the guards off, telling them to forget it.

But I couldn't. Someone wanted me dead.

CHAPTER
SEVEN

I redoubled efforts on the granaries as the rainy season came to an end. The sky flung itself out like a blue shout of joy that echoed high over the land. Clear and pure, it rose up and up and grew thin and then cracked. A white mist fell through and settled over the sky like a whisper. Spun by unimaginable winds, it whipped out into gaudy patterns. A brave bird, red-shouldered and muscular, edged its way loose from a tree and stumbled into the sky. It circled and, finding a piece of wind to play with, soared high and higher until it shot into the sun, a tiny, red-flecked arrow launched by its own boldness.

The sun felt hot on my shoulders. The ground's heat rose, piercing my leather sandals like a palpable thing. I flipped up the hood of my old desert cloak, which I had taken to wearing while working outside. Many of my workers were wearing them now.

I walked down across the rise of the palace grounds to the great flat plain of the temple area. Already the laborers, under the coordinated efforts of my foremen, were in full swing, a vast human mechanism for moving, forming and fitting rock. The sound of hammers, of rock moving on log rollers, of the shouts of foremen and workers, filled the plain from temple to river. Barges were backed up ten deep waiting to unload rock. With the foundations laid the work would move more quickly now.

It made me feel good. This was my plan. My execution. But it was only a part of the plan. I had to train the farmers to grow extra crops to fill the granaries.

I walked past the temple plain to the promontory of rock along the river, from which height I could survey the farmlands.

A full year had passed since I began the project, and, while I took pride in the orderly pattern of work, something made me anxious to finish. Letting myself be consumed by work, I had seldom been in the palace since that day last autumn.

Old habits were hard to change. At first the farmers stood and grinned at me when I explained the methods I wanted them to use. Instead of whiling away the dry autumn months telling stories and sleeping, they needed to dig irrigation ditches. But they would come out in the morning, chip haphazardly at the soil for an hour or so, then find their way back to the village square. Nor did they find any advantage in the idea of a surplus crop. They would grow what they needed, they thought.

But what of the time when they couldn't?

Since the threat of drought did not move them, they needed another incentive. My answer lay in a game, for these people were obsessed by games. Like children they would drop their labor and cheer on runners in village races or match skills in dozens of competitions they had.

So I made a game of their survival.

I divided the workers into cadres and let them compete against one another. For the farmers there were competitions in use of the land—the best irrigation, the most land planted, the neatest farms and, ultimately, the best crop with the greatest donation to the granaries. For each, I provided stepped prizes, the largest cash awards—the chief being a single gold coin from my own purse, stamped with the House of Kush—going to the largest producer.

The attitude of the people changed overnight, not so much for the anticipation of reward as for the joy of competition. Whole families surged into the fields. They hacked at the soil, uprooted weeds, carried water, tended plants. But, most important, they did so with eagerness, singing their weird chants as they worked.

From where I stood on the familiar rock promontory above the river, the landscape looked entirely changed from the dusty, piecemeal plotting I had seen upon arriving at Jebel Barkal. It was a land now of green regularity, of neatness and promise. That in itself was a reward. The people were living *with* the land, rather than merely using it.

Even the fishermen were involved; for now, rather than having them dump the guts and scrapings of their catches back into the river, I had the mess immediately turned into the soil. Young boys from the farms made bargains with the fishermen for scraps and each evening carried huge, stinking baskets of entrails to the fields. For their task, the fishermen got a small cut of the anticipated produce from the land.

The people worked for themselves, for their land, but also together.

My gaze swept finally to the temple plain. The chaos of workers had also been divided into cadres of workers under trusted foremen. I had made one concession to the increasing urgency I felt. Rather than using large, cumbersome stone to build granaries that would last for decades, I permitted them to divide these into smaller blocks, which were thinner and easier to handle, and moved more quickly. With the thinner walls, I had to reduce the height of the granary from twenty-four to eighteen feet, lest the pressure of the weight of grain inside collapse the walls. After they were mortared, I had to let the mortar cure for months before trusting grain to them. Thus I left the conical roof, made of timber and wood shingle, until after the curing. Even when a granary was constructed, it would be nearly a year before it was ready for use.

I stood and almost willed more urgency into the cadres of workers. Each group of ten cadres, under the care of ten foremen, lay under the authority of a captain. I chuckled to myself, watching the beehive of coordinated labor on the plain. I had formed something worthwhile in military orders after all. Balthazzar would be proud of me.

Balthazzar! He was last person I wanted in my mind. I shook my head angrily and climbed down the promontory.

I could not forget him. He was in me, undeniably rooted in my soul, my mind, like some obscene growth. Magus who misled me! Father who forsook me! Friend who deserted me!

I found myself squeezing the amulet about my neck so hard my fingers hurt. Why, then, wouldn't I rip it off—the heavy golden bauble—and fling it to the muddy carpet of the river below? Bury it, as his bones lay buried somewhere under the blowing dust of the desert, picked clean by buzzards, bleached and whitened and dry and lifeless.

Yet he lived in my mind. I tried, while walking toward the temple plain to view the work on the granaries, to determine just how many years it had been since the day of that madness. The years all seemed to fade and fuse. The long sea voyage. The years in Tamal, the coastal village. The time here in Jebel Barkal. Had it been nearly a decade? Why then couldn't I rip the curse of his memory from my life?

* * *

The temple plain throbbed like a hive. Slowly but methodically the work progressed, clusters of workers meshed in one large design that only I fully understood. But it moved toward order. I walked among them to get a sense of the parts.

I kept walking, past the temple itself. Wamala stood alongside it—as he did every day as if protecting his palace—and scowled fiercely at the dust and noise. I wandered over to greet the crotchety old priest. If his little beetle eyes were any more sunken, they would stare out from the back of his head. They peered out from under his headdress, passing judgment upon the day. The day was not good for Wamala. They seldom were. The tufts of white hair on the end of his nose quivered.

"Do something!" he shouted.

"I am, Wamala. Oh, I am. And how are you this morning?"

"I'm wonderful!" He spat vehemently. "Just wonderful. I step outside to get a bath in dust. No wonder the gods are silent. They can't hear with all this clamor."

"Oh, they'll hear you, Wamala. They'll hear you. You're the best of them all."

He nodded agreement and turned into the temple, his anger placated temporarily.

I no longer had any problem with his gods. If they were not for me, they were his problem.

I needed a vantage point. From the bluff above the river, my favorite spot which had become a kind of outdoor office for me, I could see much of the work, but not all. I walked back past the temple to the west, sensing the ground elevate slightly. I looked up.

The precipice loomed above me like some dark, foreboding presence. Although the day baked under the sun's dry heat, I felt a chill course over my body. The stone of the mountain took on a sandy brown hue in the light. It seemed to pulsate with heat: thick, tumescent and disturbingly treacherous. I craned my neck back and stared up at the tiny point at the end of this stalk of rock. It arched out from the lesser promontory, leaning out over the plain.

The sand underfoot turned to broken rock, edges keen as knives, and sharp pieces of gravel. I kept walking. The slant of the rise steepened. I stood panting. The rock collected heat, encasing me like an oven. Heat waves shimmered out over the plain.

For the first time, I saw my plan whole. I seemed lifted above it, looking with the eye of a god upon a living model. The unfinished canal cut a straight line toward the river. I saw certain adjustments I could make in the positions of the granaries to share equipment and speed the task. I saw the stippled indentations of the four foundations beginning to rise now above ground level.

I couldn't believe that I had been in the kingdom of Kush, at the very foot of this mountain towering over Jebel Barkal, all these years and had never, not once, walked out to it. What subconscious fear kept me from it? Despite the heat, I again shivered uneasily. One had the feeling here of not belonging, of violation of something strange or sacred.

I began to walk back toward the plain.

* * *

By noon the sun-scorched sand hammered at the hood of the desert cloaks. The sun was a raw white blister. Dry air seared the lungs. I called the captains together to dismiss the workers. A full day's pay, nonetheless, I insisted.

A long cheer went down the line of workers as the news spread. They fanned out, some toward the shade of huts to sleep away the afternoon; some to the river to loll in its receding waters.

Tomorrow I would start them well before first light. It was back to desert ways, becoming creatures of the cool hours.

On an impulse I walked to Eldrad's house, hoping to find Taletha there. Preoccupied with my work, I had not seen her for several weeks.

Inside the shade of the doorway Alsace sat on the floor grinding grain. Beads of sweat dotted her face. She worked slowly, conserving energy. Alsace leaned back against the shadowed wall when she saw me coming. I noted with surprise that she was expecting another child. She saw my glance.

"Maybe you should rest," I suggested.

"Maybe I should time babies for the cool season," she said with a laugh.
"When do you expect it?"

"Him. Not an it. This will be a boy. In about four months."

"Is Taletha here?"

Alsace paused before responding, as if studying her words carefully.
"We haven't seen you for a while," she said instead.

"I've been busy. But I told the workers to take the afternoon off. I
thought I would too."

"That's nice." She pounded the grain slowly, as if weary of the task.
It was disturbingly unlike Alsace, who seemed to attack all her jobs with
unrelenting energy.

"Well?" I asked.

"She went to the river with Kanaha and Kenetta. To go swimming."

Kenetta? That's right. Their daughter. I had almost forgotten her, so
seldom had I seen her. Yet she was a growing child by now, two or three
years old. I would walk to the river. I had never been swimming.

* * *

I heard the happy shouts and shrieks before I reached the river. From
the promontory from which I habitually surveyed the land, rocky cliffs
angled down to the river. The sides of the cliffs were honeycombed with
small caves, worn by the river's winding. In the past, they had served as
dens for smugglers or for slave-runners. Long ago, Komani's forces had
cleaned out the scourge. There were no slaves in Kush anymore.

The rocks had also been worn down by long-ago rains, creating sluice-
like troughs that ran into the water. As I topped the ridge above the river,
I saw dozens of children sliding down the sluices, carousing into the river
in a white spray. Some children scrambled back up, carrying water in
earthen pots to keep the sluice wet. The rock was so hot that little wisps
of steam eddied into the air as the water struck it. The river was low;
patches of sand rose above the current. But at the bottom of the sluice
a deep pool still lay, its water roiled and muddied from the swimmers.

The pool foamed with children. I picked out a few I knew from the
village. There was Taletha, helping some small children float.

Kanaha stood at the top of the sluice, his body already tall and muscular
for his years. He grabbed a bucket of water and tossed it down the sluice,
positioned his little sister Kenetta at the top, gave her a powerful shove

and shouted happily as she shrieked down the slide, careening into the pool in a glitter of spray. Kenetta flung her little arms about. Taletha stooped over to pull her up; water cascaded from each of them. As she reached forward, Taletha slipped on the uneven river bottom, falling headlong with Kenetta in her arms. They bobbed to the surface laughing happily, as small children splashed water at them.

A tall, muscular man, younger than I, stood up from the pool in which he had been sitting. Sitting down, the water had risen to his neck, and I had mistaken him for one of the children. He laughed loudly as he stood, and the water streamed over his chiseled frame. He reached out one powerful arm, caught Taletha and pulled her upright.

He seemed to hold her. Long. Too long. She flung her head back, letting water run off her raven hair, her teeth flashing with laughter.

Was she leaning toward him? Or was she just off-balance?

I had been walking down from the bank, surprised now to find myself at the river's edge. Small children stormed about my feet. They were angry at me because I had stepped upon the principal building of some sand city.

The man, in one easy scoop, lifted Taletha. She clung to his neck, shrieking. The children laughed. "Throw her! Throw her!" they called.

The water rose to my knees. The man lifted Taletha high, her laughter rising toward the sun. He made as if to throw her, tossing her outward, catching her at the last instant, lowering her tenderly back into the water while the children groaned. It was an act that took incredible strength. Yet it didn't deter me for a moment.

I surged forward, envy a demon raging in me. Taletha staggered backward at my passing. I caught the man unaware from the side. I shoved his shoulder, knocking him off balance. The river bottom was all uneven here with rocks and sinkholes. He must have tripped over a rock, for he tumbled sideways, arms out, splashing into the river. Even as he fell, twisting to look at me, I saw his laughing face change to bewilderment then anger.

He exploded out of the water. I waited him. "Keep your hands off her," I was saying. But suddenly Taletha stood between us, her face as set as rock. Her eyes bored into mine, hard and intense as arrowheads. "You big . . ." she began.

The man behind her began, suddenly and overwhelmingly, to laugh. The river banks rang with his laughter. Taletha hesitated, then flung her head back and laughed also. The children joined in, frolicking and splashing, then kicking water at me. I stood like stone, anger turning to bewilderment.

The man stopped as suddenly as he began. He wrapped one arm around Taletha, leaned forward, said to me, "You thought . . ." and started laughing again.

My fury gave way to embarrassment. I don't know why. For that very reason, for not knowing, I was embarrassed. They were laughing at me! Children. This . . . this imponderable woman! This handsome young man.

I had seen him somewhere before, somewhere at the palace, where I had spent little time lately. During that time, he had met Taletha. Of course. Why not? What could I do?

Taletha's anger had faded, replaced now by a gentle smile. Was she mocking me? She had every right. I felt like a little boy, and like a little boy, I turned to go. Let them laugh.

The man reached out a hand, stopping me. He wasn't laughing anymore.

"Elhrain," Taletha said, "surely you remember Arabia?"

I studied the man's face. I nodded. I couldn't place him.

"He's Alsace's brother. My brother-in-law. There," she pointed at a cluster of children behind him, "are his children."

"You've seen me at the palace," Arabia said. "I am in the palace guard. Although," he added, "there would be no reason you would recognize me. All the guards look alike." He smiled at the comment so often made about the guards. But I did recognize him, and he wasn't just a guard. He was a captain of the palace guard.

"I'm sorry," I said. I turned and climbed the side of the rocky bluff. I tried to get out of there as fast as I could, with what little bit of dignity I had left. My face burned like a coal. I only slipped twice on the treacherous rock. No one laughed.

CHAPTER EIGHT

D espite my sense of urgency, the granaries rose slowly. Another year passed before I saw the first one completed. Five more of the ten that I planned stood roofless, the mortar still curing.

I exhausted myself in labor, as much as to escape the torments of my past as to prepare the people. But they too began to sense the urgency; for the last growing season had not been a good one.

During the planting season the rain had been late. The earth grew so hot that when the rain finally came, the water seemed to evaporate as soon as it hit the ground. Either that or it sluiced off the rock-hard soil, gouging dozens of broadening rivulets that carried soil and seed to the river.

The precious seed, which I had gathered so carefully, disappeared.

To the east of city, among the hills leading toward Tamal, I had crews working among grapevines. They lugged water in great flasks from the river, trying to keep the vines alive in a battle against drought. On the few trips I made east of Jebel Barkal, I nearly despaired. The grapevines, so promising a year or two before, clung to their trellises with cracked brown tendrils.

Then the winds came. Never could the people remember such winds. Day by day, the wind battered the young crops, breaking foliage, searing the tender stalks. It came out of the north and west, traveling across miles of desert, collecting heat and force. By the time it hit Jebel Barkal, it seemed a wind out of the mouth of hell itself.

The fringes of the jungle showed the toll also. In the west the green shrubs bent to the earth. Leaves fell early from the trees, torn by the wind, wearied by aridity. The western hills, once wrapped in dense green, were now dusty brown.

Increasingly, vagabonds from those regions made their way to the city for help. They came slack-skinned, the bellies of the young bulging from malnutrition. They came in rags and with little else except for stories. They told about how the jungle was dying. How the animals disappeared. How there was no water. They told how many of them had died on the way to the great city of Jebel Barkal and begged, please, could the city help before they all died.

Eldrad set them up in a squatters' village on the south side of the city. He did not want them near the fields, the river or the granaries. Here he could manage them and their food needs. Here the refugees huddled under makeshift tents in ever-expanding numbers.

And the people of Jebel Barkal became ever more fearful for what they had. And what was threatened.

My great fear now was that I wouldn't finish the granaries in time. I had stored surplus crops in the one finished granary, topped to the brim, but also in whatever protected spaces I could find—in a few empty homes, in vats, under tents. But stored in such a way, the surplus could not be governed or protected against rodents and locusts. I needed the granaries finished.

The kingdom of Jebel Barkal seemed to be holding its breath, awaiting either a death rattle or a gasp of hope.

King Komani seemed a mere shell of his former self—a thin bag of bones and feeble muscle, part of his body and face slackly paralyzed. Yet somehow, he clung to life. His eyes burned with a powerful will. But I seldom saw him; I had a job to do.

So did Eldrad. I saw him less often, and missed him desperately. While Kurdash kept to the palace grounds, eager for the day when he could assume the throne, it fell to Eldrad to effect the king's rule in the kingdom. While Kurdash saw the emissaries who came to him, Eldrad went out among the people. Increasingly, he found signs of anxiety.

It wasn't just the unsettling weather. A mood of tension gripped the people. They greeted Eldrad with eager questions about the king's condition, and averted their faces when he told them. Eldrad inevitably carried the tension back home.

* * *

"I wish I knew what he was doing," he said when we walked together to the river one evening, after meeting by chance at the palace gate. His voice was raw, almost a bark.

"Who?" I asked.

"Kurdash! What he's up to."

"Nothing, insofar as I can tell. He hides in the palace."

"If that were the case," Eldrad said, "I wouldn't worry. But the people fear him." He stopped, shoulders slumped from weariness. "This shouldn't happen," he said. "Kurdash has spies throughout the kingdom. His police or henchmen. Call them anything you want."

"And?"

"It's his job to collect taxes. But he has his men spying on people. Why, just yesterday I found an old man accused of withholding taxes. These . . . these henchmen, they entered his home at night and ransacked it. Oh, they found some hidden coins, accused the old man and beat him."

"Have you talked to Kurdash?" I asked. "After all, you have as much right as he does."

"Yes, I have talked to him. No, I don't have as much right. Kurdash says it is his task . . . to keep the people honest. Who cares if an old man hides a few coins? But I *don't* have the right! Kurdash is heir to the throne, not I."

"Does Komani know this?" I asked. "He still lives. He still rules."

"Scarcely does he rule. And, no, I wouldn't tell him. I want to protect my father. Something like this goes against everything he has practiced. It could be just what it takes to . . ."

"Kill him?" I finished.

Eldrad nodded. I saw tears on his cheeks as he stared up at the full moon. He seemed utterly weary, nerves played out.

"I want his last days to be peaceful," he said. He looked at me. "Is that asking too much?"

I thought back to that conversation I had had with King Komani two or three years ago. "Your father doesn't want Kurdash to succeed him," I said. "He told me so."

Eldrad nodded. "I'm well aware of that," he said. "But there's nothing to be done. To break the rule of lineage in the House of Kush, well." He spread his hands hopelessly.

"Kurdash would be a disaster," I said.

"Yes." He paused a long time. He sat back against the rock, watching the thin crescent of a moon dim and brighten behind a screen of cloud. We both watched it, mesmerized by the silver loneliness of the night, while we talked.

"I had a sister I've never known," Eldrad said. "I wonder what she would have been like. Maybe that's where it all went wrong—allowing her to marry a foreigner, breaking tradition. Still, she had my father's blessing, and some say she married a god."

"Do you believe that?"

He laughed harshly. "I don't know what to believe."

The dark loneliness of night plays tricks on people, breaking down the reserves we so carefully erect during daylight hours. I suddenly felt compelled to ask him about Taletha. I had seen her all too seldom during the last few months. Since that day at the pool, I felt awkward, like a shamed boy, a buffoon. Sometimes I told myself, so what? Who cares? But when I saw her I always sensed a slight reserve. I didn't know how to tell her my feelings because I scarce understood them myself.

I decided to chance it.

"There's something else I wanted to ask you about," I offered tentatively.

Eldrad smiled wearily. "Go ahead," he said.

What could I tell him? How at night I lay on my cot and saw her face in my dreams. How I sometimes wandered the city hoping to catch a glimpse of her. And then, when I did see her, how I stood at a distance, afraid even to meet her.

Those dreams—how mingled and troubling they were. Sometimes I saw Taletha's face, smiling and open to me, then it merged with Doval's, looking at me with eyes as wide and haunted as death, Kruspian's scimitar at her throat. I would awaken then, sweating and trembling.

Eldrad waited, a half smile on his lips.

"It's about Taletha," I muttered. "I wonder about . . ."

Eldrad's weary smile broke into a grin. For a moment I saw my dear friend before me, not the haggard administrator. "Taletha, is it?" he said with a twinkle in his eye. "I was wondering if you would ever get around to that."

"What?"

"Man, the woman's in love with you. You are about as dense as rock not to see that."

"What?!"

"You're blind, Elhrain. We've been wondering how long it would take you. And how long she would bother to wait for you."

"But . . . your father."

"What? Doesn't approve? A quirk of his. Don't try to second-guess Komani. In his own way, he may have been nudging you." He studied me for a moment. "You're a free man, Elhrain. Don't be blind—the woman loves you."

"How do you *know?*" I insisted.

"Look, Elhrain. Taletha is a sister to us. More than that, she is Alsace's best friend. Some things don't need words. But she has talked with Alsace about it."

My head reeled.

"How long has it been since you've been over for dinner?" asked Eldrad.

"I don't know. A month or so."

"Too long. We're both too busy. Tomorrow we'll see you, and maybe you'll start doing something."

* * *

That night Komani's condition slipped once more, irretrievably, it seemed, toward the abyss of death.

Eldrad himself came early the next morning to get me. I was at the temple plain supervising the roofing of the second granary. I saw the despair on his face instantly and turned the work over to the cadre foreman.

"The king is dying," Eldrad said simply. The words chilled me, however long I had expected them.

"How can I help?"

"He has asked to see you," Eldrad said.

The request stunned me. "Shall I change my clothes?"

"I don't think you have time," said Eldrad. "Please hurry."

When we hurried past the temple, I heard, echoing from within, the eerie lamentations of the priests rising toward the blistering sun. One priest prostrated himself at the temple entrance before the sun. Blood ran down from his forearm and pooled in the sand. I shivered as we passed. The offering of blood.

At the palace I was surprised by two things. First, that Taletha was there also, kneeling by the king's bed alongside Alsace. She lifted her head and smiled at me through tears. Even then I wondered what Eldrad or Alsace had said to her about our dinner tonight, a dinner that would never happen.

The second thing that struck me was Kurdash's absence. I asked Eldrad where he was.

"Attending to the affairs of state," Eldrad said bitterly.

We stood by the bed and began the death watch.

Kurdash entered once, at noon. His huge body seemed a dark cloud, an intrusion in the room. He stood there uncertainly, surveying the room. He seemed unnerved by it and left shortly.

Toward midafternoon Komani's breathing turned to a harsh rattle, like heaves of storm breaking in upon the long silences. Each time I expected that frail, twisted figure to succumb to the silence; each time, somehow, he battled back.

When he failed to do so, it took us by surprise. Eldrad started. He leaned forward, peered into his father's eyes, then closed them gently. He fell forward, weeping, across the spent form.

"I'll tell the priests," I said. Eldrad nodded and I left.

Whatever Komani had meant to tell me, whatever he had meant to summon me for, would remain forever untold.

* * *

I was going to leave by the side entrance, avoiding the maze that Taletha had shown me long ago. A guard was posted there. He asked me to follow him. I didn't protest. The stupor of loss lay upon me. Until I realized our destination and stood looking up into those eyes full of dusky cunning.

If anything, Kurdash had grown even more obese. His eyes, mere slits in the puffy folds of his face, peered out malignantly. His robe fell sloppily across his body, layers of flesh seeming to spill out of its folds. A nearly animal odor emanated from him, a stench of fire and grease.

He sat on the throne like a preposterous pretender.

"Is he dead, then?" he asked when I stood before him.

"Yes."

Kurdash nodded. His eyes closed briefly.

"I needed to talk with you, Elhrain."

"I am here," I responded. I could not bring myself to the courtesies of the court. I refused to bow or kneel before this sickening sack of humanity. I had come to loathe him.

Irritation flickered across Kurdash's eyes. He took note of my indifference. The people had grown to fear him, and the rumors that had been passed about in the fields gave good reason. The people spoke the name of Kurdash with a shiver.

"You're a proud man, Elhrain. I find myself wondering if you're too proud to accept a gift."

"A gift?"

"Yes. Perhaps your life." He rumbled on now, as if he had rehearsed his lines. "You see, the people begin to talk about you, Elhrain. They think you bring a curse."

"That's hardly true, Your Majesty." Yes, I uttered the words. "Were it not for my efforts many would be dying."

"Ah, your granaries. Yes, but it was all a trick, you see."

"A trick? I don't understand."

"Well, to have their rations, of course, a fee must be paid. The people resent it."

"I never set a fee. I didn't even know there was a fee. The people produced it. I saved it. Let them have it."

He rumbled with laughter that choked in his throat like water behind a dam. He cleared his throat and spat mightily to one side, striking a guard on the leg. This induced more laughter. He lifted his hand and pointed; the guard ignored the slick trail winding down his leg. I recognized him as Arabia. His face was rigid, but his eyes burned.

"You did it!" Kurdash exclaimed, turning back toward me. "But with whose money? Who really built the granaries? I did, with the taxes I collected, that's who. Of course the people pay a fee, you fool. There's no such thing as a free gift in the government. But, you see, the people hold you responsible. Of course it was all a trick. They think you brought the curse."

He leaned forward, breathing heavily.

"Had we granaries before?" he hissed. "Of course not. We had no need."

"It was inevitable," I said. "There had been droughts here before. It's in your records." I kept trying to sense Kurdash's point. He habitually laid deceit upon deceit, trick upon trick. I wondered if even Kurdash could keep track of his own lies and puzzles.

"Oh, yes," he said. "Of course we had droughts. Peasants died. We took their lands and resold them. Now! Now, we have . . . granaries!" He spat the word like a curse. "Besides," he said, "no one remembers the old times. Too long ago."

"You had an offer for me?"

"Yes. Yes." His voice slid to an oily tone. "A hundred drachmas to see you on your way out of here. Back to Tamal. To a ship. Back to where you came from."

"You yourself just said it, Kurdash. There are no free gifts. What do you want?"

"Your accursed self out of my sight, foreigner!" His voice rose again, as changeable as the wind. "That, and the possessions that belong to the House of Kush."

"Meaning?" I knew exactly what he meant. Now.

"The medallion you wear. Stolen, bribed, bought from the House of Kush. It belongs to me!" he screeched. His body shook in a paroxysm of anger.

"No, Kurdash. It doesn't. It belongs to me."

"Were it not for that accursed father of mine, and that fool Eldrad, I would hang you with it." He reached ponderously over the arm of his chair and hoisted a goatskin bag. He lifted it and held it in one hand. "A hundred drachmas, foreigner. Take it and leave." He hurled the sack at me.

It landed at my feet, bursting open. I slid the coins aside with the side of my foot. "Your Majesty," I said as obsequiously as I could manage, "I am not yet ready to leave the kingdom. I have people to worry about. Nonetheless, I am more than ready to leave the court."

I turned my back on him and walked out, fully expecting a weapon to be buried in my back. Instead, the guards stood rigidly and let me pass.

CHAPTER NINE

The purge started in March, only days after King Komani was
embalmed, wrapped in white linen sheets and placed in the Tomb
of the Emperors at the northern end of the temple.

The mausoleum was a low building of white marble that had been
quarried far to the north. Komani's body was carried through the grieving
crowd, past their eerie wails and sweat-streaked bodies, past the dust
kicked up by shuffling feet enacting the death dance. It was carried on a
bier by the palace guard, those stone-faced men, with Eldrad leading the
procession. In a position of honor at the head of the body bearers walked
Arabia. His powerful shoulders flinched not a bit under the weight.

Prince Kurdash, now King Kurdash, followed on his throne. Eight
strong men carried the poles on their shoulders, trying hard not to grimace under his ponderous weight. The burden of the chair alone was
sufficient to bend the back of an average man. But these were not average
men. Each was tall, with a body that seemed chiseled out of stone. Each
fixed his gaze dead ahead and did not bend or flinch. Guards surged about
the entourage, beating back mourners who, hoping one last time to touch
the body of the dead king, darted too close to the funeral bier.

As he rode above the crowd, Kurdash the king gazed upon the crowd
scornfully. His eyes, fixed in their fleshy sockets in the round, bulbous
head, stared straight ahead as if plotting. His body, draped in a crimson

robe and bedecked with royal feathers, jiggled with each step of the carriers. When the entourage reached the gate of the mausoleum, the guards guided his chair slowly to the ground. Kurdash rose, a mountain of black flesh, and waited for attendants to stand on each side of him. Then he walked ponderously to the mausoleum door. He violated custom even then. He handed the key, attached to his belt, to a guard and ordered him to open the door. The guard hesitated. The crowd gasped audibly, the wails dying out in bewilderment. Only the king and the high priest were permitted to touch the Tomb of the Kings. Kurdash waved the guard forward. The man unlocked and unbolted the heavy door with trembling hands.

The priests, led by old Wamala, stood aside as the massive doors swung open, hinges groaning. A ray of morning sun fell into the open mausoleum, illuminating a large, gold insignia inlaid against a block of marble at the rear. The twined serpents, backs flared, lay suspended forever in fiery gold—the sign of the House of Kush. Absentmindedly, I fingered the amulet under my vest.

Kurdash didn't bother to inspect the chamber, as was the custom, before waving the priests forward for their purifying rituals. The priests entered the tomb nervously, peering about, as if a sacrament were being broken and they were about to be struck dead. They muttered their chants, flung incense smoke about the death chamber and backed out holding hands over their faces. Komani's body was lifted to its place in a low, shelflike vault, the door slammed and bolted, the people dismissed. They stood about, confused and uncertain for a moment, then wandered away. The streets fell as silent as the tomb itself.

All this I observed from my place at the fringes of the royal family, there by long association.

The younger priests, who had gouged new cuts of grief upon their forearms, prostrated themselves to the ground, flinging dirt upon their bowed heads and bent backs so that the cuts congealed in a dirty plaster.

I did not much care about rituals, but Komani had been precious to me. I grieved for him and for the people's violation. Now I felt fear rise in those people like a tangible thing. It seemed they were drowning in fear. Uncertainty violated everything they once knew as ceremonious.

The violation had only begun.

In the morning three heads hung upon the spiked poles before the palace gate—a warning to traitors of the kingdom. It was a ceremony of vengeance that I had not seen enacted in all my time in Jebel Barkal. And now, in one morning, three of them. The objects of this new ceremony of vengeance were none other than three of the chief priests of the temple. Among them I saw the head of old Salaam Oblah, his mouth fixed in the rictus of a scream, his eyes already gone—gouged out or plucked out by birds, I could not tell. I did not recognize the other two. Somehow old Wamala had escaped retribution.

I rushed into the council room, expecting the royalty and elders to be there; I wanted answers. The room was vacant. I turned toward the throne room, but the door was barred and guarded. When I protested, the guard on duty simply shook his head. He refused to speak to me. He denied my presence. My anger turned to cold fear.

The world seemed changed overnight. A reign of terror began. I knew even then that it was only a matter of time for me. I strode through the palace, desperately seeking Eldrad. He was not available, I was finally told by an attendant. He was in the throne room. It was not to be entered.

Within days a cloud of stark fear had permeated the palace, a cold, chilling thing. It emanated from that grotesque pretender to the throne. A darkness, massive and distorted as his own body, seemed everywhere present.

It should not have bothered me. My life had been lived in the midst of palace intrigue. But always, especially in the Palace of the Magi at Babylon, I had been one of the untouchables. Babylon too had seen the battles for political power, the deadly purges. There too stakes before the city gates had held the heads of enemies, a royal proclamation written in blood that dissent would not be tolerated. But I was the untouchable, and these affairs of common people were petty things that did not concern me.

The common people did concern me now, I realized. I now thought like one of them, not like one of the untouchable elite. It was a shocking revelation to me as I wandered the dark corridors of that silent palace. I too was susceptible.

*   *   *

I left the palace for the only secure place I knew. My work.

A weight seemed to lift as my feet were drawn to the old, familiar promontory of rock by the river from which I could survey my workers.

I clambered up its rise, mounted it, stood and looked out . . . upon vacancy. A hot wind blew across an empty plain.

The three finished granaries stood like a mockery. Two more had the roofs half-finished. Piles of rock lay scattered in place. It was as if some virulent plague had struck, killing off all life and leaving behind these circular monoliths to confound future generations. It was a landscape as vacant and lonely as death—my death, for this was my life.

I wandered to the granaries, feeling like some grim voyager of distant shores. The wind scurried about deserted huts, then fell silent. As I wandered, I was distracted by a noise in one of the worksheds. I walked toward it, noticing the absence of tools that customarily littered the work area. Even the ropes had disappeared. It was as if the work here had stopped years, rather than hours or days, before.

In the workshed I found one of my cadre foremen, a large and quiet man named Al Shabah, staring at a litter of broken forms. He kicked a scrap of wood aside.

He looked desolately upon the smashed forms for squaring the granite blocks. He didn't even turn when I entered.

"Al Shabah?"

He looked up at me with blood-shot eyes, full of . . . what? Anger. Sadness.

"It is more than a building," he said.

I didn't know what he meant. The workshed?

"They don't understand," he said bitterly. "When men come together, and they work like this. They sweat together, and they work together. And some are inspired by their work. They do great things, true things that others see and follow. Together they see the rocks rise, slowly, like a living, growing thing."

His voice cracked. He picked up a piece of wood and waved it at the granaries.

"Like a child," he said. "You raise it and care for it. It's part of your life. These are not just men working. They are one body. That's the shame!" he exploded.

He hurled the stick against the wall of the shed with such force it rebounded against his own kneecap.

"Why?" I asked.

"Why?" he said. "Why?" He fell to his knees, his hand running restlessly across the sand floor. He made a choking noise, like crying.

"I mean, why did they all leave? Who did it?"

"During the night," he said. He lifted aggrieved eyes to me. "We were given until daylight to disappear."

I could guess the origin. He certainly hadn't waited long. But what insanity was this? It was a death sentence if . . . *when* the drought came in full force.

"Don't they understand?" said Al Shabah as if reading my mind. "They aren't just killing the project. They're killing the men who gave their life to it. That's what they don't understand."

Yes, that too. It was a death sentence to the hundreds of men who had labored here, supporting families. My workers—all gone in a night. Where did they go? Back to the withered jungle? Impossible. To the desolation of northern deserts? No. Perhaps to the coast, with nothing but hearts full of broken dreams.

"Madness," I muttered.

Al Shabah choked out a laugh. "Yes. Oh, how right you are. Madness." He began laughing hysterically, flinging handfuls of sand about the littered hut. I left him.

Across the plain, worksheds stood vacant. The tools had disappeared with the men. The wind moaned in the vacant doorways, and it seemed to be crying.

Answers! This time I would have them.

* * *

But it was not Kurdash I saw. I didn't even get near the throne room.

As I strode toward the palace grounds, I saw Eldrad stomping down the palace steps. His dark face seemed nearly purple with outrage. He saw me and angled across the grounds to intercept me by the gate.

The vein in his neck seemed to swell and throb with his anger. He placed a hand on my shoulder to stop me, and his grip was like steel.

"You're not going in," he said.

"Oh yes."

"No!" It was a command. "No, you're not. You don't understand."

"That's exactly why I'm going to see that fat, bloated sack."

"Stop it!" he shouted. "Don't you see? Even now I'm taking a risk. In there . . . I wouldn't stand a chance."

"Taking a risk? You mean . . ."

"You're in danger, Elhrain. How blind can you be, man? He's been plotting all day. You have to get out of here." His grip on my shoulder had not relented. He steered me away from the palace.

At that moment, I did see. In Jebel Barkal I was an outsider. A coldness slid through me. An outsider as dispensable as any worker or any priest.

Nonetheless, I fought it. "You can't mean it, Eldrad. Leave you and Alsace and the children? Leave my work?" Especially, I wanted to add, Taletha.

"There is no more work. For my sake, Elhrain, there is no time to lose."

"But—"

"Taletha?"

"Yes."

"You must take her with you."

"*She's* in danger too?"

"Don't you understand?" Eldrad pleaded. "It is a purification. Kurdash wants to remove all foreign influence."

"That's right. Taletha is also . . ."

"Not of our blood," finished Eldrad.

Yes, I did see. I should have been first to see, first to *have seen,* years ago. Now the facts fit.

By slaying the priests the terror turned inward. It would strike the people in their hearts. Rip out their beliefs and their security.

By uprooting the workers, Kurdash would destroy a unifying direction. And so many of the workers came from outside the kingdom. Thus, the purge—a demented cleansing of the old race.

But especially, and most dangerously, he would root out the foreign influences in the highest places. Elhrain. Taletha. Cancers in the royal family itself!

"There's not a minute to lose," Eldrad said.

Suddenly he seemed mindful of the fact that we were standing in the open court itself. He grabbed my arm, pushing me out to the streets. "Alsace has your things packed," he said. "I took the risk of sending her a message through Arabia. We have two horses hidden by the river."

"Two horses?"

"One for Taletha. Quickly."

"I don't need anything," I said. "I'll go now."

"Don't be a fool. You'll need money. Alsace has it ready for you. And . . . she wants to say farewell."

He had turned me behind the houses in the direction of his own.

My mind whirled. Flight! Not again. But even then the old feeling of distrust surged up. Where is he leading me? To a trap! I can trust no one but myself!

I looked at Eldrad, hurrying next to me. His gaunt face was set like a flint. As if reading my mind, he said, "It will be short. But it is my fight now, Elhrain. As long as I have breath in my body I will fight this. But my way. My way only. Still, I thank you for all you have done for me. And I will never forget you."

Tears thickened behind my eyes. How could I mistrust him?

We turned the corner to his home.

* * *

I recognized them, but I did not know their names. They had always been . . . just soldiers, palace guards. I never thought of them as individual men, having personalities, lives of their own, wives and children. They were what they did. Their function now was clear—to arrest me. The leader stepped forward from the door of Eldrad's house as a dozen of his men stepped out at his signal from nearby alleyways, surrounding us.

The leader bowed formally to Eldrad, who stood next to me with shoulders slumped. Even then I wondered why he didn't rage against them—order or counter-order. I wondered again if he wasn't part of it.

Then I saw the reason. Behind the captain stood Alsace, holding their infant in her arms, the two older children hiding fearfully behind her.

It had all been calculated so that there would be, *could* be no resistance. And I knew the cold and cruel mind of the calculator.

"You've come for me?" I asked.

The captain nodded.

"Well, get on with it then," I said.

I felt powerful arms twisting my own behind me, lashing my wrists with rope to lead me like an animal on a leash. I turned with one comfort in my heart. I had not seen Taletha there. Perhaps she had already fled to the river.

Or, perhaps, she was already in custody!

My mind reeled. For an instant I turned back, twisting against the ropes. A guard jerked viciously at the rope, wrenching the muscles in my shoulders. But in that backward glance, I saw Eldrad on his knees in the dusty foreyard. Tears were on his face, but also a look of terrible wrath.

Stumbling under their shoves and the pressure of the rope, I was hurriedly led up the palace stairs. Entering the throne room, the captain pushed me forward so that I fell to my knees before the throne.

"Grovel, Elhrain. Crawl to me." His voice was a thick hiss.

I refused to answer or even to look at him.

"How long I have waited to have you thus, you arrogant, slimy . . ." Kurdash's words sucked off in a breath as he heaved himself upright from the throne.

His sandaled feet stood only inches before me. The flesh fell down his legs, covering the sandal straps that climbed his mountainous calves. The edge of the white robe brushed my face.

"You . . . pretender. Bow to me!"

The guard pulled on the rope, twisting my arms. The pain pulled me down, face to the floor before those stinking feet.

"Still arrogant? For fifteen years I have wanted you thus." His voice was a high whine.

Fifteen years! That long?

"Bow!" he screamed. I sensed the rush of the scepter, tried to avoid it, felt it smash against the back of my head with a force that drove my face into the stone floor. When I tried to lift my head, blood flowed into my eyes from my forehead. I was dizzy from pain. My forehead throbbed like a white fire. Blood thickened my lips. I spat and saw with satisfaction the spray of crimson on the hem of Kurdash's white robe. Then the scepter fell again, and there was darkness.

Vaguely, I sensed them lifting me. I heard cries uttered merely as sounds.

Then came a shout.

"Wait!" Kurdash's voice was a snarl in the throne room. The guards held me, dangling above the floor like a rag doll.

"The necklace!" he hissed. "Under his cloak. It is *mine!*" One guard ripped the necklace off. I felt suddenly naked—flagged and defeated—without it, especially when Kurdash's voice rose like a bull roar behind me as the guards dragged me over the stones out of the room. I twisted my neck around and saw him raise the necklace skyward and bellow between rumbles of laughter, "Elder brother! Indeed!" His voice rose to a maniacal howl.

It sounded like the death cry of the desert hyena in my ears.

CHAPTER
TEN

The guards dragged me down a long corridor that led off the central hallway into a dark tunnel. The tunnel sloped downward. Jagged rock walls narrowed around us. The floor was slick with ooze. Torches hung in wall sconces, casting a feeble light against the darkness and filling the air with a choking smoke. The air was dense, unmoving, in the bowels of the palace.

The tunnel opened at last into a wider area before a thick wooden door. Two guards fumbled with the bar securing the door. When I looked up, someone kicked me. I twisted, taking the blow on my ribs. Voices muttered, cursed. The door swung open.

More steps led downward. My body bounced as they dragged me over the steps. I tried to take the force of the jolts on my hips and thighs. The air turned fetid and damp.

They stopped to light a torch and fumbled at the lock of another timbered door. The hinges groaned. The guards cursed under its weight.

"Better to just leave it open," one guard said.

The others laughed.

"Busy enough," one agreed.

I did not recognize these guards. Kurdash's men.

The corridor beyond was thick with ooze; the floor, puddled and muddy; the passageway, narrow. The walls pressed inward, curving up like a cave hollowed out of subterranean rock. We passed a door, and as the light fell upon it, a moan rose from the other side.

Insofar as I knew, the dungeon had never been used in Komani's time. Now, wails echoed from the black vaults like cries from the dead.

They stopped before another door. More fumbling at the lock. A guard sliced his sword through the ropes on my wrists and flung me in. I recoiled when I hit the muddy floor edged with jagged rock. I tried to stand but fell to my knees, head hanging, gasping.

The door slammed. The torch disappeared with the sound of booted feet. The groaning of the far door echoed down the corridor, and then there was an emptiness as thick as the earth itself. The moans diminished in the cells.

I screamed into the blackness, "Eldrad! I'll get you for this, Eldrad!"

Someone muttered in a cell nearby, the words indistinguishable through the rock and wood. Then there was silence. Silence unimaginable. A drop of water splashed at the far end of my cell, and it seemed an avalanche.

I thought there was another person in the cell, but it was only the ragged heaving of my own breath.

I leaned back against the slimy wall, and let the darkness take me. I wanted it. Wanted its oblivion. I needed to escape from the world gone insane. From Eldrad, my betrayer.

* * *

When I awakened, I expected it to be miraculously morning. This place disappeared. Light. I wakened to nightmare instead. As thick as liquid lay the darkness, broken only by muted curses and moans.

I reached out a hand from an arm that ached from the movement. I felt bruises covering every inch of muscle, so that my hand seemed oddly detached out in the darkness somewhere. The fingertips tingled, as if touching something more tangible than nothing. The air itself seemed palpable. I needed definition.

I stood, spreading my feet slightly in the slime that threatened my balance. Hands raised, I probed the blackness, taking one step, then another. It was like wading in the dark, except that even underwater light pierces the closed eyelid. Here there was only a solidity of blackness, more profound than the blackest night.

Tentatively, I stretched one hand, feeling ahead with my toes, maintaining balance. I felt the wall rising even before I neared it. It seemed to palpitate with a living ooze. Years of underground seepage—possibly all the way from the river—seemed accumulated on the wall in a thick mucus.

Something stirred under my fingers! Small living bodies moved. Slugs. These shapeless bodies lived on the ooze like a wall itself. I withdrew my hand nervously, wiping my fingers on my sodden cloak. Under the stirring, shapeless creatures, water trickled.

I moved in the other direction, finding the side walls drier and firmer. By the thick wooden door, I found a dry spot on the floor where I huddled as if hiding from the slime.

* * *

I awoke feeling hungry. My body was a living fire of pain, but the pain of hunger seemed most intense.

How long had I been here, in this place that knows no day or night? I was aware only, and very suddenly, of this terrible hunger. With it came thirst. As if my body dared adapt to the horror, it reminded me of the routine. It was a mockery. I denied it. You are dying, I insisted, and you dare thirst!

Yet it persisted.

Would they feed me? Any of us?

I called out, hoping someone in this charnel house of darkness would answer. I could not bear being *alone!* "Answer me!" I screamed.

Through the thick walls came some dull, inarticulate sounds, moans of pain. A stronger voice cursed.

"Do they feed us?" I shouted. My lips were swollen from thirst, and they cracked as I spoke. Suddenly it seemed terribly important. To starve to death in this black hole? What a tragedy.

The stronger voice cursed me.

Why feed us? Those brought to the dungeon would see the light of day only upon their execution. It would be a taste of freedom before final imprisonment in death.

I would not capitulate! Vengeance saved me once. It would again. Hatred was a more powerful emotion than fear! I would hate perfectly until the moment I died.

Food! I thirst!

Very well, water I had. I crawled to the sunken end of the cell, feeling the cold slime under my hand. I pressed down, letting a little moisture slip through my fingers into my palm. I lapped it greedily like a dog.

Laughing, I shoved a hand down into the slime and pushed it into my mouth. And fell back, choking and retching at the foul stuff in my throat.

I huddled back against the dry wall, sobbing through dry eyes and a dry throat.

* * *

In the darkness my mind began to work backward, crawling down corridors of memory. I could not stop it. My mind fastened on Eldrad. Maybe he had been threatened: the lives of his family for the life of the foreigner. Nonetheless, I was betrayed.

But, my mind insisted, why should he? The guards could have taken me *any* time. They had no need of Eldrad. And he had been leading me away from danger.

But he deceived me! Led me into the trap. I hate him.

Did he?

To avoid the questions, my mind careened further back. Balthazzar. Him also I have hated for betraying me.

Did he? And what *was* he about to say at the fire in the desert that night before the madness?

Eldrad, my brother!

Balthazzar, my father!

Delusions of a mind in darkness. Wish fulfillment, and, like all my wishes, unfulfilled.

In a moment, in a terrible shock of recognition, this other truth from days long past struck me. I *wanted* a father, someone to turn to with the everlasting *why*. Balthazzar!

Not even his name had entered my thoughts for years, buried by an act of will so deeply it wouldn't leak out, unearthed now by fear and bewilderment. We had sat across from each other over the sputtering fire in the desert. How he had struggled for words to say it: "The fruit of a king's daughter and a Magus!" It is too late not to tell the truth, he had said. But he had had no time to speak the truth, which I could only guess at and which, therefore, lay buried deep in the tomb of my memory. "The

Seeker." Balthazzar the Seeker. Was he the father I had never known? Why couldn't he have told me? Torn between royalty and commoner as I now was, why couldn't he have told me! Forget what I *believed*; I *needed to be told*.

What had he said? "King and Magus." Had the quest been more important to him, than my father was to me? He had warned me about the land we had set out for. "Bitter enemies" he had called the people. Ah, you're my enemy, Balthazzar, for not telling me enough.

But he had no time, a part of me wailed out. "Your father!" another part screamed. I dug my fists, muddy and ripped, into my face. I didn't want to think about it! Didn't want to think! King! Magus! *I* was the enemy now. Had Kurdash, the consummate deceiver, known all this from the start? And was it true? Balthazzar my father. The lost sister my mother. I—heir to the throne of Kush.

Suddenly it all made sense. Just when the world went mad, and all sense was destroyed.

* * *

I don't know how long I slept. Time had lost meaning. From pain and weakness, I seemed to keep passing out. When I awakened next, my stomach felt on fire from something in the offal I had shoved in my mouth. I craved water to quench the fire inside. I crawled to the low end of the cell, carefully palming water from the slime, sucking it in to avoid pieces of debris. Each drop moistened my parched throat and cracked lips.

The weakness moved from my stomach and crawled through my body. That's right. I had been on the way to Eldrad's house for dinner when they seized me. How long ago? No, Eldrad could not have deceived me! He would not. The look of fear on Alsace's face! But Alsace was not Eldrad. Who knows what he had done.

Maybe . . . nothing.

I was famished. I reached out a hand to brace myself against the wall. My fingers fell on the squirming ooze along the rock. Slugs!

Tentatively I took one between my fingers. I held it for a long time before my lips, wondering how to do this. A quick swallow? But I would choke. I thrust it into my mouth, biting down once, hard, on the oozing body. Swallowing convulsively, I choked it down. I fell to my knees, gagging, gasping for water to swallow the lump caught in my throat.

My hands fell on a hard, rounded shape. I touched, probing: a snail. I had seen them along the river. I smacked the shell against the rock, plucked out the body and ate that too. It was firmer, and I swallowed it easily. Then I crawled back to the dry part of the cell, hunger still twisting my stomach.

* * *

I awakened to the dull grating moan of hinges.

They have come, I thought. Now it's all over. The execution.

I heard no other sound in the corridor. Wait! A shuffle of feet. A whisper.

"Elhrain."

Silence. I dared not answer.

It came again, closer now, at the very door. "Elhrain."

I stood. "Is that you?" This is what I meant to say. The words sounded, even in my own ears, like the groan of a dying man.

A key grated in the lock. In my desolation, it seemed like a storm of noise. The door swung inward.

I shrank from him, from his mere presence. Then he knelt beside me, pressing a flask of water to my lips. I sucked at it greedily. Eldrad pulled it away from my clutching hands. "Not too much," he whispered. "Here." He pressed something into my hand, moist and plump. "Figs," he said. "Chew them slowly. Then we have to get out of here."

Fighting the temptation to gulp them whole, I forced myself to chew them, letting the juices accumulate in my throat, swallowing, sucking nourishment. A banquet. I felt the energy work in me.

Eldrad lit a small candle. The light seemed blinding. My eyes clung to it, greedy for the light. "Don't look at it!" Eldrad commanded. "Look to the side."

He peered around the cell and sucked in his breath. I heard him groan at the sight of it.

"How long have I been here?" I asked. My body was limp. I needed time, strength.

"Three days. I came as soon as I could. We're in danger even now. As soon as you think you can . . ."

I struggled to my feet. "I'm ready." I swayed in the darkness for a moment, one hand on Eldrad's shoulder.

"It stinks like death in here," he said.

I took a step and staggered. Three days! It seemed a year. Or a day. Impossible to tell. Was it night or day outside?

"Easy," Eldrad said. "Once we go there is no stopping. Make sure you're strong enough."

He handed me the flask. This time I swallowed sparingly.

"Taletha will go with you. She too is in danger. Horses and supplies are by the river. You must go north from there."

"North? We'd never make it. It's all desert."

"It's your only chance."

"Tamal? By the coast."

"That's what they'll expect. There are troops all over the coast, doing Kurdash's . . . business."

"And you?"

"Let me fight this my way, Elhrain."

"Let me kill him."

"No! That is Kurdash's way. If truth . . . justice . . . can't prevail, then . . ."

"We are all in hell."

"I'll find a way."

I grasped his arm, found his hand. "Thank you," I said and took the key from him.

"What are you doing?" Eldrad hissed.

"Letting some others out."

"We don't have time to think about them!"

"I'm not. I'm thinking about us. About you."

"Diversion?"

"Precisely. If I'm the only one missing, where do you think they'll look?"

"Quickly, then."

I unlocked a door, flung the bar to the ground, heaved it open on groaning hinges. By the light of Eldrad's sputtering candle, I saw a shape hunched like a white sheet on the floor. I kicked lightly at what I took to be a leg, and shivered at the recoil. I leaned forward with the candle.

The man was dead.

Eldrad retched behind me, falling to his knees. "How did you stand it?"

he asked. "How?"

I looked at him, and for the first time he held the light of the candle to my face. He withdrew it with a shudder.

"Diversion or not, we have to get out of here," he said.

"No. You must be protected."

"They'll come for me anyway."

"Not if I can help it."

"What do you mean? What can you do?" Eldrad's voice was a panicked rush of words.

"What I said. I'm going to kill him."

We checked the next cell. The man was living. Barely. He staggered to his feet, blinking at the candlelight like a crazed creature, eyes starting from a gaunt face. I saw myself in him and shivered with fear.

Quickly I opened another cell. The man was stronger, more recently interred in this grave of humanity. I gave him the key, handed him the flask and some figs and told him to free the others. Eldrad and I hurried back along the dungeon.

Behind us we heard the sound of the man gorging himself on the figs. He choked. By then we were at the dungeon gate.

I heard a lock turn in another door behind us and nodded at Eldrad. He set the candle down on the floor, leaning it against the wall. We passed through the gate and climbed toward a thin trickle of light above us.

My footsteps were slow and uneven. Halfway up the stairwell, I bent over gasping for air. The food Eldrad had given me twisted like a cold lump inside, and I was afraid I would vomit. The rock walls of the stairwell pressed against me.

"We have to hurry," Eldrad said. He pulled at my arm.

I clung to him, climbing up. The very act of moving energized me. "Where are we going?" I hissed.

"I drugged the guards' food," Eldrad said. "But it can't last much longer."

Again, I sensed a trap. There were too many guards. I pulled his arm. "Drugged? How?"

"Sleeping powder in the evening meal, the porridge." Eldrad fixed me with a glance. He saw the questions in my eyes. "Elhrain, trust me. You are going to die anyway if you don't. What do you have to lose?"

I cringed. He saw through my doubt. Of course, he would. He knew my heart like a brother. "Go on," I said. My breath came easier now. The muscles felt looser, warmer; the cramps were easing away.

We squeezed through the doorway into the corridor. A pair of guards sat slouched over, as if stunned by sleep. We crept forward as quickly and soundlessly as we could. The entire palace seemed a prison now, everyone in it our enemy. We had only broached the first level. At the end of the corridor a guard lay sprawled out, floored not by sleep but by a blow. Blood trickled from his temple and lay pooled about his head on the floor. I looked at Eldrad. He nodded. "He wasn't tired enough," Eldrad muttered.

"Kill him," I said. "Or lend me your sword."

"Not necessary."

"But if he awakens and remembers you."

"I'll risk it."

The noise from the dungeon suddenly seemed to erupt. The living dead had awakened, and fury moved the pitiful men to the stairwell. I had no idea how many yet lived in that stinking pit. Surely one could not live there long. But those who had been freed were making no effort to be silent in their escape.

Or they could not. Chains that had been beaten loose rattled on the stairwell. A feral growl rose from the men.

Eldrad and I turned and raced up the corridor. It had seemed interminable when the guards had dragged me down it days before. My legs felt played out as we reached the end.

Desperate as I was for freedom, I looked back.

Far below, a wall of gray men surged through the dungeon door and into the corridor. They staggered uncertainly, desperate for one moment of freedom, one glimpse of light, before dying. Their hair hung wild as a nightmare. Eyes started blindly in the light. Some still dragged chains from wrists or ankles. Blood and filth caked their wasted bodies.

Without pause, their leaders seized the guards' weapons and unceremoniously slew them. They grabbed the torches off the wall and began staggering upward.

Eldrad tugged me into another doorway. I protested, driven by instinct toward the main gate and escape.

"You'll never make it there," he ordered. "Follow me."

The passage led back down, and the old fury of deceit rose in me. But

I followed. The passageway opened onto the side of the palace courtyard.

Stars spun in the black sky. I sucked in the night air like a man drawing his first breath after being held underwater.

Eldrad led me alongside the palace toward the river.

"I know the way," I protested. "Get back to your family."

Suddenly a light blazed in the palace. Flames licked at the windows. The tapestries had been torched by the rampaging prisoners. Shouts echoed through the great hall.

"Listen," Eldrad hissed, pushing me forward. "Under the bluff by the river." I nodded. "There is a cave, a recess at water level. Fresh clothes are there. Some of your things. Food. Money."

In a flash an idea crossed my mind. I didn't know if it would work, only that I had to try. It was so preposterous that I dared not even outline it to Eldrad. For once, I ordered him.

"Wait," I said, "the priests. Do they still favor the House of Komani? Or are they in Kurdash's pocket too?"

"You mean the priests that are left."

"Whoever. Are there any you can trust?"

"I think so."

"Then you must do this. Get as many of them as you can. Have them stand on the temple plain at sunrise and blow their horns."

"What!"

"Can you do it?"

"I don't know. Time . . ."

"Right. Jebel Barkal is mad. There is no time. But do it. Don't ask me why."

"I'll do my best. Hurry now. You have to get away as quickly as possible. Beat them, Elhrain." He laid his hands upon my shoulders, looking into my eyes. "Take Taletha. She is waiting."

My heart jolted. Yet I had to ask him, "You won't come along? You? Alsace?"

"We can't. Our fight is here. Wish me well."

Those strong arms on my shoulders pulled me to him, clasped me—stinking and filthy—to him in an embrace.

In one deft movement, Eldrad slipped something over his head and draped it about my neck. Instantly the weight felt familiar, reassuring. I lifted the heavy medallion upon the golden necklace, recognized it like a lover—a part of me restored. I glanced up, questions on my lips.

Eldrad was gone.

A scream sounded through the palace. Fires flared in an upper room. Figures scurried down the front stairs where guards met them. The clash of weapons rang shrilly in the night.

Already my mind whirled with the impossibility of escape. I needed a plan! I ran on through the night, driven by the instinct for freedom.

CHAPTER ELEVEN

The village seemed deserted, as if the people had disappeared from its streets. I knew they cringed with fear inside their huts, trying to escape the terror by sitting in the dark, pretending, like children, that it would soon go away. As I ran toward the river, the clamor of the palace grounds grew muted; the flames flickered to a red glow behind me.

By memory and touch I traced the switchback trail that cut down the rocky bank below the familiar promontory. I moved slowly, despite my haste, allowing the idea I had had to form into a plan in my mind.

A hand plucked my sleeve.

I heard horses stamping softly in the damp ground.

Taletha pulled me to her, embracing me. I raised my arms to return the same, and she suddenly broke away, laughing.

"What's the matter?" I asked.

She kept laughing and raised two fingers to her nose in a universal gesture and pointed at me.

Had I grown so accustomed to my own stench! For stink I did. How could I not, plastered from head to toe with mud, ooze and caked blood? How could anyone stand to be near me?

Taletha pointed at the river, still laughing. Couldn't the woman be serious!

"We have to hurry," I said.

"Yes," she replied in that low, guttural voice. She shoved me, and I toppled to the river.

I stripped off my filthy rags and flung them aside. The necklace caught for a moment and glittered furiously in the moonlight. The medallion! I paused and hugged the heavy medallion about my neck. Oh, but it felt comfortable there, its golden weight warm against my flesh.

How had he taken it? Had the sleeping drug affected Kurdash also? How had Eldrad dared creep up to that creature, lift that bulbous head and undo the medallion?

And why? Was it the act of a fool? This denial of . . . What? A birthright? Thereby, surely, he had jeopardized himself.

No, I thought. We had given the other captives freedom, such who still lived anyway. In so doing, we had also given them a reason for living— defiance, ransacking of treasures. They had torched the tapestries! And if the medallion were not found among them? Would Kurdash dare accuse his brother?

It wouldn't be found. That would drive Kurdash insane. How he had coveted this . . . this weird symbol, which was meaningless to me, save as a gift from a dead Magus, a remembrance of one whom I had wished to blot from my memory.

So Eldrad laid his own maze to torment Kurdash, still a pretender to the throne. In that instant I understood. Eldrad had taken this risk for one reason only: to begin to restore order and to place it where it belonged. It was all true, then. I was of the House of Kush. Here I belonged, but I was fleeing.

I smiled into the darkness. Oh, but this world is a warped and bewildered place!

While I washed, scrubbing at my skin and hair with the fine river sand, Taletha got some clean clothing out of the cave where the supplies were hidden.

The rocky shoreline was speckled with such caves through here. Some were mere recesses, others deep and wide from years of the river's abrasion. Over the years, they had been used by smugglers, by people on the run, even by casual travelers who could not afford an inn. There were so many caves that only a careful search could cover them all, but I had no doubt that such a search would be mounted. In fact, the caves would probably be the first place that Kurdash's troops would look.

We needed a diversion. My plan took shape.

But first, I had to rest a moment. My body, especially after bathing in the warm river, trembled with weariness. Taletha had the horses saddled and ready, but she also had set aside bread and figs and a flagon of wine. I sat on the cave floor, leaned against the wall and stretched luxuriously. Enjoy it, I told myself. It would be the last rest for a long time.

The moon slipped between wisps of cloud and silvered the river. The low, sluggish river looked like a field, solid enough to walk upon. Indeed, parts of it, dried by the drought, were solid ground as the water slipped through underground channels. Here before us the water pooled in a bend of the river.

The light reflected into the cave. For the first time I saw Taletha as more than a shadow. She rested on her knees, leaning forward, studying me. Her brown eyes were nearly luminous.

I chuckled. "Do I smell better?" I held out my hand.

Taletha took it and nestled beside me.

I could have stayed there forever.

I kept tossing the idea through my mind, looking for weaknesses. It was full of them. It was stupid, insane. But the alternatives? We could go to Tamal; I knew the area, and the coast represented final escape. But Kurdash would expect an escape to Tamal for those very reasons. Or, second, we could go north; for to the north was vast desert, stretching aimlessly and impossible to patrol closely. But they would patrol it, and the drought-blasted desert would only invite a few extra days or weeks before death. So, the coast it would be. So Kurdash or his generals would think.

Of course not, surely not, to the south or west. The south was a ravaged wasteland of jungle; wild animals crept to the very edges of the city. And the west was blocked, of course. Blocked by the towering monolith of rock, by its arching rocky spine tumbling down into further drought-ruined jungles. The west, of all ways, was the worst way.

Besides, no one could scale the monolith.

"I have to unpack the horses," I said.

Vigorously she shook her head, pointing toward the north.

"No, listen." Her face paled as I explained my plan. Even as I tried to do so, it seemed impossible to me. Yet it was the only way I could think to give the people of Jebel Barkal a chance. To give Eldrad and Alsace a chance. For I was utterly certain that it was only a matter of time until

Kurdash plotted an excuse to heave Eldrad into that same dungeon. I owed him the chance at least.

"Quickly," I said. "We must leave now—right now—or everything fails."

Taletha nodded. Her hands trembled on the reins of her horse, but she set her face bravely toward the night. I paused there among the rocks, watching the silver moonlight flooding her face. "I love you with all my heart," I said.

Her answer was a whisper. "I love you too," she said.

Moments later we rode the horses back toward the center of Jebel Barkal, gliding along dirt paths I knew as well as my own hands.

We each carried one pack, formed from our heavier desert cloaks, slung about our shoulders. Squeezed into them were provisions, some clothing and a few tools. Into my own I placed a small leather sack of seed grain, thoughtfully stowed by Taletha into the larger packs. It had been my life here. I wondered for a moment if it would be worth the effort, but I decided finally to take it as a memento, if nothing else.

We had strung together as many water flasks as we could carry, tied about the throat and cinched tightly to belts about our waists. This was the most precious thing we carried.

I also bore a purse under my tunic, where it flapped heavily against my stomach. In it was a random supply of coins and jewels that Eldrad had scrounged out of my gear. Some of them I had carried since the day I left Babylon years ago. Save for the few coins I had used in Tamal, I had never had need of valuables, so I had all but forgotten them.

All the rest of the provisions—the more civilized clothing, the extra tubes of dried figs and meat, the water casks—had been left at the cave.

Although the packs and waterskins seemed to weigh us down, we rode easily through the night. I felt rested now, full of nervous energy.

We neared the palace grounds and reined at the west corner. The fires inside the palace had been put out. Guards and soldiers milled on the grounds. Orders were barked into the night. At one gate a log fire burned to light the area. Soldiers had formed in ranks, horsemen alongside of them. They were preparing to sweep the village. Down a side street I saw torches bobbing from troops already sent out.

I touched Taletha's arm and pointed past the main gate. That was our route. She nodded. The packs I wore seemed suddenly very heavy. I wanted to leave Taletha out of it, but they had to believe both of us were in flight. We had to attract everyone's full attention. I sucked in a deep breath, kicked the horse's flanks precisely at the same moment as Taletha and thundered down the street.

In a moment we flashed by the gate, through the milling hordes of soldiers. Several jumped out to stop us. We wheeled the horses directly at them. I felt the satisfying thud as two of them didn't get out of my way quickly enough. I shouted, screamed. But it was unnecessary. The torches were swallowed in our wake as men came running.

The sudden gallop had the effect I wanted. The palace horsemen were momentarily caught up in a melee of bodies at the gate. We were far ahead of them as we thundered to the city's edge. I glanced at Taletha riding next to me. She seemed born to a horse, her body fluid with the gallop, merging with the powerful animal. Her face in the moonlight was intense, lips parted. "She enjoys this!" I thought. She seemed in a trance.

Suddenly, feeling my glance, she pointed. Troops patrolling the edge of the city had milled into the street. They stood with weapons raised like a wall before us. I shook my head. There was no stopping now. I kicked my horse harder, forging into the lead. Sweaty foam flecked back over my body. I felt the animal's muscles strain as the road bent uphill to the higher grounds east of Jebel Barkal.

The men fell back as I charged upon them, preferring to heave their weapons rather than be run down. I ducked as an axe spun by me and felt blows upon my legs and upon the horse as we thundered past. My horse faltered. But Taletha charged alongside, and the horses swept on, leaving howls of anger behind.

As we neared the village edge, I veered slightly to the north, remembering the vineyards I had so painstakingly nourished there. The rows appeared on the hillside, dark tangles spreading to each side. I hauled back on the reins, and Taletha followed my movements immediately. In a moment we were off, slapping the nervous animals on to gallop up the hillside.

Even as we raced down the rows of tangled vines, their dry branches plucking at our shins, the first horseman surged past. Men on foot ran after him. Voices screamed in outrage. It was chaos.

We dashed back down a row and headed back to Jebel Barkal.

Already my plan was breaking down. Or, it had worked too well. I wanted one vast surge after the horses to the east, toward Tamal. I was convinced that our terror-stricken horses, relieved of our weight, would lead them far out before faltering. We would have all the time we needed, then. But the chaos in the village was profound. Men surged down narrow alleys, clustered together in knots at intersections. Shouts and orders and torchlight filled the night.

I steered Taletha to the outer edges of the village, an unfamiliar part to me. Here the close-packed huts gave way to the rude tents of vagabonds and refugees from the drought-stricken lands to the south. They had staked out a few meters of ground and scavenged for scraps to live on. Here and there goats brayed. People stirred.

We slowed to a walk, darting from shadow to shadow to conserve energy. I felt my body weakening, but we had to make it across the village. We had to be at the monolith—be upon it!—before daylight to keep to the plan. We were wasting too much time darting about this litter of tents. I guided Taletha back to the village itself, willing to take our chances.

We turned up a narrow street clogged with carts, baskets, storage casks. We darted through the darkness, into the twisting maze of an alleyway that wound like a serpent's body. Every time we hit a clearing, I scanned the heavens for the stars that pointed us west. It seemed we were running in circles. At one such clearing, a small communal square for butchering, I noticed a dull red pall in the sky ahead.

We were heading back toward the palace grounds. Back to the fires.

I lunged down a narrow alley to the west. Taletha panted behind me. We broke into another of the seemingly random squares, peered down the intersecting alley before crossing and saw the glare of torches approaching. I pressed back against a doorway.

"Soldiers!" I whispered.

Taletha shrank back. She bumped something. It tumbled to the ground. A ladder.

I looked up. The houses here were larger. Often the second story served as a kind of patio. During a good season, figs would be hung to dry on trellises on the patios. Trays of brick would cure under the sunlight. Some of the patios actually held gardens. For these, the villagers used ladders to scurry up and down.

I raised the ladder against the building. We scrambled up, and I drew the ladder up behind me. I just about had it raised over the rooftop patio when a guard shouted, having seen the movement. I froze, motionless.

Feet pounded toward the building.

I wrenched the ladder up, carrying it across the rooftop. Immediately seeing my aim, Taletha grabbed the other end. Weighted by the ladder, by the packs at our backs and the flasks slapping about our waists, we raced down a row of adjoining roofs.

We came to another alley. Raising the ladder upright, I let it fall across the space, praying that it would reach the other side. It thudded firmly against the flat roof. Slowly we crawled out across the space. There could be no hurry. The wooden rails seemed to sag under our weight. The wood groaned. Behind us I heard the shouts of the guards, pulling themselves up to the rooftops we had crossed. They had dropped their torches, following our sounds like dogs on the chase.

We set foot on the other side. I gave the ladder a pull. Its weight, spread out over the alley, was too much for me. It crashed, clattering on an ox cart below. At least the guards couldn't cross without climbing down.

The rooftops undulated in a long flat line. In the night sky I could see the monolith rising to the west. We ran headlong, leaping the short distances between houses, clattering noisily across the tiles. Then we hit the end of the long line of houses, not at a square but at the plain itself, leading to the temple and, beyond, to the monolith.

I swung over the side of the house, dangled and let go. I turned to guide Taletha down and felt, more than saw, a man run around the corner of the house. One guard had anticipated. He ran on ahead while his fellows had scrambled up to the rooftops. He had taken the chance and guessed right. He drew his sword, breath heaving. He saw his glory at that moment. There would be no calling out for others. He wanted the trophy for himself.

He lunged out, his sword ripping through the night with a long sighing sound. He chuckled as I dodged and stumbled. I circled out of the way. Don't lose footing! I whirled, looking for something—anything—to fight back with. The sword hissed again and the guard chuckled. Had he not been out of breath he would have had me. I stumbled out of the way, feet catching clumsily at some rocks. I sprawled backward, head banging against the wall.

I looked up and watched his sword rise. Oh, he took his time! Enjoying it.

Above him a white object seemed to flutter momentarily like a bird. Taletha stood on the edge of the roof, gathered herself and leaped with feet rigidly stretched before her, landing with full force upon the guard's back. His breath exploded. His body slammed forward, colliding headfirst against rock-hard ground.

I bent to him. His forehead was split open and blood streamed down his face. His eyes were wide and staring and turned into little red pools when I turned his body over.

I ran to Taletha. "Are you okay?" She nodded, stunned. She refused to look at the guard.

"You had to," I said.

She nodded again, trying to rise.

"You saved us both."

"Just get going," she hissed.

I grabbed her hand, and we ran down across the plain.

Twisted and solitary, its scaly rock flung like a cry against the darkness, the butte jutted from night-cloaked hills and shadows. It seemed to ripple like a snake as clouds writhed across the face of the moon. Then the clouds bunched together, the moonlight shut off like a wick, and there was only this sensation—a purely physical sensation—of dense rock ahead.

At least this part of my plan had worked. All sounds of pursuit had been lost at the plain. The guards that had pursued could not be sure it was us they chased; we might have been just some vagabonds. They had never gotten close enough to identify us. Perhaps they had turned and joined forces with the others heading east.

And the guard who fought us? Maybe the other guards wouldn't find him in the darkness. Maybe they wouldn't spot him until morning when it would be too late.

Maybe! My head whirled. I breathed deeply, trying to relax. We sat high on the gravelly slope, sipping from water flasks and chewing figs. I was weary, so bone-tired I couldn't even think about the climb ahead. Taletha lay back on the broken shale and seemed almost instantly to fall asleep. I had decided to rest an hour or more before attempting the climb. For once we started, there would be no rest. Either I reached the top, or died trying.

And still I fought for an answer to the question she had asked: "Are you sure you want to do this?" Not, "Do we have to do this?" We didn't.

We could go north or south. To the north there was hard rock giving way gradually to the desert sands, almost impossible to track for many leagues. And who knows? If we had taken the horses that way, ridden them to death, we might have made it to freedom. But to the north also lay desiccation so profound it sapped the life out of a person in no time, an endless maze of aridity. And to the south, the blight was laden with starving beasts roaming the edges of the village by night, hiding in the hills by day. No, we would do this. Climb this mountain. Go west, if my plan worked.

But the *why* of it! That I could not fully put into words. It was a miracle enough that Taletha trusted me without explanation.

I could have given a reason. I wanted to do something that would give Eldrad an edge. Something so brash, so foolish and yet so dangerous it could not help swaying the people. If I could not kill Kurdash, I could nonetheless destroy him. That plan was still taking shape in my mind.

But this other reason I could never give, not even to Taletha. My need. By overcoming the mountain, I would overcome another—Balthazzar. There in the darkness, munching the soft pulp of a fig, I understood. It had been there in my mind since the first moment I had laid eyes upon this grotesque monstrosity. It was the mountain of Balthazzar, God of the Mountain. And I, the god's son, would meet a father and overcome an enemy upon it.

I shivered. The night had grown cold. I shook Taletha awake. "It is time," I said.

She shook herself groggily awake and sipped from a flask. "No," she said.

"We have to! It's our only escape!"

Her halting speech seemed to take forever, as if each word required enormous concentration, an act of will.

"Not for me. For you only."

"I can't leave you."

"I . . . cannot."

"Cannot! What do you mean? Of course you can. Follow me. I will guide you. Just step where I step."

She shook her head.

"Taletha. It's only earth. I am an earth-master!"

She stared at me with searching eyes. They clouded with a film of tears. "I am . . . afraid!" The words came out like a wail.

I seized her shoulders. "Taletha," I said, and my heart seemed to split open, "I could not live without you. Please. It is our only chance."

She fell into my arms, sobbing. I felt her head nodding against my shoulder.

CHAPTER TWELVE

From a distance, the mountain one hopes to climb stands like a mere upthrust of rock against the sky. Nothing seems dangerous; nothing seems unusual. It is there: solid in mass and sharply defined. One simply begins at the bottom and works to the top, like an awkward flight of steps.

From the mountain itself every perspective is redefined. Its mass is overwhelming. Defiant. Rising like a dark mockery against the sky, it breathes reproach. Who are you, little man?

And the surface that seemed so even, so smoothly tilted, now reveals itself as a maze. The facing is weathered and brittle. Toeholds and finger-holds disappear at a touch into a landslide of gravel. Angles that from a distance seemed to curve up now seem instead to lean outward, defying gravity.

Even height seems different. Judged from a distance, the height of a man against the mountain does not seem like much. But climb to even that small height on the mountain, and already the earth seems to tilt and spin.

This is the way one climbs the mountain. You start with the first step and enter the maze. For the first twenty or thirty feet you skitter across loose shale, the ground shifting at every step. It's like walking on water, except you don't fall through. The mountain is not solid; it is a maze of deceit. Understanding that, one begins to know the mountain.

Then, moving up, seeking with nervous fingers the steady places in the face of the mountain, one is tempted to embrace the rock, to lean in and become one with it. Then the mountain has you trapped.

Only when one leans out from the mountain, distancing the body from the precarious toeholds and fingerholds, can one defeat it. To climb the mountain, pretend you are the fly, dancing vertically up its sneering face.

But then all is changed at night, for even by moonlight the silvered rock is pocked with shadowy chasms. Then one has the right to fear, for there are no longer any rules.

* * *

I attacked the rock, lashing at it for footholds, stumbling, slipping. Within seconds sweat seared my eyes and ran in rivulets down my body. The bulky cloak tangled and pulled at every movement. For a half hour we battled the unyielding rock, gaining little.

Taletha had it the worst. Slightly below me, she caught the loose gravel across her body. I heard her whimper. I looked down and saw her climbing *with her eyes closed!* Enough! The mountain is a monster. There had to be another way.

I stopped and helped her up to me. I pointed to the left. About twenty feet across there was a ledge. We worked our way toward it and sat down, gasping, leaning back against the rock, feet dangling out into space.

It was all wrong. Who did I think I was? Balthazzar? God of the mountain? I sat heaving for breath, listening to Taletha's sobbing lungs.

"I can't make it," she said.

I was too weary to reply.

"The height . . . it terrifies me."

I nodded.

"I want to let go!"

I stood momentarily on the ledge and tried to study this obscenity of rock. Around the curve of the mountain I could see lights winking past the plain of Jebel Barkal. Of course, the soldiers were making a house-to-house search, terrorizing and pillaging their own people!

But what struck terror in me lay further east. Over the hills east of Jebel Barkal the night sky lightened perceptibly. It was false dawn, to be sure, but dawn, nonetheless. So I would be too late after all.

Give it up then. Why do this? Because Balthazzar did? I am not Balthazzar! I'm Elhrain, god of nothing. God of fear and flight, rather.

Go west, then. Climb around. Hadn't Balthazzar said there was a path down to the western hills, out of sight of the people on the plain?

Wait! If there were, it was also a path *up!*

I roused Taletha.

"Listen. Only a little farther. There is a path to the west you can take. You can wait for me."

She stared up at me with uncomprehending eyes.

"You won't have to climb any farther."

"I can't leave you."

"No," I said, as I lifted her up. "You won't leave me, and I won't leave you—not ever. We'll follow this ledge around. You can wait for me."

Even as we began inching around the mountain, feet clinging to the narrow ledge that seemed at places as slippery as water, I realized that I had spoken a vow, the first I had ever made in a lifetime of denying vows.

The ledge broadened miraculously. We found ourselves on the back side of the mountain, facing rocky hills to the west. They were tangled with dead trees, dried brush and withered vines, but we could climb into them. What Balthazzar had said was true!

I found a place among the rocks where Taletha could rest.

"You'll be safe here."

"Where are you going?" she asked. Her voice was heavy with fear.

"To finish the mountain."

"Please don't leave me."

"I'll be back." I touched a finger to her lips.

I left my pack and the belt of water flasks by her, dropping them hurriedly upon the brush-littered ground. A way out! For the first time I thought it was possible to finish this madness.

I turned back to the mountain. If I could make it. If Eldrad could get to the priests in time. If. If. If wasn't good enough. I turned back to the pack, dug through it and found my flint. I stripped the waterskins from the belt and bundled some brush and broken branches together, draping them firmly over my shoulder. I didn't know if I could make it with them, but I had to try. I couldn't count on the priests.

The path. If Balthazzar was correct, it would have to start back here. *If*, again. I studied the rough face of the mountain, walking around this back side. I reached the edge of the bluff we had climbed to, where the rock fell in a tumble a hundred or more feet down. The cliff was lost in shadows and darkness. I saw nothing like a path.

I walked back, crossing close to Taletha. This had to be it—a ridge of broken rock. It was not a path at all, just wind-riven and blasted stone, loose and treacherous, arched crookedly upward. I took a deep breath and began to climb.

Winding up the back of the promontory, the ridge gave out shortly. The rock simply split here. I fumbled in the darkness. Reaching out precariously, my fingers touched the opposite side of the rift. Too far to cross. But if I could squeeze my body into it, I could use it for leverage.

The wood bundled on my back hampered my balance. I thought about just letting it drop. No, I had to do this. For myself now. For her. Looking ahead, not back, I twisted out, feet slipping on the rock. I swung across the darkness, fingers clutching madly, trying to fling my body into the vertical crevice.

For a moment the world seemed to open in a great chasm and I was falling.

I touched the other side of the rift. For a moment, arms and legs braced, I hung there in the darkness, far above an unseen space. My head whirled. Vertigo. I reached hands out to each side of the rift to steady myself. I found footholds on each side. I could rest a moment. My knees trembled. I gasped for breath.

After a moment, I began to climb slowly to the top. If this was Balthazzar's idea of a path, he was even more insane than I thought. For a moment, in the darkness, a smile crossed my lips. I was doing it.

When I reached the crest, dragging myself over the lip of rock like a drowning man, I saw the sky brightening in the east. Too late, then. Between me and the light rose the higher promontory. The serpentine neck of rock arched above me, its edges tinged with a pink glow. It made me feel defeated all over. I couldn't go on any more. It was impossible. The two peaks split apart over a distance of twenty or more feet. In the growing light I could see definition in the gray rock, its surfaces turning pink and brown and tan. And something else. In the light at its very peak, rising another fifty feet above the flat cliff where I stood, I saw the glint of shining gold: the hammered plates. It was all true!

I crawled across the flat surface of the lower bluff to its edge. And crawling so, my fingers sank into a declivity, touching something soft and coiled. I fell back, whimpering in fear. A snake! I loathed them.

Up here, though? No serpent could crest this serpentine rise.

I reached out tentatively. Coiled ropes. That's right, Balthazzar, or the priest, had carried ropes. I chuckled nervously as I pulled them out, still fearing the bite of a snake. But they would be worn, fragile after . . . how many years of exposure? I had been here over fifteen years. Long before that, Balthazzar had made his climb.

They were coiled tightly in the leather casing. If the wrappings were tight, it could be that they were still serviceable. I tore the bundles apart, ripping away the leather casing that was as dry and cracked as papyrus.

The casing had served its purpose; the ropes seemed sound. I tested their strength, pulling, jerking. It had to be done. I knotted one end to an outcrop of rock, wrapping the ropes twice, three times around its rocky base.

I saw a flash of white light in the east. The sun!

It had to be done now!

I marked out twenty feet of rope, hand-over-hand, measuring its length to approximate the distance to the opposing arch. I coiled the slack about my waist and lowered myself over the edge.

My body banged against the cliff face like a sack of old rags. I came to a stop dangling, head down. I felt my legs kicking frantically like someone else's legs. Blood raced to my head, pounding like waves against the ear drums. Kick out! I twisted, caught a rock with my foot and somersaulted, sobbing for breath. It was light enough now to see needlelike rocks below. Long claws waiting to impale me. But I twisted upright and was free for the moment.

There was no time to waste. The crown of the sun slid above the horizon like a red boil. The eastern hills turned dark for a moment, then pink as they caught the light.

I kicked out, beginning a long pendulum swing. Again, wider, higher. Again. My feet nearly reached the arching protrusion of rock across from the cliff. The earth tilted madly. Sunlight flooded my eyes.

Again. I marked the spot where I wanted to land.

Once more, arching high, higher. Too high! I released my hold on the rope, letting it trail free from my waist. Grabbing for the cold rock, I clutched it and held fast.

I hung there straddling the rocky incline. Quickly, I pulled the rope free from my waist cinch and twisted it around some rock. I would need it. I began to climb the last few feet to the crest of the pinnacle.

As I pulled myself over the narrow ledge, I lay panting, face pressed flat against loose bits of shale. I wanted to rest but was surrounded by an unbearable brightness. I twisted my neck to look up. The golden plates glowed in the morning light like a second sun, bright mirror to its cousin in the sky. I raised one hand, slowly, and touched the thin plates. They were so delicate, like tender metal flowers that trembled under my touch. But they burned with such a deep fierce heat that the whole mountain seemed to glow. This alone would have made the climb worthwhile. My eyes began to hurt, and I turned my face aside. Ahead of me lay a weathered tool, a warped piece of an old mallet. I grasped it and seemed to feel Balthazzar's hand under my own.

I wanted only to lie there. To give in to the soothing warm metal at my back. To rest and avoid the world forever. My eyes began to close, the lids heavy.

Suddenly an eerie ululation floated up to me. I thought at first it was some wounded animal. A noise like a lamentation, a wailing. Then another tone—lower, richer—rose, and I started awake. The horns!

Clinging to the rocky precipice I leaned out. Before the temple stood three priests, clad in flowing white robes complete with glittering headdresses. In unison they raised horns to their lips. The sound was so far below that it seemed to rise from the roots of the earth itself. The men looked like rigid little stick figures. But, oh, the sound—melodious and rich—was calling the people. Already I saw villagers pouring onto the plain, coming from a night of terror to the promise of hope.

Three guards on horseback suddenly came galloping out of the gate across the plain, their animals kicking up tiny spirals of dust. They circled the priests. Still the horns blasted. They held back the guards by some mysterious power. People hurried now, excited by the horns and the horsemen streaming into the temple grounds.

I watched in weariness. They seemed like so many ants so far below, almost as if I could reach out one oversize foot and stamp upon them all in one blow. God of the mountain!

And I remembered my task. With swollen, fumbling fingers I unfastened the bundle of wood and brush at my back, dropping it into a small pile. I tossed on the weathered mallet for good luck. No wind stirred; only the merciless eye of a white sun broached the horizon and stared scornfully upon the earth.

With my fingernails I shredded dry bark into a little pile, struck the flint again and again. A spark fell. A pitiful puff of smoke came, then the hard, pure flame. In moments a fire licked against the golden plate work.

I stood and stared below, waiting for their attention. The fire turned hot, flames licking behind and around me.

Heads began to turn upward. Fingers pointed.

Still it was not time. Ah, there! From the palace gate, borne on his chair on the shoulders of guards. His fat, bulbous body like a thick lump seen from this height. Kurdash. Yes! This is what I awaited.

The people gave way. Soldiers beat them aside. Still they pressed toward the mountain like some great, black wave of flesh. I could not see Eldrad in their midst. It was simply a mass of flesh below, save for the king. My scorn grew thick and hot in my throat. People on the fringes jeered the mad pretender.

I summoned every ounce of energy in my enervated body and thundered one word: "Silence."

The word echoed down the flanks of rock.

The people stopped, stunned. All heads turned up now. First the priests—ah, those faithful ones!—then the people fell to their knees. And yes, the guards also. So this is how a god spoke. In sounds of thunder. So be it.

The flames licked behind me, flaring up. The sun burned against the golden plates. A frenzy of light shone all about me.

"I have come," I shouted, "to restore the House of Komani."

The people moaned, a long, dull sound flooding the plain. They prostrated themselves before the mountain. For a moment, the whole scene seemed oddly comical to me. Who was I to toy with their beliefs, however foolish they seemed to me? Is this how a god looks upon his people?

"Look at me!" I thundered. "Yes, look."

Slowly I lifted the gold medallion from my neck, held it high like an offering.

"Eldrad!" I shouted. "Let Eldrad come forth."

I saw him then. He raised his homely face to the sky, and I looked down upon him for the last time. Even then, Kurdash lumbered from his chair, his large body billowing through the crowd. He thrust people aside like twigs.

"The House of Komani," I thundered, "belongs to Eldrad. People! Greet your king." I held the medallion for a moment, letting the sun flash off its hard, glossy surface. It seemed, for a moment, terribly heavy, almost as if I were holding a piece of myself. I flung it out. It twirled like a great golden bird, singing through space.

Eldrad had not moved. I understood why. If he were to rule these people it would be at their request, not Eldrad's demand. That was his nature. For him, it was worth the risk.

Nonetheless, I was surprised to see a guard step forward to catch the heavy necklace. It seemed the people were paralyzed with fear. Their wails rose even as the gold fell. Terror from on high. But the guard stepped forward. I could not tell from this height who it was. It may have been Arabia, perhaps not. It was, nonetheless, an act of awful daring.

Not only to clutch the necklace, its heavy weight plunging through the air, but also to make a choice *against*. Against terror. Against Kurdash.

He plucked the heavy medallion cleanly from the air, letting his arm follow through like a true athlete, so that his whole body entered the act. Even his knees flexed. Then he stood erect, necklace held high. Turning to present it to Eldrad, he stood face to face with Kurdash.

In a blur, I saw the huge man lunge forward. There was a flicker of metal. A silver blade. Others milled forward. A howl of rage rose from the people. Again I saw the flash of a silver blade. Kurdash's arms flung wide. The huge body buckled, collapsing in upon itself, the mountainous legs giving way.

Again, the guard thrust the medallion high.

My task was finished. I turned and scrambled over the ledge, sliding down the ropes to the lower bluff.

Every choice is a choice *against*. It cannot be otherwise. Yet I wondered, even as I swung between the two opposing precipices and hauled myself up with trembling, straining arms to the bluff, when it would ever be otherwise.

Perhaps now. Now to Taletha. I had kept *my* promises.

The western back of the mountain still lay in darkness. Ahead I could see the mountain's long shadow thrust against the cluster of hills. These were wild hills, full of imagined ghosts and inspirited by gods. So the people believed. They would not follow us there.

I looked down the long sloping incline, amazed that I had climbed that in the darkness. Vertigo attacked me. Balthazzar had made it sound so easy: "There is a path down the back side someone could walk down!" Madness.

I peered into the gloom trying to spot Taletha but saw only tumbled rock and dried brush far below. Behind me the wails of the people turned to cries of celebration. A god had appeared; a king was proclaimed. I could imagine their frenzied feet kicking up dust clouds as they danced, these simple children of faith. And I had to climb down, assaulted and bone-weary.

I spotted the rift I had climbed during the night, lowered myself gently over the ledge into its cavity, finding toeholds, and descended. So it always goes—the way up or the way down begins with one step. "Like an act of faith," my mind said, and I shut it out. I became, once again, one with the redeeming rock.

Taletha was waiting at the bottom. Even as she saw my body crawling down through the darkness, she asked, "The noise?"

I slid the remaining feet, taking her rudely by the elbow, and steering her to the packs. I was in a hurry now. "They have a new king," I said as we went.

"Who?"

"Eldrad, of course. I'll tell you as we go. Now we have to disappear."

"The packs are ready."

"Good. Let's go then."

She stopped, hand on my sleeve. "Where?" she said. "If Eldrad . . ."

I looked at her distraught eyes and nearly wept. It was one thing for me to flee—quite another for her. "I'm sorry," I said. "*I* have to go. You see, I appeared as a god, and gods have no place among humans. Everything would be lost then."

Her bewildered eyes flickered.

"But it would be safe for *you* to return. You're free to go."

For a long moment she looked at me, and my heart bled. I could not, I believed then and know now, live without her. Nor could I live with her had I not given her the choice.

She turned and picked up her heavy pack, tightening it without a word about her thin shoulders. Without waiting for me, she stepped through the brush into the maze of hills, leading the way.

BOOK THREE
KINGDOM OF LIGHT

CHAPTER ONE

That first day, upon leaving Jebel Barkal, we were exhausted—as if we were two dried husks blown into the brittle hills. It was a strange, bewildering landscape, blasted by drought. After several hours we stumbled across a small declivity that had once been a water hole. The bones of small animals lay scattered about, picked clean by carrion birds. In the shade of some rock outcropping, we huddled together and slept.

The day passed into evening. Awakening, we nibbled at some figs, sipped some water, and we slept again. During the night, I lit a fire. I had no fear of pursuit, but even so it was not wise to light one this close to Jebel Barkal. Members of the old guard *could* be searching these hills. We certainly didn't need the fire for warmth, although like the desert the drought-blasted hills were cool in the night. We needed the fire for its life and comfort, to lie there near its flames enfolded in each other's arms. To be able to awaken suddenly, and see the other was there. To be able to think that this presence, at least, was real.

Looking back now, I see that moment as a marriage—this rare, intimate, mysterious interpenetration of spirit, this certainty that one could not live apart from the other.

But in this wilderness there was no place for the ceremony of marriage. I was content, but even then sensed in Taletha the longing for formality, the recovery of order through ceremony itself.

* * *

In the morning we trudged on, heading southwesterly. Occasionally, we passed deserted villages, the mud and straw huts collapsing, all belongings taken. The inhabitants had fled the devastation of drought—in the very direction from which we now fled. These people had become the refugees who squatted around the city of Jebel Barkal.

In one such village, and with our own supplies nearly depleted, we stumbled upon a small pig rooting in a garbage dump at the edge of the village plain. It was a gaunt, starved creature, probably escaped from its owner, and would have gone unnoticed by us except that it had gotten its snout stuck in a broken piece of pottery. The wretched beast staggered blindly about the dump, bumping its masked head into rocks and branches. Seizing a heavy piece of wood, I sneaked behind it and felled it with one blow. Quickly I bled the animal, gutted it and cut it up. By the time I was done, Taletha had a fire roaring in the pit at the center of the circle of huts. We spitted a chunk of meat on a dried branch over the fire, watching with excited eyes the sizzling meat. Before it was thoroughly cooked we attacked it.

I sat back across the fire from Taletha and studied her, it seemed, for the first time in days. Never once, as we slogged pace by pace over the barren land, had she complained. But her spirit seemed drained. Her brown eyes were empty pools above wan cheeks. No life seemed to lie there.

I walked around the fire and drew her to me.

"Soon," I said, "we will find something. I can feel it. We'll make it."

She lay her head on my shoulder without responding. I wasn't sure anymore what I felt. My promises were crippled.

I believed that if we moved far enough south we were bound to hit water. The tribes, I thought, would be uncivilized, but I didn't worry about them. I worried about us.

We dried the remaining meat by the fire that night, and, invigorated by it, walked more rapidly the next day. Here and there we found trees in the blighted jungle that still bore shrunken remnants of fruit, most of them completely unfamiliar to me.

Slowly and subtly, the landscape changed. I noticed it first in the air—

in a vague sense of humidity, which after the searing dryness, struck with a physical weight. We had been traveling for weeks by then.

The earth itself changed, ever so slightly. The trees showed some brave spots of green. We found dew on the leaves in the morning. A marshy sinkhole yielded fresh water under a layer of green growth. I caught a turtle by the swamp's edge, cracked its shell and roasted it.

The next morning only a few hundred yards away, we found a small current leading out of the marsh. We followed it throughout the day. It broadened to a flat, low stream. The jungle growth thickened about us; vines and branches slapped at our skin. In the evening insects swarmed out of the jungle floor to attack us. But the broadening stream gave a better way. Taletha spent the next day resting while I gathered some heavy logs. Laboriously hacking at branches, I cleaned the logs and bound them together with vines, and so fashioned a raft. We had had enough of walking.

The stream broadened as we poled down its angular course, passing now and again under a jungle canopy that shut out the sun. Strange birds called sharply in the trees. A flash of red or yellow feathers shot through the canopy as a bird soared over the river's edge.

The land was strange, primeval, a spawning place for life. The deeper we went upon the broadening river, the more eerie it became. The canopy thickened to a dense veil, admitting only scattered shards of sunlight. Huge trees lay uprooted along the river's edge. Some of them sprawled into the water so that our little raft collided against them, and only with much pushing was I able to free us from the current's grip. Our solace was that we moved in moisture. It was impossible to believe that the fierce drought lay only a few weeks' journey to the north.

We stopped against a mudbank one evening and clambered ashore, sinking nearly to our knees in the ooze. On a spit of dry land I gathered wood and built a fire. By its light I dug clams from the river muck, cleaned them out and roasted them.

Taletha sank against me, a cloak of profound exhaustion settling almost tangibly about her. She looked into the brush beyond the fire and spotted the red and yellow glint of eyes watching us.

"They are only animals," I said. She huddled against me. "We're safe."

Her body felt rigid even as she clung to me. I regretted now her coming. This was not for her. And as I thought, for the first time in weeks, beyond mere survival, I realized that I had not heard her speak a word in days. It was almost as if she were slipping back, recoiling into the fearful self she had once been.

* * *

We made our way slowly upon that shadowed river where it seemed forever evening, and I, who had rejected all beliefs, all gods, began to feel I was traversing a land of demons, so savage was the land. Animal calls and bird calls endlessly shocked the air. A cacophony of noise greeted us at every turn and twist.

The river continued to broaden and quicken, driven by the rush of many tributaries, some of them now far larger than that small current we had started out upon. The wetness was profound. After years at the edge of the desert I had never thought I would weary of moisture. But this was thick in the air, even in the lungs. Driven by heat that seemed to burn up from the earth's core, the jungle steamed.

Rashes appeared on my body. Raw, abraded skin oozed infection. Taletha suffered in silence.

I banked the raft that night, wondering if we would ever find firm ground again. We built a fire and dozed fitfully while the jungle eyes stared out upon us.

* * *

They stood about us. Eight of them. Naked. Facial features distorted by pieces of ivory that pierced lips, noses, ears. They were wiry little creatures with distended bellies that seemed to bulge even larger because they stood on one leg, the opposite foot resting upon a rigid knee while they leaned against long spears.

When I stood up I towered over them, and they shrank back like wary animals.

We watched each other for a long time, immobile, rigid. They made no threat. Even though they held spears and there were eight of them, I was certain I could destroy them if necessary. I didn't want to. I—we—needed help. Rest and restoration.

I pointed at my mouth and rubbed my stomach in a sign of hunger. I repeated the motions, pointing at Taletha, who cowered behind me.

They jabbered for a moment. Then one handed his spear to another, grabbed a vine, swung into the canopy and was gone for several minutes. He returned, swinging down on a vine, holding several oblong pieces of fruit by their stems between his teeth. He set them on the ground before us and stepped back.

I reached out, took a fruit and bit into it. And smiled, I believe, for the first time in countless days. The fruit was like a fountain of sweetness exploding in my mouth, charging in a dizzying rush through my body. I sighed. The men jabbered knowingly. One smiled and rubbed his stomach. I handed one to Taletha. When she stood from the shadows behind me to take it the men fell back in fear. Despite the dirt and muck of long travel, her skin seemed, beside the rest of us, terribly pale.

She bit into the fruit, then devoured it greedily.

One of the men gestured to follow and without a word disappeared into the jungle. I gathered our packs, and we followed. We had nowhere else to go.

Thus began our time with the Beshali.

* * *

I was grateful, once again, for at least one result of my time as a Magus—the intense study in language. This was a language unlike any I knew, consisting of a series of shrill barking sounds, a mindless jabbering and ululating wails. Yet language it was, and in time I deciphered enough of it to communicate.

It was a gift from the Magi from a time so long lost on the shores of memory it seemed infinitely remote and irretrievable.

The Beshali's jungle home seemed crammed with as much life as possible, billowing up to the tree tops, flowing out over the surge of the river. This was a great green bowl into which rivers, trees, plants and animals had been thrown with abandon. All the plant life seemed slightly exaggerated, a bit bulbous and overlush, as it fed upon the rich soil and the nearly constant moisture.

The trees had strangely thickened trunks and swollen root systems like giant tubes plunged into the earth. Stumps of roots protruded from the ground like small chairs.

Through these trees, swinging along a network of vines, the tree animals moved, chittering raucously. Birds like bright arrows shot from branch to branch. Enormous butterflies, with wings larger than my hand, floated about flowers that hung *down* from the trees. It was an inverted world, pressed toward the moisture and nutriment that the earth held in such abundance. All was a richness that seemed impossible of depletion.

But it was also a predatory world in which death struck savagely and swiftly. The chatter of a tree animal could snap off under the jaws of a great cat lurking in the branches. In the life-giving rivers great crocodiles lurked, enormous jaws working like traps. The jungle fed upon itself, all plant and animal life in a tense balance as fine as a trip wire. How fragile, finally, was this desperate beauty.

This was also a land of lost time. The jungle provided food and shelter, there simply for the taking. I taught the Beshali the art of fire with my precious flint.

* * *

But surely the most precious thing I bore was the small leather sack of seed grain. We had been with the Beshali several months when I began my experiment.

They laughed as I worked to strip back the brush behind the tangle of huts, bound by a wooden stockade fence, that they called a village. They jabbered relentlessly, shaking their ivory-sprung heads, as I used their crude axes to attack a mammoth tree to let in the sunlight. I picked the largest tree I could find, as thick and hard as hope, and hacked at it all day, barely denting the corded bark. Yet I returned to it the next day, working at a small, saucer-shaped gouge. Then, for no reason I could understand, the village men joined me. Their muscular little arms flailed at the wood. With a sudden loud crack, then a dull groan, the tree fell. They jabbered and danced. They attacked another. It was a new game.

This jungle soil, enriched by eons of leaf-mold and river effluvia, proved wonderfully rich. I wanted to get the seed in before it rotted, and I worked ceaselessly.

That first year I cleared only a tiny space and set each seed like a precious jewel in a small black necklace of land at the edge of the compound.

It flourished; in weeks the grain shot up to the light. Together, Taletha and I built ovens out of river-clay bricks, thickened with ground reeds and dried in the sun. We taught them how to grind with a mortar and pestle and how to bake the flour. At last we ate bread together. Heavy bread it was, but it was like a rare gift to these people.

Carefully, I stored away seed grain in leather pouches.

The next year we broadened the planting space, doubling and then tripling its size. We traded with other villages in the jungle, whose people came to see this wonder of bread and grain.

And in all that time Taletha hardly spoke.

Oh, when I think of her agony now. How she endured! It terrified me.

Yet, for several years—I lost count in this place where time stopped—we remained.

* * *

When the ending came, I should have been more alert to the signs. It is easy to see, looking back, how one sign led to the next, and how, in the end, I had had to struggle to ignore them.

The people who came to the village then came from further away, and about them there were signs of a gauntness and desperation I chose to ignore. My pride fed me. I was hero and savior to these people. I chose to deny it.

But I could not deny the nervous tension that throbbed among my own villagers upon the leaving of the vagabonds. The drought was encroaching upon even this mighty fortress of moisture.

Drought had seemed years distant—not just miles. But the people who came now, in ever-increasing numbers, were starving people. They came not for the novelty or the luxury of bread, but out of desperation.

Finally, I had to take a trip north with several of the warriors of the village, these same, odd little creatures with the long spears whom I had first met. We prepared for a journey of several weeks, but did not have that far to go.

Along the way we met small groups of people in new encampments. These were the strangers heading south. The encampments were precisely that, not villages but mere groups of people seeking food and safety in the jungle. Then we met a small band, a family of seven people leading a small goat by a leather thong, wandering nearly starved through the jungle. We shared food with them, but even as we sat and ate we felt the change.

The jungle was still thick with heat, but the heat was oddly drier, and the jungle was oddly silent. Birds and animals too had fled further south.

The next day we stumbled across the first sand, a wind-driven film that layered the jungle floor. Vines were brittle. We did not have to go further, but I insisted. I wanted to touch the terror, to see it for myself.

The sand built up on the ground inches thick. Then waves of it undulated around trees that were dying, and there was no water. There was only sand, with mere scattered clumps of green bravely defying the sweep of the desert. The desert was eating the jungle alive. The trees were stripped and dried posts. Shredded leaves blew in the wind.

We turned back. The jungle was dying.

Everything looked different on the way back. My warrior companions were silent and nervous as we moved rapidly through the jungle. Even the moist zone no longer seemed safe. We arrived at the village and saw a dozen or more vagabonds encamped outside the gate. They reached out trembling hands, begging of us as we passed by.

The family of seven with the tough little goat had made it. I saw them camped around a fire, their hollow eyes reaching toward us like hands.

The council meeting that night went long. I was permitted entrance by the status I had gained over the years as bread-provider. The grain had proved a huge wealth to the people, and with their wealth my status had grown.

Because of that wealth they didn't want to leave. They were primitive children, really, knowing no other place but this. The very virtues of the Beshali—trust, security, loyalty, tradition—seemed to work against them. Yet the choice was inevitable. We—and I counted myself among them— could relocate to the south now, while we had ample supplies and a good chance to start anew, or we could wait and become like the vagabonds around us. We returned to our stick-and-mud huts, determined to leave as soon as we could harvest the grain.

Taletha was waiting for me by the fire, staring into the flames. I collapsed on my cot, exhausted by days of travel.

"We will leave within a week," I said.

I had become so used to her silences I expected nothing.

But then, after a long pause, she spoke in a nearly guttural tone, as if her voice dredged her very soul, "No."

I propped myself on an elbow. "What?"

She shook her head, her back toward me. "I will go no more."

"We have no choice," I said. "The drought . . ."

She whirled upon me, her face dark against the firelight, framed by hair that had grown long and plaited.

"I have . . . a choice." She struggled with the words, as if summoning every ounce of strength within her thin body. She was still beautiful, this woman, however worn with the years. I moved across the firelight to study her.

"Go on," I said. "Tell me."

Her face was a mask.

"If you have a choice, make it. At least tell me about it."

"I will . . . not go." She seemed to cough the words out, struggling for each sound.

"But you can't—we can't—stay here. The drought is moving south. To stay here is to die. We have *no* choice!"

She stared at me, firelight glittering in her eyes. I leaned toward her, exasperated with this woman, in love with this woman. "What *do* you want?" I asked.

"I will go home." The fire crackled, filling the silence. "Home." She bent her head. "Before I die."

"Where . . ." I hesitated. It was one thing we had never dared talk about. "Where is home?"

She pointed north. "The other side."

"Taletha, there is no other side."

She nodded adamantly.

"No! The other side is death. It is all drought. It goes on forever."

She shook her head.

"Tell me," I waited a long time, "about home."

Again she pointed. "Far away . . . on the other side. Hills and grass . . . and water. No drought can touch it." Her voice seemed to quicken.

"How do you know?"

She looked surprised, as if wondering herself. Then she said, "It is the land God gave us."

"Tell me!"

"I cannot." She shook her head. "I was . . . a little girl. With my people. It is *my* land."

"And it is north?"

She nodded.

"Can we reach it?"

She did not respond.

"No. On the other side of this . . . of life . . . is death, Taletha. It's insane."

She nodded, infuriating me.

"God's land, you say?"

She looked away.

"Well, well, well."

* * *

I did not sleep that night; nonetheless, I dreamed. I was a young man again, setting out with the Magi to see a king. On the other side. Of course it was only a dream. There is no other side. No king. Yet, I felt the dream pulling me. Perhaps there was a journey left to finish after all, as insane as it was at the outset years and years ago.

The next morning I bartered a small sack of grain with the family for the goat. I tried to use the gold coins I had kept, but they were meaningless to them. The grain, however, was the sign of a promise. Throughout the day, I made packs and collected waterskins while Taletha worked at mending the desert cloaks we had not needed for years. For another day I burned and chiseled out two large sections of a tree trunk, reducing the wood to a thin, casklike container. Both proved to be watertight. I fashioned a kind of harness for these to place on the back of the goat, balancing them over large sacks of ground meal for padding. It was heavy, and the animal stumbled about getting used to it. But, like these people themselves, the animal was a strong, wiry creature, and it adjusted quickly.

So it was that we parted from the Beshali after years in their family. They were good years, for the most part. The Beshali stood in a large band, ready to travel south, while we faced north. None of them waved or smiled. They stood with grave faces, like ones bidding farewell to those already dead. Those going to the other side.

CHAPTER
TWO

Even though I had traveled with the warriors to the edge of the desert, I was startled by the severity of its attack upon the jungle. When one is in the dense, canopied and thriving jungle it seems far too powerful ever to be destroyed. But there is a far greater power, and it is the power of aridity that breeds in the desert. The jungle is self-contained, its own system for life. But the desert's dryness always attacks.

That is surely why the Beshali spoke of the desert always as a demon. Worse, it was a demon with a host of lesser devils attached to it. The cutting wind that carried sand like whips. The voice of the low crying wind. The subterranean bodies that carried sand on their backs so they became fiery-hot dunes. It was a place of demons.

I had always discounted such mythologies. I had no need for them. I had braved the desert north of Babylon, battled there and endured. At the edge of the desert in Jebel Barkal, I had taught the people how to farm in the very face of such demons.

I was less inclined to discount it as Taletha and I made our way out of the jungle and into the arid wasteland. For a certain distance there were clumps of green surrounded by sand, as if the desert played some mad children's game, leap-frogging into the jungle. Then came only sand and dried growth. Then only sand. The demarcation was as rude and sudden as being struck. A few paces this way, and one walked toward life. A few the other way, and one walked toward . . . the other side.

We crossed over resolutely, the little goat poling along on its thin legs as if it never discerned the difference. Indeed, it seemed born to the desert.

Remembering my earlier battle with the desert, I carried a Beshali spear on my back. Our waists were belted with water flasks. Our packs, holding extra sandals and food, rode high on our shoulders. I carried an extra length of cloth to use as a sun-screen during the heat of the day, or for mending our desert cloaks as the need arose. It surely would; for the blowing sand sawed at the material from our first steps.

But this desert quickly proved different from that north and west of Babylon. There, only vast rolling hills of sand, ever-moving, sprawled in waves to the horizon. This land seemed twisted somehow, like some horrible dance between life and death.

In this desert the sky seems so huge that it pressed like a weight, a blue loneliness blanketing the grinding sand. Its wind sawed among stony ridges, grinding the rock to toothlike fangs.

Like the wind, the sands of the desert shifted and slid. They had nowhere to go, only the ceaseless, lonely grinding upon themselves. But they never held still.

One can travel for days in the desert, feeling as if no distance is covered. It is nature's living deceit, an affliction of spirit and body. The desert annuls life. The feral heat of the sun scorches the earth, its fire eating into the core.

Yet in this desert the great emptiness is punctuated by resilient touches of life that refuse to admit defeat. Proud bunches of tough scrub grass clot a valley, pushing broom-straw heads up through the marl. Beyond a rise of sand, an oasis might appear like a low, clenched fist of defiance.

In these places, to our amazement, people sometimes still lived, tending a few fig trees, herding a few sheep. But they had nothing to do with us, and we had nothing to trade with them. They permitted us a bit of water from the oasis and urged us on. Any change in their environment threatened the fragile balance of life they daily walked.

In the early stages of our journey, we were encamped near such a settlement one night, just outside the circle of their huts. I had scrounged a few sticks to build a small fire. We leaned back against rocks that still held the sun's heat, watching the orange tongues of flame.

We had found no respite from these particular desert people, only sullen glances and averted faces. A mood of desolation crept once again through me. I studied Taletha's sun-darkened features. They looked even more strained in the firelight.

"So this land we're going to," I said. "Can you describe it? Name it?" My voice was harsher than I intended.

"It is just pictures in my mind," she said softly.

The words made me wince. A mind can play terrible tricks. "Pictures?" I asked. "How long have they been there?"

She shrugged, poking a stick into the flame. "Always, I suppose, Elhrain. Don't look at me that way. I know it sounds silly."

"What way?" I asked. She wasn't even looking at me! "Okay," I said, "but can you tell me more about it?"

"Your trouble is that you always want facts."

"Of course. I have been misled by enough delusions. By what people think they believe."

"And I am weary of facts, you see." The stick cracked under her fingers. She flung the pieces on the fire. "I wanted to listen to my heart. To study the pictures it made for my mind."

"And?" I prompted.

She shook her head, the long hair, unplaited now in the desert, falling across her face like a veil. "Just pictures. But they are . . . so real. I was young then, in the pictures."

"With family?"

She nodded. "A brother and a sister. Both younger than I. Parents. Odd, I can't picture them very well. And I can't even remember their names. I just . . . see them."

She threw me a glance of exasperation, as if I were some slow learner trying to keep up.

"What are you—they—doing in the pictures?"

"Playing. We played together."

"Your family?"

"Yes. On the land. It was so green. This is not just a picture, Elhrain. It is real." Her breath quickened. She clutched her knees to her, the way a child does. "Rivers and streams and flowers are everywhere. It's so beautiful. It is the Lord's land."

I felt a terrible spasm of fear. For too long, far too long, Taletha had lived in wasted places. It was all a dream. I was afraid for her.

"The problem is," I thought, "there is no turning back now."

* * *

We had traveled many more days. The desert was different from that of Babylon, a mixture of sand and littered rocks. Yet, it was the same—always dangerous.

The greatest danger, beyond the obvious one of thirst, was losing our way. If we followed the landscape, setting a course around dunes or piles of rock, for example, we could walk all day and wind up only a few paces from where we started. Or we could wind up going in the wrong direction. For that reason we traveled only by night, when I could read the stars and chart a course directly north.

The stars do not lie, I reminded myself. I also remembered the sign in the stars years ago.

Each night I pointed out to Taletha the constellations that lay like a map overhead in the clean sky, remembering as I did so old Melchior's hand upon my shoulder as he sat outside with me in my youth, carefully naming and charting each firefly flash in the heavens. "How odd," I thought. "The further in I go, the further back I seem to go." The Magi felt like living presences around me as we walked through the night.

At the first light of dawn Taletha and I began looking for a hiding place, deep among the rocks, protected from sun and from wind. I wanted rock at my back, also, in case jackals or hyenas came. We lit a fire if we found wood, by a dried oasis or a stand of brave, desert trees, and then used it to bake the small, flat, unleavened rounds of bread from our supply of grain.

We traveled for many days beyond any sign of settlements. A ceaseless current of fine sand flowed over the flat, hard land, like gritty waves flailing our ankles. Our sandals broke down, were patched, and wore out, until our supply of leather dwindled.

We found it difficult to sleep now during the day. It wasn't the heat only, which seemed nearly unbearable as the marly rock collected it and held it like an oven. It was a dull, nagging anxiety. I confess I would have given up had it not been for Taletha. It was she who comforted me during the fierce heat of the day as we huddled under our canopy among the rocks; it was she who roused me at evening, forcing me to eat and drink.

The flasks at our waist grew dangerously light. Long ago we had emptied the casks into them, sparing the sturdy goat's energy.

Day by day we adapted to the desert's ways. One night, exhausted, we stayed in our camp to rest. Noting some tracks in the sand near the rocks, Taletha fashioned some string snares. All night she waited while I slept. In the morning I wakened to the rich scent of meat roasting over a tiny fire. She had snared a desert hare.

We began to scour the land more closely for signs of life, alert to the track of the lizard or hare. Still, the desert was full of deceits and surprises. One morning we were startled to see an ox standing in the distance, locked in sand up to its belly. As we drew nearer, its mouth appeared open in a soundless bawl. We hurried across the landscape, thinking we could surprise and butcher it for fresh meat. But as we approached the truth became apparent. Mummified by the dry desert air, the ox was long dead, its jaw still open in a death bellow, still propped upright by the locking weight of the sand about its legs. Its eyes were pecked clean and filled by sand, but somehow it had been missed by the desert predators for weeks or months. Its hide was dry as papyrus, its teeth white and shining by the polishing action of the gritty wind.

"At least it shows we're going the right way," I observed.

"How so? It's horrible," said Taletha.

"Obviously, it strayed from a caravan and got trapped in a sandstorm. If we're near a caravan route, we can't be far from civilization."

But whether a day or a month from civilization, the desert is still a deathtrap for the unwary.

There came a day when I smelled sea-salt in the air, and thought I was going delirious. I had heard the stories since childhood. The desert wanderer begins to see water just above the eternally distant horizon. In the later extremes they begin to run for it, dive for it, suffocate in the sand. But the heady scent grew stronger throughout the day. And when, early the next morning I saw a gull wheel in the eastern sky, I scrambled up the dunes, Taletha and the goat running hard to keep up.

Indeed, a sea it was. I thought at first that we had wandered impossibly off course, somehow skirting Jebel Barkal and winding up north of Tamal at the coast. But this coastline was altogether different. The harsh sands seemed to end right at the water's edge. Along the sea by Tamal, inland tributaries watered the land, greenery was abundant, the land fertile. This was a weird land of sand and water standing in absolute contrast.

We plunged in. The salt grated upon our weathered flesh, but the water seemed unbelievably cool and refreshing, nonetheless.

When we dragged ourselves back to shore, brushing the salt that instantly condensed on our drying skin, I couldn't help saying it. "We're lost."

Taletha shook her head.

"This is sea water," I said.

"Yes," she said simply and pointed north.

"Don't you understand? We wandered east somehow. The stars lied. Or . . . I read them wrong." Impossible.

Again she shook her head. "It is near," she said ambiguously. The woman was always a puzzle. "The other side," and she pointed north.

Although we saw signs of caravan travel, the prints grooved deeply in the crusty sand here, we saw no sign of human life. No towns. No squatters. No bandits. It was wasteland still.

We continued north, following the shoreline, finding at last an area of tiny springs feeding some wild trees and desert grass near the water's edge. We camped there for several days, replenishing our water supplies and resting. We would have stayed longer had not our food begun running low. The grain was completely gone now. Our supply of dried meat and fruits was reduced to a few thin packages. Nonetheless, we replenished our water supplies and rested.

It was at Taletha's urging that we continued. I believe I would have been content to stay until a caravan passed this way, as it surely would. The watering ground had to be an important resting point for any route. But, after several days, we packed our gear, loading the replenished water casks on the faithful little goat, and followed the coast north.

In time, we saw the opposite shore constricting to a point ahead of us. Then there was only a flat, effluvial plain, and we turned east across it. Taletha's face radiated excitement as we crossed over. Into desert once again.

Everywhere lay the sun-scorched wastes, and everywhere arose the winds that drove the fine grains of sand like needles. Only in the night and early morning hours could we travel with any degree of safety, guided by the crystalline points of the stars.

Rock formations appeared like fingers of hope. We traveled far past our normal time to arrive there, willing to brave the afternoon heat in order to find deep shadow among the rocks.

The rocks broke the desert emptiness. Granite monoliths rose to brave the winds, to halt the shift of sand mountains. They also brought different hardships. The sharp stones sawed at our leather sandals. The ragged formations reduced the rate of travel, since we had to climb over or around them. The stone held the sun's heat long into nighttime, turning some level stretches into scorching infernos, which we had to traverse quickly, sometimes at a weary trot, to find the next pocket of shade.

In the hollows, between stretches of sand and burning rock, we found respite. Some held a stand of thorn bushes. Some held small clumps of grasses. We dug up the deep, leaching roots, brushed off the sand and sucked them for moisture. We found bugs that held a drop of moisture. In one hollow, thick with sharp-edged grass that flayed the skin, we found a colony of toads. Here we rested for two days, feasting on the tiny pieces of flesh, before continuing.

We pressed on, the faithful goat clanking alongside. Until the morning it bolted.

* * *

I wonder if some delicate scent, floating above or around the low, shifting dunes, drew it for miles like a tug on a leash. Suddenly it broke free, empty water casks bouncing crazily on its back, tearing over the dune as it barked harsh, challenging coughs. I thought the heat had finally driven the tough, runty creature insane, that it ran to its own death. I was too exhausted to do anything but stand there, beyond hope of chasing it.

I turned to Taletha. "Too bad," I said. "I was just about to kill him for food."

Taletha glared at me, then began to chase it in the sun. I caught up, holding her arms.

"No!" I shouted. "We have to find shelter."

"We can't lose it!"

"We can't lose each other, woman!"

We sank to the ground, exhausted. Taletha pointed suddenly. "Look," she said.

"What?"

"Its tracks. We can follow it."

221

"We have to find shelter." Already the sun fried the land with its white glare.

"It's going somewhere. It wouldn't just run away!" she insisted.

"It's gone crazy. That's all."

"No. It knows."

"Knows what?"

She shook her head. In the end I gave in. Pulling up the hoods of our cloaks to ward off the sun, we followed. At points the tracks wandered. I could tell where the goat hesitated, circling the ground. Then the tracks straightened as clear as a path. Following them, we scrambled up over loose hot sands and crested a hill.

The goat stood proudly butting its scrawny head against the flanks of the sheep. I counted six of them in the hollow below. An oasis lay at one end of the valley, ringed by living greenery. Across the rocky floor, clumps of grass broke the surface. By the oasis stood a low hut constructed of loose branches and mud. And before the hut lay a body, face down in the sand.

Weariness disappeared as I ran down the hillside, tossing off my pack even as I ran.

The man lay against sand that had been stained dark with his blood. His body had been ravaged, flesh torn by tooth and claw. I turned him over and had to step aside. One cheek lay open, torn so terribly his teeth were exposed through the flesh. I bent, retching dryly.

Taletha darted past me. She bent to his nostrils.

"He still lives," she said. Her voice was sharp, quickened by need. "Help me," she ordered.

I staggered back to the human wreckage, avoiding looking at the terrible wounds. Somehow we carried him to the hut.

"Get water," she hissed.

"Where?" I felt stunned.

"The oasis. Here!" She flung a waterskin toward me.

She tended him throughout that afternoon, while the sun rose and battered the tiny hut. There was no room for me. I lay down by the oasis, under a stunted palm tree, rising occasionally to check on them.

Taletha bathed him lovingly, wrapped him in a linen cloth she had found and laid him upon a blanket cast over the dirt floor. With a knife she found in the hut she cleaned his wounds, cutting back the mutilated flesh and stitching what she could with a needle and thread from her pack.

It was hopeless. We both knew that.

During the night the man began to thrash and moan. I held a waterskin to his parched lips, squeezing drops between clenched teeth, trying not to look at the stitched-up cheek, which seemed to pull his whole face awry.

Even then I noticed a resemblance to Taletha—not familial to be sure, but of race and people. He bore the same olive-colored skin, the glossy, curly hair, the deep probing eyes.

Taletha watched me study him and murmured, "He is from the other side."

"Your people?"

She nodded. There lay a fierce eagerness on her face.

In the morning he was calm. And awake. And dying. He lay holding Taletha's hand as morning light flooded the doorway of the hut. We knelt beside him. His words came in slow gasps, like branches shedding leaves. He clutched Taletha's hand as if it were life itself, a life slipping away.

He spoke in quivering gasps. A language I had never heard. Taletha bent to him, and in low, halting tones, replied in the same speech.

Long silences interrupted the few words they spoke. His eyes searched her face and calmed under her gaze.

"What does he say?" I felt like an intruder. I did not like the feeling.

She glanced up at me, then ignored me. But when he spoke again, she translated, slowly, groping for words.

"He was in a caravan. A trading caravan."

She halted, listened to the sounds that were barely audible.

"A sandstorm. He was separated from the others with his flock."

The man made frail, birdlike motions with his hands.

"Forty sheep. And this is what is left."

She paused, but the man did not speak. "The wolf," she continued, "killed the sheep that the storm left alive. And the wolf attacked him."

He gripped her hand, speaking rapidly. He choked and a pink foam gathered on his lips.

"It is a demon, he says. And it must be destroyed."

"Does he know how far it is yet?" I asked.

She didn't bother to ask him. Instead she cast me a look of scorn. "Of course not. Do you think he would be here if he did?"

The man spoke again.

"He begs us to kill the wolf. For that, the sheep are ours."

I nodded.

"He wants your promise."

"Give it to him then."

She stared at me. "A promise is sacred," she said. "It may not be as easy as you think."

"He's dying," I pointed out.

"Nonetheless. He is of my people."

"Very well."

She spoke rapidly to the man. He nodded. Then again he seized her arm, raised himself slightly from the blanket. He spoke in a rush, then, choking, he seemed to smile. He stiffened and fell back.

"What did he say?"

Taletha leaned forward. She listened to his nostrils, placing her cheek by that gouged flesh. I watched dispassionately. Then she lifted two fingers and gently closed his staring eyes.

"What did he say!"

She turned and looked at me. Sighed deeply, exhausted.

"Well?"

"He said . . . the messiah has come."

Something seemed to howl in my mind. No! It is madness. I turned and fled from the hut, staring at the desert sun as it reddened in the west.

* * *

I scooped out a shallow grave at the edge of the oasis by the light of a fire. My digging tools were pieces of wood stripped from the palm trees. I had corralled the sheep with a piece of rope I found, keeping them alongside the hut. Sweat dripped from me as I dug. Nonetheless, I kept the fire blazing. Once, in the distance I heard a howl and I shivered nervously.

We slept by the fire that night, between it and the hut, leaving the body wrapped in the blanket inside.

By the first morning light, I carried the body of the shepherd to the grave and laid it there. Taletha helped me scoop the dirt in with our rude tools. The sun was full upon us as we finished, leaning wearily on the stick shovels.

I looked at her. Tired, she was slumped over the piece of wood, black hair blown forward over her face. Her arms were thin but strong. Her body was as lean as a desert breeze.

"The reason you seldom spoke in Jebel Barkal?" I asked. "Was it because you did not know the language?"

"I did not know I remembered this language," she said. And she smiled at me.

"Something else then?"

She nodded. "But because I could not speak, no one taught me the language," she said. Then added, "Until you came."

"Will you tell me about it?"

She stared for a long time at the grave. "I don't know," she said. "First, we have something to do."

Yes. I had to kill the wolf.

CHAPTER
THREE

T he hyena I knew. The jackal I knew. And feared them both. I did
not know the wolf. But I had seen the ravages it had inflicted upon
the man's body, and I was afraid.

Armed with the Beshali spear, and wearing the man's knife in my belt,
I scouted the valley the next morning. It was a most peculiar place here
in the desert. The desert's power was illimitable; the creatures of the
desert held absolute sway. Humans merely fought the decay a little while
before they themselves succumbed. The Magi reached the end of a line,
despite their frantic questing. The people of Jebel Barkal clung to different
gods but finally killed each other. The Beshali fled the onslaught of aridity.

Grim thoughts on a grim morning when I went to track the wolf. But
what an odd place! Here in the heart of the desert the land was surprised
by life. The oasis held fresh water fringed by palms. The sheep had scrub-
by grass to feed on. There they were, led by the pleased goat that stood
guard over his new harem like a proud master. Playfully he butted the
flanks of his ewes. They danced away like coy girls.

The valley was rimmed by rocky outcroppings that held back the desert
sand. To the east the hills narrowed to a gully. And it was from there,
I believed, that the wolf came. Probably he lay up in the further rocks,
coming to feed and water as he had need.

In the gully the rocky walls seemed to close in and press upon me. I found a litter of bones by some rock, a sheep's skeleton. Further up, more jagged pieces of bone, scattered and picked clean by other predators. I nodded. This would be the way of the wolf.

I came to a point where the rocks narrowed above a sandy basin. I spotted huge flat prints of the wolf and had an idea. I returned to the hut for tools and wooden poles for digging, and I worked until the sun was overhead. Then I returned to the shade of the hut to whittle stakes with the knife.

It was something I had seen the Beshali do to catch wild pigs.

I went back in the evening to scoop the hole deeper. It took several days to complete. I drove the stakes into the bottom of the pit, now as deep as my own shoulder. I wove together palm fronds into a tight matting. Then we butchered one of the sheep.

Taletha protested at first, but knew it was inevitable. When the sheep saw me coming, they sidled about nervously as if they *knew*. I had found some salt, hard round cakes of it, that the man had carefully wrapped in his pack. He treated his animals well. I enticed them with a salt cake, waiting while they stepped forward, bending their ruffled necks to the salt lick. I jumped up, finally catching the smallest among them. The screaming goat came at me, butting me painfully in the back when I turned. I kicked him angrily, and he headed his harem away from me, looking back over his shoulder with disdain.

We built a fire, and Taletha immediately began roasting and drying the meat. Except for one large chunk that I cut raw from the haunch.

I carried it, slippery and wet, to the matting over the pit, placing it at the center, balancing it so as not to collapse the fragile matting. Then I crawled into the rocks to wait and watch.

It had been nearly a week now since we arrived, and whatever kill the wolf had made must be exhausted. I thought the wolf would come to feed in the early morning, but I was prepared to wait all night. I had food and water with me, the spear and the knife ready at hand. But the wolf was wily.

It was deep night when I sensed, rather than saw, its presence. Something was out there. I stirred. The stars were hard, cold lights in the sky. The wolf, unlike the jackal or hyena, was a night hunter. I froze among the rocks, staring out into the starlit gully until my eyes hurt. I dared not move.

It seemed a dark shadow slinking along the rocky wall. It did not walk down the center of the gully; it stalked like a shadow. And whether it was magnified by the uncertain light or not, the creature seemed huge as it moved low-bellied, legs bent up around its back. For a moment I thought it would bypass my trap altogether, that it would circle by it to the hut and seize another sheep while I waited helpless in the rocks.

Then it froze. I held my breath. Let it out slowly. Immobile, the beast hung there, a carved gray statue under starlight, only seeming to be real. Its huge head twisted as it studied the unexpected scent of fresh meat. It fell to its belly in the sand. Inch by inch it crept to the pit. I felt my heart hammering, squeezed the spear until my hand hurt. The stars dimmed. Soon it would be dawn. I wanted to see this killer! See it fully—impaled upon the stakes. Then, the starlight faded into that indeterminate grayness before sunrise, and I saw only shadows below. I stared hard, thought the wolf had left, and was about to rise when I heard the low, feral rumbling of its growl.

Faint light spilled into the gully. The wolf had crept to the very edge of the matting and lay there studying it. Something in its primitive consciousness told it this was a trick. Something was not right. Perhaps the human scent still clung to the palm fronds. The enemy. Yet something in its deeper, more urgent consciousness also recognized the scent of fresh meat. Feed! Eat!

It slunk around the matting, its sensitive nostrils testing every inch of its edge. In the growing light I could see the beast clearly. It was a thing of terrible beauty; perfect in its lean muscled body, the powerful shoulders bunched as it moved. A perfect killer. A monster of an animal. No wonder the man had called it a demon!

For a moment I thought it would step on the matting, and my heart leaped. The wolf pressed one paw delicately upon the surface and withdrew. Then it selected one corner of the matting, clamped its powerful jaws upon it and with infinite care slowly began to pull the mat toward itself. No!

Yet I watched with amazement, expecting the matting at any moment to collapse, the meat to fall into the pit. What would it do then? Would it follow? But slowly it pulled, so gentle in its terrible power. Then I saw to my dismay that it would succeed. It had the meat nearly within reach of the edge of the pit.

Enraged, I stood up and bellowed at the wolf. I flung my spear hopelessly, watching it fall far short of the animal. I hurled rocks and screamed at the wolf.

It stared disdainfully at my futile efforts, tugged the mat the last few inches and clamped its jaws upon the meat. It stood there a moment, proud and defiant. Then it turned and loped gracefully, in magnificent long strides, up the gully into the hills.

I stood there sweating in the new sun, heart hammering in my chest. Then retrieving my spear, I kicked at the futile matting and went back to the hut to nurse my anger.

* * *

This is the way I killed the wolf. I thought like the wolf, predatory and mean. I sat all day in the hut thinking like the wolf. And thought of the salt cakes. The way I would kill the wolf: I would let it kill itself.

First I corralled the sheep. They came willingly, sensing no threat. I let the randy goat wander free. Somehow, I believed, he could fend for himself, and he loathed the rope.

Then I located a stone from the hills. I spent the afternoon sharpening the knife against the stone. I washed it carefully, pressed it into the mud, rubbed its handle with palm fronds, trying to eradicate all human scent from it.

I moistened the salt cakes, sticking them together in one blocky lump, placed the razor-edged knife within it and left it in the sun to dry.

Later I took the salt block, wrapped in a piece of cloth I had washed in the oasis, like a deadly offering to the gully. Beyond the trap I had set, I placed it among the rocks near the wolf's trail and climbed high into the rocks to wait.

I knew the wolf would come. After eating, it would lie up in some hollow during the day. At nightfall it would come for water. This was the way with animals.

It did not come during the night. Perhaps it had water elsewhere. Perhaps it would lie up another day. I was about to return to the hut when I saw its shadow round a rock. Ah, but the wolf was careful, scouting every inch of the trail. The dawning sun was behind it, and its shadow was long and ominous.

Then its shoulders appeared, and I had to force myself not to gasp aloud. The beast was mammoth, and magnificent by morning light. I marveled at the size of it, gray head bent under huge rolling shoulders. The body narrow and long, stretching to powerful hindquarters. It paused and sniffed the air, sensing something amiss. I froze high in the rocks, feeling a tremble of fear run through me. I had left the spear behind. The knife was unreachable. Slowly I sank down, peering through a slit between two rocks.

The wolf approached one slow step at a time, its nostrils picking up the tantalizing scent of salt. It stalked the block, walked around it, fighting its impulses. Its long tongue reached out tentatively, merely brushing the salt block. It sank to its belly, sniffing of it. Rose, turned away. Returned. Then it bent, avidly lapping the block. Its pink tongue became frantic for the salt, and it lapped to the knife's razor edge. When the blood dripped from its tongue, the wolf lapped harder. Driven wild by the fresh, salty blood, it lapped its own life. Harsh mewing sounds escaped it, but it could not stop. A pink froth spread across its cheeks like a horrible grin.

The wolf stopped lapping, blood running down its jaws. It shook its head in bewilderment, pawed its mouth. The wolf stumbled up the rocks. At the head of the gully it lifted its bloody jaws to the sky and cried out its undoing. The howls rang among the rocks, and I had to bend my head away. No! I wanted to weep for the wolf. The wolf growled savagely and ran off out into the desert.

I could not leave the wolf to die thus, so degraded by its own nature. It seemed evil to me. It was evil! A violation worse than the wolf's compulsion to feed.

Dying! I had had enough of it.

For what reason? A promise made to a dying man who deliriously babbled away about demons? I would have no demons! No more than gods!

I stalked back to the hut in a fury, thrust some dried meat and a waterskin in a pack, grabbed the Beshali spear and turned back to the desert. Taletha watched in bewilderment. I spoke not a word. At last, as I strode to the gully, she ran and seized my cloak, holding me back.

"Where are you going?" Fear suffused her voice. I turned, and the anger fled before her anguished eyes.

"Don't leave me alone!" she pleaded.

I took her, held her, hugged her. How I loved her!

"I have to finish it," I said. "The wolf is dying."

"That's what we wanted," she begged.

"Not like this. I'll return. I promise you."

She sank to her knees, weeping. I turned back to the desert, never having felt so hollow in all my life. There was nothing left. No hatred that I had nursed all my days. Nothing. Only fear, and a task. And love for this woman I left.

* * *

The tracks lay like an arrow shot into the desert—long, loping strides at first, pace after pace. They slowed to a walk, and I could see flecks of blood on the trail. It was noon then, and I had to find shelter. I stopped to drink, holding the cloak high above my head.

I studied the land through a blinding glare. The rocks had disappeared behind me, falling to flat wasteland. For a moment I realized, with a sickening understanding, that if a wind rose, effacing the tracks, I would never find my way back.

And there was no shelter. I staggered to a walk, following the tracks. End it! Imagine the wolf's agony. Your own is nothing.

The sand shimmered like a white sea, blindingly bright. I pulled the hood of my cloak down about my face, screening my eyes. There! The wolf stumbled. The blood formed a small, brown pool against the sand. It got to its feet again, its prints splayed and uneven.

I stumbled myself; the sand under my hands was as hot as a flame, searing the palms. I reached into the pack, sipped from the flask. I should have waited. Several flasks were necessary. Already this one seemed depleted. Another sip, then, a small one. My head whirled in blinding lights. I took a piece of meat and chewed slowly. It turned dry in my mouth, and I choked on it, coughing it up. I rose and staggered on. Still the tracks wound ahead of me.

It was evening then, the sun an inflamed wound in the sky, hovering on the rim of the desert. But I saw ahead a gray spot against the burning sand.

My legs would not move. I fell to my knees and began crawling toward it. The heat in the sand blistered my hands, my knees. It seemed to rise and scorch my belly. I drank. The flask felt flat. I had to finish this and return during the night. It would be cooler. I could make it.

I lay on my belly only yards from the wolf, unable to move. I didn't know how I got there. Perhaps I crawled in a dream. Passed out. It was night, the whole land silvered by starlight. I rose to my knees, crawling to the wolf.

Did its flanks move?

I tried to raise the spear.

I could see its jaws now. The tongue hung like shredded ribbons. Obscene. A pool of blood surrounded its head like a dark nimbus.

I was there. I rose to my knees, raising the spear above my head and felt the strength leave me, suddenly drained away. My knees quivered and buckled. The spear dropped, striking me as I fell.

During the night I opened one eye and was staring into the cold, open eye of the wolf. It did not move.

* * *

I awakened and my mouth felt dry and gritty. I reached for the waterskin at my belt and felt its flatness with terror. When I fell it had landed between my body and the ground, my weight squeezing the water out. A faint damp pool lay at my waist. I groaned and tried to stand. I had to get back. No, rest a bit first.

In the night I heard the fan of wings. Carrion birds. Come to feed on the wolf. I fell back beside it. Then I knew why my mouth felt gritty. The wind was blowing. For some reason a part of my brain insisted that was terribly important. I didn't understand. I was too tired.

* * *

The years had reeled back. I was alone on the desert north of Babylon in my cage, and the animals were out there waiting. I tried to weep, but my eyes were too dry, blistered over with a film of grit. Forsaken! I tried to call his name—Balthazzar!—and tasted sand blown against my cheek.

The beasts were out there. Waiting.

Let them come.

* * *

The wolf had me. I felt its teeth on my arm, shaking my arm. I twisted away. Its teeth sank upon my neck, fastened, lifted me shaking. I whirled frantically, screaming and kicking at the wolf. No, not the wolf. A white, ghostly shape hovered overhead. The starlight had faded. The moon seemed to walk in human form above me. It wouldn't let me be.

"Balthazzar," I croaked. I felt for the spear. It seemed miles away.

"Elhrain," her voice was insistent, pleading. "Elhrain!"

A beast stood at her side.

Then she knelt, this moon creature, and slipped the nipple of a water flask between my lips. Sweet water. I choked, clearing the sand from my throat.

She held my head on her lap, helping me drink.

"That's enough," she said.

"Taletha?"

She bent, cradling my head. Her voice was music. "Oh, you crazy fool." Her tears wet my cheeks.

I heard the goat bleating, anxious to be out of the blowing sand.

Taletha helped me stand. "Lean on me," she said. "We have to head back. Now."

I nodded.

She handed me the spear. "Use this to walk with."

I hobbled forward a few steps, then took the spear and flung it as far as I could into the desert night. I heard the heavy fan of wings.

"How . . . how did you find me?" I was bent over, panting.

"I followed your tracks," Taletha said. "Until the wind blew. See," she pointed ahead in the faint last light of the moon. The tracks were nearly effaced by the wind.

"We're lost," I said.

She shook her head. "The goat," she said. "He'll find his way back to the sheep." She shook the rope on its neck, clucked her tongue once and let the goat have its way.

"The goat," I breathed.

We had gone a short way when I stopped and turned. Soon the sun would be upon us. Thinking I needed water, Taletha handed me a water-skin.

"I have several," she said reassuringly. "And food when you're able."

I held up my hand against it. I gazed out over the barren landscape. I could just make out the gray shape against the desert sand, blown and collected by the wind's draft against its body. A heavy bird lifted from the desert nearby, circled in the air and landed awkwardly above the wolf.

233

I saw its head jerk down once, again. I half turned to go back. Taletha grabbed my sleeve and held fast.

She forced the waterskin upon me. "One more drink," she said. "Now let's get out of here."

The goat tracked northward, occasionally sniffing the ground, then turned its blunt head into the wind and forged steadily on.

CHAPTER FOUR

We made it to the edge of the rocks late that afternoon. I don't know how. A dozen times I would have fallen, simply given in and collapsed. Each time Taletha encouraged me, succored me, led me. I don't know where she got that fierce, indomitable strength.

The wind rose, blowing the sand in slanting curtains, harsh and needlelike. Our skin was raw, our cloaks abraded by its sawing force.

I leaned upon her. Oh, I leaned upon her. She was the strength in me, as the stubby-headed goat was for both of us. It shook its head angrily against the wind. It stopped often to sniff the air where all scents had now been blown apart, but still it led us unerringly to the rocks.

When we saw them we staggered up into their protective outcroppings, locating a hollow out of the wind. We collapsed to the ground and fell asleep exhausted.

When we awakened night shadows crept over the desert. The sun was setting behind us, casting strange beautiful lights through the wind-blown sand that whistled above. Deep purples entwined against a scarlet canopy in a fierce beauty.

The goat was gone.

I stood up, startled, looking for it, felt the force of the wind above the rocks and ducked back down.

Taletha chuckled. "Let him go," she said. "He was anxious for his ladies. They will be all right."

"But . . . how . . ."

"Don't worry. I can find the way now. I took markings when I came to look for you."

* * *

We spent another night and a day huddled in our rocky shelter, and, oddly, I remember it now as one of the most precious times in my life. We ate, we drank, we rested and watched the storm blow itself out. We lay in each other's arms. I stroked Taletha's gritty hair and thought I had never held anything more precious.

The third night the storm blew itself out. Taletha roused me. "Come," she said. She hoisted her pack, and I followed her lead.

We arrived at the hut before morning. The proud goat bleated its greeting through the morning air.

I felt strangely morose thinking of the wolf's death. The creature was magnificent for what it was, a cunning killer. I tried to shut the wreckage of its body from my mind. My promise was fulfilled—and a foolish promise it had been, made at the moment of a man's dying need.

Yet I could not stop thinking of the wolf.

I looked at Taletha. She sat on her knees by the entrance to the hut, watching the sheep. I could almost feel the yearning in her, an instinct as primitive as the wolf's feeding, a yearning for her home. Yet she would wait until I said the word. I knew that and resisted it. *She* had extracted the promise from me. For her kinsman. And now she waited. Was she fearful, thinking I would renege? But where else could we go? Back to the desert? Stay here? Impossible!

"The wolf," I said suddenly, speaking the thought in my mind.

She turned to me slightly, her eyes still fastened on the sheep.

"It is not native to the desert, is it?"

She shook her head.

"Where could it come from? It couldn't have crossed the desert as we did. And I have never seen . . . never even heard of a wolf before."

"I think," she said, "it followed the caravan."

"The one the man was in? After the sheep?"

She nodded. "That is what I think," she said. "It followed the sheep and went too far."

"Too far?"

"Past the point where it could turn back. It had to follow then."

"And in the sandstorm," I added, following her train of thought, "it was able to pick up the scent of the sheep and come here."

She nodded again.

My mind whirled. The wolf's dying was so futile! It gave itself up—killed itself—and, finally, lay as nothing more than a heap of fur and bones in the desert, to be buried and forgotten by the desert winds. Yet I was trembling as I saw the significance of the wolf's being here, at *this* place. It was a sign that could mean life itself.

"But wouldn't that mean," I persisted, "that this . . . northern land isn't so far away? I mean, these travelers couldn't be fools. They wouldn't broach the desert unless—"

"A short-cut," she finished. She looked at me with excitement in her eyes that she hadn't dared to show before. "I don't think it is too far to the other side."

"Are there wolves there?" I asked her. "In your homeland?"

"There are wolves in the hills. By the shepherds. I don't remember seeing one. My father . . ."

"Yes?"

"Was not a shepherd."

"Tell me?"

She bent, staring at the ground. Her body went rigid.

"Taletha. I killed the wolf. My promise. You owe me this."

It was the wrong thing to say. I knew that. Don't force her! Who knows her past? I saw her body stiffen as if struck.

"Forget it," I said. "We'll set out whenever you're ready, and I'll see this . . . other side for myself."

She shook her head. Slowly the words came.

"My father was a merchant," she said. "We lived in a city. I hardly remember it." She was silent a long time. I thought she was going to stop, and I leaned back upon the rocky floor to rest. Heat waves danced off the rock.

"He traded," she said, as if groping for the right words. "Sometimes he went along with the caravan. I . . . think he was a rich man.

"Then, one time, he took us all along—my mother, my brother, my sister and me. It was a long voyage. He would be gone many days, and said he would be lonely. So he took us along. A long journey, but exciting. We stopped at many strange cities where my father did business. This was long ago. I was a young girl. I do not remember where.

"I remember only the traveling. The porters. A few guards, I remember. But we were welcomed in the cities. There were many parties." She heaved a huge sigh. She picked up a handful of sand, letting it trail through her fingers.

She turned and smiled at me. "Parties," she said derisively. "I was young then.

"We were to make a final stop at a distant city, then to return. It was a place famous for spice trade, I think. I remember Father talking about it. And the city had gardens."

I felt my pulse quicken, sat up. "Do you remember the name?"

Taletha shook her head. "We never made it. We were attacked by bandits. They . . ." Her voice trailed off in a choking noise.

"That's okay," I said. "You don't have to go on."

". . . killed my mother and father. In front of my own eyes." She knelt sobbing, her body trembling. "I have tried to forget!" she shouted, pounding a small fist into the sand. "I cannot! Over and over!"

"The rest of your family?" I asked after a few moments.

She shook her head dully. "I don't know. My brother and sister . . . I didn't see them. I . . . think I passed out.

"Anyway," she said, shaking her head, "they took me south. I was sold to a merchant. After many days' sailing I arrived at a port."

"Tamal?" I asked.

"I think so. Someone took us inland. And that's when King Komani saw me. He grew angry with the traders. He said he did not permit slavery in his land. As a lesson, he took me into his own household. Honoring me." She looked up with a crooked half smile. "He gave me my name," she added. "I didn't know who I was anymore.

"So that's where I grew up," she added. "Until I met you." She smiled.

"Look where it got you," I added as a bad joke.

She laughed. "A home in the desert? Elhrain, I loved you the first time I saw you!"

Now I laughed. "Me? I thought I was courting you. I was afraid of you. I was the outsider."

"What do you think I was!" she said. "But you were special. From the start. So handsome then."

"Then?" I teased.

"Yes. Now you're just a homely traveler. Like the goat, I keep you around."

I snorted. She threw sand at me, I tugged her to me, and we rolled on the ground laughing. I held her then, looking into her eyes. Ah, those secret eyes, like brown pools I could swim in.

"Taletha," I said. My voice cracked on her name. "I have to ask you one question yet."

She nuzzled me, the points of her hair tickling my neck. I stroked her back gently.

"The names of your sister and brother? Do you remember them?"

She sat up. Her face furrowed into a frown. "I was very young," she said. "So much I tried to forget. And it doesn't work, does it? You can't forget."

I nodded. Oh, my own efforts to forget!

"My sister looked like me, I think. Maybe I only see myself in her."

I nodded. Again my heart hammered wildly. I was seeing *her!* All these years past.

"I think," Taletha said, "we called her 'the little bird,' because she was happy, so lively. Doval, we called her."

The sound that escaped me must have been a shriek. I grabbed my head like some curtain was splitting, as if I were seeing something whole for the first time. Taletha pulled at my hands, suddenly afraid. I seized her shoulders, looked into her eyes as if trying to peer into her mind itself.

"Listen," I said. "Your brother."

She shook her head. "He was so young."

"I know. His name. Could it have been Haggai?"

She frowned, remembering. "Haggai. It means 'the precious one.' Yes. Haggai. But—"

"How do I know?"

Her face was stunned, torn between fear and joy.

In slow tones, as we rose and walked back toward the hut in darkness, I told her my story. At the end, a link was forged between us that had never quite been there before, and which now seemed incapable of breaking. In the linking we knew there was only one way to set our pasts at rest: to reach the other side.

* * *

There was a certain sadness in leaving this hidden oasis. We debated leaving the sheep along with the goat. Here was water and stubby grass. But if the oasis was life to them it was also a sure death. It would only be a matter of time until the jackal came or the hyena slunk through the rocks. But better, perhaps, was a sudden, sure death than the long agony of not having enough water; for we could not carry enough for them all.

In the end, we left them behind. The goat stood watching us walk up the gully, as if he were making some terrible decision. In the end, he turned his back on us, going back to his small flock. We were glad of his choice.

From high in the rocks we looked back down upon the plain. "Who knows," Taletha said. "Perhaps in a few years the place will be full of sheep." I chuckled. Both of us had the sense that we were heading home.

The desert no longer seemed as virulent as that to the south. We were amply provisioned with dried meat from the one sheep we had butchered. In lieu of the wooden casks, we each weighed ourselves down with water flasks. We left with confidence.

We crossed a caravan route heading north, its wagon and animal tracks grooved deep into the desert's crust, and followed it. We came to a place where there were springs, then one morning peered out from the rocks and spotted a small village. Remembering the bandit enclaves north of Babylon, I did not want to stop there, and we had no need. We skirted it during the night and took it as a sign that we were heading in the right direction.

I was startled one morning to feel a change in the air. I couldn't place it at first. I thought of the strange desert sea we had skirted before, but there the line between desert and water was as sudden as a fence. Here the atmosphere itself felt different. It was something I had not felt for months and months, since the jungles far to the south—moisture. The sun rose in a haze. A gray bank appeared in the northern sky and grew in size and density.

"Rain," I murmured.

The cloud darkened. Lightning streaked its black flanks. The earth shivered under peals of thunder. The rain hit, sudden and hard as a sheet of metal. We ducked under some arching rocks and watched it rampage across the earth. We stared amazed at the onslaught of rain.

"We have to be near a sea," I said.

"We passed one." Taletha pointed out.

"But this comes from the north."

Throughout the morning the tempest assaulted the land. Then the sun broke clear over a clean and shining ground. By late afternoon the sand was baked dry, but rocky pools held fresh water and we replenished our flasks.

We traveled by day then, anxious to see what lay ahead. On the following day we saw before us the broad expanse of a sandy shoreline and the huge blue bowl of the sea.

"The Great Sea," Taletha murmured.

"You know it?"

She nodded. "We turn east now."

"More desert?"

"Not for long. You'll see. We're almost there."

But we weren't. Here was a land of such striking contrasts it took my breath away. Stark, rocky desert collided with sea water. Waves thrashed the sand.

We followed its shore until it curved north, then Taletha turned us east. There was an eagerness in her, a raw vitality, that disturbed me. Did I feel I was losing her?

The inland desert here was a strange, dry mixture of broken hills and plains. Often huge rocks, wind-worn and grotesque, littered the ground. The land rose steadily. We climbed into rocky hills that chewed up our sandals. Our cloaks were mere rags now, patched and stitched countless times. Taletha seemed oblivious to it.

We crossed a long range of hills, arriving at last on a promontory. We surveyed a scene that took my breath away. In all my wandering, in all my imagining, I had never seen such a land. All the land I had seen—stark desert and fragile farmland, salty coast and fierce jungle—seemed primeval in contrast to what lay below, so serene and perfect.

A blue haze covered rolling green hills. The haze threaded above a river as sharp and clear as a sign. The haze spread up over the surrounding land like a foggy quilt. Green hills tumbled to the east.

We clambered down the hill, slipping, urgent in our hurry. We ran down a grassy plain, hearts hammering, the grass like velvet under our feet. And stopped at last at the river's edge. The pebbles in the river winked bright, little white eyes. They shone like polished gems. Even the sand at the water's edge shone like a sheet of burnished brass where the water rushed against it. Then, without a word, we flung our packs aside and plunged into the river.

Taletha shouted with joy. She ducked under and came up with water streaming from her. She picked up handfuls of river sand and rubbed at her hair until it shone like glossy varnish. She flung water at me while I lay back in the river, letting its current lave my body.

Then she paused, looked at me and smiled. She crawled over to me on her knees. "We're home," she said and bent to me. I held her, falling back into the current, letting the water wash and wash the desert from us.

CHAPTER FIVE

I soon discovered how little royalty meant among a people who followed priests, believed in a God and privately loathed the political domination under which they found themselves. They honored a person for what he or she did and how they functioned in a community, not for what he or she *was* by accident of birth.

I solved the problem easily, for what counted here also were coins, and the gold I had carried around in my pack all these years—virtually worthless to my position either among the royalty of Jebel Barkal or the tribespeople of the Beshali—came to good use. I bought a farm.

* * *

Taletha and I had continued to walk inland, passing shepherds in the hills, stopping in small, bucolic settlements, until we reached a larger community. The surrounding land was neatly cultivated, and I marveled at the sheer expanse of fertile soil. It seemed constantly like a dream I was waking up from, rather than a reality about me. Fig trees littered the countryside. On distant hillsides, vineyards sprawled in lush purple clumps. Fields were planted and pieced into stands of waving grain, including crops unfamiliar to me.

We stayed at an inn for several weeks, recuperating, blissfully content. When I heard through the innkeeper that a nearby farmland was up for sale, I quickly purchased it. It was not cheap. Taletha laughed at my rude attempts to barter. I would have paid any price I could afford, and since I had more gold than necessary, my heart wasn't in it.

So we prepared to become farmers. We needed to purchase some supplies before leaving the village, and I left Taletha a free hand in that. I exchanged jewels and gold for common currency, determined to stake out a homeland for ourselves here.

There was one more thing to do. Taletha wanted a proper marriage.

It made no sense to me, and I told her so. "I love you!" I protested. "What more do you want?"

"A marriage," she said.

"I'm content," I replied.

"So am I. Contentment isn't the issue."

"What *is* then?"

"I want a blessing."

"From whom?"

"The priests," she replied.

In the end I figured a few words, the waving of some hands, couldn't hurt me. If it was important to Taletha, I could go along with it. She had gone along with enough on my account. "Let me think about this thing," I said.

"Think? You have to think about it?" Exasperation fired her eyes.

"Maybe a husband should have a working farm to offer."

"Or a wedding trip through the desert," she retorted.

A week later Taletha had made arrangements.

*　*　*

We moved to the farm, a small place tucked into the hills, surrounded by a flat pasturage in the valley, room for planting grain, and some vineyards crawling up the hillside. The farm had belonged to a couple too old to work the land and who wanted to move to a larger city to be near the holy places in their last years. Their age and infirmity told on the land. The vines were overgrown, desperate for pruning. The whole place needed work, hard work and plenty of it. But from the first moment I laid eyes upon it I had seen the promise it held and had fallen in love with it.

Taletha went to the village one morning and returned with five sheep and a belligerent goat that she had to drag by a rope over her shoulder.

I smiled, watching her lead them into the pen. Five sheep. Of course, there would be precisely five. She also had made a date with the priest at the local temple.

It would be private, she said. A simple thing.

On the matter of privacy she couldn't have been more wrong.

The people in the village were a friendly people, and while I took some affront at their bewilderment over my black skin at first, I found their hearts earnest and honest. Of necessity, I had begun to learn their language. One can't deal with people long without that. But I also began to learn respect. They were interested in my farm, and some were too quick with advice. Some of it I heeded, surprisingly. However much I wanted to make this land mine, and however much I knew about earth, this was a foreign land to me where I now made my home, and I wanted to succeed.

It was different with Taletha. Day by day her wariness left her; she quickly made friends in the village. I shouldn't have been surprised, then, that a small band of people awaited our coming on our marriage day. Taletha tugged my hand toward them.

Some I already recognized or knew. Manasseh the carpenter, who had done some work readying our home and supplying furniture, and his wife, Meridivel. Tomit and Althea, the couple who had sold Taletha the sheep and the goat. The shopkeeper, whose young daughter Taletha had hired to help set the home in order.

It was a joyful and smiling crowd. And my heart recoiled. Thus Taletha tugged my hand.

"Private, you said," I muttered under my breath.

"They're friends," she answered gaily.

I forced a smile.

These people had more customs than do kings! Before we could go to the temple, we had to stop by Tomit's home to feast.

"It's morning," I protested.

"Is it ever too early to feast?" shouted Manasseh. His rotund belly shook with laughter. But the man had forearms like an ox. He could be dangerous, I thought.

At Tomit's house, the shopkeeper's two daughters worked busily over an oven in the kitchen. My head began to whirl. The people shouted, laughed.

I pulled Taletha aside. Her eyes danced. Never had she looked so beautiful. The weeks of rest had stripped years from her; her features were again smooth. Even her skin, wrinkled by desert winds and sun, seemed younger, healthier. I saw her joy and my heart melted.

"Can we ever get this thing done?" I said.

"Soon. As soon as I get dressed."

"Dressed! But . . ."

Just then one of the women—someone I didn't even recognize, they just kept coming!—motioned Taletha aside. She darted away from me and disappeared into another room, past a drawn curtain, with the women.

The men gathered around me. Someone pressed a wine flask into my hand. "I've got work to do," I protested. Somehow this struck them as terribly funny. The men roared. Someone slapped me good-naturedly on the back.

At last the curtain parted, and my knees nearly melted. There were a few audible gasps as everyone turned, and then silence.

I had seen her in the home of Eldrad and Alsace, shy, bewildered, ducking away like a frightened child. I had seen her in the palace of Komani, doing a princess's work. In the deep of the jungle, withdrawn, patient, she had been a shadow among shadows. I had seen her, thin and burned by a relentless sun, brave the most fierce desert, going out alone, with only a raggedy-headed old goat, to find me.

Now I saw a queen. She took my breath away. She wore a white linen garment that fell to the ground. Flowers were entwined into her jet-black hair. Her eyes—oh, those eyes in which I had lost myself so often—were singing with joy. I sucked in my breath and straightened my back.

This . . . this is my beloved!

The whole room seemed to bow in waiting.

Then Manasseh bellowed with laughter. "Come," he roared, "for all is ready."

The men circled me in a phalanx, cutting me off from Taletha. Behind us the women followed. I kept throwing glances over my shoulder. Taletha walked gaily, a smile of pure serenity upon her lips. I wanted her by me.

As we turned into the main street of their dusty little village, children began darting ahead of us, shouting. People stared from doorways, nodding happily, waving. A dog charged out, barking furiously. One of the men landed a kick, and the men roared with laughter as the dog limped down the street nursing a sore behind.

Celebration! I began to give in to it. For it was not just for me. Nor just for Taletha. The town was throwing itself a party. The people needed to *rejoice*.

Someone in the vanguard started singing a rollicking tune that others joined in. Feet began to stamp the beat. Dancing! The wedding party danced. The people could not restrain themselves. Dust rose under the stamping feet.

The small temple that served all the surrounding villages stood at a crossroads. It was a simple building, made of brick with the requisite portico, a tiled foyer, the altar tucked back inside. Behind it the river flowed, a clean blue ribbon. I was anxious to get in, get this blessing and get out. Inside, I saw an old priest bent on his knees by the altar. He was an ancient man. A young boy prepared the altar for him.

The people gathered in the forecourt. Half the village was there now. The women led Taletha to me as if presenting a gift. I understood. They were. They were giving me themselves!

Yes, I understood! And my eyes filled with tears. I could not help it. My knees trembled. Taletha walked to me and placed her small hand in mine, and I squeezed it gently.

The singing subsided to a gentle murmur. We took a step forward, surrounded by smiling faces. A small boy, dressed in a lovely white robe, held a sheep to one side.

Then there was silence, and with it a sudden chill in the air, as if the sun had disappeared. Heads bowed, averted. People turned rigid, fearful. I looked about, bewildered, thinking someone was hurt. Something terrible had happened. A woman made a fearful choking sound. The men bent their heads.

Through the crowd strode a tall, haughty man dressed in a black robe. Two younger men flanked him and carefully followed a step behind.

The man strode slowly, purposefully. He seemed to stand a head higher than all the others. The old priest stood up and shakily walked to him. The priest was trembling!

The man turned, fixing his penetrating glare upon the crowd. A thin black beard framed his narrow face like a cape. But those eyes! They were black as ebony, blacker than my own, but they seemed cold as metal.

For a long time he said nothing. I stepped forward, but Manasseh stepped quickly ahead of me. My use of the language was not good yet. I forced it, nonetheless.

"Who is this?" I rasped at Manasseh. He shook his head, not turning to look at me. I felt someone pluck my sleeve, shook it off.

Manasseh stared back at the man, unafraid. "Your Grace," he said.

The man nodded.

Silence settled like a gray cloud, thick and suffocating.

The man's voice was a rapier. "What are you doing?"

"A marriage, Your Grace," answered Manasseh. "By your leave."

The man shook his head, a mere twitch, showing disdain nonetheless.

"But—"

"He is not of our people. You would violate the law!" His words lacerated the people. His eyes narrowed.

He raised a long arm, draped in black, and pointed at me. "A foreigner! Infidel!"

I pushed Manasseh aside.

People began to shrink away from the edges of the crowd.

I could not find the words I wanted in this language. I stood glaring back at the man, feeling his absolute scorn, returning it.

"Who do you think you are?" I said. The words were rude, stumbling.

The man drew himself up, livid with anger.

"You provoke the Lord God!" he hissed. "No infidel shall enter this house of God."

I stepped forward, outraged. Manasseh's powerful hands closed like a vise on my arms.

"There will be no marriage here!" stated the man. His words were spoken slowly, deliberately, like a curse. "Begone!"

He turned his back on us and entered the inner room of the temple.

The altar boy and the old priest scurried out of the way.

I stood for a long time, staring at the desolate little building. Anger raged against sorrow in me. This was my gift to Taletha! It was for the people, too. What right had he to dash their joy?

It was also for me. And I nearly wept.

At last I turned. Taletha stood beside me. Oh, the flowers in her bent head broke my heart. Nearly all the people had left. Manasseh stood there yet, his broad face still as red as fire. Meridivel was there, her hand on Taletha's shoulders. Tomit. A few others.

Manasseh looked at me. "I would like to break him apart with my bare hands," he growled. He raised his hands, clenched in fists that made the muscles of his forearms bulge in knots.

"Let's get out of here," I said.

* * *

We were back in Tomit's house. I returned for Taletha's sake. I would have fled back to the farm and never set foot in the village again. But I sensed her need for the comfort of the women and willingly remained. I realized that I stayed also for myself; I needed comfort. I needed—and this is the first time since I left Eldrad that I had thought this—I needed friends.

It was evening, turning to darkness, when Meridivel and Althea prepared a meal for us. The wedding feast. It tasted like ashes. We ate in silence, watching the foreyard through the open door turn dark. We had avoided talking about it. I could avoid it no longer.

"Well?" I said. "I am a foreigner. Surely I am an infidel! But who on earth was *this*? A priest?"

"No," Manasseh said quickly. "Not a priest. The priests are for the people. At least in the villages."

"Right," added Tomit. "In the big cities they may have sold out. Not here."

"Who, then?"

"One of the religious leaders," spat Manasseh. "The keepers of the law! No one will mistake them for the true servants of God."

"What right—"

"That's the problem," Manasseh interrupted. He spread his beefy palms in a gesture of despair and shook his head. "It's hard to explain. The keepers of the law of God . . . well. They're supposed to keep our religion pure, you see."

"No," I confessed. "I don't see. The people were happy. Rejoicing. He killed that joy. *Taletha's* joy. What kind of a religion is this that goes around killing joy? Is this a God or demon?"

Manasseh drew back as if struck.

"He doesn't know," Tomit apologized.

"That's right," I said rudely. "I don't. All I know is that when gods start ruling people's lives, this is what happens."

Manasseh sighed. "Don't mistake God for what people do," he said. "We loathe these people as much as you. They've only become more fanatical during these last years."

"Threatened," said Meridivel. "That's what they are."

The others nodded.

"And when people are threatened," she said, "they do all sorts of desperate things. Using the law to protect their own power."

"Well," I said, "what on earth were we doing . . . rejoicing . . . that would threaten them?"

"It's not you," Tomit said quickly.

"Not the infidel, then?"

Manasseh smiled. "Everything has changed here. We're far away from the big cities, and sometimes it hardly seems to touch us. But during these last years, a man has gone about those eastern cities . . ." He raised his hands, as if to say the matter is too complex to explain.

"They say he is the messiah," Meridivel finished. There was a note of defiance in her voice. The others nodded eagerly.

I shook my head and drank from a flask of wine. It was time to leave.

Suddenly there was a small, bent shape at the door. Hunched over, the figure was hard to see against the darkness of night. A polite knock sounded against the doorpost.

"Come in," Tomit called.

The old priest, bent and shuffling, entered the room. He had put on a cloak against the chill of night, and when he threw back the hood there was a bruise across one eye.

Manasseh sucked in his breath. Tomit hurried to bring the priest a chair. He waved Tomit off.

The ancient priest, his body bent like a crooked stick, smiled. He fastened his gaze upon Taletha. He drew her into his smile like an embrace.

"We have something to finish," he said warmly.

The others began to nod. I could feel the excitement. It dawned on me what he was suggesting. I shook my head. "I have had enough of this," I said.

Manasseh bent to me, speaking earnestly into my ear.

"Elhrain," he murmured. "The man risks his very life to do this for you and Taletha."

Chapter Five

I pondered a moment, looked at Taletha, her face suddenly radiant again, expectant, and nodded.

We returned to the farm late that night, officially married, at least in the eyes of the villagers and the brave old priest.

CHAPTER SIX

I thought that would be the end of it. We were married. We could live at peace. Instead, the act seemed to awaken something in Taletha. I didn't know or understand what it was. Perhaps the best way I can describe it is like a hunger, a raw hunger for self-knowledge.

We were at peace in all other ways here. Throughout that growing season my crops flourished. What a joy it was to work this land! The soil, rich and deep, seemed endless in nutriment. The rains, broken by the hills, were gentle and soaking. I planted barley in the field, fencing it off from the small flock of sheep that Taletha kept in the pasture. On the hillside, the pruned-back vines at first looked like dead stumps. I was ruthless in my cutting of the overgrown tangle that had not been well-tended for years. Taletha came out to see it and left shaking her head.

"I know what I'm doing, woman," I muttered at her back. But when I saw the pruned stumps, I wondered.

They sprouted new growth, which I trellised and nurtured carefully, continuing to clip away thin tendrils, steering the life in one concerted direction.

I was so often in the vineyard for a time that I scarcely noticed the transformation in our house. Taletha had a magic touch. It was a large, airy place, which Taletha decorated with curious little pieces of furniture she brought back from the village. The front of the house was adorned with flowers and herbs. When I walked down from the hills in the evening it seemed a warm, smiling house.

In the spring her flock gave birth, one sheep dropping twin lambs that Taletha had to tend almost constantly for several days. She babied them like a worried mother, and I teased her about them.

"Just keep your eye out for predators," she said curtly. "And you might grow some grain for them."

"Grain! Sheep graze. People eat grain."

"My sheep are going to have grain," she replied.

Together we fenced off a small area and planted grain.

At least once a week Taletha went into the village. It was a long way. She set out early in the morning and returned well after the sun had set. It was at such times, after she returned, that I noticed the change in her. She would return pondering, reserved, supplying abrupt answers to my casual questions. Her comments were strange and beguiling.

"They say that records are kept in the city," she said once.

"What kind of records?"

"Taxation. They keep family records."

"Taxes! So I have to pay taxes to live here?"

"Not yet. But you will. They're collected in the village, though."

* * *

"I think my family lived in the capital city," Taletha said one day.

"How do you know? Do you remember?"

"No. I only think that is the way it would be. My father was a trader. Wouldn't he have lived in a big city?"

"Perhaps."

* * *

And, again. "The boy?" she asked. "My brother? Are you certain he is dead?"

"Yes. I saw his body. *If* Haggai was your brother."

"But my sister? She is alive?"

"Sold into slavery, Taletha. And for that I have only the word of a corrupt, dying man. If she even survived the desert; she was so young."

"I survived," Taletha said simply.

"Yes," I replied.

* * *

And, one evening. "My sister," she said. "Do you think she could be alive?"

I sat down across from her, facing her. "*Could be,* Taletha?" I looked into her searching eyes. "I suppose she could be. But I must confess I don't believe so. You have to understand the way it was. The sandstorm. The bandits."

She nodded. "But she could be."

"Yes."

Taletha was silent for a long time. Her eyes never left my own. She seemed to be searching herself, not pleased with all she found.

"Could be," she murmured again. Then, her voice like flint, she said, "I would like to go."

"Where?"

"To the city. To search the records."

I groaned. She turned away from me and began pounding a mound of bread dough on the table. Her small fists slammed into the dough like mallets.

At length I said, "May I at least harvest my crop first?"

She turned and broke into a huge grin. She flung her flour-caked arms around me. "I knew you would understand," she said.

"Woman," I said in the sternest voice I could muster. "I don't understand a thing of this!"

* * *

The crop was a fine one. The barley was adequate, the grapes promising. I was pleased.

We arranged for Manasseh's son, a boy named Liske, to stay at the farm and tend the sheep while we were gone. On the day of our parting, Taletha bustled about, citing a long list of orders to the lad. He nodded obligingly.

Manasseh finally said, "Taletha, the lad knows sheep like an old goat himself. He fled my carpentry shop to the hills nearly as soon as he could walk."

The lad grinned.

"I know," Taletha said. She picked up her pack and walked out to the wagon Manasseh had loaned us for the trip. Manasseh rode back with us as far as town. "Listen," he called as we left, "if you find any mahogany, buy all you can. That's why I loaned you the wagon!"

* * *

I had traveled vast distances by myself. Even vaster distances with only Taletha by my side. Now I had taken up life in the hills, working the land by the sweat and strength of my body. I had grown comfortable with silence and space. That comfort waned as we followed the broad road to the capital, especially as it grew more congested by the hour. We stayed the first night at a crowded village inn, and we paid what even I considered an exorbitant rate for a tiny cubicle shared with another couple.

"You're lucky to have a spot at all," the innkeeper muttered.

Our roommates, a shy, young couple, explained that a high feast day was approaching. Of course everyone wanted to be in the city.

The next day the road grew still more crowded with ox-drawn wagons, foot passengers, people on mules or leading mules, and, increasingly, soldiers on horseback. For some reason the soldiers fascinated me. There was something familiar about them, even in the way they exercised their authority and barged through the crowd. But I was too preoccupied with my own task to pay much notice. I was no driver, and the press of people made me as nervous as the tired ox that pulled us.

That second night we simply slept in the wagon itself, forgoing an inn altogether. Campfires sparkled by the road during the night. As I stretched my legs, walking down to the river that now ran parallel to the road, I heard over and over the word I had come to recognize: messiah. It was on everyone's lips.

Despite the press of traffic, I found myself enjoying the pristine beauty of this land. Several times, for lunch or just to rest, Taletha and I pulled off the main road into a field and let the ox graze for a while. White clouds crumpled down over the northern hills. Fields of green were awash in bright flowers. The ox chugged over the meadow to where it nosed aside the grass and watered at a spring. Suddenly and freely flowing, the spring bubbled up around shiny white and tan pebbles. I watched the thin stream trickle off to the river, and got down and drank from it. In the desert what a treasure this would be. It seemed I would never shake the sense of aridity from me, never find water fresh enough to slake my thirst. I walked out among the flowers, studying each luminous shape like a jewel. They were jewels, a field flung full of them. When I returned to the wagon, Taletha was curled up, fast asleep.

The crowds of people and wagons congested hopelessly near the city, finally coming to a complete standstill. Thousands of people had arrived for this feast day. Wagons and mules stood bewildered by the side of the road. Far in the distance we saw the city gates, the low towers of buildings standing behind them.

"Well," I said. "You've seen the city. Can we go back now?"

Taletha elbowed me in the ribs. She grabbed the reins from my hands and steered the ox and wagon off the road into a field.

"Now," she said, "we walk."

I groaned, hoisting the pack to my shoulder. "This thing is a part of me," I muttered. Taletha skipped happily on ahead.

At last we neared the city, forging our way through the throng, and entered its streets. Curiously, it seemed less crowded inside the city. People gathered on its main thoroughfare, so we slipped along side streets. From those streets it was a lovely, quaint, endearing city, full of red-clay brick homes, well-kept shops and municipal buildings. Beyond the city wall, hills rose to the north like green waves.

"Does it seem at all familiar?" I asked Taletha.

She shook her head and shivered, rubbing her arms.

Suddenly a great cry arose from the crowd some distance away. The roar was overwhelming. The very ground seemed to shake. We threaded our way through narrow alleys, passing tunic-clad soldiers, some on horseback, as we went. The soldiers clustered near the edges of the crowd, but held back, letting the people have their way. For one moment, we saw a man who rose slightly above the crowd, riding upon some animal lost in the press of bodies.

But we were far too far away to see whatever was happening. The noise careened through the streets, then moved toward the heart of the city, to a gleaming building that rose above the others.

We turned back. As I did so, I saw a soldier, a man of rank, standing in a portico with guards at his side. He stood absolutely still, arms crossed over his chest. But his gaze was leveled on me with a fierceness as predatory as the desert. I averted my glance, but it unnerved me. I took Taletha's arm and continued.

We tried several inns on the way back to the wagon, knowing it was hopeless. I agreed to stay overnight, to spend one more day in the city to locate some records that might give answers to Taletha's questions. After traveling this far, it seemed the proper thing to do.

We were back in the city by sunrise the following morning.

"There are two places to look," Taletha pointed out as we walked into the city. Here and there small groups of people already collected. Even though I had mastered the language by now, they spoke so rapidly and excitedly that I caught mere noise. Taletha told me they were talking about a king who had come into the city. She would say no more about it.

"The temple keeps records of my people. If there were an old priest, he might even remember," she said.

"And the other place?"

"The civil authority. They keep records of taxation."

"I don't understand this. The people seem ruled by religion, but also by politicians. These soldiers and such, they are foreign."

"Roman, I'm told," said Taletha. "Worse yet, the Romans appoint their own king from the area."

"Pretty confusing," I observed. "Whom do the people follow? I mean, who gives the orders?"

"God," she said.

I looked at her with undisguised scorn.

"Sorry," she chuckled. "That's the way it is."

"So everyone and nobody rules. Pretty confusing indeed."

We neared the temple, figuring out the building by directions some fellow travelers had given us. The place looked disheveled. By the door, two of the lawgivers, enigmatic men in black robes, stood silently surveying a litter of tables and cages in the forecourt. Off to the side, a group of soldiers stood watching. I took one look at them and decided.

"Listen," I said. "We'll divide the labor and we'll get out of here sooner. You do the temple; I'll find the tax people. There's only one problem."

"What's that, Elhrain?"

"I have no idea what to look for. I mean, your family name."

She flared at me. "So you think I do? That's why I'm looking. You have clues. My father was a trader. He had three children—Doval, Haggai, and . . . whatever my name was. Count back the years. Search the records a few years either way. Oh, and I'll need some money."

I handed her some coins without counting. With the conversion of my gold coins and some jewels, money was the one thing we had plenty of, even after buying the farm. Still, "What for?" I asked.

She nodded to the lawgivers. "Payoff," she said.

I cursed and turned down the street. I looked over my shoulder and called back. "Sunset. I'll meet you here."

Taletha waved and climbed the steps to the men in black robes. Curiously, I saw the soldiers detach themselves and walk toward me. For the next block, as I headed toward the municipal buildings, I sensed them behind me. They are probably going off shift, I thought. But at the beginning of the day?

I slowed, glancing over my shoulder. They were right behind me. Five of them. My pace quickened. I heard their footsteps nearing. I spotted an alley and turned to run.

Suddenly hands clamped down on each arm. The leader of the band stepped in front of me. He nodded. "That's the one," he said. I fought against the grip of the two guards. It was like fighting iron bars.

The leader grabbed my collar, letting his fingers bunch against my neck. "Listen," he hissed. "Come quietly, or I'll carry you like a sack of grain. You won't be harmed if you cooperate."

With two guards gripping my arms, I relaxed and let them lead me.

CHAPTER
SEVEN

The soldiers took me through streets that grew increasingly crowded, arriving at last before a long rectangular building that seemed a military post. Soldiers came and went. In the side courtyard tents were pitched in neat rows. A large back building stabled horses, and many men were busy rubbing the animals down and forking them hay. The grounds were well-kept, orderly and efficient.

We walked around the building to a side entrance, where a heavy wooden door was standing open. We stepped inside. It took a few moments for my eyes to adjust to the dimness of a room lit only by the light from the open doorway. It was large, about twenty feet square. Benches lined the walls. Directly ahead was a large desk with several chairs around it. On the desk a litter of maps lay open, weighed down by an unlit lamp. Behind the desk sat a large man, wearing the cape of an officer. I could barely see his face in the shadows, but I had the feeling I had seen him before. I tried to place him. No, there were too many soldiers around here. After a while they all looked the same. Wait. He seemed like the man whose gaze I had met . . . was it yesterday?

The guards led me directly before the desk. They relaxed their hold on my arms, but did not remove their hands. The officer in the chair stared at me a long time in silence, studying me. I grew impatient.

"Well?" I said.

Still he stared. His eyes were as unsettling as the gaze of some predatory animal. They seemed to ransack my very mind.

He leaned forward, hands clasped on the pile of maps.

His features had something unnerving about them. Strangely, though, I didn't feel afraid before him.

"There are a great many people here," he observed, as casually as if we were sharing a flagon of wine in easy company. I just then noticed a reed-wrapped flagon on a small stand next to his desk. "Yes," he murmured, "They are not your people."

"What do you mean?" I asked.

"You seem . . . out of order. A black man here? A bit unusual, I think."

"Since when is it a crime to look different?" I asked. My voice was abrasive, though I tried to control my impatience. "You don't exactly look like them either."

He chuckled and leaned back. "Yes, I suppose you're right. May I question you, nonetheless?"

"You're asking my permission?"

He nodded at the guards, who backed off and stood by the door. I detected a fierce loyalty in these guards, the kind of men who placed allegiance in a person, a leader, rather than in some idea or a state.

"See," he rubbed his forehead with the back of his hand, "we have quite a mob here. And," he observed, staring past me through the doorway, "a mob ripe for insurrection. Already they're claiming a new king. A regular coronation party yesterday. But what do they mean by that? A replacement for the local potentate—a paranoid old man whose every child is ready to overthrow him and claim his spot? Or for the emperor? That, you see, is my concern. Now, if it's merely a local mob . . . we give it a few days to burn itself out. If someone is bringing in outside insurrectionists, well, that's another matter."

"And I'm obviously from outside."

He nodded. His brooding eyes settled on me, unsettling me. "Tell me," he said, "what do you think of kings?"

"What if I told you I was one?" I replied.

"I'd probably believe you. Seems like everyone around here lately wants to be a king. Unfortunately, I'm responsible to an emperor."

"I am responsible to no one."

"I see." He reflected, murmured casually, "Lord me no lords," turning aside to reach for the flagon of wine. The words snapped in the back of my mind like a whip. He took the flagon, handed it to me.

"Would you like a chair?" he asked.

"I would prefer to stand."

"I thought so. Do you have a name, stranger?"

"Stranger? I am a stranger no place in this world, save only for *this* world where I live. My name is Elhrain."

He smiled to himself, as if chewing over some secret knowledge.

"So, no one knows anything about you?"

"Yes. But here, only my wife knows."

"I see. Does she know you came from Babylon originally?"

"I originally came from . . . how did you know!"

"Let's say, Elhrain, I simply have never forgotten."

I leaned forward, awestruck. The full beard, the graying hair. But that same piercing, unforgettable gaze. "Can it be?" I whispered.

He chuckled.

Then I said the really foolish thing. Gasping, I stammered, "You're . . . so much older!"

He laughed outright. "So are you, Elhrain. Oh, so are you!"

"Lycurgus!"

"The same." He stood up. He moved about the desk and wrapped his huge arms around me as the startled guards moved back uneasily.

"May . . . I have that chair now?" I gasped.

He laughed, grabbing a chair in one of his powerful arms and tossing it toward me. He sat down still laughing, drank from the flagon, handed it to me, then leaned forward. "So," he said, his eyes full of an old warmth. "Thirty years, Elhrain. More than thirty. And so much to tell. Who goes first?"

I did, and I took my time. It was an act of restoration. A healing. I understand that now. Here was a link to something before, a link upon which I could build a series of connections. Lycurgus listened intently. Once again I understood why his men were unusual, why they had such a fierce loyalty to him. He cared about them and dared to show it.

One of the soldiers, without being asked or ordered, brought us food and drink after a while. I lost track of the time. Lycurgus insisted upon hearing every detail, prompting me now and then: "Why did you do that?" "What happened because of that?"

261

I was startled to see the sun on the stone wall slanting and diminishing. I bolted upright. "Taletha!" I exclaimed.

"Your wife?"

"I left her at the temple." Quickly I explained.

"Well," said Lycurgus, "I think we should meet her, don't you? But tonight, and as long as necessary, Elhrain, I want both of you to stay with me. Enough of this nonsense of staying in a wagon."

He dispatched two guards with me to meet Taletha. Another two were sent to fetch the wagon.

Lycurgus rented a small but comfortable home on the southern edge of the city, just a stone's throw from the river that wrapped around the city like an embrace. The door stood open to a pleasant breeze.

A servant prepared dinner, resisting Taletha's efforts to join in. She and Lycurgus seemed like old friends from the first moment. "It isn't every night I have royalty in my household," Lycurgus said. "Let me enjoy it."

"Come off it," I growled.

"No," said Taletha. "I like it."

We finished the meal, and I was about to prod Lycurgus into telling his tale when one of his men respectfully coughed by the doorway. Lycurgus walked to him, listened, turned back to us. "I'm sorry," he said. "We'll have to wait. But meanwhile, my house is yours. If I can help you with the municipal records, let me know."

"When will you be back?" Taletha asked.

Lycurgus frowned. "I'm not sure. The madness of the crowds. Already things are changing. The paranoid old man on the throne here is scared silly." He paused. "Tomorrow night for sure."

* * *

Taletha had learned nothing at the temple. By the time she had paid off the lawgivers and an old priest so deaf she had to shout in his ear, she knew it was a hopeless case. One of the younger priests tried politely to help. "Tribe?" he inquired.

"I don't know," Taletha said.

"Can't help you much," he said. "In fact, we haven't kept decent records for years. If you knew your tribe and genealogy back, oh, say two hundred years, maybe I could do something."

Still, he let her pore over some old records, and after a day of fruitless

262

pondering he suggested she try the political offices. "Taxes are much more accurate than faith," he said knowingly.

"I certainly hope so," Taletha retorted.

* * *

The disgruntled clerks at the municipal building were already over-worked, overtired and overbearing. They were as willing to help as sheep are to give wool, and I had a mind to throw one down, tie him between my knees and shear his hair to get a straight answer. I flipped a few coins through my fingers, dangling the bribe. At least the religious people were overt, I thought. These creatures just sneered at it.

We were about to leave when a Roman guard rushed in, brushed past us with a nod and presented a letter to the clerk. The fellow jumped up and ran for his superior, who eventually waddled out, smelling of onions and wine. He wiped his thick lips with a dainty white handkerchief. He was a fat older man, stuffed full of his own importance. He fingered the note, read it and stiffened. "Lycurgus," he said obsequiously. "By all means."

He turned to us with the predatory grin of a hyena. "You are Elhrain?" I nodded. "How can I help you?" he said.

The guard smiled at us and left.

We worked in a room stacked with papyrus records rolled into tubular cylinders—the precious tax rolls. There we labored for most of the day.

The records were cross-divided: by family and by trade. We worked through the list of merchants. By midafternoon we had found nothing even vaguely resembling Taletha's family.

The magistrate returned near the end of the day. "Any answers?" he inquired.

"None," I muttered. "Maybe it's a dead end."

"That can't be," he said. "I assure you, my records are impeccable."

"Maybe we have the wrong place."

He turned to Taletha. "Your father is a merchant?"

"Was," she said dully. "I saw him killed."

"Oh, my," sighed the man. "That is another story, then. I misunderstood. The rolls of the deceased are destroyed of course, I simply don't have the room."

I groaned.

Perhaps he remembered Lycurgus's note, for he quickly added, "But perhaps I can help you, nonetheless. Do you know what he dealt in? With whom? Where? Where did he die?"

Taletha shook her head. "We were in the east," she said.

"Ah!"

"Trading for . . . I think for spices. On our way to a large city."

"Babylon," I added.

The man stroked his beard knowingly. "Ah, yes. That would be Solomon, of course. Rich man. No heirs. The whole family lost, from what we heard. The shop was taken over by the state."

"Not quite all heirs lost," Taletha said. Her face quickened. "I might be his daughter."

The magistrate registered concern. "Understand, we could not know. The property was taken for accumulated taxes. It would be a very long process, very *expensive*, to get it back."

"We're not interested," I said. "All we want is information."

The man relaxed visibly. He sat down in a chair. "Let's see what I can remember," he began.

"Names," I prompted.

He looked surprised. "Names?"

"Of the family."

"Oh, my. I'm not sure I can help. We really don't pay much attention."

"Unless, of course," I added, "there are taxes to be paid."

"That's my job," he said simply, opening his palms in a gesture of helplessness.

"Or survivors," I added.

"Let me see," he reflected. He was a prim, officious man. And with more locked in his head, I guessed, than he was willing to admit. I took a gold coin from my purse, flipped it in the air, let it land on the desk before him.

"Solomon was ambitious," he remembered. "He traded with the northern kingdom. He brought in some ivory from Egypt. But the people here had a longing for spices. You may remember our great king by the same name—Solomon. Yes? He introduced spices by the great Queen of the South.

"Well, this Solomon of whom we speak. Your father," he nodded to Taletha, "sought such spices. I think that was the reason for his travels and what got him killed.

"I think I remember the story now," he let the gold coin slip through his fingers. He looked at me inquiringly. I nodded. The gold was as much as he made in salary during a year. And he was remembering Lycurgus's note. The coin disappeared in a blink into his garment.

"Some would call Solomon . . . your father . . . a great man. His wife was from a small village north of here, as I recall. Naomi, I believe her name was. From one of the lesser tribes then. Although who knows nowadays. They all take different names."

He was wandering, wanting to impress us with his knowledge. Or to make sure he earned the gold.

I cleared my throat noisily. "Naomi?" I reminded him.

Taletha was leaning forward, eager for knowledge, for understanding of herself.

"Three children, I think. Yes, I remember. He took all of them to his shop. Set them to work there."

"The shelves," Taletha said suddenly. "A little brush made of sheep's wool. I dusted the shelves. There were . . . I can't remember what was on the shelves. Little jars I think." Something was opening in her. I found myself suddenly frightened by it. I don't know why.

"Probably spice bottles," the man said. "And that would be like Solomon. He liked to have his family with him. Part of the business. Even took them here to pay his taxes. There was a boy, a fine, brown-haired boy I remember. Hagar or Hag—"

"Haggai," I prompted.

"Yes, that was it. Not a businessman, though, that boy. He was too thoughtful. Private, you know? A thinker.

"Two girls, I think. Although I never paid much attention to them."

"Of course not," Taletha said with disgust. "They wouldn't pay taxes."

The magistrate agreed that that was probably true.

"Doval," I said. "Do you remember the name Doval?"

He shook his head. "No. There was a little tyke. Curly-haired girl. An older one. I think I heard her name once. Beth . . . Bethan—"

"Betharden!" Taletha blurted out. She shouted it, "Betharden! Betharden! That's my name."

The man nodded. "Could be. Means 'beautiful garden.' Or 'precious land,' I think. Yes, that could be it. Betharden."

We thanked him. He nodded obsequiously, fingering the coin in the pocket of his cloak. "My regards to Lycurgus," he said.

As we left, walking into the late afternoon sun, Taletha seemed to glow. She skipped down the steps like a child.

When I caught up with her, I turned her to me. "One problem," I said.

"What is it?" she exclaimed. Her face was alight. I saw a happiness in her eyes that I never believed possible, and I thought then that every step, every inch of the desert, had been worthwhile if only for this moment. I looked at her for a time, simply enjoying her joy.

"Well?" she said.

"What do I call you now? Taletha or Betharden?"

She laughed gaily and flung her arms around me. "To you, husband, I am Taletha. And I always will be. But to become Taletha I also had to become Betharden."

She reached back and looked at me, arms twined behind my neck.

"Do you understand?" she asked.

I nodded. I didn't understand any of it. But I knew her joy, and that made it all worthwhile.

As she held me, Taletha looked past my shoulder. A cloud shifted over her eyes as suddenly as storm, and she trembled.

"What is it?" I said. I whirled, looking behind me.

"That woman," Taletha said.

A thin woman with long, flowing brown hair was just disappearing into the crowd. She seemed in a hurry, hands pressed to her face as if weeping.

"What? What about her?"

"I thought . . . Nothing." Taletha grabbed my hand, and we walked back toward Lycurgus's house. The hand tightened in mine to still its trembling.

CHAPTER
EIGHT

As we walked back through the streets, my ear suddenly caught the furious rasp of a saw. I steered Taletha down a side alley toward the sound.

The carpentry shop was set back in a small square. In front of it long beams of lumber cured in the sun—lumber stacked everywhere, upon wagons, over support pieces on the dusty ground, piles of raw lumber. Inside the long, sprawling workshed men labored over huge, two-man saws, attacking timber in a cloud of sawdust. Before the shed, standing by the long, open wall under a tarp that could be lowered to keep rain out, stood a short, stocky man, hands braced upon his wide hips. The bald spot on his head was flame red in the sun. Sawdust clung to his meaty arms.

I approached him, coughing slightly to get his attention.

He turned to us, his face an angry red glare. He saw Taletha and stopped the curse that had sprung to his lips. He nodded to her. Then, turning to me, he barked, "Well?"

"Good afternoon," I said. I poured courtesy into my voice like warm syrup.

"Nothing good about it. Two saws snapped today." He pointed to a glowing forge across the square, well back from the lumber, where a smith was hammering metal. "What do you want?"

I heard Taletha chuckle. She turned sideways from the man, leaving him to me.

"Do you ever get any mahogany?" I asked.

"Mahogany!" exploded the man. He turned his head and spit powerfully into the dust. "No. I get pine and spruce. What I wouldn't do to get some good cedar again. Mahogany!"

"Do you mean you *can't* get it?" I pulled my purse from my belt, dangling it surreptitiously at my waist.

The man's glare softened in an instant. "Well, now. That isn't what I mean. Of course I can get it. It's just that people don't want really good wood anymore. They want this stuff," he waved angrily at the wood. "It's quick and cheap. Trouble is, I've got to sell ten times the amount of it to make any profit. And it doesn't last. Mahogany—can't remember the last time I had any call for good wood."

"A wagonload of mahogany," I said. I opened the purse, letting my fingers enter it.

"A wagonload!" He caught himself, squaring his shoulders respectfully. "It might take a month. And expensive! Ach, how expensive! The cutting, understand. I would have to do it myself. These kids . . . these children, they just don't know. Pine! That's all they know. Which is nothing."

"How much?"

His voice softened to a whisper. "Five hundred drachmas. That's for prime wood, understand."

"I only want the best." I drew out some gold coins.

"Cut by the master."

"Of course." I paid him, leaving Manasseh's name and village for the address. The delivery would cost another fifty drachmas. I heard a disgusted snort behind me.

Taletha laughed aloud and poked me in the ribs when we walked back out of the alley. "You could have had it for four hundred," she said. "Including delivery."

"Really?" I lifted one eyebrow, studying her. "Then it's high time you took care of this." I handed her the purse.

She chuckled and slipped it into her garment. "There's not enough left to worry about," she said.

* * *

Lycurgus was sleeping when we returned at evening. With the uproar in the city, I knew these were demanding times for him, and we decided

268

to slip out of town without disturbing him. As quietly as we could, we gathered our things.

As we were about to leave, we found him sitting in a chair in the kitchen. The man looked exhausted. Still, he smiled when he saw us.

"Leaving so soon?" he asked.

I stammered an apology.

"Were you successful?" he asked. "At the magistrate?"

"Yes," said Taletha. "Oh, yes. And thank you for your help."

"Help me eat my dinner," he said. "And then tell me about it."

The servant had the table set and the meal ready. In quick, excited tones, Taletha told him about the day's events. He smiled tiredly, nodding encouragement throughout. When Taletha finished, he said, "And now I have to fulfill my bargain."

"Are you certain?" Taletha said. "You look exhausted."

He waved it off. "I have things to say," he said thoughtfully, "that may be important for you to hear. In fact, I want to tell you. But maybe it would be easier if we walked a little."

We stepped out to a silvery night. A path led from his house to the river, its broad expanse lying like a white sheet, smooth and unruffled. Under an overhanging tree a fish broke the surface, splashing noisily back into the water and sending concentric rings toward us. They dissipated partway. Lycurgus heaved a rock into the water as if to complete the cycle.

We leaned back against some rocks.

"They made it, you know," he said.

I had to think a moment to pick up the thread of his thought. "The Magi? Impossible!"

"So you would have thought. But, indeed, they did. For a long time they told stories here, about the old one of them who rode in here like he owned the world, riding a knock-kneed camel ready to collapse in the street. He shrieked at the people, ordering them about, barely under control by the others. The way the story goes, the old one dug into a sack, pulled out some gold coins and shouted something like—'Well, here's to your king, then! Gold to anyone who can lead us.' Oh, that got recruits fast enough.

"They made it to the child, so the story goes. I was in the east, of course. All this I learned secondhand, but it was also the reason I was recalled here. If only half the stories be true, they presented their gold,

269

and some rare incense."

"Frankincense and myrrh," I muttered, my voice wondering.

"Could be. I wasn't here. But it got this potentate, this local ruler's attention. The fool started killing off babies like a madman, believing he was threatened. By a baby! The place was ready to blow apart. I got my summons from the emperor himself, to come back here and try to get things under control.

"By the time I returned, the family had used the gifts as a resource to flee. Wise people. They must have lived off the gold and incense for a few years; for they were a poor couple, from what I hear. But the kings—these Magi of yours—were clever men. Not only did their gifts save the child, but one of them, the one that survived, misled this demented potentate by giving him some false directions. The couple then had time enough so they *could* escape.

"The governor knew he had lost by then. I returned, and under the authority of the emperor, put an end to talk about kings soon enough. The governor eventually caught your Magi, by the way. He sent out troops to follow them and bring them back. One of the old men died on the way back. The other died in prison."

Lycurgus looked at me for a long time.

"One survived," he said. "I freed him from prison under the emperor's authority."

"His name?" I prompted him.

"Balthazzar. He was a man consumed, Elhrain. By regret. And consumed by success. Such a man this world sees too seldom."

I nodded and waited.

"When he heard about my travels in the east and when I mentioned you, he was ready to plunge off into the desert to find you."

"Did he?"

"No. At my urging, I confess. I liked the man. He had much knowledge, great courage. I took him back to Rome with me where we have . . . oh, fewer prejudices about a man's color or caste. Where a man could be honored for the things he knows, or does. He became one of my chief advisors. There seemed no limit to his knowledge, and I hold him accountable for my rise to general in the emperor's army."

"He *seemed*? And general, you say? But you're a captain now if I'm not mistaken."

Lycurgus nodded. "The rest of the story, then. Yes, I rose in the army. But always with men of my choosing. That has always been my way.

"Balthazzar was with me. Friend as much as advisor. It was at an insurrection—northern tribes attacked, and I was sent to put it down—that he died. Died in my arms, Elhrain."

He was silent a moment, as if choosing his words carefully. "He said this to me, Elhrain. These were his words: 'It has been a glorious quest,' he said. And, 'If ever you see my son, give him my love.' Those were his words. Today I fulfill them."

I bent my head. A shiver trembled through my body, and I could not stop the weeping. It came as sudden and hot as a storm. Taletha wrapped her arms around me and held me like a child. Child I was. He loved me truly.

Lycurgus left us. He returned after a few minutes with a platter of cheese and some wine. We ate it in silence.

"Thank you," I said.

"The thanks is mine," Lycurgus said. "Whatever happened, whatever he did, he was a great man. He had a huge dream. He dared search mysteries. And every moment he loved you deeply. I'm glad I knew him."

I smiled. "But there is one mystery yet."

"What's that?"

"The rest of your story. From general to captain. A centurion, to be precise."

"Yes, well. That's another matter. I think I began to see too many things through Balthazzar's eyes. Or perhaps my own kingdom had changed too much—into a nest of petty thieves and political fighting. Such wars I was not interested in. And the new emperor was a madman.

"In short, when suspicion is everywhere, no one escapes. I was, perhaps, too insolent. Perhaps I gave cause, but I was never untrue. I think it was only because of my family background that my life was spared at all. Instead, I was simply demoted to the harmless rank of captain and given a posting wherever I chose.

"I didn't hesitate. Balthazzar's thinking had infected me. I began to believe there might be something in it all. If there was something in this, I wanted to see for myself. I came back here."

"To this? Is there anything in it?"

He shook his head. "I don't know. You can see for yourself if you want.

Tomorrow. You see, this same baby that Balthazzar came to see . . ." He stopped, frowning. "I believe it's the same man the people are proclaiming out there. Except that already the lawgivers of the people are turning things against him. For the last day and night, I have been deflecting the conflict."

He shook his head wearily. "I don't think I can anymore. They have him in prison at this moment. It's curious," he mused, "how we want to kill our kings."

He stretched, yawned.

"A day and night," Taletha said. "Then, not another word. You're off to bed."

He smiled at her.

"Now," she said.

"I don't think I can," he replied. "You see, I'm in charge of the execution."

* * *

I awakened long before dawn, strangely disturbed, unable to sleep. I slipped out of bed without waking Taletha, thinking of the long journey we had to start today. She murmured in her sleep, a curious half-smile on her lips, as I slipped past her.

I walked down to the river, staring across the face of the water, now dark and vaguely malevolent under the predawn sky.

"I am like the river," I thought, "a dark shape under which darker currents course. Who knows the way of the river?"

When I returned, the sun fumbled above the temple, setting its dome glittering in pink light. Both Taletha and Lycurgus were awake.

"I don't have to be there until shortly before noon," Lycurgus commented. "Only to make sure the Emperor's order is observed. This whole . . . mess is in the hands of the local governor. His troops. The local guard. Still," he said, "I am curious."

He carved a loaf of bread for us. "Are you still leaving?" he asked.

"I don't know. We may stay."

He nodded. Taletha said nothing. I had the feeling she was holding her breath.

"Do you think it's the same man Balthazzar found?" I asked.

Lycurgus sighed. "I can't be certain of it." He stared at the table, as if seeing beyond its hard wooden surface. "But I think so."

"I think I would like to see him," I said hesitantly.

Taletha surprised me. I thought she would be anxious to return. Instead, she said, "I would too."

"Go along, then," Lycurgus said. "I'll come later. My men don't relish this task at all. It's not pretty." He reflected a moment. "But it would be even uglier if we left it to the locals."

* * *

This was no king. Whatever he was before, he was now changed, utterly changed. A desecration. A ruin.

A few people peered hesitantly around corners of buildings at the newly empty square. The cheers of the people, the waving hands, hearts fired with expectation—all seemed muted like the stillness of air before a great storm. As if the world held its breath.

They clung to the shadows now, then slipped away.

Where were all the men who had heralded him? Only a few women stayed now. Only those fiercely strong women.

He walked across the cobbled square to a small forecourt, herded by a straggling band of rabble-rousers. One foot jerked painfully ahead of the other in a stumbling gait. Exhaustion draped him like cerement clothes.

The guards looked disheveled and sloppy compared to the disciplined soldiers I had seen in Lycurgus's troop. Loud, insolent men these were. The mob behind them increased as they crossed the broad courtyard. Then I saw one of the black-robed lawgivers, his eyes like a green glaze, cold, vindictive. He walked behind the guards but seemed to guide the mob.

Taletha gasped when she saw the direction they were headed. Involuntarily she squeezed my hand. A few people were clustered there. Roughnecks, some still drunk from a night of carousing. Taletha tugged me forward. Every impulse in me wanted to resist. I did not *want* to see this! It sickened me. The sun seemed suddenly very hot in the square. The booted feet of the guards kicked up dust, and the air was thick, too thick to breathe.

One of the four guards was a thick-set man, whose bare arms rippled with muscle. The brassy sun accentuated each knotted muscle with beads of sweat. He held a multiheaded whip loosely coiled in his hand. His narrow, piggish eyes had a look of expectation.

They arrived at a slightly sunken pit, filled with sand that was stained and dirty. Flies spun up from it, like little bits of blue-green metal flung into the air. The prisoner was shoved toward a scourging post in the center of the pit.

Suddenly, a woman darted through the few bystanders. She tried to interpose herself before the burly man. With one swoop of his arm he sent her sprawling, her brown hair falling in the dust like broken feathers. The onlookers jeered, calling her names. Before I could stop her, Taletha darted forward to help the woman.

More people began to show up then, and the lawgiver looked pleased. He seemed to feed on the crowd, while the guard with the whip strode back and forth like a caged animal. Wine flagons passed through the crowd. Jeers and curses fouled the air. I lost track of Taletha, mesmerized by the primitive rite in the scourging pit—a ritual of brutality that I couldn't believe still existed in any civilized country. One of the guards pulled down the man's cloak, exposing his back. Great blue-bellied flies settled on the naked flesh, and the man's shoulder muscles twitched involuntarily. He seemed to struggle for a moment to free his hands from the scourging post, simply to scratch himself, then fell quiet.

When he judged the crowd of sufficient size, the lawgiver motioned to the thick-set guard. Something passed between them, something pocketed by the guard. "I don't want him killed," murmured the lawgiver.

"I know my trade," growled the guard.

"I want him degraded." The lawgiver studied the man at the scourging post, his wrists now roped firmly in place, with a kind of aloof dispassion. The man was subhuman to him, a creature. Either that, or the lawgiver feared him terribly. "Utterly, thoroughly degraded," he said. "I want these people to see an animal. To despise him!"

The guard smiled, but it was the cruel smile of a predator, toying with its prey. He stood for a moment with the flagellum in his hands, enjoying the attention of the watchers. He flexed his arm muscles, nodding at the approving hoots of encouragement, pulling the leather thongs of the whip through his fingers, letting the abrasive shards of lead fastened to the tips ride across his palm. He wanted the onlookers to see! To feel this.

I glanced around at the onlookers. Who would want to see this? I was surprised to see that there were women present, some children even. One man licked his lips eagerly. Their mood was feral, predatory. A few more people joined the rabble, rough people elbowing me aside, pressing in for a better look.

The guard's arm jerked up. The six leather thongs flashed back, shattering the sunlight. They cracked behind his head as his arm snapped forward. The first lash opened a fiery streak across the man's shoulders. Again the guard swung, working his way steadily downward, laying the streaks in a pattern down the back, the buttocks, the upper legs.

The man's legs gave way, the leather thongs securing his wrists to the scourging post now bearing his weight. It seemed that the bones in his wrists would separate. A second layer of blows descended, working from the top down again, this time pieces of flesh breaking loose. The man's eyes glazed. The blood began to run in a pulsing curtain down his body. I was sickened to the core of my being; I bent away, looking at the street behind me, sucking at the hot air. I could not shut the relentless crack-crack of the whip from my ears. I seemed to feel each blow upon *my* flesh, my body quivering. But my flesh was untouched!

Thirty-nine blows were laid, calmly, methodically, each with the full force of the guard's muscles. He was sweating hard by the time the last blow landed. He was tired.

Another guard stepped forward and slashed the ropes that held the man's body to the post, letting him fall into the dust. With the toe of one boot, he twisted the body over.

"Still alive," he observed. "Behold the king." The guards laughed and patted the big man with the whip on the back. He had done his job well, taking the prisoner within an inch of his life.

Another guard took a filthy rag and draped it over the man's body. He had a crooked stick that he shoved into the limp fingers. "Here's his scepter," he laughed. "Let him rule: Lord of the bugs."

Others joined the taunting. One took his sword and hacked branches from a thorn bush, weaving the branches together with a piece of leather thong. "No king is complete without his crown," he announced gaily. He shoved the thorns down upon the man's head, cursing a sudden cut in the palm of his hand.

They left him lying on the ground. The blood pulsed past the thorns, pooled on his forehead and dripped into a little dark spot in the dust.

For some reason, I thought of the wolf, lying flat against the desert floor, its life leaked out by its own lapping. "When," I thought, "will there ever be an end to it?"

The lawgiver stood to one side, wishing perhaps that there were more people to witness the degradation. Suddenly a tall, authoritative man hurried across the square. He carried a small bag at his side and elbowed his way angrily, pushing people aside. Glaring at the lawgiver a moment, he then bent to the body, brushing away at the flies, which floated into the hot air, hovering, waiting.

"So, physician," mused the lawgiver to him. "So much flesh and bone at the end?"

"And a great deal of blood. It's a wonder he still lives."

"Oh, that guard is an expert. Proficient, well-trained."

"I suppose you picked him yourself."

"Oh, but physician, you can't imagine I had anything to do with this. The temple must be kept separate from politics at all costs."

"Yes, and dogs don't bark." The physician stripped back the filthy rag from the man's shoulders. Blood pooled upon the ravaged flesh. Quickly the physician dabbed and pressed with a clean cloth.

Suddenly a woman, the one that Taletha had helped, knelt by the physician, attending him, ripping pieces from the hem of her garment to stanch the blood. The physician nodded, accepting her help. Then, with astonishment, I saw Taletha on her knees beside them.

"It was a political issue, pure and simple. The man claimed to be a king." The lawgiver's voice held an edge to it as he looked dispassionately upon the wounds. People began to turn away now, wandering out across the public square, their voices recounting the blows.

"No. That isn't true. Not true at all," said the physician as he worked. "He was acclaimed the Messiah."

"A sign of his madness."

"That's the only other alternative, isn't it?" The physician pulled an ointment from the small bag. Tenderly he salved the wounds.

"What do you mean, physician?"

The physician turned, looking at the lawgiver. "Either he is what he said, or he is a madman."

"It's really perfectly clear. Besides, it's safer for the people this way. It's all just as well in the end. King or Messiah, he is a threat to order."

"Why is it safer? What harm had he done?" muttered the physician angrily. He bent back to his task, dabbing gently with the ointment.

"Doctor, you above all people should know," rasped the lawgiver. "Those healings, or pretended healings, anyway, don't they rob your stock in trade?"

"They were the very thing that attracted my notice. I'm a man of science, priest." He spat the word. "The healings were not feigned. Several of them were patients of mine. And they were incurable; now they are well. In the final analysis, there is nothing quite so convincing to a genuine man of science as a miracle."

A flicker of doubt moved like a shadow across the lawgiver's face, as quickly disappeared. "Suppose you join me for breakfast, Doctor?"

"No, I think I'll stay with this."

"Perhaps I'll see you again, then. The execution is scheduled for noon. I can forgo the parade." He turned angrily to the guards. "Come on. He stinks," said the lawgiver. "Get his cloak on him." He turned aside, walking back across the courtyard with that stride that seemed to proclaim his ownership over the entire world. His robes billowed like dark wings.

Quickly, two guards heaved the body upright and pulled on the cloak. They dragged the man to a wall, allowing him the respite of a tiny band of shade.

The guards themselves rested for a few minutes, slouching in the shadows as if they had completed some enormous task. One of them leaned against a heavy crosspiece of wood propped against the wall.

For a moment all was silent, save for the faint muttering of the physician to Taletha and the other woman as they attended to the beaten man.

The sun grew cruelly hot. No wind stirred. It seemed that time itself was suspended, as if the world held its breath.

When the man spoke, it seemed preternaturally loud.

"Water," he croaked.

"Water!" hooted a guard. "You're a king! Ask for wine. Make it rain."

"Come on, get up," another barked. "You've slept long enough."

"He'll sleep longer before this day is over," said another with a laugh.

They waited until the man's legs steadied, then dragged him up. Two guards raised a heavy patibulum and dropped it across the man's shoulders. His knees nearly buckled. He kicked one leg out to steady himself, grimacing under the weight. The wood twisted his torn skin. His knees trembled and buckled, and he collapsed.

"Come on, time to go, king." The guard prodded him. Another jerked at the man's arms, splayed out under the weight of the patibulum. "Time to join the others."

Suddenly the crowd fell silent. The sound of booted feet echoed over the hard cobblestones of the courtyard. The clash of armor echoed. I whirled. At the head of a column of soldiers, Lycurgus entered the courtyard, and his face was suffused with outrage. Four of his men led two prisoners between them, but Lycurgus was oblivious to them. He stalked the courtyard like a storm. The people fell back.

Lycurgus strode forward, stopping before the muscular man with the whip. The guard raised the whip slightly. "Don't," said Lycurgus. His word was itself a whiplash. "Who gave you permission?" he snapped.

The guard drew himself up. He hated the soldiers closing in on him. He fell into a fighting stance by reflex. "Don't you give me orders, you Roman pig," he snarled.

His arm, huge muscles bulging, raised the whip.

Lycurgus surged forward. In movements so swift they seemed like flashes under the sun, he ducked under the guard's arm, seized it and twisted, sending the guard sprawling into the scourging post. Lycurgus's soldiers didn't move a muscle.

The guard came up bellowing, charging like a battering ram. Lycurgus bent, meeting the charge. The guard flipped up on Lycurgus's shoulders, spun through the air, fell flat on his back against the cobblestones. His head cracked against the rock.

Curiously, I noted in that moment, that Lycurgus wore no armor and bore no sword at his waist. His men made no movement toward theirs. And I understood. His men knew, with absolute confidence, that there was no need.

Again the guard pulled himself up, his small, piggish eyes whirling. Muscles twitched across his thick shoulders. He howled with rage and charged again. Lycurgus whirled, striking blows with such a terrible fury and quickness the eye couldn't follow them. The guard collapsed in a heap at his feet.

Lycurgus drew himself erect. He didn't even seem to be breathing hard. He looked around. The rabble fell back. He strode to the whipped man and knelt by him.

"He can't do it," the physician said. "It's physically impossible."

I noticed then that the two other prisoners carried heavy crossbeams across their shoulders. So this was the way it went. They bore the means of their own deaths upon their backs. I nearly spat with disgust. So this was civilization. In all the lands, among all the people and places I had traveled, never had I seen a torment so degrading and primitive.

Lycurgus looked at the collapsed man. His eyes searched the crowd, fastened for the first time on me and stopped there.

I nodded.

I stepped past the fallen man, knelt down, touched the rough wood of the patibulum. The fallen man worked himself to his knees, kneeling beside me. His eyes seared into my own.

I stood over the fallen man, then I bent and reached out a hand to him. His eyes never left me. His hand closed on mine, and a fire trembled through every inch of my body. He spoke something as he staggered to his feet. Or perhaps I only thought I read it in his eyes. But at that instant, I swear he named me.

I swear it.

"You have come, Elhrain—I accept your gift," he said.

At that very moment, as I was about to kneel to accept the man's crosspiece upon my shoulders, a bystander stepped in. He was a slim, but powerfully built, young man, his features sharply refined under curly, black hair and beard. He bent quickly to the patibulum and with powerful ease swung it across his shoulders.

"I am Simon," he said quietly. "One of his people. I want to do this." He paused, then said, almost apologetically, "And I am younger. The wood is heavy." His eyes beseeched me.

I looked at Lycurgus. He nodded, and we fell in behind the crooked train of the condemned.

CHAPTER
NINE

The procession wound slowly up the hill. The women followed us. I knew Taletha would be there, with the woman she had helped. I didn't look behind. Some men darted fearfully from the shadows, following at a distance. A few of the rabble-rousers followed but the jeers were weak. Simon's feet did not falter under the weight of the patibulum. His shoulders were straight as we followed the blood-stained cloak of the man before us.

Lycurgus walked at my side, his face as unmoving as stone. His men marched in step. Once he leaned toward Simon, aware of the heavy weight of the patibulum that bowed his shoulders. "Can you do it?" he asked. The younger man nodded.

He caught sight of the physician. "Stick around, doctor," he said. "You can pronounce their deaths."

The physician merely glanced at him, but fell in step with us, his eye on the whipped man who staggered slowly in place.

"You don't fear death, do you captain?" the physician said to Lycurgus.

"Shut up, doctor."

"What is it then? The truth? Is that what you fear?"

Lycurgus didn't answer. He looked grimly ahead, to the crest of the long hill.

"What if there is truth in what the man says?" persisted the physician.

"Enough, physician. We're almost there. I've got work to do."

We rounded the crest of the hill. The cobbles stopped at a weed-swept path. Wind lifted little eddies of dust that choked eyes, nostrils, mouths. The air itself had a gritty taste. Three stipites, upright posts, cast their gaunt brown forms against the withering sun.

Simon walked to the middle stipes and laid the man's patibulum on the ground before it. He stood for a moment, panting, then shrugged his powerful shoulders and stepped away, a look of fierce anger hardening his refined features. I seemed, for a moment, to feel the ache of the wood upon my own shoulders, and was grateful for his strength.

The condemned man collapsed to his knees at the foot of the cross, his breath flagging hollowly. The eyes seemed like pools of light in his worn, haggard face. Only Lycurgus's tug at my cloak drew me away. "You'll have to step back," he said gently.

I moved away to stand alongside the physician, who seemed to watch with clinical interest, perhaps a bit surprised that something within him stirred beyond his customary medical dispassion.

The soldiers moved rapidly. They took small pleasure in this task. It was a job that had to be done. One of them carefully removed the cloak from the man, tearing the clots off his wounds once again. The soldier laid him down against the patibulum so that he lay full length in the dust of the windy hilltop. Two soldiers held the arms outstretched. The third fumbled in a leather sack at his waist, extracting two heavy, squared nails, hammered out of wrought iron. He felt with one hand for the depression at the wrist, placed the nail there, and slammed it in with the hammer. The nail squirted into the wood. The soldier leaned his weight on the arm to hold it in place, surprised that he met no resisting force. Two more blows and the nail was driven home, set at a slight angle to hold the weight of the body when the patibulum was raised. If the nails were set at the wrong angle, the body could fall off, necessitating a repetition of the entire procedure. The soldier didn't make any mistakes.

Just three blows, and the same for the other wrist.

"The soldier is proficient, at least," observed the physician. I was surprised to see him still standing next to me. He glanced around behind him. A group of people stood along the edge of the hillside. The physician let his eyes rove over them. The common town rabble. He started suddenly as his eyes came to rest upon a small group huddled by some rocks across the hill. He recognized some of the followers of the man. They had decided to come, anyway, defying the authorities.

I followed his gaze, seeing Taletha among the women. Her eyes met mine briefly, and then seemed to turn inward.

On order, three soldiers stationed at each cross hoisted the patibulums. A groan escaped the man's lips as his weight fell upon the nails. Then, in one fluid motion, the three soldiers, spaced along the beam, lifted the body clear off the ground, hoisting the patibulum to the notch on the stipes.

They moved quickly now. One soldier grabbed each victim's left foot, twisting it so that it rested upon the right foot. The knees were kept flexed. A second soldier set the nail against the ankles while the third raised the hammer and drove the heavy spike through flesh into the wood. Their task finished, they walked in a group and stood aside. Lycurgus walked from cross to cross, inspecting the work of his men. It was satisfactory.

The physician stood quietly. There was nothing to do now but wait.

The task that each one faces, and yet each faces alone, I thought: the task of dying. Inevitable, universal, and yet horribly personal. One dies, always, alone.

The physician seemed about to say something to me when we heard the words murmured softly across the hilltop, so softly but they knifed the silence of the expectant crowd. For the first time his medical composure cracked. He said wonderingly to me, "He asks that they be forgiven?"

"It is a wonder," I replied.

"Did you know the man, then?" asked the doctor.

"I never saw him before this. But I think I have been looking for him all my life."

"Odd that you should be the one to help him, then."

"Not really. Any of my people would have done the same. Your people mystify me."

"Yes. I quite agree. They mystify me too."

"You're a doctor?" I asked.

"As much as the people allow me. They hang onto their own cures, you know. They prefer their poultices to medicine. If I could get them to practice basic hygiene many of their folk remedies wouldn't be necessary."

"I overheard what you said to Lycurgus."

"Oh, the centurion? He's not a bad man. Just a man doing a bad job."

"I mean about the healings. That the man healed people."

"Indeed. That is why they call him a criminal. It is why I refused to do so. And now the hard part starts for him."

"The people still mock him. That loudmouth calls for him to heal himself."

"He's frightened. People always are with what they don't understand. Frightened or angry, the end is the same. Destroy the threat. But I'm afraid it would be too late now for him to heal himself."

"How is that?"

"If he were going to do so, he would have long before. His body is dying now. This is simply medical science. The body—that fragile connection of nerve and tissue and muscle and blood—will soon be dead." He paused a moment to reflect upon the mystery of it all. "Finished," he said simply.

"It is an ugly death."

"The very ugliest. He should be in shock from the loss of blood by now."

"But he is not. He just called something to that other man on the cross."

"Yes. Odd. It would be easier to let go. And he will. His body will insist upon it. You see, even now his lung cavity is starting to fill with fluids."

"Fluids? You mean he's drowning?"

"Drowning. Suffocating. That's how they die. You see, in order to breathe, the weight of the body must be pushed up. The body is a marvelous support system, the muscles holding the skeleton upright, but when the muscles can no longer do this, the system begins to collapse. All he has to push with are the nails in his ankles. All he has to pull with are the nails in his wrists. So he can draw a breath, but cannot much longer push himself upward to exhale. The chest muscles become paralyzed. He has to push down on the nails to breath out and the nerves no longer permit that. The pain is too great. Pretty soon the soldiers will break their legs to ensure it. That's why it's an ugly death. It permits the body to destroy itself."

"By all that's holy, what a cruelty."

"Oh, yes. Barbaric. The chest begins to fill with fluid. It presses upon the heart. Fills the lungs. So, in time, he drowns as you say."

I tore my gaze from the man on the cross and looked at the physician. I saw his keen, dark eyes blinking against tears, belying his objectivity.

The physician wiped a handkerchief across his eyes without shame or apology. "Forgive me for sounding so clinical," he said.

I nodded.

"The worst is that it takes so long. The body wills to live. That is its design. Breaking their legs is actually a kind of mercy. A strong man could hang there a day without death."

Just then the man upon the middle cross called out, his words like a groan flung into the wind. The words were lost to me. I looked upward. "It's getting dark, but I don't see any clouds."

"Yes. And the wind has died." The physician studied the prisoners upon their crosses. The darkness seemed to deepen moment by moment. Many of the spectators, expecting rain, stood up and left for their homes. The physician walked to a small group at the edge of the hill.

Taletha's voice knifed the darkness, as clear as a bell. "Do you hear that, Elhrain?"

"What? I hear nothing. I can see nothing. Just a blur."

"Listen. It's growing louder."

"Drums? Is that drums?"

"Many drums. Like a great army marching." The earth seemed to shake under its beat, a steady, rolling swell of sound. The noise gathered to a long peal of thunder.

A soldier cried out in fear. "I can't stand this darkness," he shrieked.

"It's a rainstorm," called Lycurgus. "I hear thunder. Hurry now. Let's get this business over with before the rain hits. Justin, you know what to do."

The man Justin turned to a comrade grumbling, "I haven't liked this business from the start. Since when do we go about hanging a people's prophets because the people weary of them?" Taking a heavy hammer, he smashed the kneecaps of the man on the far cross. His body sagged grotesquely. Justin hurried on.

The darkness swirled like a tangible thing in the air.

Justin ran through the darkness to the second man. Again he slammed the heavy hammer against the kneecaps. He moved to the last.

"Captain," he bellowed. "This one is dead."

"Make sure."

For some reason, Justin's arm would not move. He raised the hammer but could not bring it down. A second soldier rushed past him with drawn sword. "Let's get out of here," he shouted. He thrust the sword up to the man's side. The sword drove through the chest, pierced the heart. The fluids pent in the chest cavity erupted through the wound, followed by the blood of the broken heart.

The soldier fell back as another blast of thunder rocked the earth.

Gradually, after long minutes during which time seemed suspended and as if parting from above rather than from east to west, the curtain of darkness fell back. In the appalling gloom, I saw the figures hanging as before. I had half-expected them to be swallowed up by the shaking earth.

All the people had fled save for the tiny band of mourners and the soldiers. I looked for Lycurgus, found him kneeling on the gore-spattered ground at the foot of the man's cross. His head was bent to the wood, and it seemed, in that weird preternatural light, that the figure was standing on Lycurgus's shoulders. I stepped closer to him, my legs still gripped by the cataclysm of noise and darkness.

Lycurgus heard my shuffle. He turned his head slowly. His eyes were aggrieved pools. Slowly his lips moved. "They were right," he murmured. "They were right all along."

He stood up, motioned to the soldiers to lower the bodies, and turned his back. The last time I saw him, he was walking slowly to the path. He paused, removed his cape, and flung it aside.

I walked to the women. They were crying piteously, Taletha among them, comforting, providing solace, holding them in her arms. The woman of the desert. The woman with no home. She stood and faced me. The woman she had attended stood beside her.

I sucked in my breath. The resemblance was uncanny. My eyes flicked from face to face, from brown hair to brown hair, from dark eyes to dark eyes. I peered without mercy at the woman, for in the pupil of her right eye was a flash of golden light. She stared at me without recognition.

"Shall we go?" I said.

Taletha nodded. She turned to the woman, embraced her and spoke a few urgent words in her ear.

On the pathway I saw Lycurgus's cloak, its scarlet cloth mud-splattered and stained. I took it with me.

* * *

On the homeward way, riding in the wagon behind the plodding ox, the roads now virtually empty, I asked Taletha about her.

"Did you know her?" I asked.

Taletha pondered, then shook her head.

"She reminded me . . ." I began. Then I couldn't find the words.

Taletha's voice was calm, knowing. "She has lived here many years," she said. "She doesn't remember her past. She lived . . . by selling herself. For that, because of that, she can no longer remember. Until she met him."

"And?"

"She became one of his people. She is at peace."

"But didn't you think—"

"Just a woman," Taletha said, and her voice was like steel. "Just a person . . . who had questions and found answers. It doesn't matter now. She knows who she is. She is happy now. Sometimes that is best left as it is."

I nodded. I understood nothing and, therefore, nodded, keeping silent. Then Taletha's voice broke. "Still," she said, "I hope to see her again."

"Perhaps," I said. "All things are possible."

* * *

We arrived at our village two days later. How sweet and simple it was. Manasseh rushed out to meet us, booming his great laugh. He didn't seem to notice that there was no mahogany in the wagon.

The sky was a high dangerous blue, so clear and powerful it hurt the eye. The fields lay like lush green quilts. It was good to be home.

* * *

Several weeks later we visited Manasseh and Meridivel. We tried to find the words to tell them of what we had seen. The words seemed empty, insufficient, yet they listened avidly, and nodded knowingly. We were sitting in their forecourt when a wagon appeared far down the road. It was pulled by a full team, for it bore a heavy load. It grew larger, pulled toward the carpenter's shop and stopped a few yards away from us.

Manasseh stood up.

"You've got the wrong place," he said.

"Not if your name is Manasseh," the driver answered.

"I am," Manasseh said, scratching his head. "But I have no order."

I nudged Taletha. She chuckled and winked at Meridivel, who was staring wide-eyed at the load.

"I don't know about that," the driver said as he got down. He flung back the tarp on the wagon, revealing a load of gleaming mahogany. "But someone paid for this to be delivered to you. Now if we can get it off, I have a long way to go."

The driver stayed for dinner. He wanted to talk about events in the city. He repeated the tale of the crucifixion, and we listened as if hearing it for the first time. But he had more to say. About events in the days following.

I don't know what to make of his words. I don't know if such things can be. I only know what I saw.

These words I have tried to render accurately. I sit now in my home in the hills. The sheep are bawling. They want to be fed. There are so many of them now.

I wish Taletha were here by me. She returned to the city with the driver. She wants to learn more of these things. Perhaps she will bring the woman back with her. I think I would like that.